PRAISE FOR *THE ORCHID TATTOO*

"*The Orchid Tattoo* is a fast-paced, finely wrought thriller that will keep you turning pages late into the night. When the sister of social worker Georgia Thayer disappears after trying to help a runaway teen, Georgia finds herself thrust into a nefarious underworld of human trafficking unlike anything she could've imagined. This is an important, timely story that needed to be told, and social-worker-turned-author Carla Damon is the one to tell it."

—**Cassandra King**, bestselling author of *Tell Me a Story: My Life with Pat Conroy*

"*The Orchid Tattoo* is a story of heartache, tenacity, and courage, and the lengths a woman will go to uncover a horrible truth and protect those she loves from a world of our nightmares."

—**Yasmin Angoe**, editor's pick and bestselling author of *Her Name Is Knight*

"In *The Orchid Tattoo*, Carla Damron creates that rare, superpowered thriller where a page-turning reading experience sheds important light on social justice. Georgia Thayer is a gem of a lead character—smart, sensitive, strong in her own struggles, driven to help others. I'd follow her wherever she goes next."

—**Ashley Warlick**, author of internationally-acclaimed *The Arrangement*

"Part thriller, part social commentary, *The Orchid Tattoo* is a fast-paced journey through the darkest part of the American Dream. Damron's human trafficking novel breaks your heart at every turn but reassembles the pieces by the end, leaving the reader both emotionally moved and angry at the inhumanity of it all. This is an important book that needs to be read and shared."

—**Stephen G. Eoannou**, author of *Rook* and *Muscle Cars*

"*The Orchid Tattoo* is a taut, unflinching novel, evocative and well told, full of surprising twists and turns. Author Carla Damron deftly mixes an engaging plotline, and a host of gritty characters with a remarkably probing, insightful, and compassionate examination of human trafficking in a modern American city. Highly recommended."

—**Robert Steven Goldstein**, author of *Will's Surreal Period,*
Enemy Queen, Cat's Whisker, and *The Swami Deheftner*

"In *The Orchid Tattoo*, Carla Damron takes the serious issue of sex trafficking and brings it to our doorstop for perusal and introspection. Although it can be a triggering topic, her background as a social worker allows Damron to treat the issue and the girls it impacts with compassion and empathy. While we find ourselves embroiled in the lives of young women robbed of their bodies and autonomy, Carla Damron's attention is not centered on the salacious and debauched parts of this industry but on the agency and resolve of her finely developed characters, intricate dialogue, and the unexpected twist of her novel's ending. She is a powerful writer, an activist in her writing, and an outstanding storyteller who brings attention to a vile industry and a group of girls who find strength and power in each other as they doggedly pursue their freedom."

—**Marina DelVecchio**, author of *Dear Jane* and
The Virgin Chronicles

"In *The Orchid Tattoo*, Carla Damron blends crisp, clear writing with detailed knowledge of one of the most dangerous and heart-wrenching social injustices of our time: human trafficking. Told from multiple points of view throughout a trafficking enterprise in South Carolina, the story leaves readers longing for Kitten's freedom, Peyton's safe return, justice for the perpetrators, and redemption for those within the fold whose greed drives them to commit unspeakable crimes.

"Damron's heroes are hardworking social workers and law enforcement officers who refuse to stop fighting for justice."

—**Beth Uznis Johnson**, author of *Coming Clean,* coming 2023

"Damron's book unleashes a primal scream; sex trafficking and exploitation are happening now. Through Damron's richly imagined protagonist, social worker Georgia Thayer, internal voices amplify and pry eyes open to see culpability in this beautifully written, thrilling mystery. Evil's torn, surprising petals fall, and friendships bloom in *The Orchid Tattoo*'s visceral story."

—**Tim Conroy**, author of *Theologies of Terrain*

"In this stunning thriller, it's not only the writing that made me keep turning the pages. This story of human trafficking in South Carolina kept me on the edge of my seat as I watched the struggles of the main characters play out on the page. Ironically, this fictional telling brought to life for me the reality of what people who've been trafficked as farm or sex workers go through, and how hopeless they must feel. That's because the author's characters were drawn as real people—each one had a story to tell, one that made me empathize with their situation in a way bald statistics don't, necessarily. The pacing is excellent, and the twists that practically had me out of my seat made this a book I'd recommend to book clubs and anyone who wants to learn something while reading a nail-biter of a book."

—**Gabi Coatsworth**, author of *Love's Journey Home*

"Damron's genius lies in the economy with which she crafts richly conceived, unique characters, all with their own yearnings and flaws, whose collisions drive the action. She manages to explore social justice themes without preaching or in any other way sacrificing the suspense and pacing of the story, while somehow making it look easy. In the course of this wild ride, we learn about the evil lurking beneath the surface of a mid-sized Southern city along with the people working to combat those forces and heal their victims. At the end, the reader emerges breathless and satisfied. At least, this one did."

—**Bob Schueler**, author of *Second Chances* and *The 25 Years*

"Those of us who choose to address this topic head-on are always looking for ways to shine the spotlight on this universal cancer, from films to television to music and books. We try desperately to engage the public so that human trafficking is no longer just discussed in the shadows. So let me share with you a book by Author Carla Damron. It's titled *The Orchid Tattoo*. This book is highly recommended by us at the Silent Angel Project . . . I do believe that many of you will enjoy and benefit from this novel."

—**The Silent Angel Project**

"Damron deftly weaves her social work knowledge into a gripping drama of scarred humans attempting to free themselves from physical and emotional captivity. Her look at the breadth of human trafficking and how it operates without being too gritty leads to a compelling and educating read. But it also addresses the resilience of the human spirit. No matter how bleak your world, you can find a way out."

—**Marie W. Watts**, author of *Rapture by Revenge*, *Warriors for Equal Rights*, and *Only a Pawn*.

"A gritty novel that doesn't shy away from truth, *The Orchid Tattoo* is unputdownable. Narrated in Damron's signature style, the twists, turns, heartbreaks and the terror are all captured beautifully in this completely human story of an age-old crime that is still happening today."

—**Priya Gill**, author and engineering management professor

"This book was wonderfully heartbreaking and effortless to read. I started and finished it in twenty-four hours. While the passages detailing the girls' abuse were hard to read, I didn't find them to be too graphic or triggering (outside of the topic itself, which I also feel was well handled).

"This book challenged me to frame this story in my backyard/a place I consider to be a home. I shuddered at the thought of this happening there."

—**Cary Johnstone**, psychology grad student

"Carla Damron's new Crime Fiction novel, *The Orchid Tattoo*, is a quest, a relentless adventure, and a telescopic sight into the dark and persistent world of human trafficking. This book begins with a running leap into a cloudy and frightening mystery and never slows throughout its full length."

—**Eric Morris,** *Jasper Magazine*

The Orchid Tattoo

by Carla Damron

ISBN 978-1-64663-763-8

Published by

 köehlerbooks™

3705 Shore Drive
Virginia Beach, VA 23455
800-435-4811
www.koehlerbooks.com

The Orchid Tattoo

A NOVEL

CARLA DAMRON

*Taylor ~
Good luck with
your writing career!
Carla Damron*

VIRGINIA BEACH
CAPE CHARLES

Dedicated to the memory of the fabulous Ivy Moore.
You left us too soon, my friend.

CONTENT WARNING

This novel contains references to child (teen) abuse
and sex trafficking.

CHAPTER ONE

At 3 a.m., I should be home in bed like any normal person, but "normal" fits me about as well as "perky" or "has her shit together." Instead, I was in the windowless catastrophe that was my office, trying to ignore the page from the Emergency Department flashing on my phone: *Georgia Thayer to Bay Four.* The seventh time that day. I might as well move my desk down there, maybe claim a stall in the staff bathroom. With a frustrated grumble, I rose, locked the office, and made my way down to the ED.

I entered the curtained off bay to find a frizzy-haired woman sitting on a gurney, half-dressed, handcuffed, sunken in posture as though trying to disappear.

Mark Westfall, a staff psychiatrist with the girth of a manatee, bifocals askew on his bald head, motioned me left as he went right.

"What's going on?" I asked.

"New patient. Not talking. Looking like a level three."

We used codes to delineate behavioral problems. Level three was bad. It meant needing restraints to keep the patient from harming themselves or others, but this small woman sat quietly, eyeing us as though we were enemy assailants.

I shot Mark a puzzled look because nothing about her screamed "management problem."

"Just wait," Mark said.

I took a tentative step closer. "Hey there. I'm Georgia Thayer, the hospital social worker. Can you tell me your name?"

She didn't answer.

"Maybe you can tell me why you're here?"

Silence.

"She's not talking. They found her on a park bench. When the officer asked her to move on, she bit him."

She gave a skittery glance in my direction.

I put her age at around thirty, skinny, and unkempt. She swung her legs like she was on a swing, her lips moving but little sound coming out. I inched closer.

"Careful," Mark said.

What was he worried about? She seemed—

Her banshee shriek nearly knocked me over. She leaped from the gurney and scrambled to the curtain encircling the bay; two nursing assistants pushed through to keep her from bolting. She jumped atop the gurney where she squatted like a bullfrog. Impressive move for someone in handcuffs.

"Told you," Mark said.

"Hey, hey!" I said. "It's okay. We're not going to hurt you." This woman was in torment. I spent the next five minutes trying to coax her to climb down, her looking wild-eyed with paranoia, then suddenly, she quieted. Again, she sat on the gurney—mostly silent, though her lips moved like she was whispering to a ghost. A few minutes later, she flipped again, yelling, combative if we got close, Mark getting frustrated and ready to order a butt injection of some tranquilizer. Then she quieted again. Weird.

As the cycle repeated, I focused on what triggered the crazed outburst. Had one of us moved? Said the wrong thing? Then I saw it. Whenever the air conditioning kicked on, the banshee reappeared. When it shut down, so did she.

I told the med-tech to adjust the thermostat. "Are you nuts? It's a thousand degrees out," she replied.

"Just for a few minutes." As the system shut down, the woman exhaled, her face softening as the tension evaporated. "You don't like the air blowing," I said.

She shook her head with vehemence, the first meaningful communication we'd had.

"Too cold?"

Another headshake.

"The noise?"

A slow nod. Weird, because given all the cacophony of noise that filled the ED, the air switching on was hardly noticeable. "That whoosh it makes?"

"No." She inched closer, her sour breath on my face. "The laughing."

Mark's brows shot up.

"The laughing," I repeated. "When the air turns on—"

"The demon laughs. He's in there. He's coming after me." She spoke this last sentence with a somber acquiescence.

I knew much better than most how she felt. "That sounds terrifying. It may be hard to believe, but we will keep you safe here." I turned to Mark. "Think we should admit her to the fifth floor?"

He nodded. "Wish she had some kind of ID. I'll have one of the residents work her up."

"And maybe make sure they turn the vent off in her room. That'll make life much easier for her," I said.

"And everyone else," Mark whispered back.

❦

As soon as I got to my office, I'd grab my keys and bolt. That was the plan. I've had six years in this place; there is no getting to the end of my to-do list, so I needed to escape before someone else at Columbia General expected some predawn social working. Just as I reached for my purse, the cellphone buzzed.

The number flashing was my sister's home number. "What's wrong?" I answered, fighting a wave of panic at the lateness of the call.

"You heard from Peyton?" My brother-in-law's voice surprised me.

"No. She's not home?" I glanced up at the clock: *3:20 a.m.*

"No. I have no idea where she is. I got here after work, no sign of her or Lindsay. No note. NOTHING!" The last word erupted, hurting my ear.

"You try her cell?"

"About a million times."

"I'm on my way." I clicked off, flew out of my office and down the stairs to my Civic.

May can sizzle in South Carolina, and even at that hour, the hot air startled my lungs. My hands vibrated against the steering wheel as I tried not to think the worst, my mind conjuring image after image of worst-case Peytons.

Not so fast. The counselor spoke, a gentle whisper in my head. *Slow down.*

I ignored the voice as my car sliced through the humid Carolina night.

Ten minutes later, I turned into Peyton's drive, my tires bumping over the worn cobblestones, and spotted David's Cadillac, but not Peyton's Lexus. Maybe Peyton was just late getting home from the university. She'd become a study-a-holic since returning to grad school last year, joking that at thirty-six she had a "lot of catching up to do."

Something's very wrong, the advisor said. Unlike the counselor, this voice was male. Insistent. Always difficult to ignore. My voices don't come often anymore, but when I'm scared or stressed, they slither back in. Despite my psychiatrist's valiant attempts, no medicine completely stops this internal noise.

When I huffed up the stone steps and rang the bell, David answered, wearing the wrinkled linen jacket I'd seen him in at the hospital that afternoon, his sparse gray hair standing out from his scalp like quills.

"Georgia." He spoke as though my name tasted like spoiled fruit. Yep, we got along that well. "I didn't mean for you to rush over here."

I pushed past him and his disapproving glare into their mammoth house.

"I got home around midnight, she wasn't here," David said. "It's a damn puzzle."

I hadn't heard from her in several days. No message on my cell. No texts. Weird, since we usually talked daily. I had chalked it up to her being too busy with school and my being swamped at the hospital, rather than filial neglect.

"Lindsay's bed looks like it's been slept in. Like Peyton woke her up and took her somewhere in the middle of the night."

"And you're sure there's no note?" I asked. Peyton wrote things down. Messages. Lists. Things she didn't want to forget, on a rainbow of sticky notes.

"I checked everywhere," he sighed. "But she's been like this. In and out, vague about where she's going. Always says it's something to do with school."

"How about the answering machine?" I asked because David was old school enough to still use one.

His brown eyes widened. "She'd leave in the middle of the night and then call the damn answering machine?"

"No." I forced calm into my voice because one of us needed to act like an adult. "But if she was in an accident or something—"

"Oh, God." He clomped down the hall, and when I heard two beeps from his machine, I joined him.

"Monday, eight-seventeen PM," the mechanical voice stamp announced. Then, "Peyton, it's me. I tried your other phone but . . . pick up if you're there. Peyton?" The unfamiliar voice sounded Latino, maybe Mexican. The caller ID flashed "unlisted."

"Monday, ten-twelve PM," the voice said. "Peyton? We have to change the plan. Tomorrow won't work. God, I hope you get this. Call me." The same voice edged with alarm, hanging on a few seconds before disconnecting.

"Do you recognize him?" I asked. "What's he talking about?"

"Damned if I know. Why is she getting calls from some strange man?"

I ignored him and the ridiculous implication. David had been the one to mess around, not Peyton. "Maybe you should call the ER? Just to make sure she wasn't in an accident or something."

As he dialed, I decided to look upstairs for some clue, anything. Their bedroom looked normal. The brocade bedspread had been pulled back, leaving a perfect triangle of pristine white sheets. Two plump pillows lay propped against the sleigh bed headboard, as though she had just been here, curled up with one of her public health textbooks or a trashy novel. I half-expected to turn around and find her coming from the bathroom.

I made my way to Lindsay's room. When I hit the light switch, yellow walls and marigold curtains glowed against the black of night. The comforter made an untidy bunch at the foot of her bed, the pillow nowhere to be seen. My niece has always been a stormy sleeper, kicking and tossing and grumbling in her dreams, the way I had done as a child.

I heard a noise. So soft, a gentle rumble. Another voice? No, outside of me. Then silence. I took another step. There it was again. I glanced out in the hall, expecting David to be there, but I was alone.

Or maybe I wasn't. I held my breath, not sure what to do. And then came a quiet *shooosh*, like someone taking in air. I turned to the closet. If it was an intruder, I should have a weapon, but curiosity made me open the door. I saw tiny shirts and dresses. The princess costume from last Halloween. I scanned down: Lindsay's shoes all in a jumble, a stray Nerf ball in the corner. And on my right—a hand.

I dropped, sweeping sneakers out of my way to crawl closer. My niece. There. Hidden, under a blanket and three stuffed animals, pillow balled under her head. Thumb wedged between pink petal lips. I reached for her, feeling the shallow rise and fall of her chest. "Lindsay?" I nudged her. Groggy eyes opened. The hand uncorked itself from her mouth and reached for me. I pulled her into my arms.

"David! Can you come up here?" I tried to keep my voice steady against a tangle of emotions. Her little body showed no sign of injury. She looked okay, whole. But if she was here, where the hell was Peyton?

David burst into the room, nearly stumbling when he saw the bundle I held. "What the . . . where was she?"

"Hiding in the closet." She had on her favorite Dora pajamas. One arm around my neck, the other squeezing her loyal stuffed dog, School Bus.

"Honey, are you okay?" he asked.

She held out a hand for him. He took her, closing his eyes and holding her close. "Thank God. How did I miss her?"

"Lindsay, why were you in there?" I asked.

She scrunched her shoulder up, pressing her face into her father's neck.

"Do you know where Mama is?" David asked.

Lindsay turned to blink at me. She had soft blue eyes, topped with thick lashes.

"Sweetie, it's important. Do you know where Mama went?" I asked. She keyed into the tension in my voice and pulled back, frowning.

"Did she say anything?" David pressed. "Maybe she said she had to go somewhere? Do you remember?"

Another head shake, which troubled me. This kid's a chatterbox, a thousand questions for every situation. Her eyelids pulled down, thumb taking its usual station in her mouth.

I reached for her. "Maybe I should put her to bed." As I placed her between the yellow sheets, she hugged School Bus at his stuffing-depleted neck, her face against his ear, a perfect fit.

"Did Mama tuck you in tonight?" I asked.

She blinked at me as though the question confused her.

"How did you get in the closet?"

She shifted on her side, lashes fluttering against the pull to sleep.

"Please, Peanut. Think about it. Did Mama say where she was going?" Her eyes closed, thumb in mouth. I would get no more answers from her. I stroked her blond hair and whispered, "I love you, Peanut."

When I went back downstairs, I passed the narrow marble-topped table where Peyton dumped stuff: her purse, umbrella, books, and travel mug. Her purse was gone but a hardback on statistics rested on top of a pink plastic case. Peyton's cell phone. I swiped it with my thumb, but it was out of juice. Odd that she left it, but maybe that was why.

I showed it to David. "You know where the charger is?"

"In her purse I expect. Mine won't work on her phone."

"Okay. I'll take it home and juice it up."

He nodded. David is a small, sloped-shouldered man, and looked dwarfed in his easy chair. He held a glass of what I suspected was his favorite scotch.

"The police are on their way," he said.

I sat in the rocking chair Peyton always used, gripped the arms like she always did, her missingness a pall over me. "When was the last time you talked to her?"

He lifted the glass, downing the rest of it. "Yesterday."

"Yesterday! Where have you been?"

"I've been here. I came home late last night; she was already in bed. This morning when I got up, she was gone. Jenny was here. She said Peyton was going to work on her research project."

Jenny was Lindsay's sitter. "What project?" I felt a pang of guilt that I didn't know.

"No clue. Like I said, she's been like that for weeks. Acting mysterious." He eyed the telephone beside him, probably thinking about the man who had called.

When David stood and crossed over to the window, blue lights flashed through the glass. "The police. Maybe they can find her."

Not likely, the advisor said. I hoped he was wrong.

CHAPTER TWO

The lady said she would come just after sunrise.

These words thrummed in Kitten's mind as she stared out the window, hoping for the first trace of light and her chance to escape. Even at that hour, the trailer had a strange percussion. Roman's snores rumbled in the living room. A box fan in Dulce's room thumped against the window. The steady hum of an ancient refrigerator. Kitten wouldn't miss the smells either—pot and cigarette smoke that had soaked into the furniture. The sour garbage from the overfilled trash can in the kitchen.

Once the last buyer left, Roman had finished a six-pack and a joint before passing out on the mustard-colored sofa just like most nights. Dulce had come in from working the streets and closed herself in the other tiny bedroom. Hopefully, enough hours had passed that Dulce was now fast asleep.

Kitten grabbed the knapsack from under her bed. The secret phone—the one the lady gave her—was in the front pocket. She snatched a small photo she kept tucked in the mirror frame; Mama, her brother Brandon, and Kitten sitting on their porch steps, taken the day after her fourteenth birthday. The photo was all she had of the before-life. She placed it with the crumpled twenty-dollar bill her last buyer had slipped her.

The lady had said not to bring too much, she needed to be quick. But that wasn't a problem. She wanted no reminders of her time in the trailer when she fled. She put on a T-shirt and shorts that fit more loosely than everything else Roman dressed her in. She laced up the high-tops that she wasn't allowed to wear except to work the cantina. She was escaping Roman's rules, too.

As she tiptoed through the galley kitchen, she snatched a bruised banana to eat later. The floor creaked when she passed the ratty rocker, which silenced Roman mid-snore. She froze, backpack dangling from her arm like a caught fish, and waited. Roman turned over and the snores resumed.

He always locked them in at night, but Kitten knew he kept the key in the right pocket of his leather jacket slung over the arm of the couch. She groped the scuffed leather, found the key, and crept toward the door. She slid it into the double-bolt lock and turned it, casting a frantic look back at him when the door squeaked. *If he catches me . . .* He huffed, smacked his lips, then growled out another snore.

The rickety steps twitched as she stepped down them for the very last time. Kitten smiled, shrugged the knapsack onto her shoulder, and took off running.

She blew past the scattered trailers along the dusty clay road—almost as old as the one Roman rented. Lights blinked on in a single-wide, so she picked up her pace. Nobody needed to see her now, not with freedom so close she could taste it.

She slowed as she reached the Blue Rose Cantina, a squat cinderblock building with metal bars across its windows. This was where Roman sold her. For sixty bucks, you got a drink and a dance with Kitten. Add a hundred and Roman escorted you to the trailer for time alone with her. Add four hundred and you had her all night.

Not anymore. She looked toward the road, toward the future. Once she reached the highway, she just had four blocks to get to the meeting spot—the 7-Eleven on the highway.

No cars waited in front of the store, but the sun had barely inched over the horizon. Soon the lady would come. Kitten didn't know her name. She'd asked once, but the lady said, "The less you know the better. That's what they told me." Kitten didn't know who "they" were, but she didn't care. What mattered was her escape. "My number is programmed into the phone. Call me if something happens," the lady had said.

Kitten pushed through the front door and smiled at the whiskered man snoring behind the cash register. She'd never been inside; Roman always made her wait in the car when he stopped by for cigarettes or beer. The candy aisle overwhelmed her with its choices. She settled on a Snickers bar and a bottle of cold water from the cooler, making enough noise to rouse the guy as she approached the counter. She used the twenty-dollar bill to pay.

"You new around here?" The man slapped her change into her hand.

That word, "new," jolted her, but Roman wasn't here. New didn't always have his awful meaning.

"No," she said. "I mean sort of. Just passing by."

"Passing by without wheels?" He smiled. His front teeth crossed each other like fingers.She shoved the money in her knapsack. He leaned over. His hot breath smelled like cinnamon gum. "You one of Roman's girls, ain't ya?"

Kitten fought a wave of dread. What if he called the trailer?

"You a pretty little thing." His hairy-knuckled hand slid across the counter. "Probably cost more than I got. But maybe we cut Roman out of the deal."

Kitten could handle this guy. She handled men like him all the time. Her brows quirked up in a flirtation. "Maybe we can. But later."

"Later?" He licked his lips.

"Sure, baby. I got a customer meeting me right now, but I'll be back at noon. Will you be here?"

"For you, little lady, I'll make sure I am." She winked, spun around, and sashayed out the door.

Once outside, she hurried to the dark side of the building. She leaned against the wall, burying her shaking hands between her knees. She had to be more careful. When headlights from a lone car approached, she prayed, prayed it was the lady, but this car didn't look familiar. What if the lady changed her mind? What if she didn't come?

But she would. She had promised. Kitten sat cross-legged on the grass and retrieved the cell phone from her knapsack. She pressed the lady's number. Nobody answered. *Maybe she's on her way and doesn't want to use the phone. Safer that way.* Kitten could be patient.

A man climbed from the shiny silver car and opened the gas tank. Kitten unscrewed the top from her water bottle and downed a third. The Snickers bar went into the knapsack; fear and dread had taken away her hunger.

Her head bumped back against the brick. How long had she been in this hellhole? A year? Longer? Time had a different meaning now.

Up the road, Kitten spotted two cars approaching. Finally, enough light splashed across the road that she could see that the second one was dark—maybe gray. *That could be her.* Kitten stuck the water bottle in a pocket of her pack and stood, brushing bits of dirt from the back of her shorts. She'd dash to the car and slam the door. She'd lie down in the seat so nobody could spot her. She'd imagine Brandon and the possibility she might see him again as the lady drove her away.

She'd breathe in, for the first time in so long, real freedom.

CHAPTER THREE

I don't know why I even tried to sleep. I'd left my sister's house around 4 a.m, after answering a hundred questions from a uniformed cop who'd been excruciatingly polite but unhelpful. She had focused on the phone messages, which annoyed me. Peyton wasn't having an affair. Unlike her husband. But who was the guy with the accent who called? What was the plan that had to change?

When I got home, I crawled in bed, tucked the foam-covered plugs into my ears, and listened to a recording of white noise. Sometimes the *schweesh-schweesh-schweesh* filled my mind like an ocean surf, lulling me to sleep. But not that night. The terror just under my skin kept me wide awake.

Shortly after dawn, I showered, letting the water beat down on shoulders knotted with tension from all the what-ifs bouncing through my brain. What if Peyton had been in an accident? Or kidnapped? Or . . . or . . . *Enough!*

I climbed out to be greeted by an unfriendly mirror. My brown hair, threaded with too much silver, hung down my shoulders like limp seaweed. I've often wished I had Peyton's honey-blond curls or her dimpled smile, but I inherited the hard-edged angles of Mom's face and her mouth no wider than a green bean. Most wouldn't put my age at only thirty-eight. I blame the job for that—six years as an overworked, ridiculously underpaid social worker had taken its toll. Not to mention the little matter of my psychiatric issues.

I got the coffee going before checking my voicemail for the tenth time. *Nothing.* I lifted Peyton's cell phone, which I'd left charging while I tried to sleep. When I swiped the screen, a photo of Lindsay bloomed to life. My thumb traced her blond bangs, her squinty smile. This child was Peyton's world. What would happen to Lindsay if . . . and how in God's name had she ended up in that closet?

I got to work. I could see she'd gotten five calls last night from the same number and another this morning from a different one. I tried the first. After a dozen rings, nobody answered. I started to try the second one when my own cell buzzed. Peyton's home number. I answered with a rush of hope. "Peyton?"

"No. Me," David said.

"Any news?"

"I talked to Jenny. She worked her usual hours. Peyton came home, said nothing about leaving again. You haven't heard anything?"

"No. How was Lindsay this morning? Did she remember anything about last night?"

"She keeps asking where Mommy is. Wish I knew what to tell her." He sighed. "A detective's coming over. They were going to trace the calls from last night. I told him you had her cell. He wants you to drop it off."

"I can swing by during lunch."

He clicked off without saying goodbye.

I lifted Peyton's cell and tried the most recent number again. Nobody picked up. This was getting maddening. As I hung up, I glanced at the clock. At 7 a.m., I dialed the one place where someone would answer.

"Sunrise Community Care Home." It sounded like Bernice, a first shift nursing aide. "This is Georgia Thayer. Is Mom up?" Mom has lived at the home for three years. She's spent a good part of her life in and out of hospitals, but when Alzheimer's began to ravage her brain a few years ago, she landed in the extended care facility. She had good days and bad days, but a private room and decent meals kept her fairly stable—even though she gripes about the runny eggs and biscuits "hard as hockey-pucks." For some of us Thayers, "fairly stable" was as good as it got. Peyton and I supplement Mom's monthly disability check to pay for the home, but it's worth it.

"No, she had a rough night so we're letting her sleep in."

"What happened?"

"A tangle with another resident about her garden. Miss Adele don't like nobody picking her flowers."

"Bernice, has my sister been there? Or called?"

She must have caught something in my tone. "Everything okay?"

"She's disappeared. I hope maybe Mom heard from her."

"Oh, no. Let me check the sign-ins." In less than a minute she came back on the line. "Last time Peyton came was two weeks ago. And the last call was Saturday. That was you."

"Don't tell Mom I called."

"It ain't like Miss Peyton to miss visiting this long. I hope she turns up soon. I'll be praying for all of you that she comes home safe and sound."

I hung up, picturing Bernice with her multiple black braids and her gap-toothed smile. She meant it when she said she'd pray. I needed all the prayers I could get.

The best thing to do was to get busy, starting with caffeine. I poured a cup of high-test coffee, took a seat at the kitchen table, and started assembling a list of all the relatives, friends, and acquaintances I could think of. I'd met one of Peyton's friends from the university, a woman named Candace Galloway, though Peyton hadn't mentioned her in months. Come to think of it, whenever I asked my sister about school, I got vague answers like "a helluva lot more than I bargained for." Why was she being evasive? Why hadn't I pushed harder?

I found Candace's name in Peyton's contacts and dialed. "Sorry to bother you." I explained who I was and about my sister's disappearance. "Have you talked with her recently?"

"No. She's missed class the past couple of weeks. I made copies of my notes for her thinking she'd ask for them, but she hasn't."

My alarm heightened. My sister would never miss class without a damn good reason.

"Of course, she's been up to her eyeballs in her thesis project," Candace said.

It embarrassed me that I hadn't heard anything about this project until last night. "What can you tell me about it?"

"I'm studying low birth weight on later-school performance. But Peyton's is much more involved, something to do with migrant farmworkers and access to healthcare."

Migrant farmworkers? The guy with the accent on the phone. Was he tied to her research? How did I not know about any of this?

"Her thesis advisor will know more. Dr. Jeff Lambert." More muffled voices on the other end. "I'm sure she'll turn up soon."

Next call, the university listing for the School of Public Health. No answer, but what did I expect that early?

I scrolled through her phone log of the past few days; that now-familiar number comprised most of the list. I dialed it again but got no answer. Why didn't the guy have voicemail setup? Or call again? I scanned the other phone applications, paused on the calendar function, and tried it. Holy Cow, she actually used the thing. Her past week's activities displayed: classes, Lindsay's playtime, several hours blocked out as research, and "meet with JH," scheduled for this morning. Who was JH? The man on her answering machine?

Scrolling back further, I found other appointments. Five weeks ago—Grandy Mill, 1215 Gadsden Street, which was in the industrial district. Three weeks ago—Lakewood Peach Farm, Pelion. Last week—Blue Rose Cantina, 9 p.m.. Were these appointments related to her research? The most recent entry was from two days ago—Special Touch. Special Touch what? Why did she have to be so cryptic?

One other entry caught my attention; "lunch with G." We had planned to meet at the Café last Thursday, but I canceled because a stupid treatment-team meeting ran too long. What might have happened if I hadn't? Would she have told me about all this? Would I know where she was now?

I wrote down every entry I found, including phone numbers from her contacts and her entire calendar. Somewhere in all this was the clue to where my sister was.

Twenty minutes later, I arrived at the hospital and headed straight to the office of my boss, Clancy Jefford. Clancy was nodding into the telephone and scrolling through a medical record on her computer. "It's not here, Richard," she said into the receiver. "I'm looking at the file right now."

I took a seat. Listening to Clancy gripe was like comfort food. Speaking of food, a diet cola was on her desk beside a Payday wrapper, her standard midmorning snack. Clancy is an ample woman, comfortable in her body, in her flowing plus-size skirts and unstructured jackets, who likes eating almost as much as she likes smoking. The stress of our jobs brings out all kinds of vices.

Clancy made the brave—or maybe stupid—move of hiring me six years ago. I'd been volunteering at the hospital as a recovery group leader and when she asked me questions about the participants, she was surprised by my insights. As someone who understands mental illness from both inside and out, I see things other professionals don't. When she found out about my clinical social work degree, she suggested—or rather, demanded—I apply. "Are you nuts?" I had responded. "How's personnel going to handle my needing the same medications you GIVE people here?"

"That's what the Disability Act is for. You work your butt off in your recovery and that's what our patients need to see."

A skeptical administration kept me part-time for the first year, but Clancy went to bat for me again and I've been full-time ever since. "Everybody has to be a little crazy to work here," Clancy often says. I still get flak from a few unenlightened doctors and nurses but it's nothing I can't handle.

Clancy's voice rose a few decibels. "There are just two of us down here in social work and we get the job done. Make them find the damn reports!" She hung up and turned to me, her scowl morphing into a fatigued smile. "So. What's on your plate today?"

I told her all of it, about my missing sister, my little niece tucked in a closet. The police. Once I started, the words rushed out like water through a floodgate. I hated the tremble in my voice, not wanting Clancy—or anyone—to sense my fear.

"God, George. Where do you think she is?"

"I'd appreciate it if you could convince me that she ran off to join the circus."

"She ran off to join the circus. All that clown training's finally paying off." She studied me for a long moment. "How are you doing?"

"How do you think?"

"Why are you at work? Go home."

I glanced at the state of her desk, almost as bad as mine. The offer of leave time was a real sacrifice.

"You need to leave, just leave. I can cover things here."

The problem was, I didn't know where to start. My sister was gone. I had no clue where to look for her.

CHAPTER FOUR

L illian set the cruise control on the Thunderbird convertible at seventy as she skated from lane to lane, skirting the vehicles like she was navigating an obstacle course. A little pressure on the gas— eighty. All clear in the far-left lane. No sign of highway patrol. The road a slash through lush pine forests and farmland.

She liked to imagine this was her car. *It should be.* It fit her perfectly—the red tint like her auburn hair, the sleek frame like her carefully maintained body. But no, like everything else in her life, it belonged to Jefe. Jefe—pronounced hef—fay, though he was as American as she was.

She pulled onto the private road leading to the Orchid Estate, which occupied seventy acres in rural Saluda County. Jefe chose well. Local cops consisted of a frightened rural sheriff's department that accepted bribes. The county had even paved the road leading up to the complex. Jefe had added a helipad to make it easier for international clients to have access. Business grew faster than they could accommodate it.

Lillian used her key card to open the first wrought iron gate, then drove another eighth of a mile to where the chain link fence, topped with razor wire, encircled the mansion. Another iron gate was manned by a guard at the security booth who waved as he let her in.

Once inside the premises, the driveway switched from concrete to brick, a herringbone pattern that had cost Jefe a fortune. Palmettos lined the drive, while manicured shrubs of pink-tipped loropetalum behind gumpo azaleas flanked the steps to the mansion. Camellias stood guard at the ends—Lillian's idea—so that color greeted guests year-round.

Sunlight winked through the leaded glass door held open by the security officer. It was monthly inspection day, so she paused in the foyer to take in everything—the oriental rugs over gleaming oak floors, the velvet sofas in the parlor that somehow combined opulence with comfort. Art that should be hanging in a museum. She grabbed the clipboard from her office and walked room to room, noting any speck of dust or unpolished banister rail. Keeping the place immaculate conveyed to the guests that they paid attention to every tiny detail. She prided herself on this perfection and its effect on Jefe's clientele. While his business once focused on state officials and the local elite, the current buyers came from all over the world for discreet satisfaction. They paid dearly for it, in money and favors.

She moved to the dining room, remembering its original furnishings—a monstrosity of an oak table surrounded by mismatched chairs. It took some convincing for Jefe to agree to redecorate. When she requested an interior designer, he'd laughed and tossed her a collection of Architectural Digest magazines. "You want it fixed, then fix it," he'd said. She did her best and felt proud of what she'd created. Classy. Unique. Sexy. A modern black table that sat twenty and upholstered chairs with orchid emblems stitched on the backs. Such a vast change from when she'd come here eight years earlier.

The smell of pungent herb tea preceded Onyx's approach from the kitchen. "Would you like some?" Onyx had a spectacular accent. Nigerian, she'd escaped a horrific life of slavery to be purchased by an American businessman and brought to the States. Jefe traded a large shipment of artillery for her and confided to Lillian that Onyx was "worth every bullet."

"God no. Stuff smells like feet," Lillian said.

Onyx laughed. She wore an ankle-length dashiki and a large necklace of brass beads. They'd cropped her hair close to her scalp to accentuate her very angular cheekbones and firm, narrow jawline. In another life, she could have been a supermodel. Except, of course, for the scars, hidden by the flowing robe.

"It keeps me healthy," Onyx said of her tea concoction. "It might put some color in those pale cheeks of yours."

Lillian's pale cheeks were what attracted men to her—lily-white skin with a spattering of delicate freckles. A few wrinkles lined the sides of her eyes, which disturbed her. She wasn't really allowed to age.

When her cell rang, she didn't have to check the display. Only one person was allowed this number. "Jefe?"

Onyx left the room, understanding Lillian's need for privacy.

"How did the inspection go?" Background noise told her he was in his car, probably the Lincoln Aviator.

"We'll be ready," she said.

"I want everything perfect, Lil. Do not let me down."

She winced at his tone. Disappointing him could have deadly consequences, so she always took special care to keep him satisfied. Maybe something else had him riled. "Of course. Everything okay?"

"One of Roman's girls got away. He only has two in his stable right now, and he lets this shit happen!"

"Any leads on where she is?" Lillian understood his frustration. If a girl successfully escaped—and so far, nobody had—they'd have to assume she'd go to the police. Every one of Jefe's operations would shut down to start again elsewhere. All their hard work to build the estate, gone in a blink.

"We've got her. Or we will momentarily."

She used a tone that soothed him. "Good. That's good. Jefe, how fast are you driving?"

"Why do you ask?"

"Because you're pissed and you're behind the wheel. Please be careful."

Jefe laughed, which was what she wanted. "Gunner is driving, so you don't have to worry about me. Worry about those damn Slavs we have coming in on Friday."

"We'll be ready." She heard the phone click off.

A few minutes later, Onyx reappeared, looking decidedly unhappy.

"What's wrong?"

"I went to tell the girls about getting an afternoon off and walked in on Violet with a hundred-dollar bill. I think she took it from a buyer."

Lillian's eyes widened in horror. This kind of crime, in their world, could have fatal consequences. "Took? As in stole?"

"No. Sorry. I mean, I think she took a tip. I told her you were going to the store tomorrow and she wanted new nail polish. She pulled some cash from her wallet and a hundred-dollar bill fell out! I asked where she got it and she acted very strange. She snatched up that cash and shoved it in her bra so fast I thought she'd get dizzy! I said, 'Violet, where did you get that money?' She cursed at me in Spanish then said her sister had sent it. Her sister! And I asked, 'How? We do not get mail here!' Then the waterworks started. 'Please, don't tell Jefe. Please,' she begged. So I'm not telling Jefe. I'm telling you." She shrugged.

"Dammit. Bring her to the study. Have her wait until I get there."

As Onyx left, Lillian mulled what to do. She could be lenient. Take the money, put the fear of God in her, then lie to Jefe about finding the cash on the floor of one of the rooms. This wouldn't be hard to believe as buyers often got sloppy drunk. But Violet had always been a problem. She demanded to work in the Begonia room because the air conditioning blew strongest there. She borrowed Venus's razor without asking and lied when Venus confronted her. Complained of headaches when it was time to deep clean the house, a task requiring everyone's participation. Buyers loved her though. Those plump, dimpled cheeks. The full, pouty lips. That small, but remarkably flexible body. Some simply couldn't get enough of her.

Lillian waited a little longer before striding into the study where Violet sat on the leather sofa, hands pressed between her knees, head tilted down, like a schoolgirl summoned to the principal's office.

Lillian stood over her. "Tell me about the hundred dollars."

"I told Onyx. My sister—"

"Stop that bullshit right now! Who gave it to you, Violet? And DO . . . NOT . . . LIE." Lillian fixed a laser stare on the girl, whose sunken, humble posture morphed into a look of stony defiance.

"Why shouldn't I take money when it is given to me? I work hard for it. I gave Mr. Whitfield—"

"Whitfield? Samuel Whitfield gave you that tip?" The congressman was a regular who appeared about every two months. How many girls had he had? How many had benefited from his generosity? Troubling. Something she must put a stop to.

"He's a nice man. I gave him a very special time, Lillian. I did my job."

Of course, she had. All of her girls did spectacular work with their clientele—she made sure of it. "What is the rule about tips?" Lillian asked.

"He said—"

"What is the rule?"

She let out an annoyed sigh. "The money goes to you."

"No. The money goes to Jefe. When you took that money, you weren't stealing from me. You were stealing from *him*." She pounced on that last word, eliciting the desired response. The girl's green eyes filled with fear-of-God terror. "Hand it over."

The girl reached into her bra and pulled out a crumpled bill.

"Leave it on the coffee table. Go to your room and remain there until I tell you to come out."

"What . . . what are you going to do to me?"

Lillian glared. "Don't you mean, what will Jefe do? I don't know. The last girl who stole from him, well, we don't really know what happened to her. She simply disappeared.

"Are you a praying woman, Violet?"

She nodded.

"Then you'd better pray he shows you mercy."

Violet nodded, stood, and hurried away. Onyx appeared so suddenly that Lillian realized she must have been standing just outside the door.

"You heard?"

She nodded. "What will Jefe do?"

She looked behind Onyx's question, because the answer affected her and the other girls. Showing mercy now would only invite more conduct like Violet's, something she couldn't afford. Jefe had to know she had complete control of her stable. But if she told Jefe the truth, Gunner or Lito would kill the girl.

"Maybe I'll try to convince him that Violet admitted her crime. That she brought us that money. If he's in the right mood, he may take pity on her."

She frowned at Onyx. "Talk to the other girls. Let them know how serious this is. If nothing else, this is a message they might need to be reminded of."

"I will make sure they know. But please, Lillian. Violet is young, and the young make mistakes. Try to make him give her another chance."

She let out a dark laugh. "Like I can 'make' him do anything."

"If anyone can, it's you."

CHAPTER FIVE

Kitten ducked into a narrow strip of shade beside the store. Hope faded as the minutes ticked by. The gray car hadn't been the lady, nor had the dark SUV that came after. She gripped the phone she'd been given, wondering if she could buy a charger with the little money she had left. Who would she call? Not the lady who did not come for her. No way could she call her mother because God only knew where she was. And if she could call Brandon, he wouldn't be able to help her.

How long had she been waiting? Several hours, at least. The sun had climbed high over the trees, scorching the asphalt beneath her. Maybe it was time to move on. But to where? The police?

Tires crunching on rocks made her jump. She grabbed the backpack as she peered around the corner; a rusty brown sedan squealed into the parking lot. *Roman.*

She took off running, her feet pounding the asphalt, cringing at the squeaks of Roman's car doors opening. "Kitten!" Roman yelled. "Where do you think you're going?"

She ran faster. Roman's footfall sounded behind her, and he wasn't alone. The pack thumped against her back. She thought about dropping it, but it held her money and her photo, and she wouldn't part with them.

"KITTEN! You bitch."

She gulped in more hot air as she forced herself to keep moving. A truck whizzed by kicking up tiny pebbles that pelted her legs. She picked up her pace, convincing herself that she could catch the truck, jump on its back bumper, and speed away. Sweat dribbled from her chin.

The footsteps behind her sounded fainter. Roman was too out of shape for this chase, but she was out of breath, too. Adrenalin pushed her on.

Just as she reached a curve in the road, a sleek silver SUV approached. *Maybe,* she thought. *Maybe.* She raised her arms to halt it; she'd beg for a ride—anywhere. She didn't care, just to get out of Roman's reach. The car slid to a stop.

When she grabbed the handle of the back door it swung open with enough force to knock her down. Gravel bit into her hands as she squinted up; a shiny black shoe attached to a crisply pressed black pant leg emerged. It was him. She tried to scramble away but the man's foot planted itself on her back, digging in.

"Going somewhere, Kitten?" He didn't have Roman's thick Mexican accent. His American voice was quiet, as though used to being listened to. His dark curls gleamed in the sunlight and his pale skin held not a single blemish. She had not seen him in months, but the terror that filled her belly was as fresh as yesterday. He had picked her up at the Burger King in Pennsylvania, driven her to Charlotte, locked her in that hotel room. He'd taken her to the farm and, days later, handed her over to Roman.

Roman trotted up with Lito beside him. Sweat oozed from Lito's shaven head. His shoulders bulged like kick balls from his sleeveless muscle shirt. Roman flipped her over and placed a foot on her abdomen, pinning her like a bug.

Jefe, his boss, bent over and smiled, his teeth white and straight like fence pickets. He stroked her cheek, his fingers gentle. "She got the drop on you, didn't she?"

Roman scowled. "I was asleep. I didn't know—she stole my key!"

Jefe reached for her knapsack and dumped the contents. "How did she get a cell?"

Roman's eyes widened with fury. He smashed his heel into the phone, plastic exploding.

Jefe sighed at Roman, his thin lips pulled tight. "How many more times do I let you screw up like this?"

"This one is trouble. We should get rid of her," Lito said.

"But she makes me good money." Jefe pulled sunglasses from his pocket and slid them on his face. "Teach her a lesson, but don't hurt that face. If this ever happens again, you know what will happen."

"It won't!" Roman rushed to say.

Lito grabbed her by the arm and jerked her up. Jefe stepped closer, his nose inches from hers. He reached for a strand of her hair. "You've always been a favorite of mine. And so many of your buyers. Don't make me regret letting you live."

"I . . . I won't."

"Good." Jefe climbed into his car and drove away, leaving Kitten with his men. A rage glowed in Lito's red-rimmed eyes that she'd seen before. She knew what was coming. She looked up at the crisp blue sky, at a perfect V of geese soaring south, and let her mind fly away with them.

The second day after Peyton disappeared, my worry escalated to panic. I tried to work, but lack of sleep made it close to impossible, so I stopped by the break room for another caffeine injection. We have the worst coffee here at the hospital, more like flavored mud than a beverage, but I drank half a mug and refilled it before retreating to my office.

I work beside Clancy in a space the size of a mop closet. The surface of my desk, which was last seen when Obama was in office, held more than the usual amount of clutter—work I'd avoided, coffee cups that needed cleaning, and social work journals that would be tossed, unread.

I unearthed the telephone and again dialed the number to the School of Public Health. Luck was with me; Dr. Lambert was in his office. He sounded stressed when he picked up the phone.

"What's going on?" His bass voice rumbled. "The police were just here. I told them that I hadn't seen Peyton. She missed an appointment with me last week. I asked her to email me the latest draft of her thesis, but she didn't reply."

Not complying with a professor's request? This spiked my worry even more. "What can you tell me about her research?"

"Not much. She had a health survey she planned to administer at several local farms that employ migrant workers. But she's made changes. Lots of them. That's why I wanted to meet with her."

Silence hung between us for a moment. I could hear slow breathing as he read between the lines. "I told the police I'd ask around, see if anyone's seen her," he said. "I'll call if I learn anything."

"Thanks." I gave him my cell and work numbers and clicked off. I turned on my computer to find a long list of progress notes needing my entry—not happening today. I signed off, jotted a note for Clancy telling her I was leaving and to text me if she needed anything before I left.

When we were kids, Peyton and I operated like one creature. Wherever I went, she was my blonde little shadow. My memory of starting first grade was Peyton's teary face watching me get on the school bus. I tried to climb out the window to get to her. I was a kick-ass big sister. Nobody dared pick on Peyton. Sheltering her from bullies, from hard homework assignments, and, at times, from Mom, was a job I took very seriously. Once when Mom was in the hospital, Social Services had the nerve to put us in separate foster homes, which lasted two days. I broke into my case manager's briefcase, found Peyton's file, wrote down the address, bought a map at a convenience store, and hitchhiked to where she was staying. Twenty-four miles away, and I was eight years old.

Needless to say, Social Services was unhappy with me. Just

when they were ready to plop me into a group home for "girls with behavioral issues," Mom got discharged and collected both of us. She had days, weeks even, when she could almost be a good mom. And other times? She was a nightmare.

Summer had landed like a moist splat in Columbia. Sweat bound my top to my back when I plopped myself on the blistering vinyl seat in my old Civic. Now, where to go? Looking for Peyton, I decided, so I drove toward her usual haunts.

But she wasn't anywhere, not at the Rose and Shamrock, her favorite restaurant, where nobody had seen her in several weeks, not at the university library. I certainly didn't expect her to be perusing the shelves after disappearing in the middle of the night.

Nobody had seen her at the Episcopal cathedral, where she regularly attended services, and my desperate reconnaissance of the streets of Columbia didn't produce Peyton's car or any other signs that my little sis was even still in my zip code. The absolute absence of clues terrified me.

Then I remembered the calendar on her phone. The Blue Rose Cantina was listed. When I Googled it, I got an address on Highway 262 in Lexington County, so I pointed my car west. Fifteen minutes later, I swerved into a middle-of-the-road U-turn when I realized I'd just passed the cantina. It was easy to do; the squat, cinderblock building could have been anything—a storage room, a garage. A meth lab. Rusty wrought iron bars covered the two small windows. The battered door was covered with peeling ads for Pall Mall cigarettes and Jim Beam. A wooden sign out front sagged on its chain. Under the faded outline of a rose were the words *Beer/Cerveza.*

What was Peyton doing here?

I climbed out of the car. One of the pickups in the sandy parking lot had a rebel flag sticker in its window. The other so mud-caked I couldn't read the license plate. An eighteen-wheeler rumbled beside the building.

Anxiety crawled up my throat as I opened the door. Inside wasn't much better. My Dansko clogs made sucking sounds when I stepped across the cerveza-stained cement floor. The bar, made of plywood painted blue, extended down one side, small café tables scattered across the other end of the room. The bartender was in an animated conversation with a man in an Atlanta Braves ball cap. A few stools down, a lone man sat hunched over the bar, gripping a Modelo Negra.

"You want something?" the bartender asked.

I cleared my throat. "Yeah, I was hoping you can help me. I'm trying to find someone."

His eyebrows, dark as obsidian, shot up. "I doubt you'll find them here."

The ball cap guy swiveled his barstool to look me over. He had green eyes that didn't look in the same direction. That kind of thing drives me crazy because of the whole how-do-I-make-eye contact issue. "You could be looking for me," he said with a flickery grin.

"No, I don't think so." My hand shook as I pulled out my smartphone and clicked on a photo of my sister. Seeing her familiar face, the tiny scar between her brows from the bicycle accident when she was seven, the wavy blonde hair that I'd always envied, the forced grin that said, "take the picture, dammit," made something crumble inside me. I placed it on the bar to show the bartender.

He looked at it for a long time, then frowned. "Don't know her."

"She's my sister. She's missing. Please, take another look."

He glanced at lizard eyes. I showed the photo to him, too. He lifted his beer bottle in a toast. "I'd like a piece of that."

I wanted to nut punch him, and I wanted to get the hell out of there. The bartender crossed his arms. A dark blue vine encircled his wrist. Prison tattoo. Nice.

When I turned to show the picture to the guy at the end of the bar, he was gone. I snagged a business card and slapped it on the chipped plywood. "My name and phone number. If you remember something, I'd appreciate a call."

"Georgia Thayer, medical social worker," he read.

"I like social workers," lizard eyes mocked.

"Yeah. I'll be leaving now." I hurried out, which wasn't easy since my feet kept sticking. Why had my sister come here? Did this bar have something to do with her thesis?

I skidded out of the parking lot and drove a mile toward town before pulling off the highway. I checked my watch; four-thirty. I had one more place to go.

Driving to my sister's, I felt a muddle of emotions. *Hope* she'd be there, that she'd come home, and everything was fine. *Fear* that she hadn't, and what that meant. The large white car parked in her driveway looked like a police cruiser. Maybe they had news. Maybe they'd found her. As I rushed up the steps to ring the doorbell, I heard voices from the backyard, so I let myself through the wrought iron gate. Jenny sat on the back steps, cell phone in hand, while Lindsay was perched in a patio chair. Across from her, a man dressed in perfectly pleated dark chinos and a polo-style shirt wrote something on a pad. His thick black hair had a few threads of silver, and I recognized him as Detective Lou Michaels, someone I'd met when I dated wild-man reporter Ben Reeder. While Ben abhorred structure, haircuts, and neckties, Lou had an anal-retentive gene that made him overly prompt and meticulous. How those two remained best friends for so long was a mystery I'd never solve.

I bolted over to Lou. "Have you found her?"

He looked up at me, head cocked, "Not yet. I'm sorry."

"Then why—" I looked at my tiny niece. "Why are you questioning Lindsay? Where is her dad? Why isn't he here?"

Lindsay leaped from her seat and scurried to me, her tiny arms clenching my knees. I touched her soft hair, her warm skin, and felt a rush of sadness. "Hey, Peanut."

"I was just asking Lindsay a few questions. And yes, her father knows I'm here," Lou sounded offended that I'd suggest otherwise.

I would take that up with David. Jenny must have heard the fury in my voice because she hurried over. "Everything okay?"

"Everything's fine," I said, for Lindsay's benefit. "Take Peanut inside."

She eyed the detective before reaching for my niece's hand. "Milk and Oreos?" Jenny asked her.

"Aunt George too?" Lindsay kept a grip on my knee.

"I'll be there in a minute. Save three Oreos for me."

Lindsay stuck one-two-three fingers in the air, part of the counting game we always played.

"That's right!" I kissed the top of her head and tried not to let the tears come. *This baby needs her mama.*

After Jenny led her away, Lou flashed me an irritated look. "Guess I was done."

"What did she tell you?"

He looked at the closed door to the house, as though weighing what to disclose. "She doesn't remember anything except playing hide-and-seek with Mrs. Ribault, which is why she was in the closet."

"Peyton told Lindsay to hide? From what?"

"I think it was just a game. Your niece didn't seem upset."

"But something made my sister leave." Without her daughter. Or her phone. It made no sense.

"Any ideas about that?" he asked.

"No." I pulled her phone out of my purse and handed it to him. "All charged up. She has a few entries on the calendar I've been checking out."

He took the phone with a disapproving glare. "What do you mean, 'checking out'?"

"If your sister was missing, you'd be doing the same thing, Lou. I know y'all are trying to find her, but I can't just sit on my hands." He eased the phone into his pocket. "Look, we don't know what happened to Peyton. And of course, you're worried about her. Still, it's safer if you leave the investigating to professionals."

I flashed a tight smile that held back the words I wanted to say. *What are you professionals doing, exactly?*

"Can I ask you a few questions? You heard the message from the Ribault's answering machine. Any thoughts as to who that was?"

"No." I pressed a finger and thumb against the bridge of my nose, where someone was pounding a roofing nail into my head.

He flipped pages on the notepad. "Can you tell me about her relationship with Dr. Ribault?"

Lou was smooth, I had to give him that. He had a subtle way of probing, not just with the questions, but with his eyes that didn't seem to miss a thing. I'm not sure he ever even blinked. "Complicated. David Ribault isn't an easy man to live with. He can be self-absorbed. Maybe even narcissistic. Probably because of how he was raised." I looked at the mammoth house where my sister lived, remembering the tour she gave me when they bought it. "I could fit my bedroom in your closet," I had joked. "And who the hell needs four bathrooms? There are only two of you! Will you be inviting guests over to shower?" Peyton's reply had been an embarrassed, "I won't have to share with David anymore. I can leave all my makeup on the counter and he can't complain."

I said to Lou, "You grow up having more money than God, you come to expect the world to revolve around you."

He glanced down at his pad. I wished I could see what was written there.

"They separated once before, didn't they?"

Was there anything he didn't know? "Peyton was talking about going to grad school. I think he felt threatened by it—the very idea that she could be independent. So alpha David asserted his manhood by screwing around."

"Who was the other woman?"

"Some pharmacy rep."

"This affair—that's when Peyton separated from her husband?" Lou asked.

"It devastated her."

He looked at the house, then back at me.

"She told David she wanted a divorce. But a few months later, David dumped the other woman and begged her to let him come home. Soon after, she was pregnant, and Lindsay arrived. Things have been okay with them since then."

My sister never heard voices. She didn't have Mom's rages or my difficult-to-define psychosis. She had escaped the family curse unscathed.

"Where is the pharmacy rep?"

"I heard she moved out of state. Good riddance."

"What about your sister?" he asked.

"What about her?"

"Has she been involved with anyone else?"

The hammer picked up speed. "No, she would never do something like that." I thought about the calls on her cell. The notes in her calendar. A trail of breadcrumbs from Peyton that weren't taking me anywhere. What the hell was my sister up to?

After a moment, Lou asked, "When was the last time you saw her?"

"A week ago. She showed up at my house with Lindsay. Asked me to babysit. She wouldn't tell me where she was going, but it sounded like something important to her. She said to call her cell if there was a problem." It had seemed strange, her being this secretive. I had probed and prodded. "If you're finally having an affair then you better spill it, sister. I'll open the champagne."

Her response, an enigmatic smile. "I get it now, why you do what you do. What it's like to do something that makes a difference. Why you put up with that pathetic salary they pay you."

"Because I'm certifiably nuts?" Always the smartass. Why hadn't I asked her what she meant? And now she had vanished, without telling me what she was up to.

I said to Lou, "I kept Lindsay overnight and dropped her off at daycare that next morning. Peyton called me at work and thanked me, said she'd get Lindsay's clothes later. She never did."

"You don't know where she spent the night?" Lou asked.

"No." I pressed my fingertips into my temples and began a circular massage, wondering if anything might exorcize the headache, other than Peyton's return. "Now it's your turn, detective. What have you learned? Did you talk to Peyton's advisor at school? What was her research project?"

"We're covering all the bases, Georgia. I promise you that." Lou reached in his pocket for a business card to hand me. "I appreciate your help. If you think of anything else, please call me."

"Sure I will, detective."

I found Lindsay in the kitchen with Jenny. A glass of milk beside a stack of Oreos awaited. I sat across from the munchkin who had mounted the chair on her knees. She leaned toward me licking her lips. "I see we had cookies," I said, eyeing the dark crumbs sprinkled across her T-shirt.

"One!"

Jenny verified with a nod.

"Then you can have one of mine." I held up one finger and she snagged the top cookie, an impish grin on her tiny face. I tried to summon interest in eating, but my appetite had fled.

"Aunt George?" Lindsay helped herself to my glass, dunking the Oreo long enough that I expected it to scream for help.

"What honey?"

"When's Mommy coming home?"

Her blue eyes searched the contours of my face, searching for a truth I didn't have.

"She'll be home soon, Peanut. I'm sure of it." I channeled my inner Viking to keep my voice even, to not let her feel my fear.

She dunked her cookie again. "Mommy always tucks me in at bedtime."

These simple words sliced my heart. If I didn't find her, if Mommy never made it back home, what would happen to this precious girl? Stupid tears filled my eyes. I wouldn't cry in front of Lindsay, so I stood, nudging the table and almost toppling over the milk. "I have to go." I kissed the top of her head, the place Peyton always kissed her when she said goodbye.

CHAPTER SIX

Nausea woke Kitten. She rolled to the side of the bed, felt for the small plastic trash can, and waited for vomit to emerge once again. It didn't. She squeezed her eyes closed, mentally trying to still her quaking stomach. Strands of her hair, wet from the ice pack that had melted, slashed across her face. She touched the bruise under her eye. Roman didn't like to leave marks that buyers could see but Lito, his right-hand man, hadn't shown the same caution. Jefe might be angry when he saw visible damage to his merchandise.

The swollen eye wasn't all. She had red spots on her ribs and thighs from Roman's kicks, and the swollen bulge between her pinky and wrist. Maybe the injuries would keep her out of commission for a few days, a blessing in disguise.

When she glanced at the window, she spotted a lizard resting on the sill. Rays from the sun made its skin look neon green. Of course, it didn't feel the heat the way she did. It looked quite content, arching its head back, blinking lazily as if ready for a much-needed nap. Kitten wished she felt that relaxed, but any movement made the pain roll through her.

"You're awake." Dulce stood in the narrow doorway, her jet-black hair clipped high on her head by plastic butterfly barrettes. "How you feel?"

Kitten propped herself up on elbows. "A little better."

Dulce stepped closer, teetering on the platform shoes. Fishnet hose made her thin legs look even skinnier. A shiny gold belt topped her black satin miniskirt. "Bruises look bad. I tell Roman to take you to emergency room."

"I'll bet he thought that was funny," Kitten answered.

She lifted a shoulder in a half shrug. "*Si*. The prick."

Kitten snuck a glance at the window; the lizard had vanished. Every inch of her hurt.

"You need to eat something." Dulce pointed to the small table by the bed where a pack of crackers and glass of ginger ale waited. "Try that. Or you want me to make you a sandwich?"

Kitten took a saltine and nibbled, surprised by Dulce's concern. When that bit of food didn't reappear, she braved a sip of warm ginger ale.

"Still have a headache?"

"Yeah." It felt like doors slamming inside Kitten's head. Worse was the stark truth that she hadn't escaped, she remained trapped in a spider's web she could not escape.

"You probably had a concussion. Good thing you have that hard head." Dulce grinned, one of her front teeth chipped from a fight with a buyer. "Where were you going?"

"Huh?"

Dulce helped herself to a cracker. "When you ran off. Where were you going? Didn't you know Roman would come after you?"

Kitten didn't want to think about that. About the lady who'd promised to come for her, promised a new life away from Roman and the customers. She'd even promised Kitten that she would be allowed to go to high school and get a diploma. What an idiot Kitten had been to believe this woman she hardly knew. Twice she'd been fooled. Never again.

"I've never seen Roman so mad." Dulce spoke softer. "After he got the call, he stormed into your room, then mine. He shook me like he thought I knew where you were. Then he grabbed the car keys and took off."

"What call?" Who had told on her? The greaser at the 7-Eleven?

"Somebody sold you out." Dulce sat on the side of her bed. As the mattress shifted, Kitten flinched against a flare of pain. "Sorry."

"It's okay." Kitten took a cracker from the pack, relieved her stomach felt less rocky.

"Roman said you don't have to work tonight. Maybe not tomorrow. He promised the boss you wouldn't run again."

Kitten pictured the curly-haired man in the shiny black shoes. "Who is Jefe?"

"*Shhh.*" Dulce cast a panic glance toward the door. "We don't ask questions like that. All you need to know is that he owns you. And me. And Roman."

Kitten wanted to say that nobody owned her, she owned herself, but that was only a wish. She took a sip of the warm drink. She had so many questions about Jefe. He had come five, maybe ten times since he turned her over to Roman. The sight of him made her stomach curdle. She set the glass on the table and fell back against the pillow.

"Roman threatened to send you to the factory to work. You can't break out of there. They have guards and shifts running day and night. Be glad he changed his mind."

"Why?" The factory might be better. Sure, the hours were long, but she wouldn't have to service men who left their stink on her.

"I worked there for six months. It's awful, Kitten. Hotter than an oven. They work you till you can't stand up, then let you sleep a few hours before they put you back on the floor. People get sick. Vomit. Pass out. It is hell. You don't want that, I promise." How many businesses did Jefe operate?

"Sounds like the farm." Kitten had survived hellish days in the orchard when Jefe first got her. Blisters covered her hands; sunburn scorched her neck and arms. The hours in the hot sun had made her dizzy. She prayed she never had to go back.

The front door slammed, and Dulce jumped as though she'd been caught disobeying house rules. Now and then she'd have that kind of reaction, like she was still just a kid, but then the hardened expression returned. "That's Roman. He wants me to work Two Notch Road tonight. How do I look?" Dulce wore purple and gold eye shadow. Her eyebrows, drawn in black pencil, arched like upside-down smiles. At eighteen, Dulce was only three years older than Kitten, but she looked like she could have been more than twenty. She acted that way, too. Roman let her dress however she wanted, but not Kitten, who had to look like a young girl. It made him more money.

She squinted at Dulce, assessing. "You forgot lipstick. You can use my pink on the dresser."

Dulce bent to eye herself in the mirror as she dabbed her lips with the pale rose gloss. "I like this color."

"Not as bright as you're used to," Kitten said. Dulce grabbed Kitten's brush and fluffed her blue-streaked bangs. The butterfly hair clips stayed in place.

"Get some more rest. And stay out of Roman's way. He's still pissed." Dulce tossed the brush on the dresser and tugged the neckline of her sparkly T-shirt off her shoulder. "Be back in a few hours."

CHAPTER SEVEN

"What are you doing?" Lillian stood in the doorway to Violet's room where Onyx emptied dresser drawers and stuffed clothes into corrugated boxes with gusto.

"I'm doing what I was ordered to do." Onyx threw a handful of bras on the bed—red, leopard-spotted, feather-trimmed. Violet loved the variety and paired the lingerie with vivid garters over silk stockings. In her closet hung a collection of costumes—a glittery flapper dress from the twenties, a leather corset that took two of them to lace, a princess dress that she somehow made positively pornographic, each of which was snatched from its hanger and tossed onto the bed.

"Jefe ordered it?" She wasn't sure how he could have. He'd been gone for three days, as he often did. She knew he had a whole other life she wasn't a part of, but her efforts to probe only angered him.

"Violet won't be needing them anymore." Onyx plopped the items into a box. "Lito took her away. Lito."

Lillian heard the anger and terror behind Onyx's words. She didn't want her girls more afraid than they already were. She needed their energy, which, at times, was happy and playful. This is what pleased their buyers the most. "Because she won't need those clothes at the farm."

Onyx froze, her hand gripping a feather-topped stiletto. "The farm?"

"That's where Jefe said he'd send her. He was so mad about the theft, but I told him that Violet confessed. Guess he decided to show some mercy." Lillian reached for a cherry-red thong and tossed it in the box. "She's picking peaches as we speak."

Onyx resumed packing, her movements less pronounced. "I can just picture Violet in the orchard. She'll have much to say about the heat."

"And the hours. And she won't like the overalls they'll make her wear."

Onyx heaved a full-throated laugh. "They won't let her wear her false eyelashes! The other girls will laugh about that."

"You know—" Lillian held up the flapper dress. "One of the other girls could wear this."

"Mei Mei. She loves to wear costumes!"

"And this?" Lillian lifted a sparkly tiara, won by Violet in a highly competitive game of Hearts.

"Willow. But don't give it to her right away. Make sure she cleans the kitchen better than last time."

They spent the next thirty minutes deciding who would get what. With reluctance, Onyx accepted a rhinestone bangle that matched her purple daishiki. Lillian kept a bow-shaped hair clip, not because she'd wear it, but because it would remind her of Violet.

As Onyx left the room with the box, Jefe's man Javier entered, closing the door behind him. Lillian watched with a suspicious lift to her eyebrows.

Javier was Jefe's right-hand man. He had light brown skin with a constellation of darker freckles across his nose and cheeks. He was well-sculpted from his years as an MMA fighter. While only a little taller than her, he could disable any man who needed it without breaking a sweat. "Is that everything?"

She nodded.

"What do the girls know?"

"I told them Violet went to the farm."

Javier cocked his head. "Is that what Jefe told you?"

"No. And if it isn't true, I don't want to know." She had the right to her fantasies. To imagine Jefe had shown mercy, and Violet would go on to live a long, full life. She was very good at pretending. It helped her survive.

Lillian could picture Violet standing there, smiling at herself in the mirror, dabbing on a different shade of lipstick. Javier ran a finger across the dresser. "You lied to Jefe, Lillian."

She stiffened.

"He is . . . unhappy."

It annoyed her how he measured his words. Always calculating the best way to say something so that he came out looking how he wanted. "I see." There would be a consequence. When Jefe was angry, they all felt it.

"I told him you did it to protect the girl. That you weren't betraying him."

"Of course not."

"Still. Best to be careful around him."

"Aren't I always?" Wasn't everyone, always, cautious around Jefe?

"He's been tenser lately. On edge. Surely, you've noticed."

She had sensed a difference because she lived her life according to her internal barometer of his moods. Efforts to get him to talk had been fruitless, so instead, she distracted him. That always—or nearly always—worked.

Javier continued. "A woman was snooping around. She helped Kitten escape. We caught her, but it was a close call. Too close."

"Roman should keep a better grip on his girls."

She had never liked Roman. He smelled bad and looked at her like he wanted to taste her skin. She left Javier in the vacant room. She didn't want to picture the next girl who would use it—someone young and luscious. Someone with much life to live.

No. It was best not to think about things like that. Not if you wanted to survive. And Lillian, above all, was a survivor.

CHAPTER EIGHT

The next morning, I answered Mark Westfall's umpteenth page by heading straight to the fifth floor of Columbia General. Mark waited at the nurse's station with a hairy-knuckled grip around his coffee cup. "Your Jane Doe is responding to the anti-psychotics, but she's still not talking. Thought maybe she'd do better with you."

I glanced at my watch. I needed to get back to finding my sister, but that would have to wait. "I'll see what I can do."

"Would be great if we got her name. I'm not wild about medicating someone without knowing their history. And billing keeps asking about insurance info."

"Well, we all have our priorities."

He scanned the face sheet on the chart. "You talk to your client, see if you get anything out of her. Page me if you do."

I punched the five-digit confidentiality code to the psych unit and pressed the large green button that opened the pair of steel doors. At the end of the hall, the door to Room 528 was closed. I rapped lightly but Jane didn't answer, so I let myself inside.

She was in her bed, staring at the clear bag of intravenous fluid attached to her arm. The open slats of a mini blind let in stripes of sunlight. The air conditioning circulated chilled, antiseptic air.

"Good morning." I tried to sound enthusiastic, summoning

reserves I didn't have. Jane's gaze circled the walls of the room. "How are you feeling?" I asked.

She didn't answer. Black pockets hung under her crusty, dark eyes. Her matted hair splayed out across the pillow like tentacles. I grabbed a chair and slid it over to her bed, watching to see how close she'd let me approach. Her face held as much expression as a sheet of typing paper.

"They're giving you some meds now. Is it helping?" I waited, determined that if I lingered there long enough, she'd have to answer.

Finally, she shrugged, which I took to mean she understood.

"Ready to tell me your name?"

She turned away.

"Okay. So, we keep calling you Jane Doe." I sighed. "Here's what we know. The police picked you up and brought you to us because you were pretty out of it. You kept hearing voices coming through the air conditioning system. Do you remember that?"

A slow nod. *Progress.*

"Do you still hear them?"

A shrug. She looked at me, eyes narrowed as though assessing. Trust didn't come easy to her. Me neither, those times I'd fought to crawl out of psychosis.

"You don't know me, so you're trying to figure out if I'm safe or not. I get that. I've been in your shoes—or rather, your bed, or one just like it—so I know trust is hard." I leaned forward, but not too close. "Here's the thing. I'm your social worker. I'm here to help you figure out the next step in your recovery. For now, that may be meds, but it's also where you go when you get out of here. What you do to stay healthy. That's why I need you to talk with me."

She smacked her scaly lips.

"Thirsty?" I asked.

She nodded, so I filled a cup with water and brought it to her. She downed it so fast that droplets landed on the sheet.

"Wow. You were thirsty!" I refilled the cup.

She sipped slower this time.

"Can you tell me about the voices?"

Her eyes widened.

"They scare you."

She gripped the sheet. "Not they. One. Him."

"Him?"

"The demon." She spoke in a whisper, as though afraid to be overheard.

"You hear a demon," I clarified. "Sounds terrifying."

"He laughs. It's horrible." She pulled the sheet up to her chin as though needing it for protection.

"Is he talking now?"

"Whispers. Just whispers."

"Quieter than before?"

She nodded.

"Good. Then the medicine's doing its job."

Her face twisted in confusion.

"It's hard to understand this, but that demon you hear? It's your brain sort of misfiring. You hear it outside of you, but it's actually in your own brain. The medicine will hopefully fix it."

She looked up at the ceiling, moving her lips again, probably responding to the demon. "You don't get it."

"Okay," I capitulated. I sensed her closing some internal door and that wasn't good. "Help me to understand."

She didn't answer right away. I watched the steady rise and fall of the sheets, wondering if she'd fallen asleep. Finally, she spoke again. "He's real. He's after me and nothing can stop him. He's like—"

"Like what?"

She shook her head and burrowed deeper into the sheets. I wanted to shake her, to promise her she was safe, to beg her to trust me, but that would accomplish the opposite of what I wanted. When I'd been in her place, I fought these truths, too. Psychosis can seem like an undefeatable beast when you're in the throes of it.

Time. She needed time so the medicine could continue to do its job. "Get some rest," I whispered. "I'll check on you later."

Clancy let me have another afternoon off which was a real sacrifice, given how her day looked. I didn't let myself feel guilty; it wasn't like I was off to the pool to sip daiquiris. I was continuing my search for my sister.

Before I exited the lot, I typed *Lakewood Peach Farm* into the GPS. According to her calendar, this was the place Peyton had visited last week, out in Pelion. It had been two days since my sister disappeared. The longer she was gone, the harder it might be to get her back.

White clouds marbled the blue sky. The day offered not the faintest breath of wind. A friend once commented that the one thing that separated Columbia from hell was a screen door, and I had to agree. Every summer, I couldn't wait for my week with Peyton and Lindsay at the beach. When my town turned into an oven, and every plant and every person wilted, I'd think, two more weeks, and I'm at the ocean. One more week and I'm sipping beer under a ceiling fan and watching the sunset over the marsh. Four more days and my toes are digging into a tidal pool as I build a sandcastle with my niece.

What if I didn't find Peyton?

No. I was never going to give up. Never.

Lakewood Peach Farm was acres and acres of peach trees on both sides of the highway. I parked for a moment, scanning the orange dots between the curling green leaves. I could see workers scattered through the fields, some wearing wide-brimmed hats, with what looked like canvas buckets strapped to their chests, plucking peaches from the trees. A tractor inched along between two of the rows, a long trailer behind it loaded with wide white crates. When the tractor paused, the workers lumbered over to the crates, released the bottom of their chest buckets so that the peaches could tumble down. Then they returned to their picking.

The buckets were a clever device. They rested against the worker's torso so he didn't have to bend to pick or unload. Their backs probably liked that, but how did they stand the heat? The peach trees stood eight, maybe ten feet tall, so they offered little in the way of shade. I'd drop dead after about thirty minutes of that kind of work. I looked at the men and women, mostly youngish, moving tree-to-tree, under a parching sun. I could imagine what this brutal work did to them.

Just up the road, I spotted a roadside farm stand and drove to it. A navy canopy covered the stand where a woman stood behind tilted wooden crates of peaches. A van parked behind her had its rear doors open and a small fan blew from its rear bumper. "Care for some fresh, just picked peaches?" she asked as I climbed out of my car.

I lifted a few of the fuzzy fruits and sniffed in the sweetness, squeezed them to determine ripeness, and selected six.

"I have peach preserves, too," the woman said. She looked to be thirty, with a long brown braid snaking down her back and crinkly eyes.

"Is this your farm?" I asked.

She put the peaches in a brown bag. "My dad's."

"Looks like he has a big crew working the orchard."

"Harvest time is always crunch time. He has to bring in extra workers."

I scrutinized a jar of preserves. "Where do they come from?"

"He has a contract with a company that supplies them. I think the workers are mostly Mexican."

And illegal, I thought. I introduced myself and said, "My sister was doing some research that involved migrant workers. I think she visited your farm."

When I showed her the picture of Peyton, she nodded and smiled. "I remember her. Very nice. She wanted to give our workers a health questionnaire."

Finally, someone who'd seen her! "When was this?"

"The first time she came was . . . I don't know . . . two months ago, maybe? Then again, a few weeks later. She talked to about a half dozen of our guys. We didn't have as big a crew back then. Just our regular workers and a few of the contract help. Why are you asking?"

"Peyton's missing." I said these words without a vibration in my voice. A first.

She reached for the picture again, her smile capsizing. "My God. She's the one who's been on the news. I didn't make the connection."

"Anything else you can remember from talking to Peyton?"

"The first time she came, she asked me about the Connor Orchard, that's about a quarter mile up the highway. When she came back, she said that when she mentioned the survey to them, they pretty much chased her from the property. She wanted to know what I knew about that farm."

"They chased her?" Why hadn't my sister told me about this? "What else did she say?"

"Just that Connor said if she wouldn't leave, she'd regret it. Jeb Connor gives the farm industry a bad name."

"How so?"

She glanced at the orchard behind her. "It's hard work, but we make sure our guys stay hydrated and take regular breaks. The workers rarely get sick, but if they do, we get them to a clinic right away. We pay a fair wage, and our farm has decent housing. But Jeb Connor acts like a slave owner from the eighteen hundreds. He mistreats his crew. They don't have any recourse because most of them aren't legal. Plus he switches them out, which makes no sense. We have good workers, we like keeping them around, but we see new workers all the time at Jeb's place."

"The Connor place is a quarter mile up?"

She nodded. "But I wouldn't approach them by yourself. Not sure what Jeb will do. Think he scared your sister."

A pickup pulled over and three little boys tumbled out. The woman who drove the truck snatched their hands and guided them to the stand.

"Thanks for your help," I said, handing her my card. "If you think of anything else—"

"I'll call. I hope she turns up soon." She reached into a cooler and pulled out a bottle of water. "Take this."

I got back in my car and drove up the highway to what I guessed was Connor land—a stretch of peach trees extending deep into the horizon. How many acres did Connor have? A million? Two? I turned onto a dusty clay road that bisected the orchard. After passing a few hundred rows of trees, I spotted a small group of workers moving like ghosts along the rows, collecting peaches and placing them in large baskets.

I parked in front of the truck and climbed out. A small man in a tattered straw hat worked his row close to me. He wore a stained t-shirt and frayed pants cut off at the knees. He had dark tanned skin, and moved slowly, a hand pressed into his back like it ached. I approached him.

"Hey there!"

He squinted at me with his small, crinkled eyes.

"Can you talk to me for a second?"

He shook his head.

"Please." I eased closer. "Do you speak English?"

"A little." He looked up the road, then at the other workers, who'd stopped in their tracks to watch us.

"Good. I'm looking for someone and maybe you saw her."

"Can't help you." He started to move away.

"Wait!" I held up the water bottle. "It's ice cold. You look like you could use it."

His tongue flicked out. He looked worse than parched. He placed his basket on the ground and reached for the water, which he guzzled in desperate swallows. I wished I'd brought another. Hell, I wished I had enough for everyone working. As he wiped his mouth, I showed him the picture of Peyton.

"Did you see her? She came here with a health questionnaire."

Again, his gaze swept up to the road behind me. I saw wariness in those hooded eyes. Or fear.

"She came a few weeks ago, maybe?" I persisted.

He shook his head. "I no talk. Not her. Not you."

A low rumble interrupted us. I turned to see a large truck pull up the road, stirring up a cloud of orange dust that filtered the sun. The worker scrambled to pick up his basket as a large man stepped out of the truck. "Hey! Jao, what are you doing?"

"I no talk. I go back to work!" He scurried away.

The man stepped up to me. I barely came up to his armpits. Lines on his forehead looked like plowed furrows. Gray stubble covered most of his tanned face, except where a pale scar slashed his chin. Cool air leaked through the open window of his idling truck, and I wanted to stand on tiptoes to indulge in more of it.

"Who are you?" he asked.

I introduced myself and told him about Peyton and her research, watching for some sign of recognition that he didn't give me. I held up the photo on my phone.

"Don't know her."

"You didn't look." I thrust it closer.

"Don't have to. Your sister didn't interview our crew because my boss don't allow that. Ever. My guess is she moseyed on to one of the other farms. We got like a billion of them in South Carolina."

"Where do you get your workers?"

"Look, lady." He pulled a bandana from his back pocket and wiped his face. "That ain't none of your damn business."

None of my business because he employed illegals. Where did they live? Were they allowed to leave? I looked over at the workers baking in his field.

"How can you make them work in this heat?"

"Water breaks. That's why I'm here. Not that it's your concern."

I groped in my purse for a business card. "Here. I'd appreciate it if you'd give this to Mr. Connor. I'd like to talk to him."

"I doubt you would," he answered. "But I'll give it to him."

I climbed back in my car, angled the AC vents on my face, and did a jerky six-point turn to reverse directions. I needed to get the hell away from there.

CHAPTER NINE

Lillian removed her heels and gripped the rail as she climbed the curved stairs leading to her room. She'd been working on the financials and doing her best to avoid Jefe, who hadn't spoken to her since the Violet incident. She wanted to lock herself inside her little sanctuary, collapse in bed, and sleep for twenty hours.

As she opened the door and stepped inside, she froze. Something felt different. Off. The slats from her window blinds let in a bluish light from the security fixtures outside. She always left them closed.

She smelled it before she saw it. The haze of smoke wafting from the man in the leather chair, the orange glow at the end of his joint brightening as he toked. *Jefe.* He said nothing and switched on the table lamp. Ice clinked in his glass as he lifted it to his lips, draining it. He held out to her for a refill. She took the glass, replenished the ice, and poured from his bottle of hundred-year-old scotch.

"Pour yourself a drink," he said.

She looked at him, puzzled. "From your stash?" He kept a bottle of his ridiculously expensive bourbon in her cabinet, a reminder that her sanctuary wasn't really hers.

"Of course not."

She took her time pouring a glass of cabernet, unsure what to make of his appearance here. Usually, if he waited for her, it was in her bed, when he needed to be satisfied. He wasn't one to talk, but now his silence troubled her.

She thought about her conversation with Javier when he'd packed up Violet's things. She gulped a third of the glass before joining him by the window.

"Sit," he ordered.

She wasn't sure how close to be. *The sofa?* That put two yards between them. The ottoman, only a few feet. She chose the ottoman.

"Long day, Jefe?"

"Yes. A long day."

She nodded. Sipped. Waited. He finished the joint, never offering her a hit. He usually liked her high, saying it made her more "creative" in the bedroom. It didn't, but it made him more appreciative.

He handed her the ashtray holding the smoldering end. She carried it to the kitchen, making sure it was out before disposing the ashes in her trash. It felt like a macabre ballet, him handing her things, her tending to them.

"We need to talk about Violet."

She took a few gulps of wine, girding herself for this conversation.

"She stole from me. You knew."

The lie rested on her tongue. *She felt bad and brought me the money . . .* but it was too late for that. "Yes," she said instead.

"And you didn't come to me with this." He didn't raise his voice in anger but spoke in a deadly whisper.

"It was a mistake, Jefe. You had so much on your mind I thought I'd handle it. I berated her. I planned to have her move to the massage parlor until her behavior straightened out. But she makes you very good money. Men love her. We've already invested so much in her I thought that—"

"You thought. You don't get to THINK."

She felt a rush of anger at this. He counted on her to think. To plan. To keep everything running so he could live as he wanted.

"This kind of disobedience can be a cancer to my operation. Other girls get greedy. Push the limits. All this—" he gestured at the room and out the window—"can go away." He snapped his fingers. "I never thought you would do something like this."

She watched as he drained the glass. When he handed it back to her, she took her time refilling it, needing the time to strategize. This quiet Jefe was someone new, that danger that was always a part of him pushing to the surface.

"Violet will no longer be a problem."

She closed her eyes, picturing the girl's face, praying her end had been merciful.

"Take off your clothes," he commanded.

She finished the wine, placed the glass on the counter, and unzipped her skirt.

"Slowly," he said.

The blouse came off next, but she left the bra and panties. She sidled up close, the move he always liked, and watched him drink her in with his eyes. His appetite for her might save her from whatever else he had in mind.

Jefe slid a finger up her arm and gripped her to stand. His breath smelled of pot, booze, and Thai food he'd probably eaten on the way home. She kissed him anyway.

"Go to your bed," he said.

She nodded, submissive. "Everything off?"

"Not till I say."

She heard him refill his glass. When he was drunk, he couldn't peak the way he wanted. Something else he might take out on her, but she said nothing.

The nightlight offered the only illumination. Shadows crawled up the walls and ceiling, like ghosts watching. She imagined a life when she could tell him no. Could say, *"Not tonight, I'm too tired,"* but that was not her life to live.

He entered without turning on the light. He removed his shirt, the black hair curling around his nipples and over his soft middle. He left his pants on. No bulge, which meant she'd have to work harder.

As he lay beside her, his hand trailed up her curves, skimmed her breasts, reached her neck. His touch was unexpectedly gentle, yet she felt chill bumps rise along her limbs. His thumb scraped against her trachea, paused, and then implanted itself there, cutting off her air. She grabbed at his wrist, panic a tsunami inside her, but he would not release.

She pictured Violet.

"You will NEVER lie to me again." He pressed harder. "You will always obey me. No matter what."

Dots peppered her vision. Air depleted; lungs starved.

She nodded with what little strength she had. Her thinking muddled. Again, she tried to reach his arm, but it was as though her hands belonged to someone else. Someone distant. Unable to help. She closed her eyes, awaiting internal darkness. Then he released her. She gasped; her mouth opened wide in her desperate hunger for oxygen. He pushed off the bed and towered over her.

Air. Delicious, wondrous air. She savored every inhalation. Her vision cleared. The pain in her neck flared, but she didn't care. *I'm alive.*

"Did you learn your lesson, Lil?" he asked quietly.

She nodded.

"Say it."

"I won't ever . . . lie . . . to you," she huffed.

"And?"

"I won't . . . disobey you."

"And if another girl takes money from me?"

She steeled herself to say it. "Then you will know it. And they deserve to die."

He nodded. "Make sure this message gets to the others. I've had someone snooping around. Causing trouble I don't need. So you WILL keep things here under good control."

"I will."

He grabbed his shirt and headed for the door but hesitated there. "You are my favorite, Lil. But you are not irreplaceable."

CHAPTER TEN

Kitten pawed through the drawer in her dresser trying to find the blue skirt that went with the flowered top. The sleeves covered some of the bruises that, though faded, still glowed pale green and blue on her arm.

Her fingers lay bare against the laminate drawer. Almost two years ago, she'd look at her hand and imagine the ring Drew would buy her. He'd promised he would, and she had believed it deep in her soul.

She'd believed everything about Drew from that first moment she met him. A chilly April Saturday, she'd walked Brandon from the foster home to the ball field for Tee-ball practice. As he joined the rest of the Rockets waiting for his turn to bat, she sat in the stands to watch. While they weren't with the worst foster family, the parents had three kids of their own and little room, time, or money for her and Brandon. She made a point of staying away from home as long as she could.

"Do you play ball?" a voice said from behind her.

She turned, and there he was, maybe her height but broader in the shoulders, wearing a dark blue Yankees cap and a scuffed leather bomber jacket. His dimpled smile crinkled his coal-dark eyes. She wasn't sure about his age. Older than her, but not too old. Maybe eighteen? Twenty?

She wasn't supposed to talk to strangers, but rules like that didn't mean much, at least not for Kitten. No one cared about her safety.

"I used to play softball."

He cocked his head like a puppy. "Pitcher?"

"Shortstop. But I only played for one season." That had been three foster homes ago.

"That's a power position. Gotta be fast. Think on your feet." He climbed down to sit beside her, but not too close. His hair was so black it almost had a bluish sheen. He smelled like a worn baseball glove.

"I wasn't that good," she admitted, though she had loved it. Early in the season, she struck out more than she hit, but later on, she scored seven home runs, one that cinched a game.

He pointed to the middle school behind the ballpark. "You go there?"

"No. Northside."

Some kid playing on the adjacent field hit a ball that arced over the fence, heading for the stands. Drew hopped up and snagged the ball when it was three feet above Kitten's head. She laughed nervously. "Thanks."

Drew tossed the ball back over the fence with more athleticism than she expected. It wouldn't have hit her—she'd have caught it barehanded, too—but there was something nice in his effort. Heroic. Her life had been void of heroes for so long.

"Can't have something like that messing up that beautiful face of yours." He sat closer, and spoke in a whisper, like this was a secret they could share.

"Beautiful? Really?" She let sarcasm edge her words. She was far from beautiful. She had a pimple on her chin. Her hair needed washing. The shirt she wore had a missing button and had come from Goodwill.

"Very beautiful," he clarified, looking directly into her eyes, something mischievous stirring behind his.

He pulled out one of those expensive iPhones. "Give me your cell number. I'd like to text you."

Embarrassed, she muttered, "I don't have one."

He looked aghast. "You don't? Your parents should give you one. Just for your safety."

That made her laugh. "Yeah, well, haven't seen my parents in a while. Our foster family doesn't have money for stuff like that." She didn't say that this was their third foster family in a year. That the Garrisons might be more interested in the income than the calling of foster parenthood. That she used to pray her mom would kick Lawrence out of the house and stop using drugs, but she'd come to accept that wouldn't happen. That all she had was school, and Brandon, and a hope that once she graduated, she and her brother would move on with their lives.

"Where do you live?" Drew asked.

She shot him some side-eye. He was a stranger. *Nice. Cute.* "A few blocks away."

"Smart girl. If your parents don't give you a phone for protection, at least you know not to give out too much personal information. Not till you trust me." He winked. "And you will. I am very trustable."

His swagger endeared her. Brandon's coach blew a whistle and all the boys clustered around him. Practice was over.

"Your brother plays?" Drew asked.

She nodded. "Not very well, but he's just six."

"When does he practice again?"

Kitten felt a bubble of eagerness at the question. It meant he wanted to see her again. "Tuesday at four," she said.

"I'll be here, beautiful."

As he started to climb the stands she yelled out, "Hey! What's your name?"

"I'm Drew."

"Drew," she repeated. He tipped his fingers in a mock salute and scurried off.

"Man of mystery," she whispered to herself.

Drew came to every Tee-ball practice that month. She asked him if he had a friend or sibling on the team and he answered, "No, I'm here for you." The third time he came, he handed her a small package with a gold ribbon around it. "Open it," he said.

Inside was a smartphone, the kind other kids had at school. She marveled at the colorful icons scattered on the screen. She'd never actually held one before.

"For you, beautiful." Drew took her hand and kissed it so lightly it felt like a butterfly dancing on her knuckles.

"I . . . I can't accept this." Tears pricked her eyes as she tried to hand it back. The Garrisons would never pay for a cell plan, and if they did, one of their kids would steal it.

"You can. I've bought you three months of service. My cell number is programmed in. You can text or call me any time you want."

She took a shuddery breath. Nobody had ever given a gift like this. Not her mom. Not her caseworker or any of her foster parents. No one.

Drew reached over and stroked her hair. "Maybe we keep this gift a secret. Don't tell your foster parents. Don't tell anyone. Can you keep it hidden?"

She nodded. She was very skilled at squirreling away things. She kept crackers and Oreos in her underwear drawer, in case Brandon got hungry after supper. Her mother's turquoise earrings, which she'd borrowed the night they were taken away—rested in the toe of a rain boot.

Her phone fit nicely under the mattress when she slept. The rest of the time she'd keep it with her, in the one pocket of her book bag that had a working zipper. Her pack would shimmy during class when texts came in, and she'd imagine the sweet or funny message that arrived at least ten times a day.

She loved every moment she spent with Drew. The gifts kept coming: a sweater, a pink pair of Keds, a romance novel, and even though she'd never read one, and found it too suggestive, she told him she loved it.

Sometimes, when he held her gaze, an intensity pulled at them, like he could pour himself into her through his black irises. She couldn't breathe. She could not get close enough to him. It was new and exciting and filled every part of her. Drew was hers and hers alone—until he turned her world upside down.

Best not think about that now. The betrayal still cut deep. She grabbed the flowered top and tucked it into her skirt. Outside her bedroom door, she could hear Roman on the phone, speaking in an animated half English, half Spanish voice. "*Vete a la chingada,*" he shouted.

She wished Dulce was there to translate, though she was pretty sure he was just cussing. Frowning at the mirror, she skimmed a comb through her hair, her scalp still tender from Lito's kicks. Her hair hung like wet yarn, except for her bangs, which tilted upward in complete defiance of gravity.

Roman's voice quieted, becoming almost polite. "Yes, sir. But she's been out of commission for a few days. But we'll make it up."

Great! She'd have to work longer hours tonight. Roman was probably talking to Jefe. Just outside the window, her lizard was back. He seemed to be peering in, his pale stomach against the screen. Under his throat, a bright pink ball appeared, then shrunk as he exhaled. She loved the color of it, a Gatorade hue, contrasting against the emerald green of his skin. An anole, she realized, remembering a photo in one of Brandon's books back when he was in his all-things reptile phase. She touched the mesh where the lizard's belly rested. "Wish I had something to feed you . . . and me."

In the living room, Roman continued his conversation. "We could use another girl or two, especially working the streets with Dulce."

The lizard moved up the screen. A hole gaped open at the top, and she coaxed him to it. She would catch him, bring him into her room and hide him in a shoebox. She'd love to have a pet. Roman and Dulce would never know he was there. "Come closer, little guy," she whispered. "Just a few more steps." But he had other plans. He flared his dewlap again, *quite the showoff, this one,* and moseyed up the screen, soon out of sight.

"I don't blame you." This was better.

One prisoner in this room was enough.

She moved to the small dressing table and chose the brown eyeliner, using a heavier hand than normal, a fierce slash to frame each eye. It made her look older, and that felt right. She applied the dark blue shadow in a wide arc under her brow, then dabbed an extra stroke of blush on her cheek. Could she pass for eighteen? Twenty?

"Yes, sir, I will," Roman said, and she heard him hang up. A second later, he stood in her doorway. Sweat dampened his black hair. His unbuttoned Hawaiian shirt, covered with too vivid orange poppies, flapped open around his stomach. He scowled and said, "Not that outfit. The light pink dress. Now hurry."

She didn't want to wear the light pink one because it was so short it showed the marks on her thighs. Roman seemed to enjoy the bruises, as if they were something to be proud of.

She closed the door, found the ugly pink dress, and slipped it on. Her ribs stung when she touched them, but not as bad as before. Every day, she got a little better. A little stronger. This was important, because soon she might be ready to escape again.

When Roman pushed his way back into her room, she hurried back to the mirror.

"Take that crap off your eye. You look like a whore."

"Isn't that what I am?" Kitten spoke to his reflection in her mirror.

"Watch your mouth." When he grabbed a tissue, and rubbed it into her face, it felt like sandpaper removing paint. She snatched it from him. She could smell the weed he'd been smoking. As she swiped the makeup from her eyelids, he said, "Better. A pretty little girl. Just what they want."

"What shoes?" she asked.

"White sneakers. Pink socks. Hurry."

She did not hurry. Roman moved to the narrow hall, rapping his ring against the jamb like a ticking clock, as she slowly laced up her shoes. So what if he was pissed at her again. He was always pissed at her these days.

"Ready, Princess?"

She followed him out the door, down the steps, and up the dark, dusty road to the cantina. He didn't hold the door to the bar for her like he used to, but she didn't mind. This was more honest. Before, he'd fuss over her, walk her to the back table, order a soda for her with an umbrella and straw. It was all show, of course; he wanted the men who came there to see her as something special. Once outside of the cantina, Roman treated her like a stray dog begging for scraps.

She went to her usual table and scanned the crowd. The man with the fat arms and tattoos wasn't there, but he didn't usually arrive until late. The short man who smelled like car grease sat at the end of the bar. He would want her if he had the money. When he winked at her, she smiled coyly then looked away, a flirting technique she'd been trained to do. Getting a trick under her belt would pacify Roman and make her life easier.

Closer to the suspended TV sat someone new. He wore a dark leather jacket and cowboy boots. His gray hair, cut in a buzz, was so perfectly flat it could have been a desk. He sipped whiskey from a squat glass.

Roman eyed the bartender who nodded at the new guy, which meant he had money. Roman walked over to him and ordered a glass of tequila. She couldn't hear their conversation but didn't need to. A wad of bills appeared; he slid a few down the bar. After Roman pocketed them, he waved her over.

"This is Kitten," Roman said, his arm resting on her shoulder as though he cared about her. "She's the date you want. She's new in town." *New in town* was a code he used. New in town meant she was still a teenager, so the buyer paid extra. Roman could have entire conversations that never included the words sex or prostitute, but they all led to taking a buyer. "Better that way," he once told her. "In case the police try to scam me."

"You're mighty beautiful, Miss New-in-Town." The man brushed a knuckle under her chin.

"Take him to the trailer." Roman leaned in to add, "And don't even think about trying anything. You better be back here in a half hour."

She nodded. She took the buyer's hand and led him out. She knew the rules. She'd play by them until she had another chance to run.

When they entered the hotbox that had become her residence, the buyer hesitated in the doorway. Some buyers did that—seized by guilt or regret. "Everything okay?" she asked.

He flashed a sad smile. "You don't have to . . . service me."

"I'll give you a good time, I promise." If she didn't satisfy him, there'd be hell to pay with Roman.

"I'm sure you would, but that's not why I'm here." He moved to the center of the small living room, scanning the walls, the furniture, and the nasty rug.

"What do you mean?"

He picked up an ashtray from the scarred coffee table and examined its contents, mostly joints smoked down to nubs. When he pulled a plastic bag from his pocket and deposited two into it, she asked, "What are you doing?"

"Don't mind me." He moved the desk behind Roman's duct-taped easy chair, and opened every drawer, examining the contents.

"Are you . . . robbing us?"

His laugh was gruff. "No, I'm not robbing you. I'm doing my job." He fanned through a stack of Roman's losing lottery tickets as though looking for something, but she had no idea what.

"Roman doesn't like people to go through his stuff."

"He won't know unless you tell him. Are you going to tell him?"

She couldn't figure this guy out. *Why is he here? Should I go get Roman?*

"Are you the police?"

"Not important. Look. I can help you if you help me."

"What kind of help?"

"You ignore me for the next ten minutes. Then we'll go back, I tell your pimp that you gave me a great time. Win-win."

It didn't feel like winning, but as long as he didn't take anything, and she didn't have to have him inside her . . .

"Good." He continued his search, looking under furniture and in kitchen drawers and cabinets. In the bathroom, he clawed through the items under the sink, embarrassing her when he found sanitary products.

The bedrooms took less time, and she stood in the door to her room as he pawed through drawers and searched the closet. He paused to look at the photo of her family. She didn't like any eyes but hers to see that picture. Buyers never bothered to look.

He returned everything as it was before he'd arrived. He looked at his watch. "Been long enough?"

She nodded.

"Then let's head back to the cantina. Remember, tell nobody what happened here. That'll make it easier for me to help you."

"If you're the police—can you take me with you?"

His gaze softened. She stared at him, her eyes pleading, but he shook his head. "That's not an option. But I need you to keep quiet about my visit. Got it?"

She sank in disappointment. He pointed to the door, and she escorted him back to the cantina. *Of course, he won't help me. I can only count on myself.*

CHAPTER ELEVEN

Watching Clancy waddle up the hall, blowing by medical staff who knew better than to stand in her way, her eyes wild like a woman on a mission, made me want to both laugh and hide. She hadn't even reached our offices when she waved an arm and said, "She's looking for you! She's on her way here!"

I gripped the doorknob. "Not—"

"Oh yeah. She was searching for you in the ED. Said she'd messaged you on your cell."

She had. I'd ignored them. I dropped my keys trying to unlock the door. As I snatched them up, Clancy hurried into her office and sat, looking busy and unapproachable. What could I do? Hide under the desk? Bolt the door closed and pretend I'd left the building?

"Georgia!" Too late. There stood Tiffany, all eighty-five pounds of her, dressed in a tailored navy suit jacket that accentuated her twenty-inch waist. In her hand was a tablet in a rhinestone-encrusted case. "I need a few minutes."

"I'm pretty busy—"

"Richard asked me to speak with you." Tiffany pursed her etched lips, accentuating the *Richard*. Like he needed accentuating. He was the hospital CEO, and Tiffany was his very dedicated—too dedicated—assistant. And lover, we were pretty sure.

"About?" I leaned against the desk, blocking the chair where she might try to sit.

"First, tell me how you're doing. I can't imagine how hard it's been for you, with Mrs. Ribault's disappearance and all."

"I'm peachy. But thanks for asking."

"We saw David this morning. He looks so devastated. How could he not? It's just so upsetting. I've been so worried that I've hardly slept at all. And my appetite's fled! Richard says I've lost some weight. What do you think?" She slipped a pink-nailed finger under the waistband of her skirt, showing off her concave stomach.

"Maybe a little." I'd never in my life met someone so self-absorbed. Behind her, Clancy opened a Snickers bar, taking a massive bite.

"And you. How are you managing the stress? We don't want you getting . . . overwhelmed." She stepped closer, squinting at my face as though she, armed with her bachelor's degree from an online school, could assess my mental health.

"It's all fine. I'm managing. Just very busy."

"That's good. We don't want you to get sick over this. I mean, we have excellent mental health resources if you need them. I'm even thinking about talking to a counselor myself."

"That's a great idea, Tiffany. Don't want you losing any more weight!" I forced a smile. Clancy tossed the Snickers wrapper in the trash. I spotted a second candy bar on her desk.

"I'm just saying that we understand about your . . . problems. We want to be supportive. Whatever you need."

What I needed was for her to get out of my office. She was small enough that I could toss her, but that kind of behavior might get me in trouble. "I'm good."

"I'm so glad to hear that. Okay. So why I'm here. We can't afford to keep your Jane Doe. We need you to discharge her."

I should have known. Without an identity, we had no clue if Jane had health insurance. The hospital hated racking up the cost of free medical care.

Tiffany flipped through a few screens on her iPad and showed me a billing sheet. Therapy sessions, medication costs . . . all spelled out in dollars and cents. Mental health recovery is not cheap. "Dr. Westfall says she's not a danger to herself or others, so we can let her go."

"We don't know that! She's still psychotic. We don't know where she lives. If she even has a home."

Unfazed, Tiffany clicked the billing information. "By tomorrow."

I looked over at Clancy whose scowl matched exactly how I was feeling. Time for a different strategy. I lowered my head. "This is my fault. I should have tried harder to find out who she is. I've been so distracted by Peyton and trying to find her, and worried about Lindsay and David and I just couldn't—" I got myself worked up. Let a few tears bloom.

"Oh, Georgia." Tiffany cocked her head at me.

"I'm sorry. I'm really sorry. Can't you tell Richard that I just need a few more days? That if I can't find out who she is by, I don't know, Wednesday, that we can discharge her then?"

Tiffany sighed, her scrawny shoulders lifting up and falling. "Well, I don't—"

"Please, Tiffany. If anyone can convince him, it's you." I blinked at her, my lips pulled in tight as though I might start bawling at any second.

"Okay. I'll talk to him. Maybe we can buy you a few more days."

"Thank you." I moved closer. "You're the best."

"Let me know if you get anywhere with Ms. Doe." As Tiffany turned and exited, Clancy approached me.

"And the Oscar goes to . . ." she said.

"Shut up. It worked, didn't it?"

"Sometimes you scare me." She tossed me the remaining chocolate bar. "Want me to check on Jane?"

"That would be great."

"You're going out to look for Peyton again?"

"I've got a few more places I need to check out."

"Please be careful," she cautioned.

I pocketed the chocolate as I nodded, grateful for the time off she didn't need to give me.

Twenty minutes later, I rechecked the address on my GPS, hoping she'd entered the info wrong. Peyton's calendar had listed Special Touch Massage as one of the last places she visited, so here I was in the worst section of town, on a rutted road, passing storefronts with bars on windows and signs advertising "Adults Only Toys" and "Sexy Lady Lingerie." Finally, I spotted the red neon flash—*Special Touch Massage.*

I parked and studied the shuttered windows and brown paper covering the glass door. Not exactly an inviting place. I thought about the frightened man at Connor farms, the desperate fear in his eyes. Liked someone who'd been trafficked. Labor trafficking was, sadly, too common in our state. Peyton would have figured that out. What about the Blue Rose Cantina? Was it a venue for sex trafficking? It had that creepy feel. Special Touch Massage set off similar alarm bells in my brain. I had to get more information.

Five minutes later, I had a plan. A sucky one, admittedly, but it would have to do. When I tugged on the door, bells clinked as it opened. An older woman stood at a short counter, her hair pulled back in a tight bun. Black glasses too big for her face amplified the size of her dark eyes. A half-eaten cheeseburger rested on its wrapper in front of her. The room smelled like mold poorly covered by patchouli. A semi-circle of black vinyl chairs made up the small waiting area. Behind the counter hung a pair of dark purple curtains.

The woman eyed me as if I'd come from the IRS. "Can I help you?"

"I'm here to apply for a job!"

"A job?"

I leaned over the counter, mimicking someone who had no appreciation for personal space. "Yes! I just got my license! I mean, I haven't gotten it yet, because it's coming in the mail, but they said I'd get it any day because I passed the test!"

"The test?" She removed the oversized glasses.

"I took the class, and then took the test—twice because it's hard—and finally passed! So now I can be a massage therapist. I've always wanted to help people. What better way to do that than to help them relax, right?"

She smiled. "We do a bit of that here, but—"

"That's great! How many therapists do you have working? Cause I hope I can work with some other girls. Or boys. It doesn't matter. I still have a lot to learn! And I can work whenever you want me to. Weekends, evenings, whenever you need me!"

I used exaggerated gestures as I spoke. It's not a stretch for me to impersonate an idiot.

A young woman slid between the drapes. She had long, tan legs teetering over stiletto heels. Bright green swaths of eye shadow stretched over her black eyes. The glittery blue tube-top she wore exposed a navel ring in her belly button. "Who's she?" she asked in a thick Asian accent.

"Someone looking for a job," the bunned woman replied.

"Here? Seriously?" She came around the counter, hips sashaying, and looked me up and down. "You're old. And scrawny. And have you ever heard of makeup?"

Ouch! She had a point about the makeup. Peyton would agree.

I looked down at my outfit. "Of course, I'll dress differently if you hire me. Sweatsuits, probably, in case anybody wants a deep-tissue session."

"A deep what?" The Asian woman scrunched her face at me like I'd grown a second head.

"That's enough, Ratana. Get back to your station. You have a . . . client on his way." The older woman's clipped words made Ratana back away as though she'd been scalded. As she reached the curtains, she said, "She can work in Pearl's area. They moved her out this morning."

"Keep. Your. Mouth. Shut." The woman's words hit her like acid. Her eyes widened in horror as she snapped the curtain closed.

Seemingly undaunted, I said, "Well, she seems so nice! I'm sure I'd like working with her."

The woman pointed to the door. "We aren't hiring. You can move along."

I gave her my most wide-eyed, confused expression. "Are you sure? Because like I said, I'm very flexible in terms of hours and—"

The door clinking open interrupted me. The man who entered had on jeans and a dusty ball cap. His plump face was shadowed by black and gray whiskers. My height, but three times as wide, he pushed past me and approached the counter. "You got my message?"

She shook her head but turned to the computer and punched a few keys. "Oh. Here it is."

"Got someone for me?" It was then that he noticed me, his close-set eyes scanning me up and down like I was in a lobster tank, and he was in the mood for a steamer. I felt dirty under his stare.

"Of course," the woman said.

"Her?" He tossed a thumb in my direction.

"She's in the wrong place. She was just leaving." The woman's hand-drawn eyebrows scrunched up her forehead, and I got the hint. I exited the small business, the lock clicking as I stepped onto the sidewalk.

In my car, I let out a deep breath. *A brothel.* How many trafficked girls worked there? Where had they come from? Were the people behind this operation responsible for my sister's disappearance?

Dammit, Peyton. She should have told me about all this. She should have gone to the police. Why didn't she? I found Lou Michael's card, dialed his number, and left a message on his voicemail. "Lou, call me. I've found out some stuff about Peyton. She was looking into human trafficking. Probably a big operation. What if they have her? What if they have my sister?" My voice quaked as I clicked off.

You should have known. You're her sister! The general's drawl filled my head. I loathe his voice—always critical. Accusatory. Pointing out my faults as though they needed highlighting.

"She never told me."

She was in danger and you did nothing. NOTHING. This word echoed across my synapses.

I fumbled through my purse for the rubber band my therapist, Nora, had given me, which I slipped on my wrist.

You . . . did . . . nothing! His scream reverberated auditory poison. I snapped the rubber band, hard, savoring the sting.

"Interrupt the thought. Focus on how the rubber band feels," Nora had said. I snapped it again, and again, metronomically, until the rhythm and the ache overpowered the general's words. "Physical pain can be weirdly useful."

When his rant finally dissipated, I replaced it with my own. "I'll find her. I'll find her," I whispered. I had to.

CHAPTER TWELVE

The sunlight shining through the window assaulted my eyes. When I made myself crawl out of bed, it felt like I was moving through mud. I trudged down the hallway, which had grown longer, it seemed and stepped into the bathroom for a shower.

This day would be a killer. When the depression fights for control over me, everything becomes so much harder. Dressing. Eating. Finding a parking space. It's like my neurons fire on only half the available synapses. I couldn't decide what to wear and then couldn't decide what to choke down for breakfast. I was going to be late getting to the hospital and felt bad about that. Then as I was dashing to the door, I bumped the bookcase and a picture toppled to the floor. I froze.

It was the photo of Peyton. In it, she's sitting in a rocking chair, a yellow silk scarf draped over her shoulders, a book in her lap. She's giving me an annoyed "take the damn picture" look. I lifted the photo, shards of glass tinkling down. I don't know how long I stood there staring at the woman who was so much a part of me and now so very absent.

I didn't have time for this. I needed to clean up and get to my job. I grabbed a broom and made quick work of the glass fragments. I dumped them in the trash and grabbed a paper towel to wipe the moisture from my face, wondering just how much worse this day could get.

Note to self: Never think, "How much worse can it get," or anything of that ilk, because that's when life feels compelled to kick you in the ass. My kick came in the form of my ex-boyfriend Ben Reeder, who I found standing on my porch when I opened the front door.

"Crap." I didn't want him to see me looking like the wreck I was.

He walked over to me and winced. "That bad, huh?"

"Am I too old to go goth?"

"Just by a decade or two. Got a few minutes?"

I stepped back and let him in. His wavy brown hair nearly reached his shoulders. He wore a button-up plaid shirt he'd probably scored at a consignment shop, and chinos I remembered from five years ago.

Fenway appeared, winding himself between my legs and yowling. Ben glared down. "So, you still have him."

I lifted the black beast, suppressing a smirk about the last time Ben had been here, the night I found out about his fling with the journalism intern. Fenway had taken a swipe at Ben that drew blood, because Fenway is a great judge of character.

"I'm already late for work." I eyed the door, willing him to leave.

"Well, it ain't like Clancy's gonna fire you. I just need a few minutes." He planted himself on the sofa. "I take it you haven't heard from your sister."

"No."

"I just saw David."

"Good for you." I sat in the rocker, glancing up to where her photo should be.

"His brother was at the house. Colby. He was easier to talk to than David."

"He's always been the nicer brother." I'd heard Colby had returned to South Carolina after a few years in Atlanta and kind of hoped I'd run into him. We had one date—arranged, after prodding me for months, by Peyton—right before he moved. I'd found him to be charming and funny, so very different from the other Ribaults. Guess he wasn't similarly impressed by me.

Ben ran a hand through his hair. "David's got a lot on his plate. The guy was a wreck."

"Think he knows something I don't?"

"I doubt it. But it's been three days without any word. He's letting himself think—" Ben averted his eyes.

"That she's not coming back?" I sounded all of twelve years old.

"Maybe. Or maybe he can't deal with something beyond his control. You like to say he and his clan think they rule the universe." Ben scratched at his mustache and regarded me for a long moment. "I shouldn't tell you this, but I've been snooping a bit into David's financial affairs. Things aren't as rosy there as you might think."

"How so?"

"It's not like he's broke or anything. But he had a cash-flow issue, then suddenly deposited a hundred thou. Thinking someone lent him money, but it wasn't the bank."

"What did he say when you asked him about it?"

"Said I should mind my own f'ing business." He set the cup on my coffee table. "Maybe you can find out why he needed it. You're family—maybe he'd talk to you."

"I'm family?" I almost choked. David would no more claim me as family than he'd vote for a Democrat.

"I'll see what I can find out."

"I'm doing a lead story on Peyton for tomorrow. Anything you want me to mention?"

Before I could answer, a tune sounded from inside his jacket, "Stairway to Heaven." I imagined a tiny rock band tucked around his pocket change. When he answered the call, he didn't say much to the person on the line, but his expression changed, mouth sagging, eyes blinking too fast. He said, "I'm on my way." He clicked off the call.

"Gotta run." He avoided my stare as he edged toward the door.

"That call was about Peyton."

He slid the phone back into his pocket.

"What is it?" I moved closer, mentally daring him to not tell me.

The silence between us was a familiar stalemate that I would win. I had to.

"They think they've found her car," he whispered. "Won't know for sure until they retrieve it."

"Where?"

He sighed as he looked at me. "Not far from her house. That pond at the entrance to her neighborhood. The car's in the water. I'll call as soon as I know something definite."

I stood in my doorway and watched him leave. I didn't know what to do with myself. *Go to work?* Not likely. *Wait here?* Not an option.

I left a message on Clancy's voicemail. The next thing I knew, I was in my car. I don't remember how I drove myself out there, but soon I was pulling through the open iron gates to Peyton's neighborhood. The pond lay just beyond the unmanned guard station, the road curving around the water where Peyton and I sometimes kayaked with Lindsay tucked between us.

I parked by the police cars but didn't approach where they could see me. I slid through a small-wooded area, yards from where the yellow tape marked the sandy beach. From behind an oak tree I listened as Lou Michaels spoke to a man in a suit, two uniformed officers waiting behind them. Well beyond the tape, Ben Reeder leaned against his Explorer watching a photographer snap pictures of the still water. Overhead, plump dark clouds above promised a fierce downpour before morning's end.

I heard another noise and turned to see a black Chevy SUV marked *Crime Scene Investigation Unit* pull in behind Ben's car. The unit turned out to be one guy, not much taller than me, with frizzy brown hair, dressed like Lou.

"Mike's here," an officer said to Lou.

Lou walked over to Mike and pointed to the section of the lake in front of the old ramp. I moved a few trees closer and squinted down at the water.

That's when I saw it. A gray hump of metal protruding from the water. The Lexus.

Freeze frame. Suddenly, I was gone. I mean I was there—my body, anyway—but my mind took a step back, something it does when faced with something horrific. All that followed seemed like I was watching a movie. The inside voices spoke, but none made sense, just whispery white noise cluttering my brain.

Mike put on waders and pulled rubber boots and a camera from his car.

They returned to the shore and Mike stooped under the police tape. He took pictures of the fender, the shoreline, and what looked like a tire track that had been marked with little orange flags. He handed the camera back to Lou and plodded into the water, feeling below the surface for the car.

Next to arrive was a tow truck, which backed down to the shore to where the water lapped at its rear wheels. Mike attached the large hook from the hoist to the Lexus. The machine creaked and groaned; its cable stretched tight. I held my breath. When the lake bottom released its hold, Peyton's car erupted like a whale. Sheets of murky water gushed out from around the doors. The tow truck inched forward to deposit its catch on the soft clay banks.

The chatter in my head grew louder, but I could not make out any words.

Lou and the other man jumped back as more escaping water turned the ground a muddy orange. Mike had the camera back out, taking photos of Peyton's car from every angle, then opened the car door, freeing another flood as the door yawned open.

"Stay back!" Lou yelled at Ben. I hadn't noticed him sneaking closer.

Mike leaned into the car, Lou just behind him trying to peer inside.

It seems strange that I just stood there, an audience to this movie. *That's not my sister's car. I'm not watching my own life implode before me.* I stood there, still as a tombstone, not sure I could move if I wanted to. In my brain, the noise was deafening.

Yet I understood everything that unfolded. When Mike said, "Call the coroner," I knew they'd found Peyton's body. And when Lou held up a gun from the car, and Mike scooped up a bucket of lake water and set the gun inside, I thought, *How strange.* My sister hated guns, always had. Her laptop came next, water gushing from its pink case.

"Georgia!" Ben Reeder's voice interrupted the movie. "Dammit, George. You shouldn't be here. Why can't you just listen to me for a change?" Clever man, spotting me in my hiding place.

"It's her," I said simply.

"You shouldn't be here."

"Where else should I be?"

Lou Michaels must have heard us talking because he appeared, too, scowling at Ben.

"Can I see her?" I asked him.

"No ma'am."

"Just a quick look," I insisted.

He raised his eyebrows at Ben, and I could tell something telepathic was going on between them. "Look. I've been in this business for twenty years. There's no way I'm letting you see your sister's body. It's best if you let Ben take you home."

"Best for who?" I started to move but Ben's hand on my arm stopped me.

"You should do what Lou says."

"Did she drown?"

"George—" Ben answered.

"She was always afraid of the water when we were kids. She thought a fish might bite her." My tone was strangely matter of fact, like I was talking about someone living, not someone dead.

"She probably didn't drown," Lou said softly. "The coroner will tell us for sure."

"Then how?"

He stared at me, but I just stared right back, daring him to not tell me. After a long moment, he said, "There was a gunshot wound in her right temple."

The movie reel stopped. Something loud and guttural came out of my mouth as I folded over and heaved.

I threw up all over Ben Reeder's shoes.

CHAPTER THIRTEEN

"You are not irreplaceable." This is what Jefe had said to Lillian, and it cut deep. She needed him to need her. It solidified her place in this world, and she had no other where she belonged. She would prove she wasn't replaceable. She would expand the stable with the best girls, continue to grow his business, and keep him happy. It's what she always did best.

She scanned through the photos of the latest group of girls. The recruiter, Drew, had been slack lately—picking easy targets without consideration of market value. Sure, these three from South America were the right age and maybe the right build, but they didn't have that look—that spark, that something special, that would bring top dollar. Gunner said they could train them to look that way but what the hell did he know? You could train them to pretend, to court the buyers with a certain pouty look or a mischievous wink, but it wasn't the same. No, what Lillian looked for was something natural. Something that couldn't be taught or faked.

Jefe entered Lillian's small office, his hand trailing across her back as he sat across from her. He wore his gardening hat and dirt-dusted chinos, probably from working in his beloved greenhouse.

"Any luck?"

"Where did Drew find these girls? The Walmart parking lot? He's got to do better."

He leaned against the table and removed the hat. His dark curls, thick on top, trimmed on the sides, had started to grow threads of gray. "Or maybe you're too particular."

She didn't like his implication but said nothing.

"Drew's working a few today. I told him you'd come by."

She hated being a part of the recruitment process. It made painful memories surface that she did her best to keep underwater. But she'd never tell Jefe "no."

"Where?"

"He's working local. Over at the Baybridge Hotel. The one near the fort."

She looked at her watch. "When?"

Jefe smiled and handed her a slip with a room number. "He's using the modeling agency strategy. First interview's at one."

Lillian went upstairs to change into her business suit. As she removed her top, her gaze fell on the tattoo that bloomed beside her breastbone.

It had been a "gift" from Jefe. She'd been with him for a year the day the goateed man arrived with this magic kit. He and Jefe shared a joint while Jefe selected the image he liked best—an orchid blossom with purple curving petals. In the center of the bloom, the color shifted to gold, with threads the same color veining the petals.

It had hurt like a mother and wasn't something she wanted, but the result was quite beautiful. She knew what it meant. For some reason only Jefe knew, he had a fondness for orchids, as was clear from the design molded into the estate's entry gate and the greenhouse full of them behind the pool. He was marking Lillian as his, and she was. Yes, it bothered her that other girls were branded the same way, but she had been the first. She was always the first.

At twelve fifty, Lillian entered Room 212 at the Baybridge, a plain hotel with exterior room doors and an ice machine that rumbled like a locomotive. Drew had rearranged the furniture in the double room by pulling the desk from the wall to serve as a table, which he sat behind. A stack of manila folders served as a prop to make it look like he was conducting real interviews. He'd probably advertised on bulletin boards at high schools, the city parks, and the mall. So many girls, eager for the exotic life of a model, would take the bait.

Flyers for *Debutante Modeling* lay scattered across the floral spread on the double bed.

"Jefe sending you to the front lines. Wow." Drew flashed his dimpled smile—the one that always worked on the girls. It never worked on her.

"We need to expand the stable, and you're sending us shit for choices. So here I am."

She took a seat in a folding chair beside him. Drew had a boyish appearance that made it easy to convince girls he was in his teens. Today his persona was more executive—linen suit, silk tie, and shiny black shoes. He smelled like too much Stetson.

"How many we have coming?"

"I got thirty calls. Ten scheduled for today. We'll see who shows."

Lillian pointed to the bed. "This location doesn't make them suspicious? Shouldn't we at least be using a conference room?"

"Nope. I'd be surprised if anyone says anything about the bed. And this is a lot more private than downstairs." He always spoke with a cocky confidence as though she were ridiculous to question him, but he had a point. They didn't want the hotel staff or other guests to know about their interviews.

A firm knock signaled the first arrival.

Drew let her in. Dark hair with blond extensions, nice, rounded figure with plenty up top. Red miniskirt showed a full, well-shaped rear and long, lean legs, but her steps faltered on the five-inch heels. As she sat across from them, the girl's eyelash extensions fluttered like bat wings.

She handed them a slip of paper. On it was scrawled her vitals: Desiree McMann, height five-eleven (she'd clearly measured in the heels), weight one-twenty (no chance in hell that was right). Age, eighteen, also probably a lie.

"Desiree," Drew began. "Tell us about yourself."

"I live in Florence, and I've always wanted to be a model." She flicked back her hair, the eyelashes fluttering. "People are always telling me I should be one, you know. Teachers. Friends. Sometimes people in stores will stop me and say, 'are you a model?'" Another flip of her hair. Her nails gleamed, dark red and long like daggers.

"I'll bet." Another grin from Drew as he scanned the form. "You're . . . eighteen. Do you live alone? With your family?"

"I live with my folks, but that's temporary. Just till I get my career going." She flashed a smile that looked more sweet than seductive.

Sixteen years old, Lillian decided. *At the most.*

"Do your parents know you came to this interview?" Drew asked.

"Well, no. I mean, it's not really their business. This is my life, not theirs." *Petulant. Maybe younger than sixteen.* Desiree had potential, with her round cheeks and full, overly lipsticked lips. Her teeth needed work—crooked and brushing against her bottom lip. Braces might have been a good idea, but she'd never get them now.

"Stand up for us and walk to the bathroom and back." Drew drummed a pencil against the table, as though prepared to assess her catwalk skills. Desiree stood, teetering on her shoes, and strutted to the door, hips swinging, mouth puckered as though kissing the air. She paused to turn and gripped her hip, shoulders pulled back, breasts pushed forward, as though she'd been training herself via YouTube videos.

"Very nice, Desiree," Drew said.

She sauntered back with more momentum in the hips. Lillian felt an uneasiness deep in her stomach. Desiree thought she was about to be discovered. Instead, she was about to disappear.

"Have a seat again." Drew shot Lillian a look. She shrugged, not convinced that Desiree would work for the Estate. Maybe after a stint at the massage parlor or Roman's trailer to learn some tricks, so to speak, she could be promoted.

"I can start anytime." Desiree leaned forward, breasts nearly resting on the table. "I mean, I want to get started right away."

"And we want that, too. I tell you what. I don't usually do this, but we have a shoot in Atlanta this week. One of my models got sick and, well, you might be the perfect sub for her."

"Really?" Her eyes widened.

Drew nodded as though the idea was taking root. "Yes, really. You have the look we want. But here's the thing. We'll need to leave soon. This afternoon, as a matter of fact."

"I can do it! Just tell me what to do." She looked like a kid prepping for a trip to Disneyworld.

Drew told her to meet him back here at the hotel at six so they could catch an evening flight. "We'll get you a first-class ticket, of course." She wrote down the details, asking questions about what to pack and appropriate clothing.

"We'll take care of all that," Drew said. "But one more thing. This photoshoot—it's strictly confidential. We value the privacy of our clients, and this one is a very well-known designer about to release their new fashion line. He's very worried about spies from other fashion houses." He lifted a finger. "Desiree, this is important. Nobody can know you're meeting me or that we're going to Atlanta."

Hesitation flashed on her face. "My parents will want to know."

"Of course, they will. And you can call them the minute we land. Like you said, it's your life. This will prove to them you're ready to be an independent career woman. And, if the shoot goes well, a very rich independent career woman."

Hook, line, and sinker. She had to hand it to Drew. *He's a master at this.*

Her smile reappeared, the nails clutching at her chest. "You think I'm that good?"

He nodded. "I do. But I need to see that I can trust you. Modeling at this level—you have to show some discretion. Will I see you at six?"

"I'll be here. And don't worry, I won't tell a soul! You can trust me. I'm very trustworthy."

"I'll just bet you are." Drew showed her out and shut the door behind her. "Well?"

"Not ready for the Estate. But maybe the massage parlor or Roman's place."

"I was thinking the same thing. Linda's looking for a few girls. Massage parlor it is."

Of the next four candidates, two were promising. The one who brought her boyfriend was immediately rejected, as was the older girl who demanded pay information, references, and the home office address. No way someone that assertive would work in their operation.

The last girl arrived with a tentative knock. As she came into the room, Drew arched his brows at Lillian. The kid was stunning. Long blond hair. Lithe physique. Pale, beautiful skin, with a perfectly upturned tiny nose. She wore a simple dress and carried a book bag as though she'd just left her middle school. When she sat, her timid green eyes looked at each of them. Dazzling eyes, even without makeup.

"What's your name?" Lillian started.

She cleared her throat. "Isabelle Murphy."

"And you want to be a model?"

Before she could answer, her phone rang. Embarrassed, the girl fumbled in her pack for it and changed the setting to silence.

Drew began with his questions. She lived with her parents. She admitted to being only fifteen but knew of other models who began younger. She'd even done some modeling for a local department store. Her answers were short and articulate, another plus for Lillian.

"Do you have a boyfriend?" she asked her.

"Why?"

"Because we do photoshoots all over the world," Drew said. "You'll be traveling all the time. It's best if you don't have any ties to hold you down."

"I don't have a boyfriend."

"That's good." Lillian smiled. "As lovely as you are, it's a surprise."

She shrugged. "I've always been kind of . . . shy."

Shy? We could play on that. A timid teenager looking for a daddy figure, perhaps. We'll call her Bella. She'll make Jefe a fortune.

Drew went into his spiel about her returning at six, and not telling anyone, and the girl agreed without reservation. It couldn't be more perfect. In her mind, Lillian designed the room Bella would use, the clothes she would wear. The customers she'd satisfy.

It was when she opened the door to leave that all hell broke loose.

"There you are!" A woman burst into the room. She stood close to six feet tall, square-shouldered, streaked brown hair torn free of a ponytail, her expression one of panic.

"What is this? What are you doing with my daughter?"

"Mom!" Isabelle said. "It's a job interview!"

Drew whispered to Lillian, "Run!"

As Lillian slipped behind the woman confronting Drew, she heard shouts of, "Who the hell are you?" and "Why are you in a hotel room with a fifteen-year-old child!" She didn't know what happened next, because she ran down the metal steps to her car and sped away.

The hammering in her heart settled as she reached the outer edges of town. She wondered if the woman had called the cops. If Drew had gotten away. One wrong step and Jefe's house of cards could collapse. There was nothing more dangerous to their work than a determined, protective mom. Lillian pulled over and took a few deep, steadying breaths. She'd gotten away.

And it surprised her that, somewhere deep inside, she was glad Isabelle had escaped, too.

CHAPTER FOURTEEN

Kitten felt a little stronger every day. Her bruises had faded. Her muscles no longer ached when she stretched them. That word, *stronger,* flashed in her mind like a beacon. She would get away from Roman and Jefe and this miserable life. She should never have trusted the lady, just like she should never have trusted Drew. She was done with trust. When she left again—and she would, she was sure of it—she'd do it on her own.

She used to be fit. In elementary school, she was the second or third chosen for kickball, always after Barbara Pabst, who could kick a ball to Pluto. In her first year of middle school, she'd done fine on the softball team. In those days, she could jump rope for hours and hardly break a sweat. Yet the other day, trying to run from the store, she'd gotten so winded she had struggled just to keep moving. *Inexcusable.* She'd be stronger next time. And faster. And she'd get the hell away.

After gathering her hair in a rubber band, she slipped on a T-shirt and shorts and dropped to the floor. The first ten sit-ups came easy, but the last fifteen made her groan. Still, she did them. Push-ups came next. Less successful there—only managed three—but she'd add to this total every day. Jumping jacks had her winded before she'd finished twenty. She eked out thirty.

What else? She wished she could run because that would quickly build up stamina. When she was back in Pennsylvania, she'd planned to try out for the track team, but of course, that hadn't happened. If she could run now—just up and down the dirt road leading to the trailer—it would help her muscles strengthen. But Roman would NEVER allow it.

But she could run in place in her tiny little room. She cleared a spot in front of the dresser and started with a slow jog, gradually working up to a low-impact trot. Breath in, four steps, breathe out. The rhythm helped but sweat dripping from her face meant she'd have to shower before working that night.

"Kitten!" Roman bellowed from the living room. "What the hell are you doing?"

"Uh. Nothing," she huffed.

"Be quieter with your nothing."

"Okay." She stopped, relieved he hadn't burst into her room. Next time, she'd find a quieter way to exercise. If she snuck that scratchy bathroom rug into her room, and jogged on that, it might muffle the sound.

She'd be back in shape in no time.

Later that afternoon, Kitten wiped the sweat dripping around her eyes and tried to dab pink blush on her cheekbones. What was the point of putting on makeup if the heat melted it right off? Her sequin T-shirt clung to her moist skin like plastic wrap. She wished Roman would turn on the air conditioning, but he was too cheap and only let it run when Jefe visited, or when Kitten had the right buyer. Funny how he wouldn't spend money on cooling but paid a fortune for his stupid pay-for-view Latino wrestling matches. When they aired, all brothel business stopped. The men gathered with beer and stinky snacks and yelled at the screen like they were watching the Superbowl.

She wiped perspiration from under her nose and lined her lips with a mauve pencil. The fuchsia hair ribbon was a gamble; tying her hair up would feel much cooler, but Roman liked it hanging loose when he took her to the cantina. She tugged a few blonde strands free to frame her face, the way Dulce had shown her, and hoped he didn't gripe.

The trailer's front door banged open and Roman spoke in rapid Spanish to whoever arrived. Kitten peeked out the door. She recognized the visitor, one of Jefe's men, with slick black hair and skin the color of weak tea. He had two inches on Roman and lacked Roman's blubbery belly. The Mexican, Javier. When he spotted Kitten in the doorway, his lips curled down.

"How many?" Roman asked him.

"Three. Just got in. You'll have them till tomorrow. They're headed to the farm." Javier's English was perfect. It had been in Charlotte that she'd first seen him. After Jefe had stashed her in a nasty hotel room with another girl, Javier had brought them food and sodas, always rushed, all business, but he hadn't touched her.

Javier pointed to Kitten. "Chiquita doing good work for you?"

"Chiquita's a pain in the ass. Tried to run away a few days ago. I wanted to move her to the plant or the farm, but Jefe says she makes good money here."

When she first arrived in South Carolina, they'd put Kitten on a farm near Columbia to work as part of a small crew, mostly Mexicans but a few Thai, planting turnips and other greens. Only one other person spoke English. The air had been cool, yet the sun had pinked her arms and neck. Blisters wept on her feet. One scratch on her hand got infected because there was no way to keep it clean. The one thing good about the farm was that was where she met the lady. The promises—the broken promises—came later.

On the day Roman came for her, he called her out of the field. "Jefe has a new job for you," he had said, smiling like a cartoon cat. The other workers cursed her as he grabbed her arm and shoved her into a van. She hadn't cared; anything was better than the farm. Or so she had thought. Thirty minutes later, they pulled up in front of the trailer. She remembered relief at climbing out of the disgusting van only to be greeted by an irate Dulce, dressed in short-shorts and a halter top, regarding her from the top of the rickety steps. "Another new chica? She's too scrawny! You never bring girls with boobs." Dulce punctuated her comment with a hand shaking her own breast.

Of course, it turned out that being flat-chested made it easier to convince buyers that Kitten was twelve, or thirteen, or whatever age they needed her to be. The appetites of these men sickened her, yet she'd learned to please them. It kept her alive.

When the door to the trailer opened again, Lito entered, sweat stains covering his shirt and a wet rag dripping on his shaved head. He held the door as three dark-skinned teenage girls stumbled in. They wore dirty work shirts, pants, and scruffy sneakers. Had they come from Mexico? Did the boss promise them a beautiful life in America? How much had their families paid for them to become slaves?

"Go sit over there," Lito commanded. They stared at him.

"*Sientese*," Javier said, pointing to the nasty sofa. They moved like one animal, sitting on the sofa, all pressed to each other like beads on a string.

"I have bedding for them. Maybe she can help me get it?" Javier tilted his head toward Kitten.

Roman scowled. "Watch her. She's trouble."

Lito stepped between Kitten and Javier, glaring at her. He had a darker look than even Roman, like he'd enjoy hurting her again. It had been Lito's kicks that had done the most damage.

"Come on!" Javier commanded. Kitten followed him out to the unmarked van, the one that reeked of piss and engine oil, where she'd been stashed when Jefe brought her to Columbia. Javier jerked the handles of the back doors and they squealed open. "Come here. Hurry."

She frowned as she approached, worried about why she'd been summoned.

"I want to show you something." He pulled a folded newspaper from his pocket and held it up. "Look at this photo."

She saw a woman's face, smiling, framed by soft waves of blond hair. *The lady.*

"See the headline?"

Peyton Ribault Found Dead. She stumbled back, colliding with the bumper of the van. *Dead.* Below, a photo of a car that had been pulled from the lake.

"She's the one who helped you. When you escape."

Kitten's finger traced over Peyton's smiling face. Was she the reason Peyton had died? Jefe found out and had her killed?

"She wouldn't listen to me," Javier said. "She kept nosing around. Not just here, but the farm and the factory. When she showed up at the entrance to the Estate, I told her it was too dangerous!"

Estate? She had heard Roman use this word in his phone conversations.

Javier sighed. "Jefe's most lucrative business. I told her to be more careful. I warned her. And now she's dead."

Kitten stared at him, trying to sort through his words. Above her, a mockingbird cawed from the branch of a scrub oak tree.

"Here's the thing, Kitten. We can't try it again. Not any time soon. You have to do what Jefe, and Roman, say."

"We?"

"I will help you. In time. But for now, we can't afford that kind of trouble. You are lucky that you're still alive. But you need to be very careful."

"What do you mean, you'll help me?" It felt like the world had stopped spinning on its axis. She felt dizzy.

"I can't tell you more. But do as I say. Now, go back inside. And keep this conversation between us. *Comprende?*"

She nodded. Maybe he would help her, or maybe he wouldn't. But Peyton Ribault had died because of Jefe. This cold truth sliced her like a blade.

Someday, somehow, Jefe would pay for that.

CHAPTER FIFTEEN

I don't remember much of what happened after I saw my sister's body. I know I went home and locked the door. At some point, I went to bed, though sleep never came. I lay there, letting the sheet become a second skin over me, my mind cartwheeling from one dark space to the next. Was I grieving? My feelings could not be so easily defined. A black, cold, amorphous place, a place I'd been before and almost hadn't escaped.

The voices had a lot to say. The general demanding, *Why didn't you save her?* Maybe he was right, I didn't get to keep what was good in my life. The counselor cooing, *Sleep now, sleep,* her voice a lullaby. I wondered if maybe she meant a permanent rest, a notion that I needed to tamp down.

My cell rang ten, twenty, a hundred times. Clancy. My friend Elias. Tiffany. My therapist, Nora. Voicemail chased them all away.

I felt heavy like gravity had turned up a notch, too frail to lift my head from the pillow. When night came, the blackness closed over me.

Images of Peyton flashed through my brain. The night she attacked my hair with her pre-school, blunt-tipped scissors, her pride in my V-shaped bangs. Her terror transformed into to joy when I taught her to ride a two-wheeler. Begging me not to beat up the boy who stood her up. Gripping her hand when Lindsay screamed into the world.

All the pieces of my life she'd filled. The pieces of my fractured heart.

Morning brought a knock to my door that I didn't answer. Later another, this one more insistent. Sunlight stung my eyes so I submerged under the sheet, incapable of the effort it would take to shut my blinds.

It's hard to describe my thinking when I go to this place. The thoughts are blurred, with no edges to them, not definable by language. The general's voice took advantage. *Join her why don't you? You know what to do.* I had little energy to fight those words. All I could do was burrow in and wait out the inside storm.

Sometime during the blur that was that afternoon, another voice chimed in: *Guh*, it said.

I shook my head, trying to make sense of the nonsensical word.

Guh, it repeated. Female, maybe the counselor, except she sounded far away and different, like a staticky old radio.

Guh guh now.

"I don't understand you," I said aloud, irritated that the counselor was being so elusive. Suddenly there was a weight on the bed, a presence nudging my leg. I blinked open my eyes to find two giant yellow ones peering at me.

Fenway yowled.

I freed a hand from under the sheet and pushed him off the bed. In less than a nanosecond he sprang back up, walked the full length of my body, and yowled again.

I knew he was hungry, his bowl surely empty by now. He sniffed me with his twitching nose until he found my hand and butted it with his massive head. To him, this hand existed only to feed or pet him.

When I tried to toss him again, he wrapped his sharp teeth around my thumb. Not biting, just letting me know he might. I flipped my fingers over and tickled under his chin. He released my thumb, rubbed against my chest, and purred.

I summoned the little strength I had, untangled myself from the bed linens, and dropped my feet to the floor. Walking was made more difficult by Fenway weaving between my legs. After filling his bowl, I poured a large glass of water. I was incredibly thirsty. It was halfway through the second glass that I remembered my medicine. Two doses already missed, dangerous to skip the third.

The pills tasted bitter on my tongue, but I choked them down, sealing shut the bottle in defiance of the sudden idea that maybe I should take the rest of them. Many of these black thoughts would haunt me over the next few days, and I would do all I could to defeat them.

I heard a clatter of keys against my back door and watched as the knob twisted and the door opened. Other than Peyton, who had my key?

David Ribault sucked in air when he spotted me. "Good lord, Georgia!"

"You're the one breaking into my house." My voice sounded scratchy from disuse.

"You haven't been answering your phone." He fell back against my counter, looking lost. Actually, he looked a helluva lot worse than that. His eyes were bloodshot and shadowed in their sockets. Whiskers like snow dusted his chin. "Clancy called, insisting that I give her Peyton's key to your house. Then Ben Reeder showed up demanding it. I figured you'd rather have me come than him."

"Why?"

"Why what?"

"Why is everyone—"

"Christ, George. They were worried about you. After you found out about Peyton, nobody knew what you'd do."

I glanced at the door, willing him to leave so I could barricade myself back in.

"You don't smell good." My brother-in-law, always the charmer.

"You look like shit yourself."

"I know. I need to clean myself up." He scuffed his hand through his unkempt hair. "The coroner is releasing her body to the funeral home tomorrow. I'm working on the arrangements."

Arrangements. I pictured my sister being placed in a large spring bouquet.

"Lindsay's at my mom's," he said.

Lindsay. Dear God. "Does she know?"

He nodded. "Colby told her."

Colby, the prodigal brother returned home. "Why wasn't it you? You're her father."

"I . . . couldn't. And I'm not sure what she understands. How could she understand something like this?" He cleared his throat. "Anyway, I think the funeral will be Monday. Mom's talked to Reverend Brunson. He'll do the service at St. John's. I thought maybe you could pick out what she'll wear . . . she'd want you to do that."

I found myself staring at the curve of his mouth, the quiver of his lips which hesitated after each word. I'd never seen him like this. David was always confident. Self-assured. Now he looked the way I felt. Shattered to pieces.

"Will you?"

"Will I what?"

He wiped his eyes again. "Pick out her dress."

"Yes." I couldn't imagine how, but I would. For Peyton.

"We may not have found her if a fisherman hadn't spotted the car." He flinched. "They're saying she shot herself. That this was suicide."

I felt his words like a physical blow. "No way. She'd never do something like that." She wasn't the screwed-up one, that was my role.

"I don't want to think it. I mean, she's always been my rock. But lately, I don't know. Was it the pressure from school? Trying to balance everything?"

I shook my head. I'd never believe that about her.

"Know what I found stuck in her wallet? A prescription. Dr. Matthews wanted to start her on anti-depressants, but she never got it filled." He shook his head. "She never told me. Did she tell you?"

I shook my head, startled. She'd seen a therapist off and on over the years, mainly to talk through her relationship issues with David. I never saw her as depressed.

"The police say she pulled the Lexus up to the boat ramp with her foot on the brake. She shot herself and the car rolled into the water." He froze. Those words and their terrifying meaning hung between us. He cleared his throat. "She didn't want anyone to find her body. Like that would make it better for us."

"I don't believe it." It made no sense. She would never use a gun. She would never abandon Lindsay. This couldn't be what had happened.

"I don't want to believe it either." He let out a sigh that seemed to completely deflate him. "But I feel like there's a whole side of Peyton I didn't know. Anyway. Call me if you need anything."

"Same here."

I watched as he left, moving slowly as though suddenly a hundred years old.

My sister's dead. That cold hard fact echoed in the black space inside me. I felt the pull to return to the cave of my bed, but that was the worst thing I could do.

"I need a shower," I said aloud. This was not an easy undertaking. My body felt so wooden that reaching for soap posed a challenge. But I did it, then dressed in some old jeans, noticing extra room around the waistband. I slipped a barrette around my damp hair and shoved my feet into my antique clogs, the ones Peyton had talked me into buying even though they cost a fortune. Comfort shoes.

She shot herself. The general's voice echoed David's. It made me mad. Edgy. I kept thinking about that phrase. I needed to dance around it. Needed to get out of there. I grabbed my keys and bolted out the door.

Driving wasn't a great idea. My foot pushed too hard on the accelerator. I passed other cars just because they annoyed me. I thought about Peyton in her car and her last desperate minutes. What happened to her?

She plunged herself into the water. The general came through, clear as glass.

That made no sense. None of it did. Why didn't anyone else see how wrong that was?

I did a U-turn. A few minutes later, I pulled into the parking lot of Café Italia, owned and managed by my best friend, Elias Jasper, just a few blocks from the hospital.

I entered through the side door and headed straight to the bar. My stool is the one closest to the kitchen. In the corner, a suspended TV aired a Yankees/ Red Sox game. The Yankees pitcher threw a heater to the Red Sox shortstop. A swing and miss. "Damn Yankees," I muttered.

"South Pacific!" Elias, the restaurant owner/manager, approached from the other side of the bar, leaning over to kiss me on the cheek. "Are we playing 'name-your-favorite-cheesy-musical' again?"

"No, we're playing 'watch the Sox screw up another one.'" I wondered if he knew about Peyton. But of course, he did, Elias always knew everything. Local politics. Hospital gossip. Any news related to his friends, and I was lucky enough to be one of those.

"I think you're giving up too soon on your Sox." A wine glass and an unopened bottle of pinot noir appeared in front of me. Apparently, Elias thought this was a night for the good stuff. Who was I to argue?

"You're gonna eat something, too." He filled my glass and recorked the bottle. "Don't even try arguing with me."

I didn't have the energy to argue. I took the glass, savoring the cool, crisp liquid on my tongue. My psychiatrist didn't like it when I drank, but I was always careful about it. Elias is, too.

"Sorry I didn't call you sooner," I said. He'd been up north visiting his partner's relatives when Peyton disappeared.

"You should be sorry. Doesn't matter where the hell I am. I'm always just a phone call away." Elias propped elbows on the bar and peered into my face. He has remarkable eyes. Coffee bean brown, almost the same shade as his skin. He's a big, lean guy with a gold earring in his right ear and a shaved, shiny head. His tattooed knuckles are leftovers from his teen years when he used crack to deal with his mental illness and channeled his suicidal impulses into gang affiliation. It was a wonder Elias lived to see twenty. I'm very grateful that he did.

"I'll be right back," he said, going to the kitchen.

About eight years ago, I met Elias in a self-help group, and he became my adopted brother. We've coaxed each other through the jungles of madness more times than I can count. We don't pretend with each other. When I need to, I can talk about the darkness without scaring him off. He has rapid cycling bipolar disorder; he lived a roller-coaster life until his doc found the right balance of medications. He's standing on an even plateau now. I think he likes the view.

When Elias returned, he placed a large salad and a plate of bruschetta on the bar. I couldn't imagine choking down food, though the wine went down too easily.

"You gotta clean your plate, babe. Get some meat on them bones."

I glanced back up to the ballgame where the Sox had two on base as the new first baseman stepped to the plate. His goatee looked like a furry coaster around his lips, and I thought about how Peyton hated it when the goatee craze first hit America. Then David grew the tiny patch of hair just under his lip: "I swear, George, it looks like a rogue eyebrow," she had said, and we joked about Nairing him in his sleep.

Peyton. How was I supposed to go on without her? Tears came, unbidden.

Elias appeared again, nudging the salad closer to me. "You hearing from the chorus?"

"Oh, yeah."

"They offering any instructions?" This was his sneaky way of asking if I heard any command hallucinations—a.k.a., the general.

"Nothing I can't handle." I sounded more confident than I felt.

"You seen Nora yet?"

"Therapy session next week."

He reached over and lifted my chin so he could look me dead in the eye. Satisfied, he pointed at the plate. "Eat."

I took a tiny bite of tomato. Food felt foreign. I tried a bit of bruschetta because he was watching.

"That's a double," Elias exclaimed, pointing to the TV. The Sox shortstop's fierce line drive to right field sent the first baseman home. "We're up by one."

I nursed the wine, hoping it would dull my edges, but knowing I'd never get another glass out of Elias. He can be a real mother hen sometimes. "How's Finn?" I asked. Of all Elias's boyfriends—and I'd met a dozen of them—Finn was my favorite, a physical therapist who believed in clean living, commitment, and monogamy. They'd been together for over a year. A record for Elias.

"He sends his love. Staying up in Philly another week or so."

I heard the door opening behind me and turned just as Clancy came in. She had on a wrinkled green jacket over jeans, her hair in an off-center knot. She must have been snoozing on her couch when Elias summoned her. "Well, Dan-o, I see you sent for backup." I stared into my glass.

Clancy took the stool beside mine as Elias poured two glasses of the pinot. "You doing okay, George?" she asked.

"Uh. No."

"Of course not. How could you be?"

Elias lifted his glass and clinked it against mine. "Peyton was a shining star. A shining star."

I thought back to the last time I saw her, the comment that she understood why I do the work I do. I thought about her looking into those horrible human trafficking businesses. She wouldn't have given up on it. Not my stubborn sister.

"They're saying she killed herself, but she didn't. I know she didn't."

"Who cares what they think?" he asked.

"Peyton would care," I answered.

Clancy and Elias raised brows at each other.

I felt like the wheels had come off of my life. And despite these incredible friends, I was desperately alone.

Elias reached over for my hand. I tried to pull away, but he held tight. "Look at me! Where's your fight? Your sister died and them bastards ain't doing nothing about it."

I could feel the energy he was trying to pour into me, but I was too far down the other path, and what David had said left me questioning everything.

"She was your sister. Family. You owe her." His scrutiny was fierce, something I hadn't seen in him for a while. Clancy squirmed. She's a good friend and probably thought he was being too rough.

"It's up to you. But you got us," Elias said.

I slid my hand from his grasp, lifted my fingers to his face, and stroked his chin. "You can be a real bastard, you know?"

He winked. "Don't you forget it."

Clancy rested a hand on my shoulder. "Try eating a little more."

So now I had two mother hens. I picked at the salad and took another bite of bread, but I couldn't stomach more than that.

"I better head back home. Clancy, I may need a few days off."

"I insist on it. But you stay in touch with me, okay?"

"Sure thing, Dan-o."

Elias came around the bar and pulled me into his arms. "Whatever you need, babe. I'm on it."

CHAPTER SIXTEEN

Kitten tossed the sheet from her bed and turned toward the box fan in front of the tiny window. Thoughts tumbled like marbles in her brain. Peyton Ribault had tried to save her and died because of it. *Would the same thing happen to me if I try to leave again? No!* She couldn't let herself think that. Javier would help her escape or maybe she'd find her own way. Roman had ruined enough lives; he wasn't taking hers.

Her gaze trailed up to the ballet dancers twirled by the breeze from the fan. Moving air felt like dragon's breath when the temps nudged toward a hundred. What would happen to the Mexicans in Dulce's room? Maybe Roman would give one her room and let Kitten work the street like Dulce. She'd disappear the first chance she got.

Kitten's life imploded because of Drew. Once, during Brandon's practice, he had taken her hand and led her under the bleachers. "I've been waiting for this moment. I can't handle waiting a second longer." He cupped her chin and his lips found hers. But this kiss wasn't like the others. His tongue reached deep inside her mouth, startling her. His body molded around hers and she felt his bulge meet her stomach. Did he think she'd go all the way with him? She wasn't ready for that. She loved him, and wanted him to be happy, but not that. Not yet.

Drew took a playful bite of her bottom lip and pulled back.

"What you do to me, beautiful." He exhaled slowly, his breath warm and sweet and comfortable. "You gonna be my girl?"

Wasn't she already his? "Of course."

He grinned. He always looked older when he was smiling. "I want to take you away. Get you out of that house. Take you somewhere special. What do you think about that?"

"Can we go now?" she asked with a nervous laugh.

"Not now but soon. You won't need to bring much. A few clothes. Your phone. Don't forget your phone."

Did he mean leave the Garrisons, like permanently? "Where are we going?"

"I'm not sure yet. Got a few ideas."

"How long will we be gone?"

He kissed her on her forehead. "You won't want to come back, I promise."

Kitten shook her head. "I can't leave Brandon."

Drew looked hurt, as though she'd chosen her brother over him, but it wasn't that simple. She took care of Brandon. He couldn't count on anyone else. She'd never abandon him.

"You are a very loyal sister, beautiful." He sighed. "How about this? You come with me. Once we get settled, we send for Brandon. We'll find a place with good schools and, of course, plenty of baseball. Does that work?"

Tears of relief and love filled her eyes. They could leave the Garrisons. They'd never have to be in another foster placement. She and Drew would create their own home, and Brandon would have his own room, and go to school, and have a happy life. This was all she'd ever wanted.

"As soon as you're old enough, I'm going to marry you," Drew said with a final kiss.

A few days later he texted her at midnight. "Sneak out the back door. There's a green car parked around the corner. Get in it."

She tiptoed out of the room she shared with two other girls.

When she reached the boys' room, she inched open the door. Brandon slept on his side in the upper bunk bed. She wanted to tell him bye, to promise she'd be back for him soon, but she couldn't risk waking the other kids. Instead, she slipped a note in the pocket of his backpack. He'd find it once he got to school.

Kitten had never seen the green car that waited for her. When she started to get in the front seat, she found a man sitting there.

"Get in back," he said.

As she opened the rear door, the scent of marijuana overwhelmed her. Drew had never smoked it around her. As soon as she climbed in, the car sped away.

She didn't recognize the driver either. A mass of a man, shaved head as smooth as a kickball, shoulders bulging over the seatback. "Where's Drew?"

The one in the passenger seat said, "You'll see him soon. Be patient."

Patience was something she'd never been good at. The old car rattled through traffic lights, turned onto to entrance ramp for I-95, heading south. Where were they going? She didn't want to get too far away from Brandon, not until they had him, but something about these two men made her nervous about asking questions. She'd wait till she was with Drew. He'd tell her everything she needed to know.

"What did you bring with you?" the driver asked.

"Just what Drew said. A few clothes. My phone."

"Phone?" The passenger seat guy turned to look at her. Tanned, sweaty skin. Bad breath.

She held it up. "The one he gave me."

"Let me see it." Without waiting for a yes, he snagged it from her. The light from the screen flickered as he scrolled through apps and messages. How did he know her passcode? Had Drew told him?

"It's clear," he told the driver, and tossed it in the seat beside her.

As she snatched the cell and cradled it in her hands, a dark uneasiness enveloped her. The old car quivered as it picked up speed. She felt for a seatbelt that wasn't there. A blast of Latino music startled her, and the passenger raised a flip phone to his ear.

"Jefe," he said. "We have her."

Who was Jefe? And where was Drew?

Over the next four days, the answers to these questions came, and her old life faded away.

Drew wasn't waiting for her. Drew never loved her. He had trapped her like a rabbit. She would probably never see Brandon again. She had been stupid. Naïve. She had vowed then to never let herself be fooled like that again.

The front door squeaked open; Dulce coming home.

"What the hell?" Dulce's voice rang out, then burst into a tirade in Spanish.

"Calm down!" Roman commanded.

She slipped from her bed to peek out the door. Dulce stood just outside her tiny room, hand on her midriffed waist, swaying as though unsure of her balance. Probably high on something.

"Who are they? Why are they in my room?"

"New girls here for the night. You share the room with Kitten," Roman yelled at Dulce.

"Why do they get my bed? Did they work tonight? Did they bring you three hundred dollars like I did?" She punctuated this with a stomp of her platform shoe.

Kitten wanted to shush her. Dulce would get Roman madder and he'd knock her into tomorrow if she kept it up.

"Maybe I let you sleep outside if you don't shut your mouth!" In two wide steps, he'd reached Dulce, his eyes wide with fury.

Kitten swung open her door and grabbed her friend's arm. "Come on. We can share."

Roman bent over Dulce, his nose inches from hers. "They'll be here one night. You keep this attitude up I may put you outside just for the hell of it."

She took a step back, teetering on the shoes, and Kitten steadied her, coaxing Dulce into the room. "Come on!" she whispered. "We'll be fine," she said to Roman and closed the door.

Dulce fell back against the wall and exhaled. "It's hot as hell in here."

"Worse out there with him," Kitten replied.

"No shit." Dulce kicked off her sparkly blue heels, unzipped her short skirt, and shimmied out of it. Her eyes looked droopy and unfocused. She must have had a good night if Lito got her high.

"They got here this afternoon," Kitten said. "Don't know where they're going tomorrow."

"Probably the fields. He usually brings in new workers this time of year."

"How many years have you been with him?" Kitten asked.

She swayed side to side in rhythm with her words. "That's . . .none . . . of . . . your . . . business."

Kitten looked away. She didn't want Dulce mad at her, not with Dulce's hot temper and them sharing a bed.

Dulce plopped down her shiny yellow purse and pulled her hair up higher in its butterfly clip. "Hey. Guess what I got?"

Kitten shrugged, grateful for the change in her friend's tone. "What?"

Flipping the purse over, Dulce dumped the contents across the top sheet. A small bottle of bright blue nail polish rolled toward the pillow. She snagged it and handed it to Kitten. "I snuck into the Dollar Store and bought it. Lito was supposed to come by and get the money from me, but he was late, so—"

Kitten savored the color— a perfect pale blue, like the sky in spring.

"We should try it on!" Dulce said, animated. "It's too hot to sleep anyway."

She piled in beside Kitten and opened the nail polish. "You first?"

"I don't know how."

"Come on, Kitten! You've never done your nails before?"

She shook her head. Roman didn't let her have nail polish because it made her look older.

"I'll show you." Dulce took her hand and, with concentrated effort, stroked the blue on her nails. "There. Now don't touch anything. It needs to dry before we do another coat."

Kitten held up her hands to catch the breeze from the fan, her fingertips looking like Skittles. Dulce quickly, expertly, dabbed polish on her own nails, as Kitten watched in amazement.

"Need to wait a few more minutes," Dulce said, pointing to Kitten's hands.

Kitten waited, not wanting to mess up Dulce's work. It was kind of fun having her in the same room. Talking to her like they were best friends.

"Can I ask you something?"

Dulce blew on her drying polish. "That depends."

"Why do you stay? When you work the streets, why don't you run away? I know how much you hate it here."

"You are so naïve. I can't leave. Neither can you." She grabbed Kitten's hand and scrutinized the polish. "We can try another coat now."

Kitten tried to hold her hand still, but her friend hadn't answered her question. She repeated it.

"You want to know why I don't leave Roman? Why I've been in his stable for over three years?" Dulce's voice rose.

Kitten glanced at the door. *If Roman hears us—*

"I'll tell you why," Dulce said in a whisper. "Because this is my life now. I'm making the most of it. Lito trusts me and soon, Jefe will, too."

Dulce recapped the polish and set it on the table beside the bed.

"What about your family?" Kitten asked.

Dulce's face softened, a hint of sadness in her eyes. "They don't know where I am. It's safer for them if they don't."

Had Jefe threatened them? Lito? That's how they work. She wished she'd never mentioned Brandon to Drew.

"What do you know about Javier?" Kitten asked.

Dulce shrugged. "Roman hates him. I think because he works right under Jefe and Roman wants that job.

"Once when I was working Beltline Road and Lito was my handler, Javier stopped to give something to Lito. It was a slow night and Lito was going to be pissed because I didn't have much business. Javier slipped me a hundred. It kept Lito from blowing up at me."

"That was nice," Kitten said.

She turned back over. "That was good business. When Lito busts me up I'm out of commission like you were after you ran away. Speaking of that, you gotta be careful from now on. They are all mad at you and don't trust you. Lito thinks Jefe should have had you killed but he didn't because you make good money. But if you try something again—"

"I won't." The lie stung on her tongue.

"It can get you killed." Dulce arched her brows at Kitten, a warning, as she screwed the top back on the polish. "You can make things better for yourself here."

"What? How?"

"You act like you're a kid and you're not. Not anymore. You hate Roman and Lito and they know it. What good does that do you?"

"You hate them, too."

Dulce shrugged. "Si. Most of the time. But I know how to play them. I give them a little of what they want, they give me something back. That's the trick, Kitten. Only you're too stupid to realize it."

Kitten resented being called stupid, but maybe Dulce had a point. Roman and Lito treated Dulce much better than Kitten. Dulce knew how to get her way—something Kitten seriously sucked at.

"Go to sleep." Dulce switched off the lamp.

Kitten turned toward the window. The porch light outside shone through the bent vinyl blinds and, when she held her hand up into the light, her fingernails gleamed like pale sapphires.

CHAPTER SEVENTEEN

I had three people to see that next day, and number one would be the hardest. My niece needed me. Unfortunately, it meant visiting Peyton's in-laws.

The last time I'd been to the Ribault house was before Christmas, when Peyton insisted I attend a fancy party there. They had an actual ice sculpture Santa. My sister wanted me to like her in-laws, or at least, pretend to like them, but I could stand the Ribaults in small, white-gloved doses at best.

I pulled into the brick horseshoe drive. I've often wondered how Ribaults kept their front lawn looking like a putting green. Or why two people needed a mammoth three-story home when hundreds of homeless people desperate for shelter wandered the streets of Columbia, but I wasn't supposed to broach such topics. I parked in front of the garage, which could hold two cars and maybe a jet, and noticed a bright pink tricycle nudged against a large cement planter. Lindsay out riding her trike was a good sign.

After the third punch on the doorbell, Marge appeared. She's a tall, proud woman, with beige hair like spun cotton and a wire-thin physique. She always wears tailored pantsuits, with diamonds like headlights gleaming on her fingers. "Lindsay's napping," Marge said, motioning me to follow as she moved quickly through the foyer, her footsteps clomping on the polished wood floors. She took me to the living room, which had been redecorated since my last visit. It looked spartan, just a couple of wing-backed chairs, a glass coffee table on which bloomed an orchid, and a very white overstuffed sofa that sighed when I sat. You could tell the Ribaults had no pets.

As Marge perched on the edge of her chair, I glanced up to a portrait on the wall above her. At twenty, Marge Ribault had been a beautiful woman. Eyes, wide, wondering pools of green. Long blonde hair cascading over strong, bare shoulders. A knowing tilt of lips like she was quite aware she owned a sizable chunk of this state. But the woman under the portrait looked so much older. Creases that looked like cords tugged at the mouth, pulling it into a permanent frown. Heavy makeup didn't conceal the puffy eyelids or the dark hollows below her cheeks. Peyton said she was due for another facelift. Her disappearance must have been a great inconvenience for Marge who was not used to adapting her schedule for anyone.

"Where's Pearce?" I asked.

"My husband had something to take care of at work. Colby went with him."

"Colby's living here?" I was curious about what had happened to Colby.

"No, but he's been here a great deal. Especially since—"

"Since my sister died," I finished, those stark words hanging in the air. The only reason I kept going, kept putting one stumbling foot in front of the other, was to find her killer.

Her nod was barely perceptible. "Colby's been spending time with Lindsay. He adores that baby."

"How's she doing?"

"She couldn't sleep last night. We tried to explain what happened, that her mother has gone to Jesus." Her voice broke. Her hand came up to grind knuckles against her eye. "It's unfair. Lindsay without a mother for the rest of her life. My son a widower. This has devastated

David." She paused, regarding me for a long moment, then said, "How could Peyton do that to them?"

I should have expected this attack, but I was off my game, and I had to swallow to keep from combusting. This house inspired a lot of swallowing. "She didn't—" I was interrupted by a noise and spotted a blond head just before it vanished around the arched doorway. A second later, half a face peeked in, the small nose pressed into the wall.

"Is that my Lindsay Thayer Ribault?" I asked.

Wearing a blue dress with matching ribbons in her soft blond hair, Lindsay stepped from behind the arch and came to me. As I wrapped my arms around her, a wave of profound sadness crashed over me. I squeezed tighter, her warm little body folding into mine. *Dear God, what this baby has lost.*

Lindsay placed her favorite stuffed dog on my lap. I cleared my throat. "How is School Bus?"

"She carries that thing everywhere." Marge Ribault's voice was an odd mixture of disgust and tenderness. We don't know how School Bus got his name, but Lindsay christened him with it when she was two. Maybe she thought all yellow things were school buses. Like her mom, Lindsay has a thing for the color yellow.

Keeping a good grip on School Bus's ear, Lindsay looked up at me expectantly.

I took Lindsay's hand. "Hey, you want to show me that swing set Grandpa and Colby built for you?"

We walked to the back of the house and out the door. Lindsay scampered down the patio steps and took a seat on the swing, one of those rubber-belt types. Reluctantly, I sat on the other, the seat smushing my rear into an uncomfortable *U*.

As Lindsay swayed, her sneakered foot dug in the dirt below. Movement in one of the upstairs windows caught my eye, a curtain being pushed aside.

"You having an okay time here?" I asked Lindsay.

She scrunched her tiny shoulders up in a shrug. "Okay."

I reached over to twirl a strand of Lindsay's hair around my finger. "Grammy told you about Mommy, right?"

"She's with the angels in heaven." She spoke the words like they were a memorized Bible verse.

"That's right," I said, though I wasn't much for believing in heaven or God or anything divine at that point. "She loved you so much, sweetie. Always try to remember that." She loved both of us with such fierceness. How would we go on without her?

Lindsay's mouth sagged. Her hand found its way to her lips and her thumb went in like a little plug. She grabbed the chain on my swing, pulling herself so close that her face was inches from mine. She let go of my swing, freeing hers to sway like a pendulum.

"I want to go home."

"Grammy told me you didn't sleep well last night."

She twisted the swing to the side without answering.

"Did you have a bad dream?"

She twirled herself around a few times, the chains coiling together like strands in a rope. When she lifted her feet, the swing spun her around and around, and I fought nausea just watching.

"Do you remember the dream?"

"Mommy said I can't play with her lipstick," she blurted out. "It was a accident!"

"You dreamed about Mommy?" I asked, confused.

"It got on the bed." The tears trickling down her face nearly broke my heart. I reached for the chains of her swing so I could pull her to me. Maybe this had not been a dream but a memory. From the night Peyton disappeared?

"Mommy knew it was an accident. Didn't she say so?" I lifted her into my lap and pressed my lips into her hair. "Do you remember anything else from that night? You know, when I found you sleeping in the closet?"

Lindsay rested against me without answering.

"Did you go in there by yourself? Or did Mommy tell you to go in there?"

"It's the safe place, Aunt George. When we have storms and I get scared, that's the safe place."

"Were you scared that night?"

"I wasn't scared. But Mommy acted like she was."

Peyton scared? Did she have an idea what was about to happen? "Did Mommy say something to you?"

"She said pretend it was a storm. But it wasn't a storm. But there was a noise and she said that, and I did, I got School Bus and went in the closet, and—" her voice trailed off.

"And what, sweetie?"

"And you came and woke me up."

A noise. Someone in the house? Someone threatening?

Lindsay burrowed in closer to me as I swayed the swing back and forth. Soon I heard the odd little snores that told me she was asleep. I slowed the swing, burying my nose in her hair. We had lost so much, the two of us.

I wiped my eyes. Somehow, I managed to heave my fanny out of the swing to carry her back to the house and up to her room. Lindsay hardly stirred when I covered her with the yellow Winnie-the-Pooh sheet. "I love you, Munchkin," I whispered.

When I went downstairs, Marge met me in the hall and walked me to the door. "Pearce and I were talking last night. As awful as this is, at least now we have some closure."

"Closure?" I shook my head. There was no point in arguing. I needed to get away from the Ribault house and all their pristine white stuff. "Tell Lindsay I'll see her soon."

The air in my Honda felt like fever as I twitched the key in the ignition. I thought about Marge wanting closure. The media attention had to be making her batty. And the idea that her precious son David's life might come under a microscope. Who knew what might surface?

I had just pulled out of their drive when I spotted a silver BMW slowing to turn in. Colby Ribault stopped when he spotted my car, so I lowered my window.

"Georgia. Nice to see you." His hair was longer than before, when he'd sported a clean, corporate cut, and the threads of silver were new, too. Still those dimples though. "How long has it been?"

"Too long," I answered. I thought about our one date. How he'd laughed when I asked the question that had weighed on my mind. "What's it like to be named after a cheese?" How he'd said he wished he'd met me sooner, and I'd felt the same. But then he moved, and married, and divorced. It felt like a lifetime ago, but those dimples were exactly the same.

"I'm so sorry about Peyton," he said. "I hoped she'd turn up. Damn. She was the heart of this family, you know. I can't believe—" He shook his head.

Neither of us needed that sentence to be finished.

"You're going to hear this from a lot of people, but I mean it. If there's anything you need. Anything I can do, just ask."

Tears stung my eyes at this kindness. Maybe one person in the Ribault clan wasn't a complete asshole.

"Thanks, Colby."

I pulled into the last shaded parking spot beside the Sunrise Community Care Home. Sunrise gets a lot of traffic during afternoon visiting hours. It's a small, private facility, and Adele Thayer, my mom, likes it here.

Bernice, my mom's favorite aide, greeted me at the door with a warm hug, and my hands were lost in the mass of black braids hanging down her back. Bernice can handle Adele, even on the bad days, of which there are plenty.

"I'm so sorry about your sister."

"Thanks. Where's Mom?"

"The garden. Pretty lucid this morning."

I nodded, though I wasn't sure I wanted Mom lucid when I told her about Peyton. Lucid meant she wouldn't be spared the shock or the jolting waves of grief. When I started for the garden, Bernice stopped me.

"I'm so sorry, Georgia. She knows. Saw the news before I could switch the channel."

I exhaled in relief. "How'd she handle it?"

Bernice slipped a lighter in my hand. "We had a pastor here from the AME church and he did some praying with her. I think that helped. Miss Adele likes her prayer time."

"I'm sure it did. Thanks."

I found Mom standing among the begonias, impatiens, and vinca she'd planted last April. She's a tiny thing, inches shorter than she used to be. Her straw garden hat sat cockeyed on her head, wide enough to shade her whole body and then some. Potting soil coated the fingers of her gardening gloves. She frowned at her handiwork.

"Flowers look great, Mom."

"This heat's about to parch them. I watered them this morning, but the impatiens are wilting."

"You always called them the most melodramatic flower." When I hugged her, she felt as delicate as a baby bird. She pulled away like she always did on those lucid days.

"Can you take a break?" I asked.

She reached in her pocket for a cigarette. I produced the lighter and flicked it. Long ago, Peyton and I decided it wasn't worth the battle; Adele was going to smoke, and she'd make life hell for everyone if we tried to stop her.

She took a long draw, winking against the rising smoke.

"So, you know about Peyton," I prompted.

The cigarette dangled from the corner of her mouth. I waited, wondering if her emotions would escalate into a firestorm. Fury had always been her first line of defense. Or would more tears come, the grief bubbling up through the mire of her illness?

But she surprised me. It was one of her better days. "Wish Lindsay had a brother or a sister. Gonna be hard on her, being alone now. At least you and Peyton had each other, no matter what I put you through." She took another puff and flicked ashes into her potting soil mix.

"When did you last see her?" I asked.

She bent to pinch wilting blossoms from a geranium. "Deadheading," she called it.

"A couple of weeks ago. One evening, but it was still so damn hot. Lindsay sat in my lap. A little heat generator, that one." She slid off the gardening gloves. "The news acted like Peyton probably killed herself."

I nodded, wondering where this would lead.

Adele dropped the cigarette and stomped it out. "They're wrong. She didn't."

"How do you know?"

"Because I know her. She had too much life in her. Last time she was here, she gave me that big sunshine smile, like her whole body was smiling. Looked like that on her wedding day. And when Lindsay came, she said she was doing something important. Something she was proud of."

Her research into human trafficking? "What else did she say?"

"She hoped to save some people. She said you did that in your work. That your work was important, and she was finally doing something that mattered, too." She reached into her pocket for another cigarette. Normally, I limited her to one, but nothing about today was normal so I helped her light it. Mom squinted at me. "Who could do such a thing to her? Who would hate our Peyton that much?"

I had no answers for her. And the police weren't even asking those questions.

She gave me a long, pinning stare. "You need to take care of this, Georgia. You're her big sister. It's your job to look after her."

I nodded as her words sunk in. She was an impossible woman to defy, always had been.

Mom put her gloves back on and stooped to inspect her marigolds. "Need us a good soaking rain," she said. "The drought's about to kill my garden. You plant anything this year?"

I had, during my last visit we'd discussed my garden for over an hour. Hard to know what would stick when you talked with her. "Just the usual. I don't have your green thumb, though."

She looked down at her gloves. "Pink today. I'll wear the green ones tomorrow."

CHAPTER EIGHTEEN

Lillian sipped her coffee in the living room after her morning walk. She liked the Estate best at this time of day, before the girls were up. Jefe had been away for a few days, but due back at any moment. She didn't know where he went or why but had learned not to question him. Sometimes she imagined what other life he had. *A wife? Kids? Do they think he's a businessman traveling all over the world? Do they have any clue he'd built an empire in the backwoods of South Carolina?*

She winced at the climbing sun. The day promised to be a scorcher. Sometimes, her skin almost sizzled in Carolina's suffocating heat, her very flesh holding the memory of a day so hot it nearly killed her.

She had been only sixteen, scraping out a life on the streets. Temps climbed to 108 degrees. She'd fallen asleep on a park bench and awakened to a searing burn across her nose, arms, and legs. She shouldn't have been so stupid.

Her desperate search for a spot of shade found her in an alley behind a store, but it brought little relief. The cloth of her shirt punished her skin. She wanted to strip naked and lie in a fountain but knew the water was too warm to cool her. It seemed nothing would. Fired burned inside too. A fever?

She staggered into the library, desperate to breathe something that didn't scorch her lungs. The cool air almost hurt, and sent chill bumps across her skin, but she savored it. When she found a water fountain, she guzzled so much that she almost threw up. She wanted to lie in the stacks and sleep, but a guard followed her as though worried she'd steal all the books.

It was a public place so he couldn't drag her out, but he could make her time there uncomfortable. She kept moving from one floor to another, feigning interest in a collection of local writers and a fashion magazine. Fever made reading—even thinking—impossible.

A librarian approached her. "We're closing in ten."

Lillian stumbled to the door, every step feeling odd, as though her brain had disconnected from her body. Outside, the sun hung lower in the sky, but the concrete held the relentless heat. Where could she go? Her thoughts had fuzzy edges.

She held the rail by the steps and slid down, no longer strong enough to keep moving. *I'll rest here, just for a while. Just*—she closed her eyes.

"Hey? Hey! Are you okay?"

She sucked in a hot breath and blinked open her eyes at a woman staring down at her. "You don't look so good," the woman said.

Lillian tried to speak but no words would come. The woman opened a leather knapsack and pulled out a bottle of water. "Here. Try this."

She drank, her tongue thick and dry, letting the water slosh down her chin. The woman squinted into her eyes. "Can you tell me your name?"

No words came. She just wanted to lie down, and close her eyes, hoping sleep would save her from the fire inside and outside her skin.

"Okay, okay. We need to get you checked out. Can I call your parents?"

She shook her head and tried to stand, to run away, but the woman stopped her. "Hey, it's okay. Just sit here for a second."

Sitting was a wonderful idea. She'd close her eyes, just for a few minutes. Just until—

She awakened in a room with stark fluorescent lights. Tile walls. Something pinching her arm.

"There you are!" It was the woman again, wearing a different top, and with a badge dangling from a lanyard around her neck. "You gave us a bit of a scare but you're much better now."

Hospital. She was in a hospital room. The pain in her arm was from an IV. "What happened?"

"What do you remember?"

"Sunburn. Brutal sunburn."

"Definitely. Try sun poisoning."

"I was so hot. Having to leave the library and you were there and—"

"And you passed out. EMTs brought you here. Your core temperature was dangerously high. We used cooling blankets and medication to bring it down." She touched the white sheet covering Lillian. *A nurse? A doctor?*

"Water?"

"Of course." She positioned a Styrofoam cup with an elbow straw so that Lillian could sip the delicious, wondrous water.

"That's good. We'll try more in a few minutes. What do we call you?"

"Lily." This was the name she'd given herself.

"That's lovely. What's your last name?"

Her gaze searched the room. The door. The machines. The tile walls. "Wallace," she decided.

The woman smiled. "Okay, Lily Wallace. My name is Georgia Thayer. I'm a social worker here at the hospital. How old are you?"

"Eighteen." The lies came easier as she let them out.

"Eighteen," the woman repeated, brows arched like she didn't believe it. "Is there someone I can call for you? Your parents?"

She shook her head. There was nobody. Nobody who cared if she was well or safe. Nobody.

The woman's eyebrows rose again. "How long have you been living on the streets?"

She shrugged. She wasn't exactly sure. Time had a different meaning now.

Georgia nodded, as though understanding something she hadn't said aloud. "Okay. Here's the deal. I don't think you're eighteen, but we'll go with that for now. When medical staff figures it out, though, they'll insist I call social services. And I'll have to. That's my job. But maybe we have a little time before that happens. For now, let's just work on getting you well."

Lillian felt an unfamiliar surge of gratitude for this stranger. She nodded, closing her eyes, and letting herself fall back into the delicious oblivion of sleep.

It was soon after Lillian checked herself out of the hospital that Gunner came into her life and imprisoned her in his. She never tried to run away. Why would she? She knew what was out there for her. She'd stay with Gunner as long as he'd have her, and treat him well, and stay fed and dry.

For a month, she lived with him. She taught herself to cook a few meals and tried to keep the small apartment tidy. She did what she needed to please him, because she wanted to stay there as long as she could. He had other plans, though. "Put this on," he said that fateful afternoon, handing her a short red dress. She complied.

He surveyed her in the new clothes and commanded, "Fix your hair." She gathered the top layer in a barrette, freeing a few strands to frame her face. Gunner had bought her some makeup—cheap stuff that didn't quite match her skin tone—but she did her best with the blush, mascara, and lipstick. She wasn't unattractive. She knew this about herself. The auburn hair and green eyes, the gentle lift of her small nose, the full lips—she had something to work with, so when she returned to the small living area, she knew she looked damn good.

"Nice," he said. "Come with me."

That was the first time she came into this very room. The day that she met Jefe.

She could recall every detail about that meeting. Driving up to his gorgeous mansion in the middle of nowhere. The bright blue pool surrounded by palm trees. The tile roof, the double doors with leaded glass at the entrance, the four chimes that echoed when they rang the bell.

The cook answered the door and led them to this paneled room with a Pueblo rug and heavy leather furniture. "Wait here," Gunner commanded.

A few minutes later, he returned with the owner of the house. Shorter than Gunner, with dark hair, fair skin, and a lapis bolo tie. He was broad-shouldered with a narrow waist and moved efficiently and with purpose. "This is her?" he commented, his brown eyes measuring her from scalp to toes.

"Yes."

"What's her name?" A bit of a Southern lilt to his voice.

"Lily," Gunner said, as though she hadn't spoken.

"Lily?" He circled her, his gaze like fingers on her skin. She stood taller, angled her face so that her hair fell across her shoulder. "Not Lily. Maybe Lillian."

"What do you think of her?" Gunner asked.

"She's luscious. Leave her with me."

Gunner didn't even tell her goodbye. He fished his keys from his pocket and headed out the door, not even looking back. It pissed her off. Not that she was attached to him. She no longer saw any use in attachments. But she'd lived in his house for four weeks and did whatever he asked—and he asked a lot. How dare he treat her with so little respect.

Jefe moved to the bar beside the mammoth fireplace and poured himself a dark amber drink. He didn't offer her any. Lillian stood perfectly still, assessing. Should she run? But go where?

"Sit," he said.

She took her time walking to the sofa and perching, her long legs folded beneath her. He sat beside her; the drink cradled in his hands. "You haven't said anything," he commented.

"What would you like me to say?"

He placed the glass on a coffee table and touched her, fingers skimming up her arms, her neck, her cheek. "How old are you?"

"Eighteen."

He smiled at that, his teeth straight and as white as copy paper. *Expensive teeth.* "When I ask something, you always tell the truth."

"I'm sixteen." She didn't feel that age. She felt much older.

"Where is your family?"

She shrugged. "I don't care."

"Ah. A tough *chica.*" He smirked. "Where did you last see them?"

"A trailer north of here. My stepdad was between jobs—" She flicked her hand. She was done with them, with that life.

"They aren't looking for you?"

She thought about the last time she'd seen them, the fight with her mother about a stupid pair of boots, her stepfather slapping her so hard she nearly fell to the floor. How she jerked away from them and ran, though she needn't have, they didn't come after her. They never did. "No. Why do you ask?"

His hand sifted through her hair. "I want you . . . unencumbered."

"Yes. I'm . . . unencumbered."

He lifted the glass again and sipped. "I may have plans for you, Lillian. If you prove yourself."

She eyed him with a hint of disdain. She didn't like being a pawn in a game with no rules.

He cuffed her lightly on the chin. "Ah. Feisty. I like that. To an extent. Though it would be unwise to take it far."

She softened her expression, not wanting to push him. She didn't know him and didn't know what he was capable of. She would though. If she were to stay here, she would study him. Learn him. Understand what drove him. There had to be power in knowing.

Lillian settled into her life with Jefe. He liked sex. He gave her videos to watch, telling her to be a good student, to learn what it took to please a man. She thought that was funny because she'd found him quite easy to please. She didn't like the films—the girls were too passive, too under the thumb of the men. When she asked for different ones, he handed her a catalog. She ordered six and found four that suited her because the women took the upper hand. Some did it with subtle manipulation, with postures and approaches, others with more overt forms of domination. She preferred the former.

As did Jefe. He liked it so much that he decided she should please one of his business associates, a man who'd come from New York. She hadn't prepared for this possibility. "Why should I do this? Don't I give you enough?" she demanded.

He grabbed her by the chin, squeezing so hard it felt like his fingernails might slice through flesh. "You will do what I tell you, or you won't like the consequences."

She'd never been frightened of him before. Wary, yes, but not afraid for her safety. She nodded. She met the associate in a fancy downtown hotel, wearing the evening gown Jefe had bought her, carrying the champagne he'd purchased. When she left four hours later, he was sleeping the deep slumber of the happily sated.

The next day, Jefe was so pleased he let her buy a movie to watch on his large screen tv. She watched the latest Twilight film and after, ate an ice cream sundae prepared by Jefe's cook. She liked this special treatment so much that when Jefe had another friend for her to meet, she bargained with him for three new outfits and her own tv. They continued this way for several months; he'd set up an appointment for her, she'd negotiate for payment.

She began to learn more about Jefe and how he'd earned his fortune. He dealt in people. Real live people, some from Mexico and South America, and some from Asian countries, who supplied a large and demanding labor market. A farm that needed workers to harvest—Jefe brought in a crew from Mexico. A factory struggling to produce enough cheap T-shirts or mass-market dresses— Jefe's workers from Viet Nam could pull double shifts. Lillian came to understand how little the workers were paid, and that leaving their employment was not an option—Jefe made sure of it.

Jefe came to trust Lillian more and more. Once, when he was going over his books, she saw how much money he had made. Jefe was a very rich man from selling people. What stunned her was how much he made from lending Lillian to his friends—several thousand dollars for each encounter. She felt a little foolish for getting excited that he bought her outfits and let her watch movies in exchange; she could now hold out for a higher price.

She brought this up over dinner one night, and Jefe laughed. "You think you can bargain with me?"

She swallowed. "I think that I make you much more money than the workers at the farm or the factory. And there is only one of me!"

"What makes you think you're the only one?"

The next day, he took her to the trailer, where she met Roman and two girls who worked for him. The place reeked, and the girls looked cheap and wrung out. Worst had been Roman's eyes drinking her in like she was a cheap beer.

"I bring in two thousand a weekend when business is good," Jefe said, as they drove away.

"Who is the business? Truck drivers? You make much more money on me. You should consider a more upscale operation." She knew she was pushing her luck. Jefe didn't like being told what to do, but the trailer had been awful. She'd rather die than be sold out of a place like that. How did those girls stand it?

He looked more thoughtful than annoyed. "Where would I get the girls for something like that?"

"Where did you get them?" She waved a thumb in the direction of the trailer. "Where do you get the workers for the plant or the peach farms?"

He eyed her carefully. "We don't find girls like you every day. You're different."

"Yes, I am," she said with more confidence than she felt. "And maybe I can teach others what I've learned. Maybe I can make you richer."

He laughed. "Maybe you can."

A few days later he brought her a stack of photographs. "These girls work for me. Pick out a few."

The pictures were amateurish, but useful. She sorted through twenty pictures of girls, selecting three. She wasn't even sure why she chose them. It wasn't necessarily beauty, though that helped. It could be an expression, a physical posture, or the way she took in the camera.

Jefe looked at her selections and pulled two additional from the stack. The two he chose concerned her. They looked so young, only children, wearing a blank look as though all emotion had been leached from them.

"Why them, Jefe?" Lillian asked.

"If we can clean them up, they'll bring top dollar. My friends often ask for younger girls."

Something roiled in her gut. *How young?* Lillian had lost her virginity at thirteen, by choice, and had come to regret it. What would it be like for these girls—these children—to be forced to lie with older men?

"What's wrong?" Jefe's voice held a hint of criticism.

"They're just . . . so young."

"Young?" A wildness flashed in his eyes. "How dare you. You have no idea what they came from. How they were treated. You think you can judge me?"

"No. Never. I just—"

He jabbed a finger at her like a knife. "I give them food, a place to sleep. Clothes. They have a better life with me. Like you do, Lillian." He collected the photos, shoved them in a drawer, and locked it.

CHAPTER NINETEEN

The next day, the tension that remained between them frightened Lillian. She walked a tight rope as she fixed him his favorite breakfast, which he ate without saying a word. She cleaned the dishes and the kitchen, vacuumed the living room, and dusted every surface, keeping an eye on him, assessing. Finally, he spoke. "Get in the car." Hidden danger in those words.

He drove her through downtown and into an industrial area, slowing to turn on a gravel road that led to a cement block building. It was surrounded by a tall hurricane fence topped with razor wire like a sadistic slinky. Two beat-up-looking cars parked beside the lone entrance.

Jefe honked his horn, and a man came out to open the gate. Once parked, they stepped out of the car into oppressive, moist heat. Lillian noticed a box fan whirring in a window and prayed that wasn't the only air circulating inside.

The man led them through a battered, plain door where a wall of hotter air greeted them. A small desk with an old computer monitor sat to the right of the entrance and a Lance snack machine squatted to the left. The rumble of machines echoed from the open door in front of them.

A small woman with dark hair pulled into a tight bun entered from an interior door. She wore a dark cotton dress and athletic shoes; a yellow measuring tape looped around her neck.

"Jefe." Her voice sounded shrill. "Wasn't expecting you." Her knuckles were smeared with black grease. The tiniest beads of perspiration dotted her forehead, while streams of sweat dribbled from Lillian's face.

"Show us the floor," he ordered.

She nodded, turned, and led them to a larger, very noisy room. Two dozen sewing machines thrummed. Behind each sat a girl—some Asian, some Hispanic, some Caucasian. One who looked to be of African descent. The oldest looked to be in her twenties. The youngest, barely a teen.

The heat reminded Lillian of the time she'd been so badly sunburned she'd ended up in the hospital. How did these girls work in these conditions? In the corner, sewing at a feverish pitch, was a tall, strong-looking woman with very dark skin and black hair cut close to her scalp. Her machine stopped. She looked up at Lillian, her gaze open and searching.

Approaching them was the man who'd let them through the gate—a wide semi of a person, dressed in a blue work shirt and chinos, a shaggy auburn mustache drooping around his mouth like a swag. "Something you need, Jefe?"

Jefe ignored him and turned to Lillian. "See these girls? If you want, you can join them. If I tell Stan to put you to work, that's exactly what you'll do. You'll sit behind one of these machines. You need more help, Stan?"

He shrugged. "Sure. We're pushed today. Everybody's pulling doubles."

"How long are they working?"

"Fifteen hours probably. Till we get the order done."

Lillian felt burning bile rise into her throat. One wrong move and she'd become one of these girls. Only she wouldn't survive it, not in that heat. Jefe reached in his pocket and pulled out the photos—the ones she'd picked out yesterday—and shoved them at Stan. "I want these girls off the floor. Clean them up, bring them to me tomorrow morning."

Stan licked his lips. "Like I said, we gotta big run to finish."

"Then finish it!" he commanded. "But I want to see these girls at eleven."

Stan nodded, eyes wide with fear.

"Good." He turned back to Lillian. "You come back with me and do as I say. Or you stay here. Which will it be?"

She turned and walked to the door, letting her footsteps be his answer.

The next day, she waited in the living room for the girls to arrive. During the ride home from the factory, she'd told Jefe that the dark-skinned girl showed a great deal of promise. "I didn't see her photo with the others."

"I'll think about it," had been his reply. The distance, the chill to his tone concerned her. That night, she'd put on her best lingerie and slipped into his bed. When he didn't rebuff her, she shimmied up beside him. He smiled, so she went further, determined to please him, to win him back. She tried techniques she'd seen on one of the Asian videos. Jefe responded with that low, guttural rumble. Jefe was hers again, and he would stay that way. She'd make sure of it.

When Gunner brought the girls, the dark-skinned one led the group. They all looked unkempt. Dirty. Smelling of stale sweat and neglect. The younger ones—thank God—weren't the pre-teens. Still young, but so was she.

She approached Jefe. "Give me some time to get them cleaned up. I'll see if they can wear my clothes for now. Let me have them for a few hours."

He nodded, instructing Gunner to stand behind the locked door in case any of the girls thought they might escape. She thought this unlikely. They looked too tired and beaten down to flee, except, of course, the dark-skinned girl, who eyed them with a fierce strength and curiosity.

Once the men had cleared out, she sent each of the girls into the showers, ordering them to scrub every inch of flesh and get their hair as clean as possible. The dark-skinned one sent the youngest in first. They took their time, probably relishing the feel of warm water. As they emerged and two others went into the bathrooms, she went to work on their hair at the two card tables she'd set up to hold mirrors, brushes, hairdryers, and make-up. Lillian ran a comb through a Mexican girl's long, uneven black hair. She needed a trim, but the long strands nicely framed a round, dimpled face. "Ow!" the girl said, when Lillian found a snag.

"Dulce! Be still and let her work," said the tall, dark-skinned girl. She turned to the other freshly clean teen with Asian features, and said, "Let me brush yours."

Lillian couldn't place the girl's accent, but she sounded elegant, perhaps African. As she dried her friend's hair, Lillian noticed it had a natural tendency to curl. She said to the dark-skinned girl, "Switch with me," and, as they traded spots, she grabbed a round bristled brush to guide the curl into a longer wave.

"Nice, Mei-Mei," the dark-skinned girl said.

"Mei-Mei and Dulce," Lillian said. "Nice to know your names. I'm Lillian."

"Lillian. A strong name. I'm Anwuli. I am from Nigeria."

Lillian turned Mei-Mei's chair so that she faced her. "Hand me that eyeliner and shadow," she said. She was no expert at applying makeup, but she found that a stroke of blush in the right spot highlighted cheekbones, a dab of cover-up blurred away imperfections. Next, mascara and crimson lipstick.

"Wow," said Mei-Mei looking into a mirror.

"You're beautiful!" Dulce said, which was certainly an exaggeration, but the girls did look much improved.

"Anwuli? You're next," Lillian said.

Anwuli took less time in the shower, and when she exited the bathroom, she wore just a towel. Lillian stood across from her, taking in her lean, strong physique. "You're taller than me, but I have something you can wear." From her closet, Lillian pulled out a dark blue satin dress and Anwuli put it on.

"Anwuli!" Dulce said. "Look at yourself!"

Lillian angled the mirror so she could see. She was spectacular. Long-limbed and lithe, the satin riding her curves like a stream of water.

Anwuli turned to Lillian. "Why are we here? Why are we wearing makeup and beautiful clothes?"

So, Lillian explained everything. How she was owned by Jefe just as they were, but she didn't work in a farm or factory. She lived in a nice place and had nice things, but she had to do things to keep Jefe happy.

"What things?" Anwuli asked.

"Whatever he needs me to do. I belong to him. But I'm not a prostitute," Lillian said defiantly. "I only date Jefe and a few other men. These men pay Jefe a lot of money. And Jefe gives me things, like this makeup, and that dress, and movies and—"

"But you are not a prostitute?" Anwuli's ample brows arched.

Lillian would not use that word. *Never.* "I can't leave. Where would I go? I have no other home but this one.

"And you? Would you rather go back to the factory?" Lillian continued. "Work in that God-awful heat for fifteen hours a day? Is that a better life?" She didn't tell them that there was no decision for them to make. Better to let them think they had some control.

Anwuli looked at the other girls, assessing. Dulce said with a hint of defiance, "I can't—*won't*—go back there."

Mei-Mei said nothing, but eyed Anwuli with a look of fear and expectation.

Anwuli said, "You entertain men every night?"

"No. I mean—Jefe, sometimes. But not other men. And if I'm with them, I'm with them all evening. We have a nice meal in a nice place. I wear beautiful clothes. I please them and come home to my air-conditioned bedroom and my movies. It's not a bad life."

"And if you wanted to leave?" Anwuli asked.

"I can't leave. This is my life now, so I make the most of it. I'd suggest you do the same."

The younger girls looked at Anwuli. Mei-Mei said, "I can't go back to the factory. Please."

Anwuli scanned the room, assessing, then said, "We stay then? And make the most of it?"

The girls nodded.

Lillian gave them a wavering smile. She wasn't sure they would work, that this plan would ever amount to anything, but she had to give it a shot.

Over the next weeks, there were other girls to try out. Dulce was taken to the trailer to work on her "self-discipline." Quieter Mei-Mei integrated quite well into their household.

Anwuli though. She became a star escort, often requested by businessmen with a taste for the exotic. Together, Anwuli and Lillian decided on her new name—Onyx. It fit her well. A glossy black stone. Strong. Hard. Indestructible.

Lillian smiled into her chilling coffee. They'd both come so far since those early days. As bigger changes came, they might find themselves in different roles. While only twenty-seven, Lillian knew hers was a business for younger girls. There was no retirement plan. It was important that Jefe continue to need her.

Lillian surveyed her closet, looking for an outfit to match her mood, and her mission. She wanted comfort, but she needed something soft and pleasing to the eye. Something to work in but also enticing to Jefe. She took pride in how she'd arranged her clothes by purpose and by color. On the right: entertaining outfits, bold colors with tailored fit and swooping necklines. On the left: other day clothes, more comfortable but still flattering, in subtler hues. In the rear: the just-for-Lillian clothes, sweatpants and cotton tops and ugly but comfortable sneakers. Jefe had never seen her in those.

When she was in seventh grade, her favorite teacher had been Mrs. Chastain. She was middle-aged and frumpy but had a full-throated laugh and brought much-needed humor into English class. One day she held Lillian after the bell and asked her for a favor; her special lending library needed to be inventoried. Would Lillian stay after school on Friday? When Lillian agreed, she wrote a note for Lillian's mom, promising to drive her home once the work was done. Lillian tossed the note knowing her mother didn't give a rip when Lillian got home.

It only took an hour to complete the inventory. She walked with Mrs. Chastain out to her Toyota but before climbing in Mrs. Chastain opened her trunk. "You may know my daughter, Tiffany. She's a year ahead of you."

"I've seen her around." Of course, she knew Tiffany. She cheered on the varsity squad and had starred in the school production of *Wizard of Oz* last year. Lillian had thought her quite ballsy to perform on stage like that, especially since she didn't sing all that well.

"That kid's grown two inches in two years! Anyway. She's outgrown all these clothes and I thought maybe you could use them?"

Tiffany's clothes were gorgeous. Paris Hilton pinks, Abercrombie and Fitch camis, and Tommy Hilfiger jeans. Maybe a little big for Lillian, but with a pin here, a tuck there, she'd have a whole new wardrobe.

"So? Are you interested?" Mrs. Chastain asked. "You'd be doing me a favor."

"Yes. Yes! Thank you."

Mrs. Chastain drove her home, chattering about the weather and the new movie *Mean Girls* that had just come out. She pulled up to the drab duplex where Lillian lived, saying nothing about the stained mattress the neighbor had left by the road, or the knee-high weeds that choked the front yard. "I'll see you on Monday."

Lillian's arms bulged with all the new outfits. "Thank you" seemed not enough, but she didn't know what else to say. As Mrs. Chastain drove away, Lillian realized she hadn't needed the library inventoried. She simply wanted to give Lillian these clothes without it feeling like charity. This kindness was the greatest gift Lillian had ever received.

But she'd given her more than clothes. She'd given Lillian a way to feel good about herself. Lillian found some instructional videos on tailoring clothes and, after a few missteps, managed to turn Tiffany's tops and dresses into customized outfits with lowered necklines, added ruffles, and bejeweled accents.

Lillian finally found a way to not be invisible.

What would Mrs. Chastain think if she met Lillian now? If she knew that adapting Tiffany's outfits had become a skill she used daily to costume her girls?

A rap on her door interrupted these thoughts.

"Yes?"

The housekeeper said, "Jefe is asking for you."

"He's in his office?" Lillian asked.

"The greenhouse."

Lillian rushed to put on the purple shift with a silk scarf and inch-high gold sandals. She hurried down the stairs and out the back door to the fiberglass-walled space where Jefe grew his orchids. The air conditioning blew temperate air over his prized blooms as Jefe inspected the leaves of a rare Kovacii plant he'd illegally imported from Peru.

She started to speak but spotted the phone in his hand. He motioned her to wait as he said into the cell, "I hear you. No need to repeat yourself. Jesus."

She pretended not to listen as the animated conversation continued. He was probably talking to his business contact in DC, a man with expensive tastes in cars, wine, and girls. He visited the Estate every few months for business meetings with Jefe and recreation upstairs. He worked as a lobbyist, but had other, more lucrative enterprises with Jefe.

When Jefe hung up, he crossed to her. "This is big, Lil. Our most important event yet."

"When? What do you need?"

"The Pro-Am Golf tournament in Augusta at the end of the month. We've got six buyers coming for the weekend when it ends."

"Okay. I'll have the girls ready. And we'll prep the rooms. Any special requests?"

He nodded. "Several. We've got two Russians coming. One prefers the more exotic girls. Ratana or Onyx may fit the bill. The other, Vasily, likes them young. I'm thinking Kitten for him."

"Which means we have to get her ready. Javier will bring her here Friday. You'll need to work with her, get her used to how we do things. Use the credit card to get her the right clothes. Show her how to do her hair and makeup. I want her vulnerable and drop-dead gorgeous."

She nodded. She'd seen pictures of Kitten. She'd even requested her for the Estate a time or two, only to be shot down by Roman who counted on revenue from Kitten. Still, she had less than a week to prep her. She'd have to kick things into high gear. "I'll take care of it."

"These guys are connected and wield a lot of power. Rumor is they've done covert jobs for Putin. They need to leave happy, Lil.

"And we have a senator that we're lobbying for a defense contract vote. We'll put him upstairs with Venus. She's good at keeping her mouth shut.

"Another Hollywood producer is coming. I'm not saying his name, but you may recognize him. The girls are not to react when they see him. No requests for autographs. No acknowledgment of any kind. He's to leave here wanting to come back every month."

"Of course. We'll do our best."

"Wish we had more choices for all of them. We have to expand the stable."

Which was exactly what she'd been saying for months. "You're right, Jefe."

"This has to go well. Millions of dollars are at stake. You make sure they leave more than just satisfied."

She would, of course. She always did. They had a similar group of businessmen—half of whom were international—who came for the annual Master's Tournament, a mere one-hour commute from the Estate. Those men sometimes chose her girls over the golf; that's how good they were.

Jefe lifted his rarest orchid, "Rothschild's Slipper," with wing-like fuchsia petals seeming to stretch in the sun's rays. "Isn't it beautiful, Lil?"

"It is." But was it worth the ten thousand he'd paid to have it smuggled from Australia? *Not in a million years.* "I'd better get to work," she said, and left him. She had planning to do.

CHAPTER TWENTY

From the cobwebbed window, Kitten watched Roman's car pull away, the three Mexican girls who stayed in Dulce's room crammed in the back seat. He had left as soon as he got a call from Jefe. Roman said Lito was on his way, but she saw no trace of the nasty van.

This was her chance.

She ran to her room and stuffed a pair of jeans, underwear, and two T-shirts into her knapsack. As fast as she could, she donned the pink sneakers, still scuffed from her last attempt at running, and secured her hair in a barrette. She hefted the knapsack on her shoulder and closed the bedroom door behind her. A bubble of guilt surfaced as she passed Dulce's room. *Betrayal? No. Once safe, I'll find a way to get her out of this. I'll find a way to help all of them.*

The exterior door wouldn't open. Of course, Roman had locked her in, but that wouldn't stop her. She climbed onto the couch and tugged at the lock that secured the cheap window until it slid open, hot air rushing in. If she tossed the knapsack first, she could just about fit through the small opening, and she'd be gone. Away from the trailer, from Roman, from Lito and Jefe. Gone.

A cloud of dust drew her attention to the driveway. The ugly van puffed out exhaust as it rumbled up to the trailer.

Too late. She couldn't leave, not without getting caught. She slammed shut the window as Lito climbed out the driver door. Back in her room, she shoved the knapsack under the bed as the trailer door squeaked open. She'd gotten so close. She'd leave her knapsack packed so when the next opportunity came, she'd be ready to bolt.

"Roman! Where the hell are you?" Lito boomed.

Breathless, she peered out the door. "He'll be back in a few minutes. Went to get some cigarettes I think." *And beer, probably.*

"I told him when I was coming." Lito spat out, glancing back at the van. "I'll let them wait."

How many had he brought this time? She could see the driver window was open, but the back of the van was probably hotter than a kiln. Lito closed the trailer door and backed against it. His shoulders and shaved head almost brushed the edges of the door frame. He had on the often-worn T-shirt, bright red with a clownish devil face across the front, a picture of his favorite wrestler.

"We're alone here?" he asked.

She winced at the growly edge in his voice. She didn't want to feel afraid, but Lito was the cruelest of Jefe's men. "Yes. For now." Kitten straightened her back and met his stare.

"Roman was stupid enough to trust you by yourself?"

"I won't run away again, Lito. I've learned my lesson. Nobody gets away from here." She lowered her head.

"No, you won't."

"I think I'll go wait for Roman in my room."

Before she could move, he grabbed her shoulder, his fingers pressing into her clavicle. "Since we're alone—"

No. Not Lito. He had been the one to kick her the hardest. When he pinched her chin and brought his face close to hers, his breath nauseated her. Without thinking, she jerked away, shoving him hard and bolting to her room.

"You little bitch!" He thundered after her. She tried to shut the door, but he kicked it with the force of a stallion, banging it against her hand.

She pressed stinging fingers against her mouth as she backed away from him. "You don't get to refuse me, Kitten. You do what I say."

He loomed over her, as big as a monster, and she wanted to kick him hard in the groin, to break things that mattered to him, but his eyes blazed, and she knew he would kill her if she fought him. Terror sliced through her.

Javier burst into the trailer. "What the hell? Lito!"

"*La puta—*"

Javier grabbed him by the shoulder to spin him around. "What are you doing? Are the new workers still in the van?"

Lito nodded.

"Are you insane? It's boiling in there. Jefe will kill you if one of them dies. Get out there and bring them in."

Lito eyed her then Javier, finally lowering his fist and exiting the trailer.

Kitten backed into her bed and sat, cradling her hand. Javier stared down at her. "Let me see."

"It's okay."

He took her fingers, turning her hand so that light from her lamp shone on the knuckles. Pain sliced through her. "I don't think it's broken. I'll get you some ice."

He hurried to the kitchen, returning with a grocery sack filled with ice, which he'd wrapped in a towel. She draped it on the back of her hand, desperate for some relief.

"We don't need you damaged right now." Javier wiped his sweaty face with a bandana. "Do not get him riled, Kitten. He's like handling dynamite."

She nodded.

"I have a question for you. Has anybody else shown up here? Someone like that Ribault woman?" Javier asked.

"Why?"

"Because somebody else has been snooping around. They're going to have to shut down the factory operation."

She thought about the man who'd pretended to be a buyer,

who'd searched the trailer up and down. She had promised not to tell anyone, but what did she owe that stranger? "Roman set me up with a buyer. Only he wasn't interested in me. He only wanted to search the trailer."

"What did he look like?"

She described him. Javier nodded. "Okay. Anyone else?"

"No." Why didn't it matter? Did Javier know the buzz-cut man? Who was he?

The door opened and two Asian teens staggered into the living room. Kitten stayed on her bed, watching. The girls looked dirty and very, very tired.

Lito ordered them to sit on the living room floor. Javier backed out of her room and closed the door. Kitten sat on the bed, cupping the ice against her hand, and trying to breathe away the pain.

CHAPTER TWENTY-ONE

Dianne Grafton, the art therapist, summoned me to Jane Doe's room. I once thought art therapy was just so much hokum, but during my third hospitalization, when I'd been instructed to make a collage of my voices, what surfaced became a real turning point in my recovery. So I put stock in Dianne, unlike some of the psychiatrists who worked this floor. The unenlightened.

She waited for me outside the door. "Are you ready to meet Marilyn Wilder?"

"No shit! You got her name?"

She nodded. "Has a pretty loaded psych history, too. No surprise there, I guess. We've ordered records from Charlotte where she's been treated since she was about twelve."

"Wow."

"She loves art. In the first session she worked with watercolors but didn't say a word. During the second one, I asked her to sign her colored pencil drawing and she wrote her name."

"Sneaky. Well done."

"Her affect is better. Not responding to voices. Still not volunteering much, though. Her therapist in Charlotte said her family moved to Columbia about nine months ago. Maybe she's been out of treatment since then. She wouldn't give me her address or how to contact her family. Maybe you'll have better luck."

"I'll give it a shot."

Dianne started to leave, but hesitated. "And Georgia, I'm sorry about Peyton. Can't even believe you're back at work. Maybe you should take a few days off."

"Thanks. But distraction is just what I need right now. And ain't no place as distracting as Columbia General."

Dianne nodded sadly, and I slipped into our patient's room before her kind sympathy made me do something embarrassing.

Marilyn looked better. Her hair had been washed, combed, and pulled back in a ponytail. Her skin had more color and her dark eyes had lost their haunted vigilance. Sheets tented her bent knees. She offered a quivering smile when she spotted me.

"Hey there," I said with more energy than I felt. "Do you remember me?"

She nodded. "Georgia. The social work lady."

"Exactly." I pulled a chair close to the bed. "I'm so happy to know your name, Marilyn."

"It's a stupid name."

"It's not stupid."

"Really? Do you know anyone under seventy called Mar-i-lyn?" She accentuated each syllable.

"Okay. You have a point." I poured a cup of water from the pitcher on her bedside table. "You're from Charlotte, right?"

"Charlotte was a long time ago."

"Why did you move to Columbia?"

"My family *dragged* me here." She exaggerated the dragged the way a teenager might.

"Speaking of your family, I'd like to get in touch with them."

She shook her head. "Nope. No way. They don't control me, and they don't have a say in my psychiatric care."

More coherent Jane/Marilyn could be a force to be reckoned with. I liked that about her.

"Have you been living with them?"

"Sometimes. Sometimes in my own apartment. I don't want to talk about them."

I sighed with exhaustion. I was running on fumes, but needed to let her take things at her own pace. Besides, once we had a full set of medical records, she might be more forthcoming.

Staring at me she said, "Are you alright?"

"Yeah, why?"

"Don't be offended, but you look kind of rough."

"No offense taken. I just had a long night." Eager to switch subjects, I asked, "How are the voices?"

"Very quiet."

"I'm glad to hear it. Any other signs of . . . the demon?"

"Not too much. I know I was batshit crazy the other night, but it's pretty damn terrifying having that evil chasing me like it was."

Her gaze begged me to believe her. I nodded. I knew exactly how it felt, how psychosis can alter everything. "It sounds terrifying."

She nodded somberly. "It's still with me. The fear, I mean. I wish I could let it go."

I gave her a long, intent look, seeing something evasive behind her eyes. "Why is it hard to let go?"

"Don't want to let my guard down, I guess."

I wasn't sure if this was a thread of paranoia remaining, or if cautiousness was simply a part of her personality.

She took another sip, then stared into her ice cubes. "What if it was real?"

"The demon?" I asked, perplexed.

"I know that sounds crazy. Hell, it is crazy. But—" She tossed the cup into the trash.

"But what?" I asked.

"Nothing." She scooted down under the sheets and turned away from me, shutting me out.

❀

I took a long lunch hour to run an important errand. I needed to see Peyton's research. Her laptop had been in the car and probably wasn't savable, but she was the most anal person I knew. She'd have backed up her data.

When I turned on Peyton's street, a knot clenched in my chest. How many times had I made this drive? Hundreds, probably, but I'd have little reason to make this trek in the future. No, that wasn't true. I had a very good reason—Lindsay. I loved that kid, and I had a place in her life. David might need to be reminded of that.

I rapped on the door. When it opened, David glared like I was a evangelical missionary.

"Can I come in?" I asked.

"Sure." He looked terrible. Bristles speckling his chin, shirttail hanging out of his jeans. Haunted, skittery eyes. He walked away from me, a damned annoying habit he had. And just as my sister always did, I followed him. When we reached the dining room, I was struck by the disarray. A half-eaten sandwich on a plate rested beside three glasses and stacks of paper cluttering the table. Jackets had been carelessly tossed on chair backs. Strange, because the Ribaults liked to keep things pristine, a practice Peyton had done her best to honor from the moment she and David moved in together.

"What happened in here?" I asked.

"This is death, George." He rested a hand on the stack of forms and cards. "The business of death, anyway. Legal documents and insurance papers. Oh, and greeting cards." He handed me one depicting a bouquet of roses. "Guess I should save these for you to see."

"No thanks."

"Mother says I should make a list of people who sent cards."

"So she can send thank-you notes?" Never underestimate the power of ritual in the Old South.

"Whatever." He hurled the card onto the table.

I looked at the mess, then at the man. "I need your help with something."

"What?"

"I want to find out who killed Peyton. The police aren't doing it, so that leaves me. And you, if you'll help."

I watched a collage of expressions play out on his face. Confusion. Raw grief. He dropped into a chair, putting his head into his hands, rubbing his face as though trying to erase his skin. "The police said it was suicide. She took her own damn life! Guess she didn't love me and Lindsay enough to stick around. Do you have any idea how that feels?"

Anger now, words grunted out through clenched teeth. Peyton had told me about times when David dropped his tight control and how it unnerved her. I would have found his rage intimidating, except when he whipped his head around to glare at me, some comb-over hair sprung free of its spray to stand straight up like a little off-center horn.

I lifted a placating hand. "You don't believe that. She loved you. And Lindsay—no way she'd do that to her baby. Please, David. Just answer a few questions. Did she talk about her research?"

He shook his head. "No. Not that I didn't ask. She started spending strange hours working on her so-called project. Leaving the house late. Coming home long after midnight. When I'd ask, she'd say some bullshit about it being confidential."

He rifled through more cards. "I should have paid closer attention. She wasn't going to classes. I didn't know that. The strange disappearances. I should have seen something was wrong. I'm a doctor. How could I have missed it?" The quake in his voice was very unusual for him.

"You didn't. Listen to me." I stepped closer so he'd have to look at me. "Peyton uncovered human trafficking. Right here in Columbia. That was her project. She wasn't sick. She was incredibly brave."

David gave me a you're-out-of-your–freaking-mind glare. I get that a lot from him.

"I'm serious. I've been to a few of the places she'd investigated. I've seen it."

His stare softened, replaced with a look of puzzlement. "How could she do something like that and not tell me? Or the police? Why would she take that on herself?"

His questions matched my own. "I don't know. Hell, there's so much we don't know. But she didn't kill herself. Surely you get that now."

He blinked at me, processing. "Okay. But if you're right, then whatever she got into is dangerous. If it's what got her killed, then you need to stay out of it. Tell the police what you know and let them handle it. Lindsay has already lost too much."

That got to me. Lindsay was my Achilles heel. His, too.

He pointed to the stairs. "Since you're here, go upstairs and pick out something for your sister to be buried in. You promised you would." His eyes softened and he turned away, which was just as well. If he got all teary, I'd fall apart, and I was barely keeping my pieces together as it was.

"Okay." I wasn't sure how I would manage it but knew I had to. For Peyton.

❧

As I approached the staircase, dread filled me. Automatic pilot. I would pretend this was someone else's house. I was looking through someone else's clothes.

I took my time climbing the stairs, hoping a surge of courage might nudge me forward. When I reached the closed door to their bedroom, I glanced across the hall at the unmade bed in the guest room. David must be sleeping in there, but why? Because it was too painful to sleep in the bed he shared with my sister? Or is there some other reason? I took a deep, steadying breath, turned the knob, and stepped inside.

It was as it always was. Perfect. The bed made, a half dozen pillows scattered along the headboard. The alarm clock blinked on the nightstand. Beside it, a lamp and a textbook, *Principles of Epidemiology*. Huh. My sister reading something like that.

I crossed over to the dresser. Framed photos of Lindsay made a parade in front of the mirror. Peyton's jewelry box, which held her everyday jewelry, looked untouched. I opened a drawer— underwear. A larger drawer—bras. Peyton had dozens and dozens of them, different colors and styles. Various amounts of padding. Would she need lingerie in her casket? I shuddered. But it wouldn't be her, not really. Peyton wouldn't care if the body in the casket wore a bra or pantyhose because it wasn't Peyton I was dressing.

I went to the closet, which was about as big as the guestroom in my house. It looked like my guestroom, too, a disorganized mess. Clothes chaotically stuffed on various racks. Shoes in a jumble on the floor. This was the Peyton I grew up with before she had her body snatched by the Ribaults.

When she was a girl, yellow had been her favorite color. Mature Peyton—the Peyton who'd had her colors done—wore olive green, blues, and black. But she still had that one yellow dress. Raw silk with shell buttons, belted at the waist, and she often wore a flowered scarf with it.

I found the dress with scarf attached tucked between a winter coat and a pair of acid-washed jeans she hadn't worn since 1999. I would need to go through all these clothes and get them to a shelter. Maybe that would help, knowing bits of Peyton helped warm some homeless people in Columbia.

She always loved you. The counselor's words of comfort made something twist in my gut. Peyton had loved me even when I didn't deserve it. Peyton never gave up on me; her faith sustained me until I found my own. So much of grief is selfish—all the parts of my life she used to fill, now empty. All the ways I leaned on her when I was at my worst. Had I ever thanked her? Told her what she meant to me? And now—

The staticky voice from the other night returned.

"What?" I whispered.

Baahk. The word gurgled like it was full of bubbles. *What the hell?* I closed my eyes and shook my head, desperate for clarity.

Boxxxx.

Box? Peyton had one. A special box she'd kept from childhood. I glanced up at a wire shelf over her dresses and spotted a green metal file container. I spun it around, noting the multicolor butterfly sticker atop the lock. I almost laughed. She'd gotten this thing in grade school. She'd even carried it off to college, toting her most precious letters from friends, her Sting cassette collection, and her stash of pot.

When I dragged the thing down, I found it heavier than I expected and the top popped open before I got it to the bed. Three stacks of letters were inside, each tied with ribbon. I flipped through the first pile—old letters and postcards from her college days. Stack number two looked like legal papers and correspondence from Mom's care home. Number three contained letters from the university, a few notes from our aunt, and a bunch of postcards I'd sent during various vacations.

My fingers groped under the piles and felt a small, bulging envelope at the bottom. When I opened it, I found a micro-cassette. The outside of the envelope read, *K. March-June.* Notes on her research? I didn't have a way to play the tape, but Clancy had a dictation machine in her office.

"You find what you need?" David beckoned from downstairs.

"Uh, yeah. Just about done." After slipping the envelope into my pocket, I replaced the letters in the metal box and returned it to the closet. I grabbed Peyton's clothes and a pair of heels before hurrying down the stairs.

David met me at the front door. "Can you get that stuff over to Dunleavy's?"

I nodded, though the idea of walking into a funeral home gave me chills.

He glanced down at the clothing, wincing as he did. "Maybe after the funeral we'll—I don't know. Move on?"

Not likely. "What about Lindsay? She wants to come home."

"I know. I'll get her after the funeral. Once we bury her mother, I'll bring her back here with me."

CHAPTER TWENTY-TWO

If there had been any way to escape Peyton's funeral, I would have. My love for my sister ran as deep as my toes and I would honor her life for the rest of my own, but I needed no formal ritual to say my goodbye.

Yet today was her funeral. I had to take Mom.

I parked at the group home. The reflection in my rearview mirror made me groan. I licked a finger to wipe the dark spot of mascara under my eye because I'd put on makeup and didn't want Mom to know I'd been crying. It would be hard enough getting her through this day, and I didn't want to add to her confusion.

When I reached the front door Bernice greeted me, smiling. "She's all ready for you. Got on that pretty green dress Peyton bought her. We got her hair looking real nice."

"Does she understand where we're going?"

"She knows she's going to a funeral, but she gets confused about who it's for. We've been trying to get her straight about it, showing her pictures and all. But this has been one of her bad days."

The aides here always talked of good days and bad days, but it seemed there were so few good ones anymore. I started down the hall to Mom's room as the door opened and she came out to meet me. She looked so tiny, even smaller than last week somehow, and when I bent over to hug her, she felt delicate as Peyton's crystal. Her short gray hair lay in wisps like feathers across her forehead. Smears of makeup streaked her cheek and chin. When she smiled, I realized right away that she'd applied the lipstick on her own, making a clown-like circle of red around her lips.

"Mom. You look beautiful. But the other ladies at the church will feel jealous when they see all that lipstick." I grabbed a tissue from her purse to clear away some of the smudges.

"You never wear enough, George. A girl as pretty as you. A little lip liner, a little blush—"

I groaned the way I'd been groaning for twenty years. Mom never relished having a tomboy daughter.

"Ready to go?" I took her elbow and guided her out to the car.

We hadn't even backed out of the parking space before she lit a Camel Non-Filter, which she held between her thumb and yellowed index finger. I could track the deterioration of my mother by the pattern of her smoking. From Virginia Slim Lights to Regulars to Camels to Camel Non-Filter. From cigarettes elegantly dangled between polished nails to cigarette nubs clutched like lifelines. The downward spiral of the mental patient. I hoped I'd be spared the same course.

"You know where we're going, right?" I asked.

"Peyton's funeral. I'm not stupid, you know."

"Of course not." I glanced over at her, anxious that she was getting mad. Anger was always her first line of defense.

Mom turned to look at me, the cigarette drooping from her mouth. "Peyton isn't due back from Winthrop till tomorrow, is she?"

Yep, this was a "bad day." "No, Mom. Peyton died, remember? We talked about it the other day."

"Oh, Christ." She stared at me, defiantly at first. Then her face softened into a squinty-eyed look of confusion. Confused was better than furious or grief-stricken.

When we arrived at the church three TV vans were parked out front. A cameraman stood in the ancient church cemetery, his camera taking in the long line of people entering the sanctuary. I glanced at Mom. The last thing she needed was this kind of stimulation. I drove to the end of the block, rounded the corner, and parked beside a bank. When I held out my hand for her cigarette, Mom clutched it close to her lips, sucking out that final bit of nicotine before letting me take it. I nearly burned myself getting it to the ashtray.

"There are gonna be a lot of people in there, Mom. Remember, Peyton had a lot of friends. And David comes from a big family."

Mom said, "You have friends too, Georgia."

"What I mean is, try not to get overwhelmed by everything. This won't last too long, and we'll be out of here. Okay?" I came around the car to open the door.

When I reached for her arm, she snapped, "I'm not helpless. Why do you act like I can't take a step without your help?"

I clamped my jaw shut, praying this didn't escalate into a screaming fit on the sidewalk. Wouldn't the TV cameras love that?

Two black limousines had parked by the main sanctuary door. David had called earlier, expecting me and Mom to ride with the family, but I turned him down. I didn't care about proper funeral protocol; Mom didn't need to be the focus of attention, and if she got loud, I needed an exit strategy.

I let her take the lead, eyeing the media frenzy as we inched closer. I saw someone being interviewed, a stocky, white-haired man in an expensive gray suit—Pearce Ribault, David's father. I wondered what he was saying about my sister.

"Georgia! Over here!" Elias stood under a towering live oak beside Clancy.

Relief flooded me as we approached these friends. Clancy reached her arm around me and whispered, "We're going to sneak y'all in through the side. Less of a circus that way."

"Thanks." I turned to Mom. "You remember Clancy and Elias, right?"

Soon the other Ribaults emerged from the limos. Marge wore a black dress—simple, elegant. Colby stood beside her. He scanned the crowd and, when he spotted us, gestured that he'd make room between him and David.

I shook my head, mouthing, *"Mom."*

He replied with a sympathetic nod.

Sweat trickled down my back. My hands stroked the supple silk of the black dress Peyton had insisted I buy in a shopping trip last fall because "everybody needs a church dress." And my smartass reply had been, "I'll just need it for funerals." And here I was.

Why were so many people around us? Peyton had always been an introvert. I scanned the crowd, looking for familiar faces, but finding few. A whimper beside me made me turn to Mom. Tears streamed down her face. I froze. "Mom? You okay?"

She had a panicked look now, her gaze flitting around the room like a trapped bird. When I handed her a tissue, she wiped her eyes before gently patting my cheeks. "Don't let them see you cry," she said. "Never let them see that."

Clancy nudged me. "How you doing, George?"

"I need a drink."

At that moment, I spotted the last person I wanted to see walking in beside Richard, dressed all in black. Even the purse. She had on a pillbox hat edged with black netting, like she was a latter-day Jackie O. *Tiffany.*

Clancy nudged me when we saw her walking toward us, her arms outstretched.

I turned to my friend. "Please. For the love of God. Do not let Skeletor hug me."

"On it." She gave my elbow a reassuring squeeze and turned to intercept the grieving executive assistant while Elias guided us to seats in a back pew. The crowded sanctuary felt stifling. Ben, who sat across the aisle between two men I didn't know, gave me a sad, sweet smile. I nodded back.

I tuned out most of the service but kept an eye on Mom. She handled it pretty well, considering. When the priest said the final "Amen," and the casket was wheeled out, and the family escorted down the aisle, I took my mother's elbow and tugged her toward the door. Navigating through the throng of people proved a challenge. I was a few feet from the exit when someone touched my arm.

"Georgia?"

I turned to look into the soft, gentle brown eyes of Colby Ribault. He was taller than David, with broad shoulders and a narrow waist. He held a squirmy Lindsay in his arms. "Just bailed her out of the nursery. I think they amped her up on sugar."

Lindsay reached for me, and I embraced her, needing to feel the warmth of her young life. "You doing okay, Georgia?" Colby's soft eyes studied me, filled with concern.

"As good as I can."

He played with one of Lindsay's curls. I liked the easy connection between these two. "I'd do anything for this munchkin," he said.

"Same here." I glanced at Mom, who was rummaging in her purse, probably for a cigarette. I had to get her away before she lit up.

"How's she doing?" he whispered.

"She's okay. She's one tough cookie, aren't you, Mom?"

Mom ignored me as she continued to scavenge her bag.

"Grandma!" Lindsay held out a hand and Mom took her, making funny faces that had her giggling, a sound we all needed to hear.

Colby stepped closer to me, and I caught a subtle spicy, citrusy scent. "Just wanted to ask if there was anything I can do for you. Anything either of you needs?"

"Need? I need a damn lighter," Mom uttered, thrusting her purse at me.

"Thanks, but I better get her out of here," I said. I took Lindsay from her and handed her back to her uncle. Musical niece.

"I'm in town, if you need anything. And I mean anything, George."

Aw, Georgia. He likes you, the counselor said.

He won't once he gets to know her, the advisor added. I feared he was right. I waved goodbye and herded Mom to the car.

CHAPTER TWENTY-THREE

The next morning, I forced myself go to work. Maybe getting back into my routine would help; I had patients to check on, like Marilyn Wilder. And I had the tiny tapes that Peyton had hidden, so I would borrow Clancy's player and listen to them. Later, I'd catch up with my buddy Elias again to plan a return visit to the Connor orchard where I'd been given such a warm welcome. Though the truck driver guy had denied it, I had a feeling Peyton had spent some time there.

Sleep deprived, I was so tired I could almost feel the random firings of my neurons. Things that should be so easy—even driving— became needlessly complex. *Where is it I'm going? Is this the correct street? Did I stop at that red light?*

So far, the voices had slept in that morning, which was a good thing given my shaky state. Nobody gets my voices, even Nora, try as she might. They are annoying, yes, but they are also company. Sometimes I think of them like a Greek chorus commenting on my life. They offer suggestions, sometimes with great insistence, but I do my best to remain in the driver's seat. I listen to their guidance, but most of the time, I make the final decision.

When I was a teen, they were the first thing to come between me and Peyton. My shame and fear about the voices made me pull into myself. Made me wary. Hyper-vigilant. Whenever my sister caught me muttering to myself, she was quick to say, "This doesn't mean you'll be like Mom. You can handle this." Of course, it took ten years, three hospitalizations, and a string of medication changes for her to be proven right.

But now I was starting to spiral. I wasn't sure I could handle the internal noise. Since the moment I saw Peyton's body, they'd been active, sometimes talking on top of each other. Stress was the reason, of course, but I couldn't let them get control. I wouldn't. I'd had years with them and had a few tricks to try. As long as I was self-aware, and used my ability to reason, I should be okay.

After parking at the hospital, I glanced in my rearview mirror. Yep, still looked like something the cat hacked up. I pulled my hair back into a barrette so the humidity wouldn't totally win. The temperature approached three digits and it was hardly eight o'clock. It's no wonder so many Southerners are Bible thumpers; we taste hell every summer.

I found Clancy in the break room reading the *Columbia Tribune* as she downed a white powdery donut with her coffee. "Hey," I said.

She looked at me, folded the newspaper, and leaned back in the chair. "Hey, yourself. You kinda look like shit."

I glanced down at the wrinkled top half-tucked into my denim skirt.

"I'm not talking about your clothes."

I sat, a little uncomfortable at her scrutiny.

"How are you sleeping?"

"Not great."

"No, I suppose not." She clicked her nails against the table. "Maybe take some more time off?"

"Maybe. But getting back in a routine helps."

"Symptoms manageable?" This was her kind way of asking about the voices. I promised when she hired me that I'd never lie about that.

"I'm holding it together," I answered. "I mean, I'm using duct tape and superglue, but it's holding. I promise if I start losing it, you'll be the first to know."

She pushed her half-eaten package of donuts toward me. "Eat."

I did. The confection was sickly sweet and a little stale, but I downed it, if for no other reason than that Clancy asked me to.

"Can I borrow your dictation recorder?" I asked.

"Sure. It's on my desk."

"Thanks. Can I have it overnight?" I slid the remaining donut back to her.

"All yours," she answered, sugar sprinkling her top as she finished the package.

After retrieving the recorder from Clancy's desk, I went to my office and closed the door. My fingers shook as I tried to load Peyton's tape, though I wasn't sure why. I pressed play.

"May twenty-first. I'm hoping to get a few minutes with Kitten. She just took a john—she calls them 'buyers'—behind the cantina."

I paused the recording as a wide ache unfurled inside me. Her voice. The Southern lilt that softened her I's into ah's. The musicality of it, hitting five notes in a single sentence. My sister's voice, so completely erased from my world now. My life would not be the same without her in it.

I let the tape continue. "This is my chance to get her alone. The buyer leaves and she lingers to give me just a few minutes. She's very afraid of getting caught by her pimp." I heard the ding from her car door opening. "There he goes. He's wearing a cowboy hat and climbing into a Ford pickup with an NRA sticker in the window. What a walking cliché."

I smiled at my snarky sister.

Crunching gravel sounded as she walked. "She's usually right over . . . there she is. She's wearing a pink T-shirt and a short, ruffled skirt. He likes to make her look young. As if fifteen isn't young enough. Turning this off until she gives me permission to tape."

A few seconds later, she resumed. "Kitten, is everything okay?"

"Roman's waiting. I have to be careful." She sounded scared.

"I brought you a phone. Can you keep it hidden from him?"

A minute of silence, then, "I can keep this?"

"Yes. It's yours. My number is programmed in it."

"Thank . . . thank you." Her voice trembles as though she's close to tears.

"Last time, we talked about your time on the farm where I met you. You were there a week, right?"

"It was hard. I got sick."

"I remember."

"Jefe said he had a better place for me. So he took me to the trailer."

"Just one more question. You say Roman works for Jefe. Do you know his real name?"

"No. Nobody does," the girl said. "Just Jefe. The boss."

"Where does he live?"

"I don't know." Kitten sounded fainter now, like she was moving away.

"Remember you have the phone! Call me tomorrow when you can."

No answer.

"Be safe, Kitten."

I heard a footfall on the tape, then the squeal and ding of a car door opening. "She's so terrified," Peyton continued. "I'm trying to get a handle on the scope of this operation but he—the trafficker—controls them with fear. The factory, the farm, the brothel. What else? How many people are involved? How much money are they making by enslaving these people?"

The tape ended and I pictured my sister—a brave, activist sister, one I'd never met—taking on this important issue. Why had she not told me about it?

I inserted another tape.

"May twenty-sixth. I finally heard from Kitten. She called from the yard behind the trailer when she was hanging out laundry. She said she'd be at the cantina tonight so I'm waiting in the parking lot for her."

The cantina? That was the first place I'd gone when I was retracing Peyton's steps. This was where the trafficked girl operated?

"There she is, with another buyer. She's leading him by the hand, but they aren't going behind the building, they're headed up the dirt road. She just looked in my direction. I'm going to follow her." The recorder clicked, then clicked again.

"She took the guy inside a piece of crap trailer," Peyton continued. "I'm standing behind a tree waiting for the buyer to finish up. This makes me crazy. I want to charge in there and chase that guy to hell. I have to get her out of here. I have to get to the police."

Exactly. Why hadn't she?

Another pair of clicks, I supposed the recorder turning off and on, then she spoke again. "Kitten, how much time do we have?"

"More time than usual. Roman went off with some of Jefe's men. He'll be gone a while."

"Who was he with?"

"Lito. Someone else I didn't know. He'll get paid so he'll get high." My sister sighed. "Can you tell me how you got to Roman?"

"I told you. He got me from the farm."

"I want to know how you got into this life. Did you run away?"

The girl didn't answer for a long moment, then said, "My mom got involved with a guy who gave her drugs. It got worse and we ended up in foster homes. Didn't like that much."

"I can imagine."

"Then I met a boy who promised me a new life. I believed him. I believed he'd help me and Brandon."

"Brandon?"

"My little brother." The girl's voice softened.

"I'll bet you miss him."

A long silence followed, and I thought about Kitten's sibling, and my own. How having a brother or sister changed one's childhood. If Peyton and I hadn't had each other, how would either of us survived the wreckage of our family?

Peyton said, "You still have the phone, right?"

"I keep in under the mattress."

"Next Friday may be the time. I'll text you to make sure so leave the phone on."

"Friday?"

"Very early. We can get you somewhere safe. Next Thursday night, when you come back from working the cantina, gather your stuff and put it in this knapsack. Just before dawn, head up to the 7-Eleven by the highway. I'll be there to pick you up."

"What if Roman—"

"You said he sleeps soundly, right?"

"Yes. Especially if he's been drinking."

"Then he won't wake up until you're long gone."

"Where will I go?" She sounded both frightened and hopeful.

"My sister is a social worker. She'll help us find somewhere safe for you. Somewhere you can get back to being a normal kid again."

I turned off the recorder. My vision clouded from the tears that emerged. Peyton had planned to come to me. She would have let me help her. That lunch date I had to cancel—was that when? I felt a flush of self-anger. If only I'd realized she needed me. If only she'd told me how important it was. I'd have made sure she was safe, even if it meant dragging her ass to the police. Maybe she'd be alive.

On the rest of Peyton's recordings, I heard two other brief interviews with Kitten, who never once revealed her actual name. Half of one tape included her speculation about the trafficking operation; she seemed to be using the microcassette as a log or journal: "Finding out who Jefe is will be key. My associate says he plans to expand the business. I talked to him about going to the police, but he said he would handle that. I suppose I have to trust him.

"I have one more site to visit. A place called The Orchid Estate, close to the lake. Javier says security there is intense and I shouldn't try to approach it, but I have to see it.

"I'm going to get Kitten out of this. Then the others. With George's help, I'm ending this nightmare for all of them."

With my help. I savored those words. My brave sister. I would finish what she started.

As I started to exit my office, a familiar figure greeted me in the hall, Detective Lou Michaels. "I got your message. Hope this isn't a bad time."

"Yeah, well, lately they're all bad."

He winced at my comment. "I'm sorry about Peyton, Georgia."

I nodded. Everyone was sorry. Wished that made things different. "You know what would help, Lou? Finding the person who killed her."

He gave me a long, steady look. "Your message said something about human trafficking?"

"That's what her research was on. Did you know that? Did you know we found several places here in Columbia where people are basically enslaved?"

He didn't reply, which I found quite annoying.

"Aren't you going to say anything?"

"There isn't much I can tell you. Yes. We know there's trafficking going here. There is everywhere. But I'm not at liberty to tell you more."

I glared. "Guess it's up to me to find out who killed my sister then."

He lifted a hand. "That's . . . a really bad idea. Look, I'll tell you this. I agree, your sister most likely didn't kill herself. But what she was exposing . . . that's nothing I can discuss with you. Believe me, it's for your own good."

I wished I could believe him. That I could trust the police to do whatever it took to punish Peyton's killer. That I could have faith that they'd shut down every trafficking business in my state. On the tape, Peyton had said some of the police couldn't be trusted, and I wasn't sure about Lou Michaels.

"Message received," I said evasively.

"Good."

As he turned to leave, I said, "One more thing, Lou. Have you ever heard of a place called The Orchid Estate?"

His eyes widened just slightly, then the calm, neutral stare returned. "No. Never heard of it. Why?"

"Just curious. I'd appreciate it if you'd keep me posted on your investigation."

"Trust us, Georgia. We'll get to the bottom of this."

"I'm sure you will, Detective."

CHAPTER TWENTY-FOUR

A gentle knock on my office door interrupted my plan to finish treatment summaries that were three weeks overdue. I welcome these interruptions. "Come on in."

Dianne Grafton, the art therapist, dressed in a paint-spattered smock, entered carrying sheets of newsprint with bright colors on them. She placed them on my desk, removed a stack of progress summaries from a chair, and took a seat. "You gotta see these."

I spread out three sheets of paper. Vivid drawings filled each, done in bright reds and crimsons. In the center, a face: giant, black eyes. Flame-red skin. Cartoonish mouth set in a sneer. And horns—pointed, gold horns protruding from its head.

"Marilyn drew these. It's pretty much all she draws. She says it's the demon that she saw the night she came to the hospital."

I traced the outline with my finger. "Sounds obsessive."

"Maybe. But maybe it's how she's overcoming the fear. This gives her some power over what terrified her. She's still pretty traumatized by it."

"And maybe traumatized by what happened after. Getting handcuffed and dragged to the hospital by the police is no picnic." I almost added, *"Believe me, I know firsthand."*

"At least her psychosis is under pretty good control. I wouldn't be surprised if she gets released soon."

"Then I'd better start working on her discharge plan."

Dianne grinned. "That's why I'm here."

I gripped one of the pictures. "Can I keep this one?"

"Sure. I'll let you know if she asks for it back."

I sipped chardonnay as I studied the scraps of paper I'd scattered across my dining room table—notes from Peyton's calendar and the taped interview with the trafficking victim, Kitten. *The Orchid Estate*, written on a yellow sticky note, with a question mark beside it, had my attention.

I'd powered up the laptop to Google it, but all that popped up were trip reviews about a garden in Santa Barbara. Nothing local. I tried Zillow and a few other real estate apps; nothing remotely similar to that name emerged in any of Columbia's zip codes. How was I supposed to find out what—and where—the damn place was?

Three quick bursts of my doorbell told me Elias had stopped by. I let him inside, savoring the hug when he pulled me into his long, warm arms. "How you doing, babe?" he whispered.

"One day at a time. Or maybe I should say, one glass at a time?" I held up my chardonnay.

"Whatever works." He wandered over to the table where I'd been working. "What's all this?"

I filled him in on what I'd learned about Peyton's last days, the now-familiar roil in my gut churning like a cauldron. I should have been helping her with this dangerous project, but I'd canceled the lunch that would have been my last chance to see her.

"Trafficking. Damn, that's some serious shit."

I showed him the Post-it that had me puzzled. "You ever heard of the Orchid Estate?"

He shook his head. "Where'd you hear it?"

I told him about the tapes of Peyton's interview. "Her tone changed when she mentioned this. I don't know what she found out about it, but I wonder if it's what got her killed."

"Damn."

"I asked Lou Michaels if he'd heard of it. He said no. He's a liar."

"Cops are good at that."

Elias had a long, colorful history with the police. In his teen years, he'd been profiled, been punched by a cop when he demanded to know why he'd been falsely accused and arrested for a robbery someone else committed. He'd spent five terrifying days in jail before he got out. Elias, the successful businessman and restaurateur, hadn't forgotten that life.

I looked down at the list of places Peyton had visited, remembering my first venture retracing her steps—the Blue Rose Cantina. It might be worth a second visit. "Hey, wanna give me a hand with something?"

"Sure. What do you want me to do?"

I placed the glass on the table. "Maybe you'd better drive."

Twenty minutes later, he parked his Jeep under the half-lit blue flower. Four pickups, an old sedan, and two banged-up SUVs cluttered the small unpaved parking area. "Classy place," Elias commented.

"It's even more impressive inside." As I reached to open my door, his hand gripped me.

"What's our plan here?"

"Plan? You think I've thought this out?"

He rolled his eyes. I get that a lot from him.

"You think the trafficked girl—Kitten, right? She works here?"

I nodded. "And who knows who else."

He looked at the front door, covered with peeling beer signs. Broken bottles littered the walkway leading up to it. "If this is where the girl works, then her pimp is here. Let me go in alone, see if I can get him to offer me the girl."

"And leave me here? Nope."

"Yeah, I thought you'd say that." He rubbed his chin, considering. "We go in together, but let me negotiate. Pimps don't much care if I'm a single john or looking for a three-way. May charge more, though."

I tried to imagine what life was like for the girls caught up in the trade. How did they survive it? What kept them from giving up? Of course, many did—succumbing to drugs and other destructive choices. No wonder Peyton was so determined to help them.

When we entered the bar, the counselor whispered, *Careful, Georgia.* She wasn't alone. The staticky voice spoke too. I couldn't quite grasp what it said. *Find her* maybe. This was going to be hard enough without them.

Three greasy men leaned over the bar, tall beer glasses inches from their mouths. In the corner, a large Hispanic man sat at a table. Across from him was a teenage girl dressed in a frighteningly short skirt and sequin top. Her complexion looked Hispanic though much of her dark hair had been dyed a vivid blue. *Could she be Kitten?* I hadn't heard an accent on the tape.

Elias pointed to a corner table, and I took a seat. He removed his leather jacket, gave me a wink, and proceeded to the bar. I wished I could hear the conversation. He had two of the greasers laughing, and the bartender nodded when he paid for drinks. When Elias whispered something to him, he gestured toward the girl sitting with the big dude. Elias made his way over to their table.

Whatever he said to the Hispanic man didn't fly. Elias kept talking, the guy staring at him like he was speaking Swahili. Not to be dissuaded, Elias grabbed a chair and joined them, straddling the seat backward like a cowboy. After a few minutes, he pointed to me. I had no clue what to do so I gave them an uncertain smile. Elias laughed. He removed a few bills from his pocket, but the guy thumped the table, so Elias added to the cash.

When he stood, the girl rose and smoothed down the skirt that looked molded to her hips. Her sashay over to my table looked comical, but Elias lay an arm across her shoulder as though he'd never met anyone so beautiful. As he reached me, he whispered, "Let's take this outside."

I felt very weird walking with them out the door. Once out, we stopped under a streetlight, and I got a better look at her face. Purple and lime green eye shadow had been artfully applied in stripes above her narrow eyes. Lipstick so dark it was almost purple. The blue streaks in her hair matched her pointed fingernails. Her every exhale smelled like beer.

"What's your name?" I asked.

She twirled a bit of hair around a finger. "Call me Dool-chay," she replied, her accentuated lips puckering. She could have been from Mexico or South America. Hers wasn't the voice I'd heard on the tape.

"Dulce," Elias repeated. "What a lovely name."

"You paid for a half hour. Want to go behind the building?"

"How about you take us to your place."

She looked at each of us and frowned. "You not pay for that."

"We will," I said. "We'll pay you." I emphasized this last word and a smile flickered on her lips. I held up three twenties as bait. After glancing back at the closed door to the cantina, she nodded.

"Follow me."

The moon offered faint silver light as we trudged down the road and turned into a decrepit-looking trailer park. When we reached the one at the back of the lot, lovely with its broken window screens and bag of smelly trash by the door, she retrieved a hidden key from under a broken pot and let us inside.

The place reeked of grass. Elias sniffed the air, and I worried that the fragrance might serve as a trigger for him. Even after five years in recovery, certain things will bring you to your knees.

"Together or one at a time?" Dulce asked.

Elias wiped a sheen of sweat that had emerged on his face, which I suspected wasn't related to the temperature. "You want to wait outside?" I asked him.

"I'm chill," he replied.

I turned to Dulce. "We just want to talk to you."

She crossed her arms and stepped closer; her face pinched in defiance. "Mierda. You say you pay. No backing out of deal."

"We won't," I said. "You said we get thirty minutes. We won't need that long." I pressed the money into her hand. "Here."

She eyed the bills with a flicker of delight before stuffing them into the waistband of her skirt. "So what? We play cards? Talk dirty?"

Elias smiled, and I was relieved to see it. "We ask you some questions about this operation," he said. "The man who took my money—your pimp. What's his name?"

She shrugged. "None of your business. Besides, nobody uses real name."

"Speaking of names, do you know a girl called Kitten?"

"Kitten? Why? You like younger girl? You want some *chica* with no boobs?" She gripped her own small breasts and shook them.

Elias arched his brows at me. I could read the question behind his expression. *What do we share with Dulce?*

I pulled my cell phone from my bag and showed her Peyton's photo. "Do you recognize this woman?"

She shook her head. "Who is she?"

"My sister, Peyton Ribault. She was murdered." I told her the rest, about how Peyton went to the factory and the farm, about her attempt to save one girl from the hands of traffickers.

Dulce's stone expression never wavered.

Curious that she's not surprised, said the advisor.

She's a victim, too, the counselor added.

She's a manipulative little bitch.

Having voices in my head is not easy. When they argue, tuning them out can be a challenge. I can do it if I'm calm, well-rested, and relaxed, a condition that Nora describes as "centered." I've reached that state maybe twice in my life.

"When did she try to save this girl?" Dulce asked.

"Thursday three weeks ago."

Her gaze shot up the tiny hall but then she blinked, fixing her stare back on me. "What?" I asked.

"I can't help you." Dulce looked at her watch. "You have ten more minutes. We go back to cantina. You tell my guy I give you best time you ever had. That you've never had it so good."

"Absolutely," Elias said.

I looked up the dark corridor and wondered if Kitten was there. "Before we go, can I use your bathroom?"

Her frown told me how much she liked that idea. *Does this kid ever smile? Laugh? Emote anything other than distaste?*

"Please," I persisted.

"Second door on the left."

Elias winked as I passed and stepped closer to Dulce, effectively blocking her view of the hall. The smell changed as I moved—less smoke, more stale sweat. The first door was partly open, and I peered in; a scarred dresser, a double bed, and a mobile of ballet dancers twirling above it. Not Dulce's style.

Across from that room was a smaller one that held a single bed, a lamp draped with a pink scarf, and a dressing table cluttered with makeup and nail polish, probably Dulce's abode. As I entered the bathroom, I closed the door and made quick work of searching the drawers and medicine cabinet. Razors, shaving cream, soap. Ointment for yeast infections. Three boxes of condoms brought a tiny bit of relief; at least these girls had some protection from disease and pregnancy.

I flushed the beyond-disgusting toilet and returned to the living room, shaking my head at Elias. No, the girl wasn't here, but my gut told me this was where she stayed.

As we trudged back to the cantina, Dulce and Elias walked ahead of me, Dulce teetering on her heels like a kid pretending to be a grown-up. I couldn't stand the thought of returning her to her pimp, of how many buyers she'd have to service that night.

"Hey."

They both spun around to face me.

"You could leave with us," I said to her. "We'll get you somewhere safe, I promise."

Even in that dim light, I could see Elias's skeptical expression. He was right, I didn't know how I could keep that promise, but I would do my best.

Dulce shook her head. "There is nowhere safe, you stupid *chica.*"

She resumed her trek to the cantina, again cautioning us about what we should say to her pimp. As Elias returned her, he gushed at the service she'd provided. Her pimp looked apathetic.

Another man entered the bar and approached Dulce and the man. He had black, greasy hair and wore torn jeans and a T-shirt. It was the shirt that got my attention. A face filled the front—cartoonish, with a wide, evil smile and curved horns coming out of its head. It looked just like the pictures that Marilyn had drawn. Below the face were the words *Diablo Mysterio*.

I almost approached the stranger, but Elias was beckoning me to leave. As we climbed in the car, I asked, "Have you ever heard of Diablo Mysterio?"

"Huh?"

"It was on that guy's T-shirt."

"I think it's a professional wrestler."

That made no sense. A wrestler wouldn't have been chasing Marilyn. Psychosis could have some odd manifestations.

As we drove away, I had to shake off the encounter with Dulce and my imaginings about what her life was like. As a social worker, I see ugly stuff all the time. Pushing away the darkness was the only way to survive.

"Are you up for another stop?" I asked Elias.

He glanced at his watch. "This is late for you. But sure."

I directed him into the choice section of town where Special Touch Massage was. We passed the storefront, neon lights blinking but nothing lit inside, and rounded the corner. Elias parked and we glanced up the alley that led to the rear of the store.

"Exactly what do you have in mind?" he asked. "We breaking in? Because I didn't exactly bring my best B & E tools with me."

"I don't know." Part of me wanted to do just that. If I could get inside, maybe I'd find something that would lead me to Peyton's killer. Or we could get caught, the two of us disappearing as my sister had.

Beyond the dumpster in the middle of the alley, I thought I saw a flicker of light. Tiny, just an orange dot moving up and down—the end of a lit cigarette.

"Someone's behind the building," I whispered. We climbed out of the car into thick night air. No streetlights glowed nearby. The moon hid herself behind clouds. After Elias grabbed a few items from the back of his car, he switched on a tiny flashlight. We took careful steps over the rutted concrete. As we approached, I saw it was two Asian women, one small, dragging on the cigarette like nicotine was her oxygen, and a tall, thinner woman, her back against the dirty wall, one leg propped against it. I'd seen her when I visited last time—the worker who'd worn the glittery top.

I slid on a loose piece of gravel and the smaller woman heard. Urgent words spoken in an Asian language I didn't recognize passed between the women. As they started to hurry inside, I blurted, "Wait! Ratana, right? Please. I just want to talk to you." She swirled around, her arm outstretched. "Don't come any closer!"

"Hey, easy," I whispered, as we continued our approach. "I was here before, remember? I just want to ask you a few questions."

The smaller woman spat out something to her as she opened the door and slipped inside, handing the cigarette to the other. Ratana remained, taking a step back, as though sizing us up in the steady darkness. "You. No makeup. Pretend to look for job," her tone, agitated.

"Yes. Ratana, that's your name, right? I'm trying to find out what happened to my sister, Peyton Ribault."

"Don't know her."

I thumbed through pictures until I found my favorite; Peyton smiling at something Lindsay had done, her honey-blond hair hanging loose and wild around her face. "She was killed. Murdered. She was trying to help a girl like you—a girl being forced to do things she didn't want to do by men who threaten her. A girl being kept captive."

Ratana eyed the door but didn't leave. A long moment of silence followed. A frog croaked in the distance.

Finally, she took my phone to look at the photo.

"Do you recognize her?" I coaxed.

She nodded. "She came two times. Iva make her leave the first time. Second time, she come at night like you. She ask too many questions."

"Iva?"

"My boss. You talk to her. I tell you sister to leave. I tell her it too dangerous to talk. She stubborn, though. Want to know about Iva and who Iva work for. Ask about other girls who work here."

"Besides you and your friend," I pointed to the door the small woman had used, "how many are there, Ratana?"

She took a puff on the nub of cigarette and gave me a cold, hard stare. "Why you want to know?"

Elias stepped forward. She flinched, so he retreated. "Look, her sister wanted to help you. It got her killed. This life you live is dangerous. I'm sure you know that. Maybe we can help you escape it."

"What can you do? You stick your nose in this, it get you killed, too." She flipped the cigarette to the ground and stomped on it.

I decided to try a different approach. "Ratana, where did you come from?"

"I'm Thai."

"How long have you been here?"

She shrugged. "I not have a calendar. A year. Two."

"How did you get here?" Elias asked.

"Boat. My family pay for me to come. This man promise them I start a life here. Have a job. Place to live. I make enough to bring them over. Lies. All lies."

"How awful. Who promised this, Ratana?"

She shrugged. "A man. He a trader. Trades in people. He bring me to US, sell me to Jefe. Many of us squeeze into van. I know then, it all lies. They bring me to South Carolina. I put on farm to work. Brutal work."

The frog started up again. Ratana startled at the sound.

"Who is Jefe?" I asked.

Her eyes widened. "The boss. He... owns us."

Owns us. The words sunk in.

She went on, "Anyway, I got sick. Couldn't work like they need. So, they bring me here."

Noise from inside startled us. Ratana glared at the door, her eyes wide with panic. After a few moments of silence, we relaxed a little.

"How many are in there?" I asked.

"Five girl. One guard."

"Iva?"

She shook her head. "One of Jefe's men."

"He's inside right now?" Elias asked.

She nodded. "Playing computer games, so we come out to smoke."

I wanted to ask why she didn't run away, but I knew the answer. She was held captive by fear and threat, as are all victims of trafficking.

"Peyton came a second time?"

"Yes. Say she can help. Jefe's man catch her talking to us."

"When? What happened?"

"A few week ago? I thought he kill her, but Javier show up. He say he take care of her."

"Javier?"

"Another of Jefe's men. He grab her by the arm and drag her away."

Footsteps and voices sounded from inside. "*Shia!* Go now. I get in trouble!"

Before we could move the door swung open. Elias smacked his keys into my hand. "Run!"

"What are you—"

"Go!" He shoved me toward the car.

As I bolted toward his Jeep, I heard a thick Spanish accent yell, "What the fuck?"

Elias replied in a drunk sounding voice. "Come here for a lill . . . a little action!"

"I told him to leave," Ratana said. "I told him come back tomorrow."

I rounded the corner and stopped to peek back at my friend.

"I got money! How muh . . . much you charge?" Elias staggered toward the man, gripping the wall as if needing to regain his balance.

"*Mierda.* Fucking drunk!" The man loomed over Elias, as wide and muscular as a weightlifter, his shaven head glinting in the dirty light from a streetlamp.

"Jus . . . jus want me a lill action." Drunk Elias swayed as he pretended to grope for a wallet.

"Action? I'll give you action." He closed on Elias, reaching in the waistband of his pants to retrieve a gun. Elias took off running.

Three quick shots pierced the night. Elias kept moving.

"Oh, God." I grappled with the keys to unlock the car, and promptly dropped them. I fell to my knees, found them behind the front tire, and opened the door. I scooted behind the wheel ready for a quick getaway. *What if they shot Elias? I should have stayed with him. I should have—*

"Move over!" It was Elias.

Thank God. I shifted to the passenger seat and he started the Jeep. We wheeled away to echoes from more gunfire.

"Shit, Elias! Shit!"

"It's okay. We're both fine."

"Why are you so calm? You're the one he shot at."

"Wild shots in the dark to scare us off." Elias grinned. "It worked."

"Wild shots can still hit you."

When we arrived at my house, he flipped on the lights as I threw myself on my sofa and tried to settle my hammering heart. He went to the kitchen, returning with a glass of wine which he placed in my hand.

"Drink. But drink slowly." He sat across from me, looking a lot less panicked than I felt.

"Finn would kill me if he knew I dragged you into this."

"Yeah, we ain't mentioning it to him. Spare us both a smackdown." He gave me his wide, smart-ass smile.

"I shouldn't have brought you there. Shit. I . . . I don't know what the hell I'm doing, and if something had happened to you—" My mind filled with worse possible scenarios. "What will he do to Ratana? He saw her talking to us."

"I hope nothing. She played right along with my drunk john act. Let's just hope the bulldog-shaped dude believed her."

"I put her in danger."

I massaged my head, wishing I could massage away the internal noise.

"You okay, George?"

"Not so much. I keep thinking about Peyton diving into this world alone. I should have been with her." I would have been if I hadn't canceled that damn lunch with her.

"You could be dead, too. She wasn't completely alone. She put her faith in the person helping her. Maybe that faith was misplaced."

I hadn't thought about that. I reached for Lou Michaels's card in my purse. Speaking of faith—could I count on him if I told him what had happened?

Elias studied the phone number. "Not a bad idea."

I dialed, but it went to his voicemail. I told him what had happened. About our visit to the massage parlor and the cretin who fired shots at Elias.

"Get over there, Lou. Get those girls out of there." I gave him the address to the massage parlor and the trailer.

He won't do anything, the advisor said, and I was pretty sure he was right.

CHAPTER TWENTY-FIVE

When I left my house that next morning, a Bronco SUV waited at the end of my drive. Ben Reeder climbed out, holding a crumpled paper bag that I recognized from my favorite pastry shop. "Brought you breakfast."

I took the bag and retrieved a caramel-covered cake donut. My favorite. *Nice that he remembered.* He wore a blue denim shirt that brought out his eyes. Those eyes used to make me cave, but not anymore.

"What do you want, Ben?"

"An update. I tried talking to Lou, but he was a brick wall. Figured this bribe might make you more obliging. You got anything new to share about what happened to your sister?"

I bit the donut as I weighed it. Ben would move heaven and earth to uncover who killed Peyton if he could get a story out of it. I didn't want him involved given that it might be dangerous but wasn't sure what my options were. After another lick of caramel, I said, "Get your pad out. This may take a while."

I told him everything and he interrupted with too many questions because he's a stupid damn reporter. Then came the lecture about my poor judgment, lack of regard for personal safety, blah, blah, blah.

"So that's where we are," I said.

He gave me a long, hard stare. "You're something else, you know that? You could get yourself killed. Maybe you should let the professionals handle this?"

I tossed the donut remains back in the bag. "Who? Your buddy Lou? I left him a message last night and he never returned the call. As far as I know, he hasn't done crap."

"Let me talk to him." He saluted me as he climbed back into the truck.

"Light a fire under him. It's about damn time the police did something about all this. They need to save those girls and find my sister's murderer. You make that happen and I'll buy the donuts next time."

Fifteen minutes later, I sat in my chair in the waiting area, trying to still a leg that bounced like it was possessed. Thank God today was my appointment with Dr. Nora Harper. I was way overdue.

I started seeing Nora six years ago, the last in a string of psychiatrists; I fired half of them, the rest couldn't put up with me. Granted, I'm not the easiest of clients. I'm tough to treat because even the strongest medicines don't stop the voices. And I'm a bit of a smart ass. I know way too much about therapy—as a client and clinician. I'm very particular about who provides the services that keep me this side of the locked doors.

Nora sees through all my crap. She uses a light touch with medications and tolerates my little experiments, like cutting doses in half or skipping a few days. I hate the medicine, or more to the point, hate needing the medicine, but my current cocktail of pills keeps me stable. I describe myself as "in recovery" because it's been over seven years since I was hospitalized. I give Nora credit for this, but she would give the responsibility to me.

Which is why I like her so much.

I stood and paced around the waiting area, nervous energy bubbling up. I'm always like this when I come here. I know stuff is going to surface. Stuff I haven't wanted to face. This can be the hardest part of recovery.

Nora has plants everywhere, thriving greenery that spills over tabletops and across shelves. Stained-glass panels hang high in her windows, one with purple irises, the other an abstract woman with golden hair stretching up to the sun. Beyond the glass, I could see cars and bicycles riding by, a world that went on like it hadn't lost a sister. *Must be nice.*

"Georgia?" Nora surprised me. I bumped into the coffee table, tipping over a stack of magazines.

"Sorry." I rushed to straighten the pile.

"For what?" She strained to bend down and collect two *New Yorkers* that had landed under the table. "Come on back. Need a soda or tea or anything?"

I shook my head, following her to her office and taking my usual seat in the chair that rocked. She waddled over to the sofa, puffing out air as she dropped into the seat. Nora was eight months pregnant with baby number three, her second boy. I had guessed when she was in her fourth month by the way her hand smoothed her belly, unconsciously soothing a child no larger than an avocado. "Can't get much by you," Nora laughed.

I glanced at the window curtained by vines from a spider plant gone amok. "You need to prune that."

"You tell me that every week."

I tapped my fingers against the arm of the chair.

"Georgia?" Her tone softened. "How are you doing?"

"I spent a couple of days in hibernation. But I'm out of the cave now." This was a little dishonest. I still felt like a cave dweller. "But I'm okay. Considering."

"Considering that your sister died." She paused, letting those stark words sink in.

I looked over at her aquarium, a sixty-gallon aquatic world where a dozen creatures lived. An angelfish pressed close to the glass wall as though awaiting my reply. What could I say? Peyton was gone.

"Georgia?"

"I don't know where to start," I admitted. The angelfish swam back and forth, its cobalt blue fins shimmering in the tiny aquarium light. Beautiful in its water world. Peyton died in water. Probably not beautiful.

"When did you find out about Peyton?" Nora asked.

"I knew she was missing Monday night when David called. The phrase 'scared to death' has new meaning for me. I was there when they found her body."

"There?"

"Hiding in the bushes. Watching them pull her from the car." She had floated in the submerged Lexus. *Was it like a womb? Or tomb?*

"I'm so sorry."

"Yeah. Everyone is sorry. So very sorry." My voice sounded cold, surprising me. "She was doing some investigating. Into human trafficking, if you can believe it. Right here in Columbia." I told her the rest, all in a rush of words. The angelfish moved behind a little castle in the sand. Coy little bastard.

Nora leaned forward, something she did when she wanted to make a point. "You decided to finish Peyton's research? Into human trafficking?"

"She's my sister. I owe it to her."

"Even though you think it got her killed?" She narrowed her eyes. "Georgia, this is dangerous stuff."

"I'm okay. Elias is helping me." Bubbles drifted up behind the tiny fake castle. "And I've told the police, for all the good it does. I don't think they have any interest in finding her killer."

"But you gave them her phone. They can piece together what you did about her work." She shifted, pulling a pillow behind her. "You mentioned her tapes. The police have them now?"

"No." Why hadn't I given them to Lou?

You can't trust him, the advisor said.

Nora lifted a finger. "What happened just then?"

"What do you mean?"

"You turned your head—a voice, I'm guessing."

I hated it when she did this kind of thing. "Yes."

"Who?"

"The advisor."

She nodded slowly. "Have you been hearing from him a lot?"

"About what you'd expect. The counselor some. The general when I was at my worst." What a catalog of crazy I kept. Saying it out loud like this made me feel like exactly what I was—a mental patient.

"Tell me about the general."

"Usual crap. I tuned him out."

"He's not issuing any orders?"

"He tries. But I'm handling it." I swallowed.

"Good." Nora smiled. "That's very good. Now, back to the advisor. What's his role in this?"

"His role?" I thought back, unsure what she was getting at.

"His role. When you went to the factory, for example, had you heard from him?"

I nodded. "He's adamant that I finish what Peyton started."

She pushed back, sighing. "Even if it puts you in danger. This worries me, Georgia."

Don't listen to her, he said. I blinked, wishing that would make him vanish.

"He spoke again, didn't he?"

I nodded.

She gave me a long, assessing stare. "Where is the counselor in all this?"

I thought back, remembering her gentle voice, a whisper of comfort.

"You just smiled." Nora shook her head.

"What?" I asked, though I knew where she was going.

"Can you stand up to the voices, Georgia? I don't want you giving into them."

Now it was my turn to sigh. "You underestimate me. They aren't in control. They're there, a presence, but they don't rule me."

"They don't? If I had a magic pill that would make them go away, would you take it?"

I held out my hand. It was a lie though, and we both knew it. While sometimes they make my life hell, other times the voices are company. Guidance. Allies. I could never make Nora understand that, though I'd tried many, many times.

She lowered her head as though I'd disappointed her. "At least promise me this. If the general or the advisor tries to control you, you'll call me. Anytime, day or night."

"I will if I can't handle them."

"No, that's not the deal. If the advisor has you visiting the places where traffickers operate, it can get you killed. You make the call to me before that happens."

She'll slap you in the hospital. You can't trust her, the advisor said.

Yes, you can, the counselor countered.

I took in a deep, full breath. "I promise I'll call. I can't promise that I'll let you hospitalize me."

"I don't think we're necessarily heading in that direction. The voices are more active because you're under stress."

"Yeah. And there's something new." I told her about the new voice, who might be Counselor, except when she spoke it was garbled and echoey. "It's annoying. I don't know why she's acting so ... elusive. But it's only part of the time." And if she was a brand-new voice, I prayed she didn't bring along any friends. I needed to keep my catalog of crazy to a manageable size.

"I think you've got a rough road ahead. Maybe we should increase your dose?"

I was expecting this from her. Doctors love their medications. "Not yet. I need to be able to think straight. That stuff makes me blurry."

She smiled again, though it looked a little pained. "You remember the techniques we've used?"

"Of course. Thought stop signs. Snapping the rubber band." A million times we'd gone over cognitive-behavioral techniques that sometimes interrupted the voices. Sometimes.

"Here's the deal. How about over the next week, you call me every couple of days? If I'm in session, just leave a message with the service. Tell me you're okay or if you're not. Touch base so I won't have to worry."

Her use of the word *worry* made something warm bloom in my chest. Nora cared about me. I needed to remember that. Peyton was gone, but I wasn't completely alone.

"If you need to see me, I'll work you in. No problem."

I glanced over at the aquarium. The angelfish danced on the other side of the glass, as though waiting for my answer.

"I will," I said.

Good girl, said the counselor.

I found myself in sore need of some Lindsay time, so I invited myself to the Ribaults, only to be greeted at the door by frowning Marge. "She's already in bed."

I looked at my watch. Only eight. "Can I peek in? I won't wake her if she's asleep."

She stepped back, allowing me through the door. "Don't get her excited. She needs her sleep."

What did she think I'd do, challenge her to a hula-hoops contest? I smiled tightly as I passed her and hurried up the stairs. Lindsay's door was partly open. A lamp by her bed cast a yellow glow over the sheets. I heard a male voice, very soft and curiously expressive saying, "Annabelle Rose has eyes so—"

"Blue!" My niece filled in. I found her in her bed, dressed in Wonder Woman PJs, clutching School Bus. She was nestled in the crook of Colby's arm, her head against his chest.

"She always smiles when she looks at—" Colby pressed his lips against her hair the way I like to do. The way Peyton always did. I found it both moving and sad.

"You!"

"You are one impatient young audience." Laughter bubbled into his words.

"She's always like that." I stepped into the room. Colby looked up, his cheeks reddening. "Oh, don't stop on my account."

Lindsay grinned and held out her arms for me. I crossed to the other side of the bed and sat, our niece tucking between us like the little butter bean she was. "Keep reading! It's just getting good."

"Uh." Now he was positively scarlet.

Lindsay swatted the page. "Read."

"Her favorite toy is a bear named—" Colby paused, waiting for her finish.

She looked up at me. "Aunt George?"

"Ichabod Crane?"

Lindsay shook her head.

"Gordon Ramsey? Larry the Cable Guy?"

Colby laughed. "You're making this so much harder."

This got a giggle out of our niece. "She always does this. She never gets it right."

I hung my head as though chastised.

"I'll just finish it, then." Colby continued the story, pointing at the pictures and commenting in his softest voice about the stars in the sky. He was quite good at this. Lindsay's eyes blinked then closed, her head lolling onto the pillow. Colby closed the book and we both carefully extricated ourselves from her bed.

"Light on?" I whispered.

"Off. We have a good night light now."

We moved to the hallway and stood outside the room, making sure she was asleep.

"How do you think she's doing?" he asked me.

Better than me, I almost said. Instead, I shrugged. "As well as she can be. This has been an awful trauma, but she has good support here. She has her grandparents. And you."

"She told me she wanted to go home. David came over for lunch. He misses her but he's also a bit of a wreck. We think it's better if he waits a few more days. He said you came by to see him."

"Yeah. Kinda want to knock some sense into him, but he's going through a lot."

Colby's eyes softened. "Nobody should have to go through what he is. Or you are." He gave me a long, assessing look. "He said you've done some investigating of some kind?"

"I want to find the person who killed my sister."

He nodded. "I do, too. But I don't want you getting hurt in the process. Have you been to the police?"

His gaze, full of concern, warmed me. I continued. "Yes. And my friend Ben—he's a reporter—he's putting some pressure on them. I want this situation blown wide open. Everybody in jail. Faces all over the front page. Ben's happy to do that."

He smiled. God, those dimples. "Still got that fire in you, don't you? But we all need for you to be safe, Georgia." He cocked a thumb toward my sleeping niece. "Her most of all."

I couldn't peel my eyes away from his. It was unsettling, like something dormant deep inside me might just wake up. I expected the voices to chime in, to define this feeling, but they remained silent.

He cleared his throat.

I shifted, looked away, wondering what to say next. Finally, I stammered, "I should be going."

He reached for my hand, his fingers clutching mine a little longer than was necessary. "You know, when this is over . . . I mean, well, when things settle down at least, I'd like to have a drink with you. Or dinner."

"I'd like that too," I replied. "Both."

"It's a date then." The dimpled smile returned, and as I left him, I felt better than I had in days.

CHAPTER TWENTY-SIX

I sat across from my friend Elias, who showed up as soon as I got home from work. He had his laptop and once we sat at my dining room table, he fired it up.

"I wasn't sure if I should show you this, because I don't think the Georgia Thayer Sleuthing Agency needs to stay in business, but you probably do need to know."

"Know what?"

He pecked away at the keys. "I have a friend who does some business on the dark web. Not horrible stuff—he scores drugs sometimes and, well, other business."

"Oh great. You have a friend who's a drug dealer." Elias did not need to spend any time that close to his personal demon.

"He doesn't bring that stuff near me. Anyway. I asked him about the Orchid Estate, and he did a very covert search. He came up with these." Elias spun the computer around so I could see, gesturing that I should forward through a group of photos. Each displayed a very large house, or mansion, made of stucco, with arched windows and a slate roof. Around the structure lay some elaborate landscaping— palm trees, flowering bushes, and brick walkways leading to what looked like a mammoth garage and an ornate front door.

The next group of photos, grainier in texture, showed men exiting limousines and approaching a string of scantily clad women awaiting from the top of the steps. Beautiful women, some Black, some white, some Asian—posed like models preparing for a photoshoot.

"This is the Orchid Estate. A very big—and very fancy—brothel. It's about thirty miles or so from here near Saluda. It's well guarded by a fence." He clicked a photo of a nine-foot chain-link barrier topped with razor wire, "and a dedicated security force." He pulled up a picture of a security gate manned by two armed guards.

"It looks as protected as Camp David."

"It is. For good reason. The clientele here are billionaires, international businesspeople, and political leaders from all over the world. Think South Carolina's version of Jeffrey Epstein's lair."

"You're kidding. In Saluda?" It made no sense. Saluda hardly qualified as a town. It had maybe one stoplight.

"Yep. So rural nobody's gonna pay it much attention."

"Why doesn't the sheriff close it down?" I asked.

"He's probably on the take. Whoever owns this place can afford to keep the cops away."

"Don't know his name?"

"Everybody refers to him as Jefe."

Ratana had said that name. "So Hispanic then?" I said.

"Not necessarily. The dark web is a universe of aliases, all created to divert and deceive."

I looked at the photo of the building again, focusing on the young women posed outside of it. They looked too young to be forced to work in a brothel. "I want to go there."

Elias closed the laptop with a resonate click. "Are you out of your mind? Did you not hear the part about the security force? The armed guards?"

Elias, sweet, loyal Elias, had a point. And I had no right to drag him anywhere, not after what happened.

But you have to go, the advisor whispered. *It may lead you to Peyton's killer.*

This wasn't a time when I needed input from the voices, but they don't come with an off switch. I steeled my expression and said, "I am out of my mind. Forget what I said."

He watched me closely, like he could peer through the cracks. And I had plenty of those. His eyes widened. "Oh shit. You're snowing me. You think you're going there on your own."

Damn it. He knew me too well. "No, I'm not. It's a terrible idea."

"And you excel at those." He lifted a finger. "What's our one rule? The one we never break?"

"Chastised," I muttered. "We don't lie to each other."

"Then don't lie to me now." His gaze on me locked me in place as I mulled his words.

You can't just sit here. You have a job to do. Peyton's killer was out there, along with the girls forced to work in brothels while this Jefe dude made millions violating their bodies.

"What if I just drive by the place? I won't try to enter the grounds, but I have to see what we're talking about."

He closed his eyes as he slowly shook his head. "What am I going to do with you?"

That was a familiar verse coming from my friend. He opened the laptop again, punched the map link, and zeroed in on a county road connecting Saluda with Lake Murray, a large man-made lake heavily populated by motorboats, jet skis, and other water sport devices. "Looks like this is the main access route, just north of the lake. The Estate's connected to one of the tributaries connecting the lake with the river. Looks like a nice spot."

I memorized the name of the county road, intending to enter it in my GPS.

Elias looked at his watch. "Not quite seven. Still a good bit of daylight left. Let's go."

"Seriously? You wanna go with me?"

"No, I don't want to go with you! But it's a helluva lot better than letting you go by yourself. And this way I can chaperone and make sure you don't do anything stupid."

❧

A few minutes later, I found myself once again in the passenger seat of Elias's Jeep, heading west. Rush hour traffic on the interstate had died down. The sun hung annoyingly at eye level, causing Elias to squint, shift the visor, and curse at the insanity of our mission.

I closed my eyes, grateful for my remarkable friend and for a bit of silence in my head. I must have dozed off because my next awareness was a windy, country road that sliced through large forests of pine and oak. Green mailboxes stood sentry in random spots. Not a single car passed us for what must have been a half-mile.

"Isolated," I said.

"By design, I'm sure. Check the address again."

I compared the address I'd put in my phone with the map displayed on his GPS. "Looks like we stay on this road another five miles, then make a left turn into . . . nothing. Seriously. The route just stops."

"Probably a private road."

Of course, he was right. We passed another mailbox before coming to a black asphalt road with no markings. Elias turned, keeping the Jeep at a slow speed as we scanned our surroundings. The land was beautiful. Hardwoods and wild ferns, gentle hills covered with lush green moss. After about a half-mile, an iron gate blocked the road. Elias parked so we could climb out and approach the gate. The metal bars bent and shaped into a design—some kind of flower. I couldn't see any buildings beyond, but the road curved up a hill and out of sight. Beside the gate, a metal device with what looked like a key card insert blinked red. Elias nudged me and pointed up. On a tall electrical pole rested a camera, no doubt filming our arrival.

"We better get out of here," he whispered.

I hurried back to the passenger side as a black Suburban approached from the other side of the gate. Two men climbed out, one tan-skinned and bulldog stocky with a shaven head and the other square-shouldered and tall.

"This is private property," Bulldog said, the gate opening just enough for them to come through.

"Hey!" Elias had an unusual bounce in his voice. "Man am I glad to see you! We are hopelessly lost."

"Lost?" the taller man said.

"I told him this wasn't the right road," I added. "I told him his Aunt Edith didn't live this far out, but would he stop for directions? No. No, he would not."

"Who is Edith?" Bulldog frowned in annoyance.

"His aunt. Her birthday's tomorrow but we can't come then so we thought we'd take her out to dinner tonight, didn't we, Hon?" I looked at Elias.

"This is a private road," the taller guy said. He eyed his companion as though carrying on a non-verbal discussion about us. I sensed their annoyance morphing into something much stronger.

Elias lifted his hands, palms out. "No problem, man. We don't want no trouble."

When he started to open the car door, Bulldog pressed a mammoth hand against the window, slamming it shut. "Step away from the car," he commanded. We complied.

To his partner, he said, "Search the car."

Elias shot me a quick, worried look, which told me there was something in the car he didn't want to be found. Fighting panic, I thought through our options. Could we run? Not with them carrying what looked like assault weapons. Call for help? Not likely since my phone was in the car.

"*Vaya, vaya.*" The man crawled out of the car holding a pistol.

Dammit. Of course, Elias had a gun. His dangerous early years had won him some enemies and a healthy dose of paranoia that sometimes leaked out. Not telling me he had a gun, that was another matter altogether.

"Wedged under the driver's seat. Loaded, too."

"Man, I gotta have some protection. We in the Deep South, man," Elias said.

Bulldog inched closer to him. "Maybe. But you show up here, on private property, with a loaded gun, and we gotta wonder. Why are you here? Are you a cop?"

Elias shook his head, his hands spread wide. "A cop? Do I look like a cop? Hell no. I hate them fellas. They stop a Black man for nothing and shoot him for less. I . . . ain't . . . no . . . cop."

I had to give it to my friend, this performance was Oscar-worthy. Maybe I'd live long enough to tell him that.

Stocky dude took Elias's gun and turned to me. The next thing I knew, the cold metal was pressed under my chin.

I didn't dare move. Or breathe.

A revving engine roared behind us. I turned to spot a red convertible speeding up the road toward us, the top down, Beyoncé blaring from the stereo inside. The car pulled up to the gate and the driver, an auburn-haired woman wearing an angled straw hat and expensive-looking shades, climbed out. "What's going on here? Who are they?" She pointed at us.

"Intruders," the taller man said.

"Intruders," she repeated, removing her sunglasses and hat. She approached us, first studying Elias then tilting her head as she looked at me.

She was familiar, somehow, but I couldn't quite place her. She came closer, her mauve-glossed lips pursing. Her dress was short, V-necked, and perfectly tailored to fit her lean figure. Her hair hung in loose, shiny waves.

I did know her. Not this version of her—the girl I remembered had been homeless, filthy, and nearly dead from sun poisoning. "Lily?" I whispered.

Her eyes widened. "The hospital. You're Georgia, right?"

"Yes." I felt a flood of relief and hoped with every ounce of energy I had that she might help us.

"What are you doing here?" she asked.

"We got lost. Very, very lost," I said.

"Lost." She cocked an eyebrow in disbelief. "I go by Lillian now."

"That's a nice name. And you look . . . terrific. I'm glad to see you so healthy."

"A lot has happened since we met. When was that? Ten years ago?"

"Maybe."

"You still at the hospital?"

I nodded. "Still overworked and underpaid. And I still love it."

She glanced over at the men, one of whom still held the gun on me. "It's okay," she said to them.

They looked doubtful but didn't seem inclined to argue with her. Bulldog lowered his weapon.

To me, Lillian whispered, "You don't want to be here. You need to turn around and never come back."

I nodded. "Got it."

She approached Bulldog and held out her hand. He gave her the gun. "Yours?" she asked Elias.

He nodded.

"Not anymore. Now both of you. Get in the car and get the hell out of here. And don't even think about telling anyone you came."

"It's already slipped my mind," Elias answered.

We hurried to the Jeep and scrambled inside. Elias did a fast turnaround and a few seconds later, we were flying down that unmarked country road, relieved to simply be alive.

CHAPTER TWENTY-SEVEN

Kitten awoke to doors slamming, Dulce in one of her moods. She rolled from the bed, stiff from the tension of recent events. A curse word in Spanish, then Kitten's door flung open. Dulce stomped in, hands on her hips, reeking of pot. "Did you take my purple nail polish?"

"No."

"Sure you didn't." She marched over to the dresser and jerked open drawers. She pawed through Kitten's tops, underwear, and pants, leaving her usual mess.

"I didn't," Kitten said emphatically, untangling herself from the bedsheets. "What's the matter with you?"

"Me? Nothing. Except I'm sick of your lies." She kicked the drawer shut. "You have them all fooled, but not me."

Kitten stood. "What are you talking about?"

"I know the truth. About when you ran away. How someone was helping you. Don't bother lying. You had it planned for days and didn't tell me!"

"Dulce—"

"Don't 'Dulce' me. I met a woman tonight. She and her friend pay for me but all they do is ask questions about you. About her sister, Peyton something . . . can't remember her last name. She was the one you were going to meet. Peyton didn't show up, did she?"

"Dulce, shhhh. Lito will hear you."

"So what? Maybe I go to Lito right now. Maybe I tell him about your plan to get away. How much money would he give me? Enough to buy new nail polish like the one you stole from me." The fire in her eyes wasn't unusual, but Kitten didn't relish having it directed at her.

"I didn't steal your nail polish." Kitten took Dulce's hand and pulled her to the bed. "Sit down. I'll explain."

Dulce didn't sit, but she didn't rush out to find Lito, either.

Kitten lowered her voice. "Okay, I'll tell you what happened, but promise me you won't tell anyone. If you do who knows what will happen to me."

"Maybe what you deserve." She stepped closer. "You didn't even tell me you were leaving." She sounded hurt.

"I'm sorry," Kitten said. "The lady—Peyton—told me I couldn't tell anyone. She said she'd get me away. I'd be the first one, but she planned to help all of us—the people at the farm, at the massage place, you—all of us. She was going to shut down all of Jefe's operation."

Dulce's eyes narrowed. "By herself? Stupid *chica*. And you believed her."

"She was not stupid!" Kitten felt a flush of anger. "She was brave." So brave that she'd risked everything to help Kitten and lost her life in the process. This cold fact lay like a rock in Kitten's stomach.

"No. She was stupid. She die for what? Nothing. You are still here, taking my nail polish and telling your lies."

Kitten searched her friend's face, puzzled by the venom that normally went away after Dulce had a few minutes of shouting. "How did it go tonight?"

Dulce drifted over to the dresser and grabbed Kitten's brush. She teased her bangs so that they stood tall. "It's *mierda*. They made me work the cantina. My only buyers were the nosy woman and her friend. They helping you now, Kitten? Are you getting ready to run again?" She teased another clump of hair, using some of Kitten's hairspray to shellac it into place.

Out the window, Kitten saw a car pulling into the drive. Roman and two others.

"What do you think?" Dulce turned to face her.

"Your hair looks nice."

Dulce threw the brush onto the bed and stepped closer, eyeing her like she was prey. "Not asking about my hair. I'm asking you if you're going to run again."

The front door squeaked open. The men spoke in Spanish to Lito. She couldn't tell who they were.

"Well, will you?" Dulce demanded.

"No. I learned my lesson." She didn't want to lie to her friend but knew better than to trust her. Once Kitten escaped, she'd help Dulce and the others. Maybe she'd be the one to put Jefe out of business.

After she was free.

CHAPTER TWENTY-EIGHT

That next morning, I awoke thirty minutes late to an alarm that had exhausted itself trying to get me out of bed. I flew into the bathroom for a three-minute shower, clipped my hair into a tragic-looking ponytail, threw food in Fenway's bowl, and snagged a cup of coffee to drink on the way to work. I forgot to take my meds, but I kept a stash in my purse for this very reason.

My normal morning drive routine includes a mini self-assessment, and after recent events and the session with Nora, I wanted to be particularly attentive. Was I eating well? God, no. Getting enough sleep? Nope. Managing my stress? Sucking at that. Handling my internal stimuli? Struggling, but not as badly as Nora thought.

I made myself lessen the foot pressure on the accelerator; being five minutes late to work wasn't a capital offense. I needed to calm myself down.

In my rearview mirror, I spotted a burgundy sedan two cars back. It turned when I did. Three blocks later, when I took a left on Harden, it mirrored me.

Is he following you? The advisor whispered.

Paranoia was never my friend.

Speed up. You can lose him.

The suggestion tempted me. *Calm*, I reminded myself, but I kept an eye on the car, noticing a dent in its front bumper. When I took a quick right into the rear hospital lot, the car slowed, then passed on by.

He's scoping you out, the advisor whispered.

"Or he's just some other idiot on a morning commute." I was determined to not give credence to his words. Nora would be proud.

My first stop, after a coffee refill and checking my messages, was Marilyn Wilder. On the way to her room, Dr. Mark Westfall stopped me by the nurse's station.

"Got a second?"

"Always. What's up?" I replied.

"Your patient Marilyn." His gaze remained fixed on the iPad in his hand.

"Uh oh. I thought she was doing better."

He punched the screen. "Psychiatrically yes. Pretty stable. But she had some dizziness earlier and we did a cardiogram. It showed an arrhythmia." He pointed to cardiac readings as though I should be able to understand them.

"Has it happened to her before?"

"She says not. I was looking at her medication history and one of the anti-psychotics she was on before she came here can cause it. We've switched her to something else, but we want to keep an eye on her for a few more days."

"Okay. Does she know?"

He smiled. "We thought we'd let you tell her."

"Don't do me any favors, Mark."

"There is some good news." He flashed through a few screens to a billing page, where insurance numbers had been added. "Tiffany's thrilled that she's got coverage."

One less battle I'd have to fight, but I didn't relish telling Marilyn about her extended stay.

She wasn't in her bed, but sitting in a chair by the window, a book in her hand. The door to the cabinet where her clothes were kept was covered with her artwork, all similar to the pictures Dianne had shown me.

"Good morning." I did my best to not sound as dismal as I felt.

"Hey. Are you here to help me get out of this place?"

I smiled. "You're ready to bail on us, huh?"

She nodded. "No voices. Taking my meds like a good girl."

I grabbed the wooden chair by the door and pulled it close to her, glancing at the pictures taped beside me. "Still doing your art, I see."

She stood, snatched off one of the pics, and studied it. "Dianne says I'm painting the demons as a way to conquer my fear. Of course, Dianne might be full of shit, but somehow it is helping."

"That's great!"

"Can I leave today? No offense, but this psycho ward life is not that much fun. My brother came to see me this morning. I told them you'd be calling to set up my aftercare stuff. I can stay with him and his family until I can find my own apartment."

I mulled how to give her the bad news. I'd been exactly where she was, ready to get back to life and resenting anyone and anything that held me back. Only this time, I was the bad guy.

"I look forward to talking to him. Maybe he can come by my office next time he visits you?"

"What do you mean, next time? I'm getting out of here today, right?" It was less of a question than a demand.

"Okay, here's the deal. You're doing great, but Doctor Westfall is worried about a cardiac arrhythmia that's flaring up. He's changing your meds to see if it resolves, and we have to keep a close eye on you to make sure it does."

"Shit."

"It's not fair, I know. And we're just talking about a few days here."

"Here? On the freakin' psych ward?" She crossed her arms, her eyes wide with defiance.

"You know, maybe not here. Maybe we move you to a medical floor. Your issues now are cardiac, not psychiatric. Would that make it better?"

"It sure couldn't be worse."

When I left, she was still sulking in her bed. I felt for her. She had a life she wanted to get on with and we were stopping her. I found Mark and he had no problem with moving her to Medical. If nothing else, it freed up a psych bed. Maybe that would placate Marilyn, at least for a few days.

As I left the hospital that evening, I was tired deep in my bone marrow. When I took a left on Harden, I spotted a dented burgundy sedan in my rearview mirror. It looked identical to the one I'd seen during my morning commute.

Danger, said the advisor.

No, no. This was my imagination in hyperdrive. There were gazillions of burgundy cars in Columbia.

He's following you.

I made a quick right, and the car mirrored my turn.

"Damn it."

Speed up.

"Speed up?" Like I could lose him? My Honda had over 215,000 miles and desperately needed a tune-up. I floored it, passing two cars and a semi before maneuvering into the right lane, making sure there was no room for the car to squeeze in behind me.

He approached from the left, nudging up until he was parallel to me. "Shit." Panic clawed inside my chest.

Don't look at him.

I sped up. So did he. Ignoring the advisor's guidance, I braved a glance. Two men. The one in the passenger seat was dark skinned, wearing a Yankees cap. *I hate the Yankees.* His window glided down, and I got a better look at his face. Wasn't he the man who held a gun on me outside the Estate?

My terror swelled as I tried to go faster, thwarted by a beer truck in my lane. The red car remained at my side.

The Yankees cap guy had an arm out the window, his hand poised index finger extended, miming a gun.

Did the man plan to kill me right here in traffic? No, just a threat. *Brake. Then turn.*

I did. The truck behind me blared its horn but I ignored it as I took a hard right onto Henderson. The sedan had no way to follow, as the truck blocked it from changing lanes. I took three random turns to make sure I'd lost them, then pulled into the parking lot of a CVS. My hands quaked against the steering wheel.

Good job, said the advisor.

"Thanks," I panted out. My heart rate pushed a thousand.

I called Lou Michaels's number.

"Detective Michaels." His voice had a clipped, get-to-the-point tone.

"Uhmm. This is Georgia Thayer."

"Everything okay?" He tuned into the fear in my voice.

"Someone has been following me. First this morning. And just now. A burgundy car."

He didn't say anything.

"It was two men. One acted like he wanted to kill me."

"How did he do that?"

"He gestured with his hand like it was a gun." My voice rose. "I'm not kidding, Lou. They followed me from the hospital."

An itchy silence followed, then he said, "Any idea why they might want to follow you?"

"Maybe it has something to do with the traffickers. With my sister's murder."

This time his silence just pissed me off. "Never mind."

"Wait a second." He sounded placating now. "Can you give me a description of the car?"

"Dark red. Midsize. Oldish, I think."

"Did you get the license number?"

"No. It happened too fast. I—" I knotted a hand in my hair and tugged. "Never mind. Next time, I'll see if the hoodlums following me will pose for a few selfies. Maybe then you'll believe me."

"Georgia—"

"Did Ben call you today?"

"He did. We were supposed to meet for breakfast, and he stood me up. I called the paper and he didn't show up for work this morning. They said they knew he was on a story, so they weren't concerned, but—"

"Dammit. What if he decided to go after the traffickers himself? What if they—"

"The traffickers?"

I filled him in on what I'd learned, including the visit to Special Touch Massage and the man shooting at Elias, my speaking in such a panicky rapid-fire that I lost my breath.

"Okay, slow down. I'm not quite following you."

It occurred to me that I probably sounded pretty damn crazy just then. I forced calm into my voice and repeated what I'd told him.

"Go to Special Touch, Lou. I'm scared Ben went there. Something bad may have happened to him."

He asked for the address, and I gave it to him. "I didn't tell Ben about the Orchid Estate, but Elias and I found it and it's a very sketchy operation. Guarded like it's Fort Knox. But then, you probably knew that." I waited, hoping he'd take the bait and fill me in.

He didn't. "Do I need to tell you again how dangerous it is for you to be visiting these places?"

"Yeah, yeah. Call me as soon as you know something." I clicked off.

I took back roads the rest of the way home. No burgundy car, thank God, but what if they knew where I lived? It wouldn't be hard to find out; anybody with a little computer skill could uncover my address.

After locking the front door, I went room-to-room looking for any signs of an intrusion. Had I left the TV remote on the shelf? I usually plopped it on the table. And that area rug was it a little left of its usual spot?

And where was my cat? He always greeted me at the door. "Fenway? Fenway!" I yelled.

When I rushed into the bedroom, I found him curled up on my pillow. He blinked up at me as if to say, *"What?"* I lifted him and held him against me. He tucked his head under my chin.

"We're okay," I whispered to him. "We're okay."

Before I went to bed, I checked out the windows to make sure there were no burgundy cars parked in front of my house. I double-checked the doors, the window latches, and made sure my cell was charged and within easy reach. Sleep avoided me, my mind a jumble of thoughts of my sister, the traffickers, Kitten, and the mysterious burgundy car. Peyton's efforts to save that kid got her killed. Would the same thing happen to me?

I didn't matter, not really. I had to continue where Peyton left off, with or without the police.

CHAPTER TWENTY-NINE

To say that Jefe was in a pissy mood was quite the understatement. He roared at the maid for leaving a sock on the closet floor. He barked at Cook for the scrambled eggs being runny, even though he always asked for them that way. When Javier arrived and rushed into the dining room, the volume of Jefe's discontent hit new levels. The girls hurried to their rooms and shut the doors as though running from an imminent assault.

Lillian wanted to barricade herself, too, but instead approached the dining table where Jefe sat, noting his white-knuckled grip on the coffee mug. "What's wrong?"

He frowned over the steaming cup. "Tell her, Javi."

Javier ran a hand through his thick black hair. The dark bristles shadowing his chin were weird for him. Javier always managed to be immaculately groomed, unlike many of Jefe's men. "The massage parlor. We had to close it."

"What? Why?"

"I blame Lito!" Jefe said. "He can't keep a better grip on those girls."

"I understand that Jefe, but we let the girls go to the alley to smoke. If we let them have cigarettes inside the buyers complain. And we've never had an issue with Ratana before."

"What happened?" Lillian hoped they wouldn't get rid of her. She had met Ratana a few months ago and wanted her for the Estate.

"Lito caught her talking to two strangers. This after we had the Ribault woman snooping just a few weeks ago." Jefe shook his head in disgust. "And worse, he let them get away!"

Javier stretched out a pacifying hand. "To be fair. The guy was drunk. He tried to buy time with Ratana. She did the right thing and went inside to get Lito."

"That's what she claimed she did. But we don't know, do we? Maybe those two were working with the Ribault woman. Maybe they're with the police. Christ, Javi. This could destroy me!"

She didn't like the red pallor on Jefe's face. He generally wasn't one to overreact. While always extremely cautious, he didn't punch the panic button often.

Javier gestured to a chair, asking permission to sit. Jefe nodded. Javier took a deep breath and said, "We had another development this morning."

Jefe pushed back from the table, his glare at Javier murderous.

Javier cleared his throat. "A man stopped by Special Touch. We'd already cleared out the girls. Linda and Lito were packing up the computers. He asked a lot of questions."

"Fucking cops?" Jefe yelled.

"No, Jefe. Not the cops. A reporter."

"A reporter? JESUS!"

"It's okay. We took care of it." Javier said softly, as though calming an aggressive dog.

"How?"

"Lito handled him. He won't be a problem anymore."

Not a problem anymore. Those words made something dark stir in Lillian's stomach. She thought about Violet. About Carmen, who'd worked for Jefe two years ago until Jefe found out she'd stolen a buyer's ring left on the nightstand. Carmen drew her last breath on the cold asphalt behind a truck stop. On its surface, the Estate was like a beautiful, inviting sea, beckoning buyers to bathe in its warm water. Beneath, though, the treacherous undertow. One wrong move, one betrayal, could pull you to a brutal, merciless death.

Jefe flattened a hand on the table as he drew in deep, slow breaths. Good. He was calming himself.

Lillian leaned closer. "You talked just last week about closing Special Touch. You don't need it now that the Estate is doing so well. We have much better control here, you know that."

"Exactly," Javier said. "Lillian and I will decide which girls to bring here. The others, we'll give to Roman. In a few months, this will be just a blip. What you're doing here, Jefe—" he waved a hand to indicate the Estate, "is an international hit. We'll soon be at a point where we're turning men away."

Lillian nodded. "Next weekend we're going to make special. You're reaching a new caliber of clients, and we'll give them an experience unlike anything they've had before. And that will just be the beginning. Like Javier said, we'll be turning clients away."

He eyed each of them, took a sip of his cooled coffee, and lowered the mug. "And Ratana? What do we do with her, Lil?"

Lillian knew this was a test. She'd shown leniency with Violet, and it nearly got her killed. Still, Ratana may not have betrayed them. Plus, she had an exotic, Asian look that would fit in well here at the Estate. She shot a look at Javier, hoping for guidance. He offered only a shrug.

"What do we do with her?" She forced strength in her voice she didn't feel. "Give her to me. We can use her next weekend and that will give me time to prep her. You know we're short on girls anyway. Onyx and I will watch her like a hawk. She pulls anything, I'll give her to Lito myself."

Jefe frowned, but she held his gaze. Javier tapped the table. "I'll be here, too, Jefe. If Ratana is up to something, we'll know it. It's easier to eliminate a threat when we have some idea what it is."

Jefe sighed. "You have a point. Have Lito bring her here with Kitten this afternoon. If Lito hasn't already done it, search all her belongings and make sure she isn't hiding anything.

"Call Vince, too. I want these girls branded by the end of the day. They're Estate women now."

Kitten sat beside Ratana, an Asian girl they'd picked up from a rundown building on the edge of downtown. Lito drove, his old rumbly car bumping over cracked asphalt roads. The girls didn't speak. Ratana fidgeted, studying her nails, peering over the seat as though she had a clue where they were going. Kitten remained still, wishing she was invisible as Lito eyed her in the rearview mirror. She'd made a big mistake getting on his bad side when she tried to leave and saw no way to remedy that. Maybe with the move, she'd see him less.

He pulled into a gas station and spun around to look at them. "Don't even think of trying to pull something. I mean it."

She nodded. Lito climbed out and inserted a card in the pump. Ratana watched with careful vigilance.

"Have you ever been to this estate place?" Kitten asked.

Ratana nodded. "Once. It very nice. Fancy."

"Huh." Anywhere would be nicer than the trailer.

"Why he always watch you?" Ratana gestured at Lito.

"I tried to get away."

"Why? You stupid?"

Kitten smiled. "Yeah, maybe. I just thought maybe I could. Maybe I'd find a better life out there."

"You're lucky you still have a life at all."

She leaned back, eyeing Lito as he tapped the nozzle against the tank. She didn't say she would try again. She didn't say that she wouldn't let this be the only life she had.

"If I try to leave, they kill my parents," Ratana said. "Back in Thailand. Jefe has people there and they will kill them. So I never leave. Maybe you get away, they kill someone you love? It worth it?"

Kitten shook her head. Jefe had threatened her brother Brandon before. But how would he know how to find him? How many foster homes had Brandon lived in since she left? How can anybody trace him? Once she escaped, she'd find Brandon and make sure he was safe. Then do everything she could to stop Jefe.

Thirty minutes later, they passed through iron gates, Lito nodding to the man guarding them, and up to a giant stucco house with shingles glinting in the sun like fish scales. Palm trees with quivering fronds perched beside a brick walkway. A woman stood on the steps, arms crossed, watching as another guard opened the car door. When Kitten and Ratana climbed out, the guard spun them around, his hands patting them down.

"You think I didn't search them before I brought them here?" Lito huffed.

"Never hurts to be careful." The woman approached them. She had auburn hair and skin as pale as typing paper, her movements somehow elegant and purposeful. She had them each stand in the sunlight, turning them this way and that, touching their chins to angle their faces left, then right.

"Take them inside," she said to Lito. "To the library."

As Lito guided them toward the front door, Kitten marveled that a woman had ordered him to do something.

Inside was more majestic than outdoors. Kitten had never been to Disneyworld, and she and Brandon used to fantasize about what it was like. This was as luxurious as she pictured the castle to be.

"Go in there." Lito shoved them through double doors into a room with dark red leather furniture and towering bookshelves. Ratana moved to the sofa and sat, her back straight, her hands folded in her lap, staring ahead while Kitten explored. The books were real. A globe made of a thousand glittering stones, also real. The purple flower blooming from a planter on the coffee table—an orchid, she thought—was perfect enough to be silk but wasn't. Only the fireplace logs were fake—gas ones, she guessed, like in foster home number three.

The art included landscapes of lush country scenes, hay wagons and plowed fields, and flowers blooming on stone walls. The paintings looked old but well kept, the gold frames heavy and ornate. Lights above were angled to highlight the art, like flashlight beams showing the past.

The woman entered, followed by a tall black woman wearing a flowing purple robe. The woman said to Lito, "Vince is on his way. Send him in as soon as he gets here." She pulled the doors closed and spoke to them. "My name is Lillian. I work directly for Jefe. You are in my charge and you will always do as I tell you to."

She placed a hand on the arm of the dark-skinned woman. "This is Onyx. She's my second in command. If I'm away, she's your boss."

Onyx circled them, her head cocked to the side, appraising. "We'll need to get them some clothes."

Lillian nodded. "For Ratana, we'll stay with the Asian theme. A silk kimono over black lingerie. She can use the crimson room for her buyers." She circled Kitten again. "With Kitten, we'll focus on her youth. Not the baby doll look. That's overdone. But a minidress and Keds. We'll go minimalist on her makeup."

"Which room?"

"Begonia."

Onyx lowered her gaze, her lips drawn in tight.

"We can't avoid using it forever," Lillian said. "Violet's gone. We have to move on."

Who was Violet? What had happened to her? She knew better than to ask.

Next came a long lecture and a list of rules. Kitten tried to absorb them all, not wanting to get in trouble during her stay here. They worked whenever instructed to. They slept in a bunk room behind the main house. They would be given specific directions on how to satisfy the clientele. Nothing was forbidden except overt violence.

"These men . . . hurt us?" Ratana asked.

"Sometimes it can get a little rough, but this is a high-class operation. We don't allow our girls to get damaged."

Damaged? Like merchandise in a gift store?

Someone banged on the door and Lito opened it. An older man dressed in jeans, a T-shirt, and a vest entered, carrying some kind of equipment. Tattoos of giant cats covered much of the flesh on his arms and a scraggly gray goatee covered his narrow chin. He placed a case on the coffee table, then proceeded to assemble a tripod topped with a metal tray and a telescoping lamp.

"Who first?" he asked.

"Ratana." Lillian guided her to flatten her arm on the tray under the light. The man opened his case, which contained dozens of small bottles of ink, and pulled out a metal cylinder with a needle on the end.

"Same as the others?" he asked Lillian.

"Of course."

He went to work, first cleaning Ratana's arm with an alcohol pad, then stenciling the design on her arm. When his needle penetrated her skin, she jerked, but steadied herself and remained perfectly still for the rest of the procedure. When he was done, he leaned back so they could admire his work. In the middle of red, inflamed skin were the purple petals of an orchid blossom, three curved up, three curved down. In the center of the bloom the color shifted to gold, with threads the same color veining the purple. It was quite beautiful.

"It's lovely, isn't it, Kitten?" Lillian asked.

She nodded, unable to speak. She didn't want a tattoo, her flesh scarred forever in a permanent reminder that she belonged to Jefe.

"You're next," Lito said. "Move to the table."

She couldn't budge. Tears pushed, but she didn't let them fall.

"Move!" Lito grabbed her arm and wrenched it till she was positioned close to the tray. He slammed her arm against it, hard enough that it stung.

"Don't be afraid, Kitten. It hardly hurts." Lillian leaned over, pulling at the neckline of her top to reveal the same orchid on her chest. "We all wear this. It's Jefe's brand. We're lucky. It could be something hideous, like a barcode or an obscene word. The orchid is very important to Jefe. Wear it as a work of art."

The man used more force than necessary with the alcohol pad before starting with the needle. At first, the area stung like a bee had attacked, then a burning sensation vibrated down her arm. She looked away, taking in deep, steadying breaths, determined not to move.

Slow breaths in, slower out. She focused on this tide of air and not on the pain that only worsened as he continued. Then finally, he was done.

She turned to the artist. "How do I take care of it?"

He gave them directions about the healing process. The skin would flake, but don't peel it. It would itch, do not scratch. Antibiotic ointment as needed and no baths for a week. NO sleeves that would rub until it had completely healed.

He repositioned the light so that the tattoo practically glowed. Had she seen it on someone else, she might admire it, but on her skin, it represented all that was sinister about the life she'd been forced into. A taint that could never be erased.

She looked at Lillian. "Can I go lie down? I have a bit of a headache."

Lillian's gaze on her felt like an assessment. Kitten looked down, swallowing, not liking this scrutiny. Finally, Lillian said to Lito, "Take her to the bunk room. We'll fit Ratana's wardrobe first."

Lito seemed to relish grabbing her arm again and jerking her up from the sofa.

"Hey! Not so rough." Lillian approached him like a looming presence. Like someone in charge. He let out an annoyed sigh before guiding Kitten down a narrow hall to a room beside the back door. He flipped on the lights, revealing eight bunks, beds unmade, personal items like robes and shower caps lying in disarray atop them.

"The last one is yours. Up top." He shoved her into the room, watching as she climbed the metal ladder to the upper bunk. Lito closed in, gripping the rail. "Listen, you little bitch. I'm on to you. Jefe's giving you a chance you don't deserve, and I'm just waiting for you to fuck it up. Kinda look forward to it, myself." He thumped the rail, gave her one last leer, and left.

She wanted to sleep, to crawl under the scratchy blanket and stay hidden there for days. Her thoughts turned to her brother. *Does he think I abandoned him? Will I ever see him again? Will I even live to see twenty?*

CHAPTER THIRTY

Fitting Ratana had been easy. Lillian used a kimono that Lito had brought from the massage parlor. Once cleaned, mended, and pressed, it would flow nicely over her gentle curves. A dress from Violet's wardrobe could be altered to fit her, though the rest of Violet's clothes she was saving for Kitten. They were similar in size, though Kitten didn't have Violet's ample breasts. A stitch here, a hem there, they'd make the clothes look brand new.

She knocked gently on the bunkroom door before entering. Kitten lay on the top bunk closest to the window, covered in blankets like it was the dead of winter. Lillian switched on the light. Kitten pulled herself up, cradling the arm as though nursing a gunshot wound. "Feeling better?"

"A little." Kitten propped the pillow against the wall. "Do you need me now?"

"In a minute." She wandered from bed to bed, touching the blankets and discarded clothes, disgusted by the mess. "I'll have Onyx get on the girls."

"How many sleep in here?"

"With you and Ratana we're up to six. Have room for a few more. Let me see the tattoo."

Kitten lifted her arm. The flower, surrounded by inflamed skin, looked perfect.

"It's nice. But you don't like it."

"It's okay."

"You'll get used to it."

"Yeah."

Lillian studied the girl's face. Her expression a void except the blue eyes. A lot went on behind those eyes. "Jefe told me you tried to get away. And he caught you."

She cringed.

"It's surprising that he gave you another chance. But now that I've met you, I understand. You're lovely. Young. Valuable to him, as long as you don't pull another stunt like that."

"I won't," she rushed to say.

Lillian wondered if thoughts of escape swirled behind those pale irises. She felt Kitten's gaze on her, assessing Lillian as much as she was evaluating Kitten. "You remind me of myself at your age. I ran away from my very fucked up family. Lived on the streets. Nearly died there. A man saved me and brought me to Jefe. I've been with him ever since."

"Saved you? I didn't get saved. I got stolen."

There it was. The edge. The sense that this was all unfair, that she deserved better. The piece of Kitten that might prompt her to run off again. Lillian drifted over to the bunk across from her and sat. Kitten descended the ladder and plopped on the bed below hers.

"What happens here is up to you, Kitten. I'm inviting you to become one of us. We will treat you better than Roman ever did. You'll have a comfortable life—good food, nice clothes. This gorgeous place to live.

"Our buyers aren't from a scuzzy honky-tonk. They're important people from all over the world who come here for distraction and pleasure. We give them that and more. You won't be turning fifteen-minute tricks. You'll be offering an evening of sexual indulgence. If you're good, and I think you will be, you'll become an artist at the ways of pleasing a man.

"The better you are, the more you'll be requested. The more you're requested, the more perks you'll receive from Jefe. Nicer things. Your own DVD player. If you're really good, you may get your own room like Onyx.

"We'll make this a good life for you if you let us. But again, it's up to you."

Kitten leaned forward, elbows on her pale knees. "You make it sound okay. Almost nice, even."

Lillian mirrored her posture, closing the distance between them. "I'm not lying to you."

"I have a question, though. What happens when I'm too old? When I'm no longer valuable to Jefe? I mean, what will happen to you when you hit your thirties or forties?"

The questions pelted Lillian like buckshot. The same questions that had haunted her for the past year, that had led to longer morning runs, yoga workouts in the afternoon, and more focus on anti-aging cosmetics. Lillian was twenty-seven. Jefe's attraction to her, from the very beginning, had been her youth. When would she be too old? She knew what would happen to her. She knew, but she pretended she didn't.

Kitten stood and crossed over to sit beside Lillian. "I'm sorry. I didn't mean—"

"You didn't mean what?"

"I didn't mean to imply that you're too old. You're drop-dead beautiful. But—"

"But what?"

"But this isn't the kind of life where we live to a ripe old age, is it? Lito lets me know all the time that I'm expendable."

Lillian's thoughts went to that black place where the cold, hard truth lived. What chance did any of them have? There was no retirement plan for the girls at the Estate. In time, the undertow would claim them all. She cleared her throat, desperate to change the subject. "Lito is a prick."

Kitten's eyes widened and she let out a laugh, full-throated and boisterous. She slapped a hand against her mouth as though trying to suppress it, like a kid caught giggling at assembly.

"What's so funny?" Lillian found herself smiling.

"It's just good to hear someone say that."

"Still, be careful around him, Kitten. He can be lethal. Never forget that."

She nodded, looking less childlike now. A young woman who understood what danger was.

"Can I ask you a question?" she asked.

Lillian nodded.

"Why am I here? I mean, why now?"

"Because I need you. This weekend is very important to Jefe. Everything has to go just right. You are a part of that." Lillian realized how very true her words were. If anything went wrong, if the food was cold or one of the girls displeased her buyer, Lillian would be blamed. How Lito and the others would love for her to crash and burn. Jefe needed just one more mistake, and that would be her end. Her situation had never been this precarious.

"You're nervous about it." Kitten's words were soft. Gentle.

"Very."

Kitten's gaze probed her face and made her uncomfortable. She could feel the sweat on her forehead and cheeks, tears pushing from her eyes. This vulnerability wasn't good. Ever. Especially in front of one of her girls.

"I'll do my part, Lillian. I promise. I'll do whatever you need me to."

Lillian smiled, not quite believing. "You will? You won't try to run?"

"I don't want anything to happen to you. Or any of us. So, you can count on me."

Lillian felt like a boulder had been lifted from her chest. "Okay then. You keep our buyers happy this weekend, and I'll make sure Lito leaves you alone."

"How?"

"The Estate is my turf. I run things here, whether he likes it or not. I'll keep you safe." Lillian hoped she could make good on that promise. "Okay. Let's go get you a new wardrobe."

❧

"My name is Dulce. Why you want to change it? It's a beautiful name!"

Kitten kicked back the sheets and pivoted her feet off the bunk. The clock read 7 a.m..

"I didn't remember how huge this place is! How many people live here? How many rooms does it have?" Dulce's voice boomed from outside the door making Kitten smile. She'd missed her friend.

How long had it been since she'd slept that well? The bunk was small but the mattress practically new—no lumps to sleep around, no smells to ignore. She swiveled so that her feet hit the ladder, climbed down, and threw on a dress and a pair of Keds.

Dulce stood in the dining room, dressed in a cleavage-revealing midriff top and too-short shorts. The other girls sat around the table, helping themselves to cereal, fruit, and coffee. Kitten had learned a little about them. Two were American, like Kitten, but a little older and not much interested in talking. They'd been introduced as Zoe and Lotus. An Asian girl named Mei-Mei, probably fifteen or so, understood little English, but at least smiled when Kitten spoke to her. A large woman from Guatemala, whose dark hair reached her waist, had a boisterous laugh that got on the nerves of the Americans. Her skin was a coppery bronze. They called her Citrine.

Another orchid bloomed on the center of the table, but on either side waited an assortment of cereals, fruits, and juices. Kitten helped herself to corn flakes, milk, and strawberries. She could not believe the food they had here. Last night's dinner included baked chicken and fresh vegetables. She even got her choice of ice cream flavors for dessert!

"Good morning," Onyx said. "We let you sleep in but don't make a habit of it. Have a seat and eat your breakfast."

She found an empty seat beside Ratana.

"Dulce, sit," Onyx commanded. "We'll discuss your name later."

With a pronounced pout, Dulce took the chair across from Kitten, who slid a box of Coco Puffs—Dulce's favorite—over to her. She wanted to whisper, "settle down," to tell her that her usual antics wouldn't play well with this group, but Dulce was unlikely to listen.

Lillian entered, dressed in a snug short skirt with a matching jacket and a white blouse with a neatly pressed collar. She stopped at the head of the table and surveyed the girls.

"I want you all dressed for work at noon. Free time till then. Ratana and Kitten, you may want to explore the grounds so you're familiar with them when our guests arrive. Meet me in the study so I can review our schedule with you." She turned to Dulce, looked at the top she was wearing and frowned. "Did you bring other clothes?"

"I have a few other outfits." Dulce flipped her hair behind her shoulder.

"Onyx, you've checked them out?"

Onyx nodded. "With some alterations and repairs, two will work, but we'll need to order some additional dresses."

"Stand up," Lillian said to Dulce.

She lowered her spoon, slid the chair back, and stood, teetering a little on her too-tall heels.

"Turn around." Lillian stepped closer, assessing, as Dulce did an awkward pirouette.

"She has a nice figure. Petite, which shorter men will like."

Dulce straightened her back, obviously offended by the "petite" comment.

"Play her young?" Onyx asked.

"I don't think so. Work with the wild Hispanic quality she has. Dress her in reds and blacks. Satins and tulle." She reached for Dulce's hand. "And for God's sake, do something with these nails."

Kitten's eyes widened. Dulce took great pride in her home manicures, but her cheap polish chipped off after a few days. Dulce clenched her fist to hide the nails but kept her mouth shut.

"She's unhappy with the prospect of changing her name," Onyx said.

"Dulce is a nice name." She spoke with clarity and pride. "Why change it?"

Lillian laughed. "Well, you change it if we say you have to. But let's give it a day or so. If we costume you correctly, it might still work." Lillian turned to Kitten. "This afternoon, I'll run you through the weekend schedule. We have very important guests coming, and everyone will follow our protocols. Got it?"

Kitten nodded. She'd be the perfect worker this weekend because she'd promised Lillian. But after that, she'd look for her chance for escape.

CHAPTER THIRTY-ONE

The morning had been a crap-fest. Tiffany came by my office and had a seat before I could stop her, regaling me with tales of her yoga and Pilates classes before offering me some of a cleansing smoothie to "purify my liver." (Behind her, Clancy opened a bag of Peanut M&Ms and popped them in her mouth just to torture me.) Once Tiffany finally moved on, I opened three emails from the Quality Assurance Coordinator expressing profound condolences before pointing out that four social histories were four days overdue and strongly insisting that I get them done.

Then came the call. "Is this Georgia? This is Lou Michaels. I'm down here in the ER. I think you'd better come down."

"What's wrong?"

"Ben Reeder's been attacked. Don't know how bad—"

"I'll be right down." I dropped the receiver. Took a few dizzying breaths. *Ben, attacked? How?* I stood, almost teetering over my desk as I made my way around it and to the door. I ran to the elevator and groped for the button. It took too long, it always did when I had an emergency, so I opted for the stairs. As I ran down the metal steps, my footfalls echoed like flat notes on a piano.

When I reached the nurse's station, I was huffing. "Ben Reeder. Which bay?"

The nursing aide scanned a chart attached to a clipboard. "Bay three. Doctor Danzler's got him."

Before I approached the curtained-off examining area, Lou Michaels intercepted me. A shadow of beard darkened his chin. His blue shirt was crumpled as though slept in. His panicked expression filled me with alarm.

"What happened?" I demanded.

He took in a breath before answering. "Somebody assaulted him. We went to Special Touch Massage like you suggested. Found his truck in front but no sign of him. We did a search, and it took a while. Finally found him by a ditch a quarter mile away." Lou shook his head, the muscles in this throat working in moving lumps. "They dumped him there like garbage."

"How bad is he?"

He glanced over at the closed curtain. "He wasn't conscious. Pretty messed up. God, how long had he been there?"

I pushed past Lou and slid through the curtain, freezing at the foot of the gurney. Ben lay unconscious, half-covered by a sheet. Electrodes attached to his chest surrounded a large hematoma that looked like a crimson balloon. A long gash zigzagged over his right eye and down to the bridge of his nose. His left leg had been splinted and levitated by a foam wedge. Seeing him like that—so broken— nearly made me buckle.

"Paula?" I glanced down at the record in the doctor's hand. "How is he?"

Paula Danzler, a tiny, blonde—and one of our best ER attending docs—squinted up at me. "He's lost a lot of blood. Dehydrated. He's got a broken tibia and a few busted ribs. We're sending him up for a CAT scan of his head and X-rays of the leg and chest."

"Been conscious at all?"

"In and out. When we checked out the leg, he was awake enough to spew some obscenities. We sedated him. You have a break like that, you'd want to be sedated, too."

I could only imagine the language that had come out of him. "You think he'll be okay?"

Paula gave me one of her "you should know better than to ask that" looks. "We'll know more after we get the CAT and the films back." A nurse's aide slid through the curtains. Paula said, "Let's get him upstairs."

The aide jerked the curtain back, removed the electrodes, and wheeled the gurney out toward the elevator. "I'll call as soon as I have the films," Paula said.

I found Lou Michaels sitting in a plastic chair and staring at the phone gripped in his hand. He looked up as I approached so I dropped in the chair beside him.

"Shit," I said.

"I kept texting him yesterday. Giving him shit about not answering the damn phone. Then I got worried, but I didn't think—" He took his time about pocketing the cell. "Did they tell you anything about his condition?"

"A broken leg for sure. Tests to determine what else we're dealing with. But he's tough. You know that, right?"

"In college, I once saw him down five hotdogs from a sketchy gas station, so yeah." He let out a sardonic laugh.

I glanced back at the open curtain to the bay in which he had lain. "This is my fault."

He shook his head. "Blaming yourself isn't productive. Besides, did you make him go to that place? Have you ever been able to make him do anything? Because I sure as hell haven't."

I appreciated his attempt at humor, but the guilt weighed me down. If I hadn't told him about the trafficking, he'd be safe in his office instead of on his way to a brain scan.

Lou huffed out air as he looked around. "I hate this place. No offense, but..."

I looked at him. "It's okay. Nobody really loves a hospital. Bad memories?"

"You could say that." He blinked his eyes fast and cleared his throat.

I wondered what he was remembering. A colleague killed in the line of duty? A relative who passed away? The walls of any hospital absorbed so much grief and pain. The smells and sounds could conjure up the most brutal memories and I wondered what he was reliving right then.

But he didn't look willing to share. He pulled out his notepad and pen. "The massage place was abandoned when we got there. It would help if you'd go over everything you told me on the phone in a little more detail."

Probably because I sounded batshit crazy during the call. I repeated what I'd learned about Peyton's investigation, and my own. Lou scribbled down the details that spilled out of me. The visit to the Blue Rose Cantina. Meeting Dulce. Peyton's tapes, and what they'd told me about Kitten, the girl she hoped to save.

"I didn't know about any tapes."

"You would have if you'd bothered to return my call."

A long, awkward silence followed. Finally, he spoke. "I wish you'd left this to the police instead of pulling Ben into it."

"I didn't want Ben to investigate anything. I wanted him to talk to you. I wanted him to light a match under your ass so you'd do something about the trafficking operation." My voice quivered and it embarrassed me.

His eyes softened. "I know. Sorry about that. We'll check all this out. But Georgia, you need to leave this alone."

"No argument here. I'll bring you Peyton's tapes. They may be useful to you."

He nodded. I noticed beads of sweat on his upper lip and dotting his forehead. He was as worried as I was. "Remember Lou, people get better in hospitals, too. Have faith in Ben."

That brought out a nervous smile. "Thanks. I needed to hear that."

CHAPTER THIRTY-TWO

The guests—"buyers"—arrived in stretch limousines, fancy sports cars, and even a helicopter. Seven men of varying ages and nationalities. Kitten and the other girls were instructed to wait by the pool. They wore fancy bikinis—hers a simple black solid, not like the gold lamé Dulce had donned—each striking a pose on lounge chairs and towels, ignoring the scorching sun.

The water looked delicious, and Kitten wanted nothing more than to roll from her towel into the pool, but they'd been told not to get wet. The men were paraded through the girls, given their names, and told which had been assigned to them. Kitten spotted her buyer, a plump, jowly man in close conversation with another guest. He paid her little interest.

As they followed their luggage inside, Lillian said to the girls, "Afternoon wear next. I want you dressed and in the parlor in fifteen minutes. You'll serve drinks and let them get more acquainted with you."

So off they scurried to the dorm rooms, hurling off the beachwear and zipping into short, yet elegant, dresses. Dulce put on her highest black heels. Kitten wore ballerina flats, her simple yellow dress selected by Onyx because "it brings out your youth and your blond hair."

After quick touchups with combs and lipstick, they rushed to the parlor where Lillian awaited. She'd changed into a snug satin shift that rode her curves and revealed her lean, long legs. She pointed to the bar. Part of Kitten's instructions that week had been on basic bartending, so she filled crystal flutes with an expensive champagne, offering it to the guests as they entered.

"I'll take one." A shortish man in a white linen suit and wire-rim glasses helped himself to a glass. "What's your name?" he asked.

"I'm Kitten." She smiled, hoping she looked confident and charming, hoping the nervous shaking of her hands wasn't noticeable.

He lifted his glass. "Hello, Kitten. Though I'll bet that's not your real name."

"It's my real name here," she replied.

"My name is Greg."

She knew that. Lillian had briefed them on every guest. This was Greg H (no last name provided), a wealthy film producer from California. He liked sports and reading historical biographies. She'd also been told about the senator and the two Russians, Vasily and Pavel, who kept to themselves despite Onyx's efforts to engage them. Vasily was to be Kitten's guest for the weekend. He wore black trousers and a white shirt from which his thick, hairy arms protruded. His plump jowls quivered when he spoke. When he finally noticed her, he licked his lips.

She smiled to hide her repulsion.

Greg the producer was probably fifty years old, with brown hair thinning on top, artfully styled to hide his spreading baldness. He stood very close to her.

"How are you liking the Estate, Greg?"

He glanced up and down her body. "I'm liking it just fine."

As if on cue, Lillian appeared, taking the tray from Kitten's hands. "Excuse us, Greg. Vasily is asking for Kitten." She led Kitten to the Russian man who was refilling his champagne glass. "Why don't you show him the back garden? We won't be having dinner for another twenty minutes or so."

"Would you like to see the flowers?" Kitten asked.

"Yes. Show me your flowers."

She pretended not to hear the sexual innuendo as she let him open the French door that led to the patio. The garden lay beyond the pool, a brick walkway meandering through azaleas, irises, lilies, and roses. The colors exploded against the green foliage. He led her to a bench and sat, gesturing that she do the same.

"This is very pretty," he commented. "Not as big as some of the other, shall we say, *resorts* I have enjoyed. This is smaller, but cozier, no? Not so many girls though."

"Maybe we don't have quantity, but we do have quality." She'd rehearsed that line with Lillian.

He laughed. "Tell me about yourself, Kitten."

How should she answer? She wanted to say, "*I'm an enslaved fifteen-year-old desperate for escape? . . . I used to want to be a doctor. Now I'm just a kid trained to look sexy for pervs like you. Please don't hurt me.*" Instead, the practiced words came out; "I'm here to make you happy, Vasily."

His hand trailed up her bare arm to her neck. He pulled her close, pushing his fat lips against hers. He smelled of strange herbs, a little citrusy, a little musky.

"Mmmm," he whispered.

"I'm glad you liked it."

They heard voices and looked up to see Lillian with one of Jefe's men. "Dinner is in a few minutes. Kitten, run and change. We'll seat you beside Vasily if that's what he wants."

"That would be exactly what he wants," Vasily repeated.

Dinner was more elegant than anything Kitten had ever experienced. Jefe sat at the head of the table wearing a crisp white shirt and a bolo made of turquoise and gleaming silver. Lillian, in yet another dress, sat at his side. Jefe's men wore suits—even Lito and Javier—as they poured wine and served food. Kitten had asked about waitstaff for the weekend, and Onyx explained that Jefe wouldn't allow caterers, or pretty much anyone else, on the premises. The filet mignon, grilled asparagus, pear salad, fresh-baked bread, and chocolate torte had been delivered to the outer gate so Jefe's men could take over from there.

"How do you find the meat, gentlemen?" Jefe asked.

"As tender as Dulce's lips." An older man spoke in a European accent, Dulce smiling beside him.

Lillian had given them a crash course in table manners. Kitten knew to only eat small portions and to take little, delicate bites. She sat beside Vasily and Pavel was on her other side. The two Russians mostly spoke over her in their home language, which she found rude. Lillian had told her that Jefe had a big deal pending, something to do with weapons, and now and then they'd say something to Jefe. His animated nod signaled he was anxious to please them. Across the table, Dulce and Ratana were doing all they could to keep their guests happy. Kitten could see the anxiety on Ratana's face—the same nervousness she herself felt—so she smiled in encouragement of her new friend.

It felt like this whole weekend was an audition for the three of them—Kitten, Ratana, and Dulce. If they passed, they stayed. If they failed, well, best not to think about that.

She turned to Vasily. "Would you like something else to eat or drink?"

"More pinot."

Lillian handed her the bottle and she filled his glass. He pointed at hers, so she added a splash. She hadn't developed much love for wine, or any alcohol, because drinking never led to anything good.

"You should have more," he said.

"Our girls don't like to indulge. Their focus is on you, not on their own pleasure," Lillian said.

Kitten suppressed a smile. From her few days at the Estate, she'd seen the girls *indulge* as much as they could, in the privacy of the dorm room. Javier sometimes supplied beer. Lito brought them pot.

The smoke billowing from beneath the door had to be noticeable, yet Lillian and Onyx never mentioned it.

Jefe reviewed the schedule for the weekend for the guests. After a brief business gathering at the end of dinner, they could have "alone time" with their chosen date. Vasily leaned toward her and let out a guttural sound. She nodded back, noting the smile of approval on Lillian's face.

Yet another change of clothes. Kitten hated the white lace-up bustierre that pinched her sides and made sitting nearly impossible. She was instructed to wait in Vasily's assigned room—a lavish purple and white suite with a canopy bed, a sofa, a fireplace, and an attached bathroom with a tub that held two.

Vasily and Pavel remained with Jefe for a long time. Kitten waited, dreading his arrival. When he did show up, he didn't knock before entering and had his shirt off before he reached where she was perched on the mattress. Ten minutes later, the bustier was off, the lights dimmed, and Kitten closed her eyes.

The grounds of Orchid Estate reminded Kitten of a fancy garden she'd visited on a field trip in fifth grade. Immaculate landscaping. Brick paths that wound through blooming flowers of every color. Cement benches tucked in bush alcoves that offered privacy, if not comfort. One path paralleled the fence that encircled the main part of the estate. When given free time in the mornings, she took runs along this route. Lillian had said it was fine, and that three times around was about a mile and a half. "Don't get too close to the fence," she'd warned. "It's electric."

She was glad to have this time to run before breakfast. Vasily would be tied up with Jefe until noon, but she had to be available to him after that.

How different last night had been from her previous experiences with buyers. The canopied bed with too many pillows, which Vasily hurled to the floor. How he insisted on watching her undress, commanded her to lie beside him, and rolled on top of her with the grace of a log. Every inch of her felt his weight. It had taken him a long time, probably from the wine, and she had a moment of alarm that she might not satisfy him and what that might mean for her. But finally, he was done. He took a call on his cell phone and spoke in animated Russian for close to an hour. She was glad he was occupied. She gradually fell asleep to the low drone of his voice.

Running purged the evening from her system. She imagined the sweat purified her. The pounding of her feet against the pathway strengthened every muscle and prepared her for the moment that would surely come—the moment she could escape. She would not let herself be weak.

As she entered a shady section in the back of the property, she heard a muted male voice. Slowing her pace, she tried to follow the sound without being seen. As she drew closer, she made out the outline of Lito, tucked between two magnolia trees, talking to another of Jefe's workers. She inched toward them. The second man—short like Lito, with close-cropped black hair and tanned skin—had been to the trailer a few times. She remembered he was called Gunner, and Roman said he was Lito's older brother. Dulce had told her that Gunner was the one who brought her to Jefe.

"Should we go to Jefe?" Lito asked his brother.

"Not yet. We need to be sure."

"Do you think the senora's alone? Or working with someone?"

Gunner shook his head. "Who knows? By herself, she can destroy everything. She knows every detail of Jefe's operation."

Lito's eyes widened. "Maybe we tell Javier?"

"Can we trust him? Hell, can we trust anyone?"

"I will not go to prison." Lito's tone was more threatening than resigned.

"Not happening. If Lillian's betraying Jefe, we'll do what we have to do."

"We should tell Jefe."

"Not without more proof. One of my girls is here now. She'll keep eyes on her."

Why did they suspect Lillian of betraying Jefe? She seemed fiercely loyal to him. Kitten hated to think of anything happening to her—she was the first person who'd been nice since Kitten came into Jefe's organization.

What if they figured out that Javier had helped Peyton? They'd kill him. *He might be my only hope of escape.*

When she saw that the men were wrapping up their conversation, she inched back, not wanting to be seen. The leaves crunching under her feet seemed horrifically loud, but she heard no movement behind her. She picked up her pace, reaching the wooded path, ready to resume her run.

"Hey! Stop right there!"

Crap! Lito.

She kept moving, but he stepped in front of her, grabbing her shoulder when she tried to pull away.

"What are you doing?" His breath smelled rancid on her face.

"Exercising. It's good for me."

"Exercising? Or eavesdropping?" Lito's hand squeezed hard enough to bruise her. "What did you hear?"

She shook her head. "Nothing. I didn't even see you—"

"Don't start that bullshit with me. If you didn't see us, you wouldn't be sneaking away." Lito shook her, the vibration reaching down to her toes.

"*Mierda.* What do we do with her?" Gunner asked.

Lito reached for the gun he kept tucked in the back of his pants and pressed it under her chin. "I'll take care of her."

"Not here. Need to get her off grounds."

Kitten closed her eyes against a wave of terror. "I'm supposed to be with one of the Russians this afternoon. He's important to Jefe."

"Then Jefe will be especially pissed when you don't show," Lito growled.

"Lock her in the toolshed. We'll take care of her after the noon shift change."

The toolshed might buy her some time but promised to become excruciatingly hot; temps had been reaching the nineties before noon.

Lito pushed her along the path, Gunner close behind. When she stumbled over a root, he grabbed her arm and wrenched it behind her, snapping his elbow into her forearm and sending a blast of white-hot pain. His fingers gripped tighter and jerked, bending her wrist at an unnatural angle, her pain morphing into agony. She'd broken bones before. She knew the drill.

He nudged her toward the small greenhouse where Jefe grew his orchids. Behind it was the green toolshed with a corrugated tin roof. Gunner unlocked the door and Lito shoved her inside. "Tie her up," Gunner said.

Lito obliged, using rough hay rope to bind her hands and feet and knotting a painter's rag across her mouth.

"Bring the car here when the guards change shift. She should be nice and toasty then. We'll drive her off-campus and finish her off," Gunner commanded.

The door closed with a cold click, leaving her in darkness, save for a lone sliver of light coming in between slats of wood. The small space smelled earthy and rank. She twisted to pull herself up, wiggling to rest her back against a wall. Her wrist throbbed as the bindings compressed against the swelling. Sweat dribbled down her face and off her chin, but the heat would only worsen. *I have to escape.*

The hay ropes securing Kitten's hands looked impossible. She'd practiced knot tying with her little brother but didn't recognize the elaborate configuration Lito had used on her. Thankfully, he'd shown less care with her feet. Using one finger and two thumbs, she scratched into the tangle of rope and, with more patience than she usually had, managed to loosen the knot. A few minutes later, she kicked her feet free of the rope.

Her hands though. No way she could untether them, not with the swelling that bulged between the rough strands and the searing pain shooting up her arm. The gag around her face couldn't be removed, though she managed to lower it enough to draw a good flow of air. Hot air.

She wiped the sweat from her face with the back of her bound hand as she rose and approached the door. Even pushing all her weight against it didn't loosen the lock. The few fingers she could access shook the handle, but nothing budged, and her wrist screamed in agony. Despite the dim light, she could tell the walls were simple wood, not concrete, and there was a small gap between two planks. She felt her way to that spot, wedged her fingers in the narrow space, and pulled. At first, the wood held fast but with enough effort, she managed to wiggle one board just a little.

Using her busted wrist to pry the wood more might damage it further. She dropped to the floor and brushed her sleeve against her face. *So damn hot.* She'd kill for a glass of water, or even a sip from a garden hose. And about six ibuprofen or anything else that might dull the pain. She closed her eyes, deciding to rest for just a little while. Maybe that would settle the ache.

Kitten jolted awake. How much time had passed? It could have been hours. Frustrated, angry, and determined, she leaned back and kicked the board she'd loosened earlier. Again. And again, this time with all her might. It pulled free.

Yes! She scooted over to kick the adjoining slat of wood. This one was more stubborn but channeling her fury into her feet soon disconnected the board from its support. Once she shifted both boards, the space was almost big enough for her to squeeze through. She backed up, inhaled deeply, and smashed her foot against the first board. It broke free.

Panting from exertion and the heat, Kitten squirmed her body into the narrow open space, shoulders, then torso, then hips, tumbling free

of the building and down a hill she hadn't realized was there. Stopping
the freefall wasn't easy with her busted wrist and tied hands. She felt
every root and rock poking and scratching as her body rolled and
rolled, not stopping until she collided with a tree.

Then all she knew was blackness.

CHAPTER THIRTY-THREE

Lillian studied the spreadsheet displayed on her laptop. Revenues looked good—Jefe should be pleased. The weekend seemed to be going brilliantly; Jefe had secured a vote on a transportation bill from one guest for a friend and obtained a defense contract worth two million for a business associate. Amassing these favors was his preferred currency, and they served him well. Few turned away when he called in a debt.

Onyx appeared in the doorway, dressed in a yellow dashiki and gold hoop earrings large enough to be wrist bangles. Beaded bracelets covered both wrists. "Have you seen Kitten?"

"No. Why?" Lillian closed the laptop.

"Nobody's seen her since early this morning when she went for a run."

"She wasn't at breakfast?"

Onyx shook her head.

Lillian checked her watch; it was nearly noon. She shook her head in frustration. Her girls didn't simply disappear, though Kitten had that history. Still, how would she possibly escape the compound? The fence was electric, set to do serious damage. The gate was manned by a heavily armed security team. Besides, Kitten had seemed very sincere when she promised she wouldn't run. Something else must have happened.

"We've got to find her." Lillian reached in her desk drawer for a set of walkie-talkies, tossing one to Onyx. Lillian slipped off the stilettos she had on and retrieved some sneakers from her desk drawer. As she exited the office, she heard a male voice booming from Jefe's office.

"Where is the girl?"

It was Vasily. Lillian drew a deep breath and rapped lightly on the door frame. "Good morning."

The large man pivoted, pointing a finger at her. "You. Where is the girl from last night? I was told I'd have her this morning."

Jefe shot her a look that sent ice through her veins. "Lillian?"

"I apologize, Vasily. We certainly don't want to keep you waiting. Kitten went for a run and, well, we don't know what happened, but I assure you we will find her momentarily."

Jefe guided him toward the door. "In the meantime, we have other girls, don't we Lil?"

"Of course. Shall I bring one to you?"

He pursed his blubbery lips. "I want the girl! I have business I can take care of. Bring her to me when you find her."

"Certainly." She forced a smile as he pushed past her and stormed up the stairs.

Jefe came closer. "What the hell? Did she run again?"

"How could she? No. Something else is detaining her."

"She better turn up. I can't have Vasily suspecting anything or it'll screw up a sizeable deal we're working on. Do you understand?"

"Of course. We will find her."

"You'd better."

Lillian found Onyx and sent her with the other girls to search the yard and the area near the helipad. She headed straight for the running trail, starting where it ended behind the kitchen.

The sun throbbed overhead. Lillian wiped her forehead and looped around the pool, past the gardens, toward the greenhouse. No sign of Kitten. Woods flanked her as she moved farther from Jefe's place. They were familiar to her. The old-growth pines that provided soft needles for her footfall. The scraggly oaks needing to be thinned. The smaller mimosas waving their feathery leaves as she passed.

Kitten wasn't on this trail.

The notion that Kitten had escaped niggled at Lillian. Had she misjudged her? What if Kitten actually got away? Especially this critical weekend? Jefe would kill her.

Lillian developed a relationship with the kid. Maybe she didn't quite trust her, but she knew Kitten wasn't stupid enough to leave at this critical time. Security was too tight. The stakes too high. The consequences too horrific.

She picked up her pace, scanning the trees and the path ahead. As she approached the toolshed, something off the trail caught her attention. An animal? Something sprawled—like an injured dog. Or a coyote. Should she have brought her pepper spray? As she inched closer, she saw it wasn't an animal.

"Dear God. Kitten?" She rushed to the girl.

Kitten lay on her side, her elbows in the pine needles, her hands bound together. Leaves and bits of grass peppered her hair. A scrape across her right cheek dripped blood. A bandana gripped her chin— had it been used to gag her?

Was she dead? "Kitten!" Lillian shook her with more force than she probably should have. Sluggish blue eyes blinked open. "What happened? Who did this to you?" Lillian demanded.

Kitten looked dazed. When she lifted her hands, Lillian saw the lumps of swelling around her right wrist.

"Jesus." She went to work on the hay rope knots. As careful as she tried to be, she felt Kitten shudder in pain. "I'm sorry, I'm sorry," she whispered, working as fast as she could. Finally, the bindings broke free.

As Kitten let out a sigh of relief, Lillian slid a fingernail into the bandana tie and pulled it loose. Kitten wiped her face with the rag.

"Any other injuries?"

Kitten squinted as though not quite comprehending.

"Your head?"

The girl glanced toward the toolshed. "Fell down the hill. Hit a tree."

"Is that how you hurt your arm?"

She shook her head. "Lito."

"He tied you up?"

"Him. Gunner. They caught me listening to a conversation. Locked me in the toolshed."

Lillian swallowed her fury. *How dare they hurt this girl?* She wasn't their concern. *She's under my supervision.* "Let's get you up."

With a gentle touch, she helped Kitten stand and guided her toward the trail. Kitten moved unsteadily, her breath shallow and rapid. Poor kid had to be dying of thirst. How long had she been locked in that small, dank space?

"Besides your wrist and head, any other place hurting?"

"Think I busted a rib or two."

Lillian adjusted her hold on Kitten and wished she could call an ambulance. The arm looked bad—the hand cocked at a strange angle. The broken ribs could puncture a lung. A head injury might pose all kinds of problems.

"I'm supposed to be with my guest this afternoon." Kitten spoke in a raspy voice.

"Don't worry about that. We'll give him to a different girl."

It seemed to take a year but finally, the house came in view. Behind the kitchen, Lito and Gunner unloaded trays of food that would be lunch for the guests. When Kitten spotted them, she froze.

"It's okay," Lillian said.

"No, it's not." Kitten shuddered, her voice angry. "They said they were coming back to kill me. I caught them talking about somebody betraying Jefe. They said it was you."

"Me? Jesus." Had they gone to Jefe with their accusations? She looked at the injured girl, unsure what her next step should be. She grabbed the two-way radio from her pocket. "Onyx? I have her. Meet me behind the kitchen. Bring my purse. And a bottle of cold water. Don't tell anyone."

A few minutes later, Onyx hurried through the backdoor, Lillian's clutch and the water in her hand. When she spotted Kitten, her black eyes widened. "Oh my God."

"I can't bring her inside like this. Give her the water."

Onyx opened the bottle and handed it to her. Kitten guzzled as though near death from dehydration. "Easy there. Don't want to make yourself sick."

Kitten pulled the bottle away, her eyes closed, her head lolling back as though she might slip into unconsciousness again. Did she have a brain injury?

Lillian tightened her grip on the kid. She could be seriously injured. Lillian would NOT lose another girl. But what were her options? She thought about the social worker—Georgia Thayer. She'd helped Lillian when she needed it and been very discreet. Maybe she'd do the same for Kitten. But it was a risk—a huge risk.

Kitten started to sag, as though her legs could no longer support her.

"Shit. Help me get her to my car."

Sandwiching Kitten between them, they shuffled toward the garage where the Thunderbird waited. "What will you do?" Onyx opened the door and coaxed Kitten inside.

"Kitten was supposed to be with Vasily. He cannot see her like this. Nobody can," Lillian said.

"Ratana's guest left this morning. I can pair her with Vasily."

Lillian looked doubtful. "He had a strong interest in Kitten. Have Ratana dress very young. If he asks, say Kitten fell and hurt her arm and we're getting her tended to."

"How will you do that?"

"Good question." Lillian climbed in the car and turned to Kitten, who'd leaned back in the seat and closed her eyes.

"Kitten? You still with me?"

Groggy eyes blinked open. "Sorry. Feel a little . . . muddled." She looked down at the swollen arm cradled in the other hand. "Where are you taking me?"

She started the car, positioning the vents to point at the girl. "I'm going to get you help. This is going to be tricky. You have to do exactly as I say."

She nodded.

"When we go by security, I need you to hunch down." She pointed the Thunderbird toward the gate and blew through it like a bird escaping a cage.

CHAPTER THIRTY-FOUR

I had just finished with a thorny discharge—an alcoholic who'd finished his third try with detox, and his skeptical wife who reluctantly let him come home. I gave him a list of AA meetings and he promised to attend one that night. "It will be your lifeline," I had stressed, and I put his odds at staying sober at fifty-fifty. Odds of staying married? Less.

When my pager shimmied on the desk, I read the number and dialed the ER.

"There's a lady here with a teenager. She's asked for you."

"On my way."

The ER was surprisingly quiet. The nursing tech pointed to the interview room where a woman with auburn hair sat with her back to the door. The lanky girl who rested on the gurney looked scraped and battered, clutching an injured hand.

"I'm Georgia Thayer. How can I help you?"

The woman turned around and I recognized her immediately. "Lillian?" Odd to see her so soon after she'd rescued Elias and me outside The Orchid Estate.

"Georgia. I hate to bother you, but I need a favor. A kind of huge one."

"Okay."

She approached the girl. "This is Amanda. She's on staff at the Estate. She was rollerblading and had a bad fall."

I crossed over to Amanda, wondering if that was her real name, and took in the swollen forehead, the scraped cheek, and the large knot over her wrist. The bits of grass and leaves in her stringy hair. How she contrasted with Lillian's smooth, unblemished skin. Heavy, but artfully applied, eye make-up. Immaculate tailored crimson suit, white satin blouse, cleavage bubbling up. "Amanda, has a doctor checked you out?"

She nodded.

"He's sending her for X-rays," Lillian answered. "Problem is, well, we don't have insurance."

"You should. How old are you, Amanda?"

"She's nineteen."

"Nineteen." *Not likely.* I got it, though. I'd had to pretend to be an adult during much of my teen years. "Can I call your parents for you?"

I kept my focus on the girl, taking in the sunken posture, the dirty hair, and clothes. The look of abandonment, much like Lillian had appeared those years ago.

The girl looked at Lillian who answered, "They're up north."

Right. I'd probe further once I got the kid to trust me.

"As I said, she doesn't have insurance, but we can pay cash if it's not too much. Could you tell the admissions clerk that? And no, she doesn't have a photo ID. Something we'll remedy soon, I promise."

"So, Amanda. What do you do at the Estate?"

"She's part of the kitchen-wait staff. New though. Still getting used to things. Look—can we get her X-rayed or whatever the hell we need to do? I have to get back."

It bothered me that Lillian insisted on speaking for the girl. What I knew about the Estate, like Jefe's other enterprises, was that workers were trafficked. Was this kid being sexually exploited? "Tell you what." I turned to Lillian. "It will take a few hours for her to get x-rayed. There may be other tests to run—the lump on her head looks nasty. Why don't you head on back to the Estate and we'll call you when we're done."

Her heavily lined eyes widened. "I'm not just leaving her here."

"You can trust me. I won't let anything happen to her."

"No. Absolutely not. I'll wait."

I shrugged. "Suit yourself. I'll be back in a second."

Pushing past the curtains, I found the resident who'd examined Amanda. A kid in his late twenties with thick brown hair and Harry Potter glasses. He suspected a fractured ulna, a broken rib, and a possible concussion, he told me. "That's not all," I replied. "I'm thinking she's been sexually trafficked. Can we check her out for STDs?"

His eyebrows arched. "Jesus. Poor kid. You calling the police?"

Good question. "I need more information."

When Amanda got wheeled down to X-ray, I found Lillian sitting in the back of the waiting area and planted myself beside her. "Amanda reminds me of when I first met you. It's nice to see you so strong and healthy."

Lillian let out a sad laugh that sounded more like a groan. "You met me at my lowest point. Thanks, by the way. For helping me. But I'm not that girl anymore. My life is good right now."

I gave her a slow nod, unsure how to proceed. "Is life good for Amanda?"

"Very." Lillian met my stare dead-on, as though determined to paint the right picture.

"She looks too thin. Maybe a little undernourished. And she doesn't look eighteen."

"Everybody says that! Look. She came from a shitty home like I did. She was on the streets for a while, like I was, but now she has a home and a job."

I watched her very closely as I posed my next question. "And a paycheck?"

Lillian visibly drew a breath. Her tell, I suspected. "Yes. And a paycheck."

I let a few minutes of silence do their work. Lillian didn't flinch.

I pushed harder. "Tell you what. I don't think she's nineteen. I don't think she's legally employed. If she was, she'd have ID. And I don't think her injuries happened in a fall.

"What goes on at the Estate? If you and Amanda are in a . . . situation . . . you don't think you can escape, I'm telling you that you can. I can help you if you let me."

Lillian stroked the arm of her chair with a beautifully manicured hand. "You don't know me, Georgia Thayer. Whatever it is that you're assuming is wrong. There is no situation. I'm a businesswoman building a successful business and trying to help girls like me get a fair chance at life. You're a social worker, for God's sake. You should be glad that there are people like me out there!" She pursed her cherry-red lips in a flash of indignation.

"I am glad. Mostly, though, I'm glad you're still alive. I'm here whenever you need my help."

"I don't," she said quickly. Then added, "But thank you."

I entered the triage area and found the resident who'd treated Amanda. He verified an isolated fractured ulna and planned to refer her to an orthopedist for casting. I explained her financial situation. "No way she's keeping that appointment. Can't you cast it here?"

He mulled it. "I just finished my ortho rotation."

"Excellent. You know we have to get creative in the ER. It's part of the gig. So is doing favors for colleagues."

"Like?" He looked skeptical.

"You need to find a reason to admit her. She banged her head, so maybe we need to put her under observation. That'll give me some time to get what I need for the police.

"No way this kid is nineteen. She's a minor. We can't just turn her loose back to that life."

He rolled his eyes at me. "They warned me about you, you know. Said you were tenacious."

I grinned. "That's unfair. I'm more . . . persistent. Determined. Maybe stubborn on a bad day."

"Yeah, okay. Don't need to throw the whole thesaurus at me."

CHAPTER THIRTY-FIVE

Kitten closed her eyes against the noises. Clicks. Scraping sounds. Ka-thumps that came as rhythmically as a clock. Voices that she didn't recognize, sort of far away. Someone coughing. A laugh.

She didn't like this place. She opened her eyes to a white ceiling with a fluorescent light. She could see a cast on her wrist. A pole held a plastic sack with a tube snaking down to a needle in her arm that pinched. She felt blurry, like that time her mom gave her too much Robitussin. Her mouth was as dry as a desert. At the sound of approaching footsteps, she closed her eyes. She wasn't ready to talk to anyone yet. They would ask questions she didn't know how to answer.

The sound of scraping startled her, like someone dragging a chair.

"Amanda? You in there?"

Her eyes blinked open to find the woman, Georgia, sitting beside her. "Where's Lillian?" she asked.

"In the waiting room. I'll get her in a moment. First, I wanted to chat with you."

Kitten pulled the sheet up, tucking her good hand in its folds, dreading what was coming.

"How are you feeling?"

She heaved a shoulder up. "Okay, I guess. A little wobbly."

"That's the medicine. It won't last long. I need to go over some things with you."

"What things?"

"How did you hurt your wrist?"

"Lillian told you. I fell when I was rollerblading."

"I thought you were on a skateboard."

She licked her dry lips. Is that what Lillian said? She wished she could clear her muddled thinking. "No. I was rollerblading."

"Okay. I got confused."

Kitten didn't believe it for a second. This woman was trying to catch her in a lie, and she didn't like being treated that way. When Lillian had driven her to the emergency room, she'd given Kitten clear instructions. "You cannot trust anyone, do you understand? If you talk, Jefe will find out. Nowhere is beyond its reach. There will be hell to pay. Not just for you. For me, too." She'd slapped a burner phone into Kitten's hand and told her that if they got separated, to dial the number programmed in it. *Where's my phone?*

Georgia poured Kitten a cup of water and handed it to her. "Can you tell me where you live?"

"I'm sure Lillian told you."

"She said you were at the Estate. What's it like?"

"It's nice. Very pretty. Lots of room." She directed her gaze away from Georgia to the curtains that opened to escape. She wished Lillian would appear. More than that, she didn't want Lillian to think she was telling this Georgia woman anything that would get her in trouble.

"Who else lives there?"

"A few friends."

"Friends? Tell me about them."

She smoothed the sheet over her stomach. "It doesn't matter. Can you get Lillian for me?"

"In a second. She's with the clerk filling out some forms for indigent care. We need to keep you overnight because of the concussion."

Kitten shook her head so hard it felt like a sledgehammer pounding on her skull. "Ow."

"Easy, there. You don't want to make yourself dizzy."

"I can't stay here. I have plans . . . for later."

"Plans?" *Right, with a john.* "You need to rest, Amanda. Your body's been through a lot. Just twenty-four hours. I'm afraid your doctor is insisting."

Had Lillian agreed to that? She doubted it. But maybe she could use the time away. Maybe this was how she could escape. She could play along with Georgia for now and sneak out as soon as the sun went down.

One problem with that plan. Lillian. She'd taken a huge risk bringing her here. If Kitten ran, it would play into Lito's theory about Lillian. Jefe would have Lillian killed.

"I can see you're scared. My guess is you've been living afraid for a while. If you'll let me, I can help you." She reached for Kitten's good hand, but Kitten jerked it back. "Okay. You don't trust me yet. And honestly, why should you? But sometimes you have to take a risk. You may feel trapped, but I can help you climb out."

The woman looked sincere, but Kitten knew expressions didn't mean a damn thing. People could pretend to be anything, then screw you over first chance they got. No, she had to bust out of here and take off. She'd be gone before anyone knew she was missing.

"Where is she?" Lillian found Georgia in the hallway after she'd followed a family out of the waiting room. The nursing assistant let them into the ER bays and Lillian went directly to Kitten's to find it empty.

"Amanda?"

"Yes, Amanda. Jesus. I have to get her back." She didn't like Kitten out of her sight for this long.

"We admitted her. Just overnight. There's no reason to be concerned."

"Absolutely not." Panicked she said, "Amanda is leaving with me right now."

Georgia smiled. "That's not happening. I'm sorry, Lillian. Truly I am. For whatever it is you've gotten yourself into. For whatever it is that you're terrified of. But Amanda is not an adult and isn't ready to be medically released. And if you try to take her, security will escort you from the building."

Perspiration beaded on her forehead.

"Do you need to sit down?"

"I need . . . I need Amanda."

"And you can have her. Come back tomorrow morning. If there are no complications, she should be ready to go around ten or so."

Georgia gripped her arm and guided her out of the ED. At the door, two uniformed security guards seemed to be watching. Or maybe she was just being paranoid. She was very good at that.

Seeing no other option, she hurried through the waiting room and out to her car.

Lillian pulled her phone out. She'd ignored the seven texts from Jefe, escalating in anger as the afternoon went on. She faced a deadly shitstorm. Seeing no alternative, she dialed his number. "It's me."

"Where the hell are you? Do you have Kitten? What the fuck is going on?" His voice rumbled.

"I'm sorry, Jefe. I screwed up. I thought I was doing the right thing and—"

"What did you do?" The growl replaced, by a roar.

"Lito and Gunner hurt Kitten. She had some bad injuries. So I brought her to get some medical help. I—"

"You did what?"

"I knew somebody. Thought I could trust them to be discreet, but it went to shit. Now Kitten's been admitted at Columbia General. They won't release her till tomorrow."

"Don't you dare leave without her, Lillian. Who knows what she'll tell them."

"They figured out she's a minor. They have security people on her."

Deadly silence. Fear pulsed through her. What were her options? Drive the car as fast as she could away from Columbia? How far was out of Jefe's reach? It would take interstellar travel to truly escape him.

"What can I do?" she whispered.

"Come home immediately. Do not stop for any reason."

"But what about Kitten?"

"None of your concern anymore. I'll put my men on retrieving her. I'd better see you in my office in thirty minutes."

"Okay, Jefe." She clicked off.

CHAPTER THIRTY-SIX

Kitten awoke in a different bed and a different room: yellow walls, a small window, a TV suspended by the door. Why was she here? Oh, Georgia had told her she'd be admitted. Why hadn't Lillian prevented it?

She wore a skimpy hospital gown tied in the back. Her arm throbbed; her fingers were swollen like sausages. Where were her clothes? She spotted a sink by the open door to the hallway. Beside it, a cupboard—maybe it held her belongings. The tubing that ran from a needle on her hand to a plastic sack above her made moving awkward, but she managed to shift her legs off the bed and stand. A little light-headed, but she stayed upright. Clutching the pole, she maneuvered around the bed to the sink area, but a wave of dizziness made her clutch the counter to keep from toppling over.

"Hey, are you alright?" The woman's voice came from the hallway.

"Huh?"

She nudged open the door. "You look like you're about to collapse. Should I get a nurse or something?" She wasn't hospital staff. She wore a gown like Kitten's, though she had matching pants. She looked to be in her thirties, with black hair fraying from a ponytail, and thick eyebrows that could use a trim from Dulce.

"I'm okay. Just a little unsteady."

"Maybe you should go back to bed." The woman moved closer, offering a hand to help, which Kitten declined. When she reached the mattress, the stranger pulled back the sheet and helped her reposition the pole. "Here ya go. What's your name?"

"Amanda."

"I'm Marilyn."

Kitten wasn't sure what to make of her. Marilyn took a seat in a chair as if planning to stay for a while and Kitten didn't know what to make of that, either.

"Hope you don't mind. I'm dying to talk to someone who isn't sticking a needle in me. But I won't overstay my welcome."

Kitten nodded, eyeing the door. She needed to get out of there. Was she strong enough to escape?

"You're here for a busted arm?"

"Yeah. Just overnight though."

"Lucky. I've been here a week. Seven *loonngg* days. Heart stuff. And other issues." Marilyn swallowed as though not wanting to say more.

Kitten had no intention of asking. She hoped to end this little chat session soon, but the other patient seemed lonely, and something about her amused Kitten. How odd to talk with someone from the outside world.

"A few things you need to know. One, ask if you can go to the cafeteria instead of having a tray brought to you. They don't advertise it, but it's sometimes allowed, and the food is much better down there.

"Two. The head nurse on this floor is a brute. Don't get on her bad side, which I did when I asked her to print something I need for restarting my disability check. You'd have thought I'd asked her for the keys to her car."

Kitten smiled. "Okay. Don't piss off nursing. Got it."

"The doctors are good. Yours will have to write an order about the cafeteria though. Maybe I can smuggle you something when I go down for dinner."

She hoped not to be here for dinner, but she said nothing. A loud noise in the hallway sent a tremor through Kitten.

"Hey! Easy there. You look like you heard gunfire."

"Who is it? Can you go look?" Kitten tried to tamp down her panic.

"Okay." Marilyn stood and peered out. "Ah. Just as I thought. The clumsy nursing assistant dropped some kind of metal thing. Probably a torture devise for irritating patients. Like me," she added with a smile.

"That's all?" Kitten let out a breath.

"That's all. I promise. Jumpy much?"

"Sorry. There are some people . . . I'd rather not run into."

"Okay. There's a story there. Maybe one day you'll tell me."

A muffled buzz came from somewhere. "You have a cell phone?" Marilyn asked.

It had to be the phone Lillian had given her. "Would you mind seeing if it's in my pocket? My clothes are in there." She pointed to the cupboard.

Marilyn found her pants, fumbled in the pocket, and brought her the ringing flip phone. "Old school like me. I like it."

Kitten held it to her chest, not wanting to answer it in front of company.

"Okay. I'm going to give you some privacy. But if you don't mind, I'll stop back by later."

"That would be okay," Kitten said. As soon as Marilyn left, she pressed *answer*.

"Kitten? Are you okay?" Lillian's voice sounded off. Breathy. Tired.

"Are you?" Kitten asked.

"Uh. That's questionable."

"What did they do to you?"

"I don't have much time. Look, Jefe is sending some men after you."

"What do you mean?"

A long silence before Lillian answered. "Lito and Gunner are on their way. Lito has a cousin who works in the hospital kitchen who can help them sneak in."

She closed her eyes against this news. Another few beats of silence, then Lillian said, "I'm sorry, Kitten. If you can get away, do it. I hope it's not too late."

"What about you?"

A sour laugh. "I thought I could talk myself out of any situation. Turns out, I was wrong. Lose this phone, Kitten. Jefe will be able to track it."

Kitten clicked off. She couldn't let them find her. Out the window, the hazy gray light of dusk was settling down over the city. Good. She just had to escape the hospital and slip out into the darkness.

She wiggled the fingers protruding from the end of the cast. Even that bit of movement made the busted wrist ache, but she'd have to ignore it. With gentle force, she pulled the needle from her other hand. Fat red drops of blood oozed, which she blotted with a paper towel. She noticed some bandages by the sink and used her teeth to open one. After her third attempt she got it to stick. Now for the clothes.

She couldn't move fast. Bending over made her head hurt, and everything made her wrist scream out, but within a few minutes, she was dressed. After slipping the phone into the trash and extra bandages in her pocket, she eased out the door.

CHAPTER THIRTY-SEVEN

When I got to my office, a pink message slip from Lou Michaels had been taped to the door. "Come to Ben Reeder's room around five o'clock? Need to talk to you." It was already ten till five, so I headed straight there.

Ben was deep in the slumber of the thoroughly tranquilized. The cut on his forehead, which had been sutured, threatened to leave a wavy scar over his brow. An inch of hair had been shaved off close to his ear. I sat by his bed, remembering the times I'd run my hand through that unruly mess of curls. The times we'd argued about politics and laugh about our crazy jobs. The nights I'd lay beside him in his bed, listening to the steady rumble of his snores, a lullaby that helped me sleep. I had loved him then. Maybe a part of me still did.

He stirred, blinking himself awake, and scanned the room as though trying to get his bearings.

"Hey there."

When his gaze found my face, his lips quirked into a crooked smile. "George."

"How do you feel?"

"Like roadkill. Make that week-old roadkill." He licked his chapped lips. "And maybe a little hungry."

"Hungry is a good sign." An unopened fruit cup rested on his bed table, probably a leftover from lunch. I opened it and handed it to him. "FYI, you can expect me to throttle you once you're feeling better. I can't believe you got yourself into this mess."

"Hello, Pot. Meet Kettle." He stabbed a peach chunk with his plastic fork.

His door opened and Lou Michaels stepped into the room, accompanied by a pale, blonde-haired guy in a crew cut as though he'd stepped out of an episode of *Leave it to Beaver.*

I crossed to the other side of Ben's bed. "Y'all need to keep this short so Ben can get his rest."

The new guy said, "I'm Agent Warren, FBI field operative. Just have a few questions."

Ben turned to Lou. "Feds? Seriously? What's going on?"

The agent and Lou looked at each other like they were in a silent conversation. Then Warren said, "I'm lead on a task force looking into human trafficking in South Carolina. But that's not for release to the media."

Lou said, "Ben, can you tell us what you remember about the assault?"

Ben lowered his fork. "After I talked to Georgia, I tried to call you, Lou. Then I headed out to the Connor place. Didn't even get to where they kept the people. Some big guy intercepted me. Given how pissed he was at my questions, I knew we'd struck a nerve." He paused. I handed him a cup of water.

"Thanks." He slurped through the straw. "I didn't plan to push any further until I had backup, but this story looked to be huge. So, I decided to try the massage place."

"What time did you go there?" Lou asked.

"I don't know. Six, maybe? I parked and banged on the door. At first, nobody answered, but then a very annoyed older woman opened the door. She said they were closed. I started to ask a couple of questions when a man came from the back—some Latino dude with muscles like one of those gym rats.

"Anyway, he told her to lock the door. I tried to get around her, but he pulled a gun on me. Next thing I knew, there were two of them. Thug one smashed my head into the counter. Thug two had a metal pipe that he smashed into my leg. God, the pain was brutal. Guess I blacked out.

"Then I woke up here."

"They could have killed you." That stark reality twisted inside me. Ben could be dead right now because of what I told him.

"Do you remember any details about the two men?" Lou asked him.

"They spoke in Spanish. The stocky guy ordered the leaner guy around."

Ben was fading. His eyes drooped shut. I removed the half-eaten fruit cup from his limp hand and slid the table back.

"He's had enough for now."

"We're not done," the agent said.

"I don't care," I replied.

He eyed Lou as though expecting agreement. I gave Lou a look of my own.

"Let's let him rest," Lou said.

I ushered them out the door. Once we reached the hallway, Lou hesitated, head cocked to the side as he looked at me. "I think I was a little hard on you yesterday."

I fixed my glare on the agent. "Did you ever meet my sister?"

Warren looked at Lou, who nodded at him. "This isn't for public knowledge, okay? We've been investigating a sex trafficking ring for the past six months. Your sister came to us and told us what she'd been trying to do. It was at a very sensitive part of our operation, and we couldn't disclose much. We tried to get her to pull out, but she was stubborn. Kind of like you, I'm starting to see."

Lou said, "Local police haven't been involved. I knew nothing about their investigation until, well, yesterday."

I eyed the two men. "Might be smart for y'all to talk to each other, don't you think?"

The agent nodded. "We are coordinating with them now. You can let us take things from here, Ms. Thayer. And all this must be kept confidential. Do you understand me?"

"No argument here. But when you find out who killed my sister, I better be the first call you make."

CHAPTER THIRTY-EIGHT

Kitten thought back to her workouts in the trailer. Each time, she'd gotten stronger, able to handle more sit-ups and push-ups. More minutes jogging in place. She needed that same strength now. She had been preparing for this.

The hallway outside her door looked endless. She had to avoid the nurses' station, so she headed the other way, passed the main elevators, and punched the button for the service one. Leaning against the wall, she listened for the muted dings, and finally, the doors parted. A woman in scrubs pushing a cleaning cart came out.

Kitten straightened, praying the woman wouldn't approach her. She wheeled the cart past her and up the hall.

Inside the elevator, Kitten pushed the *G* button because she had to avoid the main entrance. After a direct descent to the garage, Kitten stepped out into a sea of parked cars. In the corner, three people huddled together over lit cigarettes. Kitten moved in the opposite direction, toward a sliver of daylight that she hoped was her exit to the outside. To safety.

Steps. A dozen of them. She clutched the rail and pulled herself up, one then the next, counting as she went, ignoring the tug of her stitches, the burn of her ribs, and the throbbing of her casted wrist. *Ten. Eleven. Twelve.* Finally. An open portal to the world.

Where should I go? She had no money. She didn't know Columbia and she sure as hell wasn't going back to the Estate. *Poor Lillian. Probably dead.*

With slow, painful steps, she moved out of the parking area to the sidewalk. A street sign at the corner read *Sumter.* Four lanes of traffic zoomed by. She turned right, for no other reason than the sun wouldn't be in her eyes, and started a slow trek away from the hospital.

She kept one eye on the traffic whizzing by. She could recognize Lito's beat-up car. The white van would be harder to distinguish—it was old with a few dents, but she'd never paid attention to the license plate. When a light-colored van pulled into the lane closest to her, she scurried off the sidewalk and hid behind a tree.

Her heart hammered against her bruised ribs. If it was Lito or Roman, no way she could run away from them. If it was Jefe, he'd kill her for sure.

She braved a look; the van sped on by.

A few shaky exhales and she was moving again. She didn't know where she was going, but once she got far enough away, she'd hitchhike. Someone would pick her up, and she'd ask to go north. All that mattered was getting as far away as possible.

Lillian sat on her sofa and waited, unsure what, exactly, she was waiting for. There'd be no talking her way out of whatever Jefe had planned for her. No more tricks up her sleeve.

Jefe had let her handle the afternoon cocktail hour, and, after she'd changed her clothes and touched up her makeup, she'd worked especially hard to make sure each guest had whatever they needed. Vasily asked her about Kitten and had not hidden his disappointment, and outright anger, that she had not returned.

"She had a fall and broke her wrist. There are other injuries, too. She won't be available to you for the rest of the weekend."

Onyx brought him Ratana, dressed in a jumper and wearing little makeup, and he'd begrudgingly accepted her when Lillian offered him another weekend with any girl of his choosing. When he asked, "will Kitten be an option?" she'd smiled vaguely and replied, "We certainly hope so."

Taking Kitten to the hospital had been a mammoth mistake. Lillian felt like an idiot for trusting Georgia but keeping Kitten at the Estate would only get her killed. What the hell were Lito and Gunner up to? Of course, if they wanted to convince Jefe that Lillian was the betrayer, she'd played right into their hands.

The gentle rap at her door certainly was not Jefe. She let Onyx come in. "Everyone's settled in for the evening."

"That's good. Is Vasily happier?"

"Ratana's trying very hard. But she is no Kitten."

"No, she's not. Come in and have a seat." Lillian welcomed the company. The distraction. Anything to keep her from thinking about her own fate. "Did Lito and Gunner find Kitten?"

"Not yet. I fear what they will do to her when they find her."

"Do the guests know anything's going on?"

"No. I promise. We have kept them entertained and content. We told them Kitten sprained her arm badly while on a morning run."

"Well done." Lillian felt a surge of pride. Onyx had taken command and managed the crisis with her usual quiet charm. "Do the other girls know?"

"Yes. Javier's warned them to keep their mouths shut. He didn't need to, though."

Lillian crossed to the small bar and poured each of them a glass of red wine. Onyx's eyes widened as she accepted the glass. Lillian never served anyone but Jefe and herself in this room. She lifted the glass in a toast. "To you, Onyx. For keeping the ship going."

"I learned from the best." She held up her glass, took a small sip, and placed it on the table. "We are—the girls and I, I mean—we are concerned about you."

Lillian took a large swallow. "So am I."

"Is there anything we can do to help?"

"I wish. No, this is for me to handle." Another sip, then another. When Onyx left, she'd drain the bottle.

Her cell resting on the table stuttered, signaling a message from Jefe. She closed her eyes, wishing she didn't have to reply, but knew she had no choice. She said to Onyx, "He's on his way here."

"I must leave you then." Onyx carried her glass to the sink before approaching the door, where she hesitated. "He depends on you, Lillian. Perhaps he won't be as harsh as you fear."

If only that were true. She stepped closer to Onyx, her prodigy. The closest she had to a confidant. "I'm just glad that— if the worst happens—I can count on you to look after our girls."

Jefe arrived five minutes later, Javier close behind him. His presence surprised, and worried, Lillian because if Jefe planned to kill her, he wouldn't do it himself, and Javier was his most trusted henchman. She stood still as they entered her room, imagining bolting from it, hurling herself into the Thunderbird, blasting through the Estate front gate to freedom.

There would be no freedom for her.

Jefe rounded her, looking her up and down, his expression strangely sad. His hand came up to her face, brushing her cheek with calloused knuckles. "I've counted on you for so long."

"You can count on me. You know that, Jefe."

"I remember when you first came to me. You were lost."

"I remember, too."

"I never thought—" he dropped his hand, his face hardening. This was the same Jefe who tried to choke her.

"Do I get a chance to explain myself?"

"I don't know. Javi, do we want to listen to Lillian's excuses?"

Javier sat on the sofa, his arms crossed, watching. "Why not?"

Lillian told them all of it. About Kitten stumbling on Lito and Gunner as they discussed their belief about Lillian. About the damage done to Kitten when they locked her in the tool shed, complicated by her rough escape. About how there was nowhere to go on the Estate that was safe from Lito and Gunner, and her need to protect their guests from this underbelly of the operation. "She was badly hurt. Her wrist. Ribs. Her head. She kept losing consciousness. We didn't need another dead girl, Jefe. So I took a calculated risk to get her tended to. I had plenty of cash and a connection at the hospital. I certainly didn't think they would keep her."

"Yet they did." Jefe looked over at Javier. "Tell her about the woman Lillian picked to help them."

Javier swiped at his forehead before speaking. "We had a problem last month. A woman snooping around. Her name was Peyton Ribault. Got too close to our operation and that proved dangerous for her."

"After they found her body, another woman has been prying. She's why we had to close most of our outside operations."

Jefe stepped closer to her, his breath like steam against her face. "She's Peyton Ribault's sister. Her name is Georgia Thayer."

Lillian closed her eyes and wished she could be somewhere else— anywhere. How could she be so stupid? There would be no talking herself out of this situation. No clever maneuver to get Jefe to let her have another chance. She should have run when she had the chance.

Lillian thought of the time when she was nine years old and they'd adopted a black dog named Martin. He'd followed her to the door when she left for school, and he waited in the same spot when came home. Her mother used to say she could burn the house down and that damn dog would still be doing his job in flames.

Lillian looked at Jefe. His house was on fire, and here they sat.

A pounding on her door interrupted them. Jefe looked at Javier, annoyed. Javier took his time about responding to the banging. When he turned the knob Roman was standing on the other side. "She got away."

"Kitten?"

"Yeah. Lito just called. Found her room but she'd bolted. They're driving around looking for her now."

"Shit." Jefe ran a hand through his hair, looking cornered. He could never stand it when someone was out of his control. "Javier, secure her somewhere," he cocked a thumb toward Lillian.

"Sure, boss."

"We'll deal with her later. I want every man scouring the neighborhood around the hospital. Kitten's on foot and injured. She won't get far."

"Will do."

"We don't get her before the cops, we're done. This fucking house of cards blown to bits. Make sure the men understand that."

CHAPTER THIRTY-NINE

I leaned back in my desk chair, trying to stretch the crick in my neck. My nerves felt tauter than piano wire, despite the dose of meds I'd downed with my afternoon coffee.

"Catch me up." Clancy said from the office doorway. She wore a linen jacket and skirt that meant she'd been in a meeting off-campus. Our hospital clothes tend to be more casual. "How you doing?"

With other people, I lied. But never with Clancy. That was the deal. "I'm holding on. Tired. Sad. Kind of in survival mode. Today I'm tackling this." I pointed to a stack of progress summaries I'd handwritten to scan into the medical record.

"Wow. You sure you're taking your meds?" Clancy's smile made me laugh, which felt both strange and good. She cocked a thumb toward the stairs. "By the way, I was just on the Med unit. I saw security and nursing going into the room of one of your patients."

It had to be Amanda. I felt a flush of panic. "Which one?"

"Marilyn Wilder."

"Marilyn? We just moved her there. I better go check on her."

I hurried down the stairs and found Carlos, a security officer, talking on his radio outside Marilyn's new room, which was just a few doors down from Amanda's. Skinny Tiffany stood beside him, shaking her head. A nurse had Marilyn sitting on her bed and was going through what looked like the concussion protocol. "What happened? Did she fall?" I shoved my way into the room.

"She was pushed," Tiffany answered.

The nurse flashed a tiny flashlight into Marilyn's eyes, frowning.

"She confronted two intruders and they knocked her down," Carlos supplied.

"What the hell? Marilyn? Are you okay?" I squatted down so we were eye level. She looked more annoyed than injured but looks can be deceiving.

"I'm fine. Tell him to quit poking at me." She swatted the nurse away.

"Let me talk with her," I said to the nurse. "You can finish up later."

He didn't look happy but complied. I stood, my knees screaming, and sat beside my patient. "Want to tell me what happened?"

"These two men barged into Amanda's room! They looked sketchy, so I asked them what the hell they were doing."

"Wait. You know Amanda?"

"I met her earlier. She's a good kid."

"Can you describe the men?" Carlos asked.

"Skin a little darker than yours. One tall. One not as tall but broad and ripped. Both scary looking. I saw them go into her room. When I talked to Amanda earlier, she was jumpy. Worried somebody would find her. So, when they pushed their way in, I got concerned."

"Is Amanda okay?"

Marilyn shook her head. "She wasn't in there, thank God. But when I said something to the men, they rushed by me, slamming me against the wall as they ran out. I lost my balance and fell."

"We've got people looking for them." Tiffany sighed. "Marilyn, I want to assure you that this kind of thing doesn't happen at Columbia General. You are perfectly safe here."

I guessed Tiffany was worried about the hospital getting sued, good little soldier that she is.

I turned to Carlos. "What about the security cameras?"

"We're checking footage."

Marilyn grabbed my arm. "There's something else."

"What?" I was antsy to go find Amanda, but Marilyn had an urgent look in her eye.

She reached toward her nightstand and handed me a picture that was just like the others she'd drawn of the devil figure. "This. One of the men had this on his T-shirt."

"This face?"

"Yes."

Carlos moved closer and took the sketch from her hand. "That looks just like Diablo Mysterio."

"Who?" I asked.

"Diablo Mysterio. He's a wrestler. Pretty famous in Mexico. Always wears a mask. My nephew has a T-shirt just like this."

Marilyn's eyes widened. "And . . . and I remember more from that night. It's blurry, but when the devil chased me, it was this—a man in this shirt. I was walking around the little lake, and I saw him and another man. There was a car. A gray car."

My sister's car was gray. It was found in that lake. She'd been killed the night Marilyn arrived in our ER.

Marilyn went on. "They were behind the car. They pushed it into the water. I remember thinking that was wrong. And strange. I wanted to tell someone, but they spotted me, and he chased me and—" She spoke in rapid-fire, the memories stoking fear.

"It's okay. You're okay. Sit back on the bed."

"I saw him. I wasn't crazy! Okay, I was a little crazy, but I saw that man and the car. It was *real*." She practically bellowed this last word.

The information roiled inside me. The car had been Peyton's Lexus. Those men had killed her. I had to tell Lou. I said to Marilyn, "Can you let the nurse finish up? He's got a job to do, and we need to be sure you're okay."

She nodded.

"Would you be willing to talk to the police? I think you may have witnessed a very serious crime, but I don't want you doing anything that makes you uncomfortable."

Tiffany's overly sculpted brows shot up. "Your sister?"

I nodded.

"I'll talk to them. But go find Amanda. Tell her men are looking for her," Marilyn insisted.

I left with the nurse and made my way to Amanda's room, only to find it empty. Completely. No clothes, no shoes, no girl. She'd flown the coop. Dammit. I should have stationed an officer outside her door.

Who were the two men? They must have come from the Estate. Did they plan to hurt her? Did they have anything to do with my sister's death?

I gave Carlos Amanda's description and told him she was an endangered teen, something they'd take very seriously. Tiffany hurried off to tell the hospital director.

What if the men found her? They'd killed Peyton. Would Amanda suffer the same fate?

You screwed up. This is your fault, the advisor said.

My thoughts raced. Too much was happening. Marilyn's attack. Amanda's disappearance. Ben upstairs recovering. The dangerous men who might still be in my hospital. Where to start?

Your fault, your fault, your fault. A chant now, loud, bouncing inside my head like it wanted to get out.

Slow deep breaths. Get your act together. One thing at a time. First step, find Clancy, the counselor said. Luck was with me. Clancy sat in her office, growling into her phone, but hung up as soon as she spotted me. "What's wrong?"

I told her everything, disjointed information like water through the floodgate. She listened intently, asked a few questions, then said, "How can I help?"

"Amanda. I don't think that's her real name. We know very little about her, but she's in serious danger. Am I betraying confidentiality if I tell the police?"

Clancy shook her head. "You think she's a minor. Child endangerment trumps just about everything else. They need to be called."

"Probably should have done that before. I was hoping to get her to trust me."

"Always a gamble we take. I think you'd better make the call. You have more info than I do. An injured kid with a broken wrist shouldn't be too hard to spot."

"I need to look for her."

"Call me if you hear anything."

After a quick trip to grab my keys out of my office, I headed out to my car. The day carried a merciless heat, the kind where the sun feels close enough to scald the earth. I hoped Amanda was somewhere cool and comfortable and—most importantly—safe. Before exiting the lot, I put in a call to Lou Michaels.

Voicemail as usual. *"So much to tell you. One of the trafficking victims was in the hospital but left—trying to find her now. Also, we may have a witness to my sister's murder. Call me."* I repeated the last phrase with as much emphasis as I could muster.

Where the hell was he? This guy never answered his damn phone.

I swerved into traffic, scanning the sides of the street for signs of Amanda. *Slow down,* the counselor said.

I nodded and complied.

When my phone rang, I pulled into an auto parts store. "This is Georgia."

"We checked the footage from the security camera," one of the guards told me. "The girl left on her own. The two men showed up about ten minutes after. I'm texting you a still shot of them."

I watched as the grainy photo appeared on my screen; two men, looking menacing, searching for my patient. The taller guy looked very much like one of the guards outside the Estate.

"Outside cameras caught the girl heading toward Harden Street."

"Thanks." Once I got the car pointed south on Harden, traffic picked up, cars whizzing by and blocking my view.

Thehhh—not the counselor this time, but the soft, staticky voice spoke.

"What?" I asked aloud, frustrated as hell.

Thehhhrre. A little closer now, like in another room.

"There? Where?" I scanned the rutted sidewalk and spotted her. There, moving in labored steps along the sidewalk, was a thin, frail-looking girl in a torn T-shirt and stained sweatpants.

"Thank God," I whispered.

Amanda stopped at a lamppost, holding on to the metal and panting. She'd gone maybe a quarter of a mile but looked like she'd run a marathon.

I parked and stepped in front of her. "Hey, there."

"Damn," she whispered. I didn't like her pale color, nor the new dark pockets under her eyes.

"I'm sure glad to see you," I said. "Where are you going?"

She shook her head. Tears emerged.

"Hey, it's okay. Come to my car and we'll talk." I reached for her elbow, moving her slowly toward the car.

She braced her good hand against the car door, declining entry. "I can't go back to the hospital. They'll kill me if I do."

"Easy. The men who came for you are probably long gone by now."

"They'll be back."

An eighteen-wheeler blew past us, sending a blast of hot air. I sucked in a breath as I tried to piece this together. "Okay. Get in the car so we can talk. I won't take you back to the hospital. Not yet anyway."

I opened the car door and helped her sit, then scurried around to the driver's side before she bolted. She was a long way from trusting me now.

"Do you know who those men were?"

She nodded. "Gunner and Lito."

"Last names?"

"I don't know. They're brothers though."

"And they came to the hospital to find you?"

"To kill me."

"How did you know that?"

"I called Lillian. She gave me a burner phone to use."

Another truck rumbled by, my old Civic quaking a little in its wake. "She didn't come back for you?"

The girl shook her head. "I think she's in a lot of trouble for helping me. Jefe doesn't tolerate betrayal."

Jefe. Peyton had talked about him in her tapes. He was the lead trafficker. She wanted to get the girl—Kitten—away from his grasp. "Amanda, do you know someone named Kitten?"

Her eyes widened. "Why do you want to know?"

I drew a breath. Trust worked two ways, and I was about to share something important with no clue as to how she'd handle it.

Tell her, the new voice said.

I pulled out my phone, flipped through some pictures, and landed on my favorite photo of Peyton. "This is—was—my sister."

She took the phone from my hand, eying it with wonder and a glint of sadness. "Peyton. That was her name."

"Right. Did you meet her?"

She nodded. "I'm so sorry about what happened to her. I didn't even know for a long time. She . . . she'd been trying to help me get away. I'm Kitten."

Dominoes fell into place. "I had no idea. Maybe I should have figured it out. This world is so new to me."

"Wish it was to me." She fingered the cast encircling her wrist.

"Does it hurt?"

"A little."

"That may be a good reason to go back to the hospital."

"No! Absolutely not. I'll jump from this car before I'll go back there." Her eyes held fire I hadn't seen in her before. I was glad to see it.

"Okay." I motioned for her to show me the arm. No increased swelling. No streaks of red that might signal infection. "Ribs?"

"Sore. But only when I breathe." Her fleeting smile broke the tension between us.

"Can I feel your forehead?"

She looked surprised but nodded. I placed a gentle hand over her brows. "No fever. Excellent." I started the car.

Pearls of sweat glistened on Kitten's face, so I pointed the air conditioning vents her way. She grasped the door handle. "Where are we going?"

"That's a good question." I didn't like her grayish pallor, but the kid had walked six blocks without collapsing. Where else could I take her? If I turned her over to social services, they'd dump her in a foster home, and I knew that wouldn't be safe enough. The police? Not until I talked to Lou.

Looking at her reminded me of myself at her age, adrift and just trying to survive. How many men had ravaged her? What part of herself had she closed off to survive it? And survive it she had. Still, a spark inside her remained that I had to protect.

Take her home. Keep her safe. The new voice commanded, stronger than before. I found myself unable to disobey her. Nora wouldn't be pleased about that.

I shifted the car into drive and said to the girl. "Looks like you're going home with me."

CHAPTER FORTY

J avier came for Lillian. He told her to grab a sweater, which she did, and escorted her out the room. "I'm to lock you in the wine cellar."

She nodded, accepting this fate. When they reached the top of the stairs, he held up an arm to stop her. Voices boomed from the foyer below. Vasily and Pavel had Jefe cornered, Vasily holding up a small black object with a slim cord attached. Pavel spoke in loud, angry Russian. Jefe held his hands up and said, "I have no idea what you're talking about."

"A camera! In my room!" Vasily boomed. "Were you recording me with the girl? Are you planning to blackmail me?"

"Cameras?" Lillian whispered. "How? Who?"

"I don't know. They're demanding to search the other rooms. Onyx and the girls were told to keep the other guests busy but with all this noise—"

"We . . . do . . . not . . . film." Jefe pointed to the object in Vasily's hand. "I have no idea how that got there."

Pavel's phone beeped and he took the call, standing off to the side and speaking in a hurried Russian.

"You!" Vasily pointed up the stairs at Lillian. "Do you know anything about this?"

She shook her head. "We would never—"

"Shut up. You are all liars. You tape me with the girl. Then the girl disappears. Now what happens? I get accused of something? You blackmail me? Do you know who I am?" His voice thundered.

"Never!" Jefe said. "Look, the trust of our buyers is—"

Vasily shook the device in Jefe's face. "Why would I believe you?"

Pavel hung up the phone and approached Vasily, whispering something in his native tongue.

"Let's get moving," Javier whispered.

Lillian didn't argue. They moved past the kitchen and down the dark stairs to the basement.

Javier unlocked the heavy door. "If there's a way to help you I will, but I'm just not sure I can. Not with what's going on upstairs."

"What do you mean, help me?"

Javier motioned her into the small, cold room. Before closing the door, he tossed her an old blanket. "I'll try to bring you some food if I can. The best thing for you to do is stay quiet." With that, he closed the door. Lillian heard the resonate click of the deadbolt, locking her in complete darkness.

She knew this small room well, having often been dispatched to select a fine wine for Jefe's guests. The light switch was to the right of the door, so she felt along the dusty shelves until she reached the cold brick wall, found the switch, and turned it on. Several boxes of a Malbec Jefe wanted to try hadn't been shelved; Gunner had been slack on the job. She reached for the doorknob and twisted it. As expected, locked.

One of the boxes became her seat, the blanket a less than adequate cushion. As she scanned the rows of bottles stacked sideways, she wasn't sure what she was looking for and couldn't imagine a way out of here, but she had to try. The very back wall held other beverages like sodas and mixers for liquor. She didn't think 7UP or Dr. Pepper would be of much use in busting down a door.

What were Onyx and the other girls doing? Would the Russians hurt her girls? Lillian leaned back, shutting her eyes, resting. If there was a way out, she didn't know how to find it. Soon Jefe would send his men to get her. The inevitability of this darkened all her thoughts. *Let it at least be painless.*

When Kitten awoke, light outside the curtained window had turned orange with the setting sun. The bedroom was small with creamy walls like the ones in foster home number five. A yellow bedspread and matching sheets topped the soft double bed. A wood dresser like one her grandmother had was by the window, and two bookshelves filled the opposite wall that bulged with piles of books. A closet door opened partway to reveal a chaos of clothes on hangers, and an unlikely tiny Supergirl costume suspended from a hook inside the door.

This Georgia woman was odd.

A doorbell chimed and through the half-open door, Kitten watched a dark-skinned man wearing a blue T-shirt and black jeans enter. Georgia walked up to him, saying nothing, and the two simply stared at each other for a long time. Finally, he spoke.

"What kind of mess did you get yourself into this time?"

Georgia burst out laughing.

"Where's the girl?"

"She may be asleep." Georgia crossed to Kitten's door, peeking in. Kitten tossed back the sheet and stood, pleased that she was less wobbly than earlier attempts. She straightened the long T-shirt Georgia had lent her. On it was a sketch of a woman saying, *Give me some coffee and no one gets hurt.*

"Hey there," Georgia said with a smile that didn't look real. "You feeling better?"

She nodded. "Thirsty."

"I'll bet. Come on out. I'll get you some ice water while we wait for the pizza to arrive."

She followed Georgia into the living room, noting that the clutter of magazines, books, and coffee cups had been tidied up from when they first arrived. Georgia pointed to the man. "This is my best friend, Elias Jasper. Elias, I want you to meet Kitten."

Thick black eyebrows shot up. "From the trailer?"

"Yes. But more recently from the hospital. She'd almost been killed by one of the traffickers. I thought she was safe, but the guy came after her there and she took off. I was lucky to find her. I brought her here."

"Broke a few rules with that, didn't you?" he said to Georgia.

"Never been that great at following them." Georgia patted the sofa for Kitten to sit, then went into the kitchen. A giant cat hopped up beside her, studied her face for a moment, then curled up against her thigh. She ran a hand along his soft black fur.

"Fenway likes you."

Elias smiled. His brown eyes were close together like a hawk's. "How old are you?"

"Fifteen."

"How long they have you?"

"I don't know." She had stopped measuring time. Summer didn't matter, because she didn't get to go to school. Birthdays and Christmases didn't matter, because nobody cared. Weekends did matter because Friday and Saturday nights were the busiest, and Roman slept late Sunday mornings, making that her favorite time.

Georgia brought her a tall glass of water which Kitten downed so fast it dribbled from her chin. Georgia handed her a paper towel. "Want more?"

She nodded.

When Georgia returned from her second trip to the kitchen, she sat beside Kitten and handed her the refilled glass, which Kitten sipped. Her thirst felt bottomless. Her wrist still ached, but not as much as before.

"What's the plan?" Elias asked.

"We're keeping Kitten safe. And shutting down Jefe's operation. I've been trying to reach Lou Michaels but I'm not having much luck."

"Let me see if I have this straight," Elias said. "Jefe has girls working out of a trailer and out of a massage parlor. He furnishes workers for the peach orchard and used to have a sweatshop. Anything else, Kitten?"

"The Estate."

"The place we tried to get to last week?" he asked Georgia.

Kitten told them what she knew, taking a brief break when the pizza arrived. It had sausage, eggplant, and mushrooms and tasted better than anything that Kitten had ever eaten. Georgia and Elias just ate a few pieces, and munched quietly, without asking a lot of questions. She liked that about them. "I haven't been at the Estate very long. It's much nicer than the trailer, but the work is . . . the same."

Georgia tossed her slice on the plate. "Meaning you have to service men."

She nodded. Although *service* wasn't a word she'd used before, it perfectly described what she did.

Elias kept eating. "How many of you are there?"

"Onyx, Dulce, Ratana, Zoe, Mei-Mei, Citrine and two or three others. Can't remember their names. Me, Ratana and Dulce are the new ones."

"Dulce," Georgia repeated. "We met her. We asked about you, but you weren't at the trailer that night." She told Kitten the rest, how they'd pretended to be buyers so they could scope out the trailer operation.

"She told me about you. Wish I'd been there."

"Wish we could have gotten both of you away from Roman that night." Georgia looked sad, which Kitten didn't like.

"It's not so easy. You and Elias could have been killed if Roman suspected anything."

"Right?" Elias raised a hand as though making a point. "Georgia's fully capable of pulling stupid shit like that. She needs a keeper."

"I have a keeper." Georgia arched her brows at him.

Kitten smiled. These two were like brother and sister.

Georgia's cell rang. She checked out the number. "Lou. Thank God." She said a few ahuh's then, "that works," before hanging up and turning to Kitten. "Okay. Lou Michaels is on his way over. He's a detective with the police department. Do you think you can talk to him?"

Kitten stiffened. It had long been ingrained in her to avoid the police, that talking to them would lead to certain death. But she was no longer a prisoner of Jefe.

"Or, you don't have to tell him anything. I'll tell him what I know and leave you out of it. You can hide in the bedroom if you want."

Kitten studied each of them. Having a choice about anything was something new and strange.

"What?" Georgia asked her.

"I'll talk, under one condition. The police have to help the others. And Lillian."

"That's the plan," Georgia said. "We shut down Jefe's operation. The girls are freed. And maybe, just maybe, my sister's death will have meaning."

CHAPTER FORTY-ONE

Lou Michaels arrived thirty minutes later. Agent Warren came in behind him, dressed in chinos and a polo shirt, his muscular arms bulging below the short sleeves. I introduced them to Elias and Kitten, who looked less than comfortable with the men's arrival.

Lou sat across from her, bent forward, hands propped on knees. He spoke in a gentle tone that surprised me, asking questions about how she came to Columbia, the different places she'd worked for Jefe, and the recent injuries to her wrist and ribs.

Agent Warren stood to the side as though standing guard. Fenway rubbed against his leg, but he didn't acknowledge him. Fenway shot me a look of contempt and planted himself beside Kitten with a rumbling purr.

"You said you started at the farm. What kind of farm was it?"

She described picking peaches, living in a crowded, unairconditioned bunkhouse. Jefe moving her to the trailer where she was violated. A dark bleakness echoed in her voice.

"Tell us more about the Estate," Lou prompted.

Her eye for detail impressed me. She talked about the different rooms, the girls who worked there, and the upscale clientele.

"It's very isolated," I commented. "West of Bumfuck South Carolina. Near absolutely nothing."

Warren wanted details about the weekend visitors and looked positively hungry when she mentioned the senator and the Russians.

I lifted a hand to interrupt them. "My concern is how do we keep her safe? Jefe's already sent his men after her."

"No problem. We have a safe house in the upstate."

Kitten's hand on Fenway froze. "What's a safe house?"

"Somewhere we keep witnesses. This one is near the NC border. We'll station an agent there to make sure you're safe."

"What agent? How long would I be there? How do you know Jefe won't find me?" Her questions sprayed like buckshot, an edge of panic to her voice.

"You're dealing with the FBI. We'll do whatever we need to keep you out of danger." Warren sounded weary.

Kitten spun around in her seat to face me. "Where's your bathroom?"

I guided her to the small room and switched on the light. There's one window in there, but only large enough for Fenway to fit through. I was pretty sure Kitten would have escaped if she could have. I held the door and whispered, "You're not going anywhere unless you agree. I promise."

Her exhale was audible as she closed the door.

When I returned to the living room, I said to the agent, "She's not comfortable with your plan."

He wiped a hand across his face. I didn't sit but approached him so that we were eye level. "This kid has had every choice taken away from her. Every damn one. She's been sold to men who did who knows what to her. She's been tied up. Abused. God knows what else. The one thing she gets to have now is agency over herself and her future.

"If she doesn't want to go to your safe house, she's not going."

Warren looked at Lou as if wanting back up. I shot him a stern look.

Elias came over to me. "George has a point. We can keep her safe here if that's what she wants."

"It won't be the same," Lou said.

"No it won't," I relented. "But if you try to take her to your safe house, I guarantee you that she will run. She's clever. And she's not exactly under arrest. If you want your witness, you better let her have this control."

Elias winked at me, approving my strategy. Unfortunately, he wasn't the only one. The counselor whispered, *Well done.*

"She's got a point," Lou said. "We can keep an eye on her here. Of course, that works better if you coordinate with us and let us know where you are in your investigation."

Agent Warren sucked in his cheeks, clearly unhappy with all of us.

Keep the girl safe, the counselor said.

Kitten emerged from the bathroom, moisture glistening on her face.

"Kitten, come over here." I sat on the sofa and patted the place beside me. She complied.

"You don't want to go to the safe house, do you?"

She shook her head.

"Then I don't want you to go there, either. What do you think about bunking with me for a few days?"

She eyed the two men from law enforcement. "I like that much better."

"Good then. It's settled."

Agent Warren lifted a hand. "One more thing. Kitten is a minor. Have you reached out to her parents?"

Kitten shot him a glare like it could burn through his skin. "Good luck finding them."

"What do you mean?"

"I mean I was in foster care. I mean they had their parental rights terminated. And if you think you're turning me into social services—"

"Easy there!" I stepped between them. "We're not turning you over to social services because that wouldn't be safe, given the circumstances. We've notified law enforcement that you were endangered." I pointed to Lou, "And you are staying with me as an emergency placement until you are safe. It may not be exactly kosher, but I don't see the courts jumping on this. I can make some calls to be sure."

"She is a social worker, after all, Agent Warren," Lou clarified.

"Let me do my job of taking care of Kitten. You do yours of shutting down Jefe's operation and freeing the other women. And the sooner you do that, the safer Kitten is."

Agent Warren didn't like it but didn't argue. He shook his head at Lou and approached the door, hesitating there. "Detective Michaels will give you my contact information. Anything happens—and I mean anything—I want to be your first call."

As Lou and Warren left, Kitten visibly relaxed. Elias smiled at me. "Nice job, George."

"I'm not so sure. I know I don't want Kitten to do anything she doesn't want to do, but I want to be sure I can keep her safe."

"You mean *we* can keep her safe. I'm sticking to you like glue till this is over."

I closed my eyes, relief like a warm blanket covering me. "Thanks."

Elias insisted on sleeping on the living room sofa, so I brought out a foam pad and sheets, hoping to make it as comfortable as possible. I'd put in a call to our local social services. The supervisor was someone I'd been in graduate school with and, while he didn't love our arrangement, he said it would have to do until a case manager could be assigned. I knew from experience that it could take a few days, especially given Kitten's special circumstances.

Kitten reclined in my rocking chair, eyes drooping. She had to be beyond exhausted, but at least she didn't look sick. I couldn't help but worry about her early exit from the hospital.

She isn't broken, the counselor said. I had to agree. Other girls in her situation might have given up. Turned to drugs or self-injury or even suicide. But not Kitten. She had a resilience in her core that kept her going.

She stirred, stretching her good arm in the air.

"You might be more comfortable in bed," I said, moving to help her up. With me by her side, she took groggy steps into the guest room and sat on the bed. I had left a nightgown for her, and she didn't flinch when I helped her remove her shirt and slip it on, careful when I touched her wrist. The bruises on her chest made me want to hurt someone.

"Thanks," Kitten said, sliding her legs under the sheet. Her gaze fell on a colorful design on her forearm, a tattoo.

"That looks recent."

She nodded. "They did it to me the day I got to the Estate."

Did it to her. The phrasing resonated.

"This is Jefe's brand. All his girls get one," she said.

I swallowed rage as big as a boulder.

"Some think it's beautiful. That we were lucky it wasn't something hideous, but I think this is ugly enough."

"It doesn't belong on you. You do not belong to him."

Her gaze searched my face, seeking truth.

As soon as we could do it safely, I'd schedule her for tattoo removal. No woman should ever be branded. I stood. "Need anything else, Kitten?"

She shook her head.

"Light on or off?" This was a question I always asked Lindsay when she stayed with me.

"Off."

As I turned the switch on the lamp, she clutched my hand. "What?"

"I just—" She winced, and I worried that maybe she needed to go back to the hospital. I touched her head, relieved to find no fever.

"What?" I asked.

"Don't call me Kitten. That's not my name. That's the name they gave me, and I hate it."

"Then we won't call you that."

Again, she seemed to size me up. Then she whispered, "My name is Tessa."

"Tessa," I repeated, stunned by this disclosure. "What a lovely name."

"I haven't heard anyone say it in so long," she whispered.

"I know. But you don't have to be Kitten anymore. Do you believe me?"

She fingered the edge of the sheet. "I'm starting to."

"Excellent." I stood. "Goodnight, Tessa."

Elias was stretched out on the sofa whispering into his phone (probably to Finn), so I crept into the kitchen to clean it up. My unexpected houseguests didn't deserve to live in the clutter that had become my norm. I loaded the dishwasher, scrubbed the counters and stove, and even swept the dingy floor, thinking about what Kitten—*Tessa*—had been through. She had not let what happened claim her soul.

CHAPTER FORTY-TWO

Lillian awoke on the cold cement floor where she'd wrapped herself like a mummy in the blanket. Was it morning? She had no sense of time. Her last contact with anyone in the house had been a quick visit from Javier who let her out to use the bathroom. That was late last night.

She was hungry. Her bladder pressed against her abdomen, screaming for relief again. Soon she'd have to squat in the corner and release it, a humiliating metaphor for the situation she'd found herself in.

What's happening upstairs? She figured that the Russians must have Jefe occupied, otherwise, he'd have ordered his men to take care of her. She heard footsteps, then the click of the lock. The door opened and Onyx appeared, her Afro like a black halo in the dull basement light. "I brought you a sandwich," she whispered.

"Thank you."

"I'm allowed to take you up to use the restroom if you want."

Lillian nodded and stood, swaying a little as she tried to get her bearings. Onyx held the door for her and followed her up the steps. All was quiet in the kitchen. Lillian used the small washroom beside the pantry to relieve herself and wash her face, then Onyx escorted her back to the cellar.

Lillian took a seat on the wine case and pointed at the remaining one for Onyx. "Can you stay for a minute?"

Onyx nodded and closed the door. Lillian bit off a corner of the sandwich and reached for the bottled water Onyx had also brought.

"The Russian men, they are very unhappy," Onyx said.

"I heard." She wiped a bit of mayonnaise from her chin. "Are the girls okay?"

Onyx nodded. "So far. Jefe is . . . very nervous. I've never seen him like this."

"What do you mean?"

"The Russians, they are bad men. They are making threats. Not just to Jefe and us. To Jefe's family."

"His family?"

As long as she had known Jefe, Lillian knew almost nothing about his actual identity. She savored the evenings he spent away from the Estate. If she ever questioned him about where he'd been, he shut her down so fast she dared not persist. She didn't think he had a wife, or if he did, it wasn't a good relationship. And if he had children, they saw very little of him.

"The mean one, the one with the jowly face, he says Jefe filmed him with Kitten and wants the SD card that holds the recording. He told the other guests to look for cameras and several found one in theirs. They left furious. They do not believe Jefe when he tells them that he didn't record anything."

"I don't think he did, Onyx. I mean, we'd know if he had, right?"

"If he didn't put the cameras in our rooms, then who did?"

"That's a damn good question."

Onyx stood. "The Russians know all about Jefe. They know where his home is in Columbia. They know where his parents live. His brother. They tell Jefe they will kill his family if he doesn't give them what they want, but he says he doesn't have the card from the camera."

Lillian tried to remember the last time she'd been in the Begonia room. Two days ago, when Mei-Mei got it ready for Vasily and Kitten,

Lillian had stopped in to check her work. All was as it should be. Of course, she hadn't been looking for something as small as a camera. It could have been there for days—weeks even—without them knowing.

"This is bad. If the police somehow planted the camera—"

"How could they? We do not allow people to come here!"

"Maybe one of the guests?" Lillian thought back to the men who'd visited in recent weeks. The congressman from New England. The hotel mogul who liked to be spanked. The Bulgarian who needed two girls to be satisfied. Had one of them betrayed Jefe?

"Where is Jefe now?"

"In his office making phone calls. He's raising his voice so much the girls are cowering in their rooms."

"And Jefe's men?"

"I do not know. Lito, Roman and Stan haven't come back from their errand. Gunner is upstairs with the other guards."

Great. Gunner would like nothing more than to kill me with his bare hands.

Onyx stood. "I should return upstairs before they miss me."

"You should. And thank you for the sandwich."

She approached the door but hesitated. "This is the extra key to the wine cellar. The one we keep in the pantry. They might not notice it is missing."

Lillian's eyes widened. "They might not."

Onyx tossed it to her. "Do you know what you'll do?"

"I have to get away."

"Don't leave now. There is still a lot of activity upstairs. Maybe tonight?"

Lillian nodded. If they didn't kill her before then, she'd find a way to sneak out.

CHAPTER FORTY-THREE

Tessa pulled the bedspread closer to her face, suddenly chilled. It wasn't as cold as in the hospital, but she was still getting used to air conditioning. A fat beam of sunlight poked between yellow curtains and lit up the framed crayon drawing of a cat on the wall opposite the bed. Who had made it? Georgia didn't seem to have children, but she did have that costume hanging in her closet. Maybe she'd ask about it. That was something else to get used to—not always keeping her mouth shut. Not pretending to be invisible. Asking questions.

Georgia was talking to someone in the living room. "I'm okay. Yes, I'm still hearing them but I'm taking my meds and have everything under control."

Nobody replied, so she decided Georgia was on the phone. Tessa wondered what the meds were for.

"I just have a lot going on. I didn't get much sleep last night. And before you say anything, I don't want sleep meds. We've talked about that before."

After a few, "a huhs," and an "I will, I promise," Georgia ended the call.

Elias said something, his voice too low for Tessa to understand. She could hear both of them puttering around in the kitchen. Tossing back the sheet, she crawled out of bed and stood on less-shaky legs. Her wrist hurt, but not as bad as before. Every day, a little better, a little stronger. And she wasn't going back to Roman and Lito and Jefe.

As she shuffled out of the room, Fenway thumped over to her and rubbed against her legs.

"Looks like you made a friend," Georgia said from the kitchen doorway. She wore a dusty blue T-shirt over jean cut-offs, her hair clipped in a chaotic knot at the nape of her neck.

Tessa reached down and scratched the cat's head. His purr rumbled like a truck.

"He likes you. And Fenway can be discerning."

Tessa hesitated before saying, "You were talking to someone about not getting much sleep?"

Georgia leaned back against the counter. "Heard that, did you? I was talking to my therapist. She can be over-protective."

Tessa wasn't sure how to respond.

Georgia must have read her reluctance. "I see a therapist because I have some mental problems. I take meds that help me. I take care of myself—mostly. I have a job. I do okay."

"She does better than okay." Elias peered over the refrigerator door.

Tessa had always wanted her mom to go to a counselor. Maybe then she'd have gotten off drugs and not married Lawrence and . . . no. That line of thinking led to anger.

"Any questions?" Georgia asked. "It's okay. I'm an open book."

Tessa studied her for a long moment, then asked, "Do you have anything to eat?"

Georgia smiled. "I do. Don't laugh, but I made scrambled eggs."

"They look fairly edible," Elias clarified. Georgia swatted him with an oven mitt.

"Have a seat."

Tessa didn't say anything about the burned edges of the toast on her plate as Georgia scraped a mound of yellow beside it. Elias fixed his own plate and sat beside her.

Georgia looked tired. She had said she hadn't slept well, while Tessa'd had the best night of sleep in forever in that sweet little guest room. "Eggs are great."

"They are? Okay, I doubt that. But thanks." Georgia kept checking her cell phone as she poked at her breakfast. A large cup of coffee rested beside her plate, and she took frequent sips. "We'll hit the store later. You can help me pick out supper."

The idea of going to a grocery store, of choosing whatever she wanted for dinner, excited Tessa. She wouldn't select anything too expensive, because that would be rude, but maybe they could even get ice cream.

"No to the grocery store. I'll fix dinner. I have to run by the restaurant anyway," Elias said.

"Okay. I want to take Tessa over to David's so he can check out her arm."

"Who's David?" Tessa asked.

"My brother-in-law. He's a doctor. I'll feel better if he can get a look at you, Tessa."

She nodded, though not exactly thrilled with the idea.

"He was Peyton's husband."

That got to her. Peyton, who'd died trying to save her. A good person, dead because of Jefe.

"Come on. Let's get dressed," Georgia said.

After quick showers and getting dressed, they told Elias they'd come by his house after running errands.

Tessa spoke little during the drive to David's house. The whole thing made her nervous. would he blame her for his wife's death? Because part of her blamed herself.

His driveway was made of artistically arranged stones and was long enough for a fleet of cars. The house was wide and brick, with columns on the porch and stained-glass designs glinting in its wide windows. When Georgia pressed the doorbell, five chimes rang inside. Tessa half expected a butler to answer the door.

No answer. Georgia pressed the bell several more times and muttered impatiently until the door finally opened.

David was a short man, thin-to-balding hair, wearing white shorts and a plaid shirt. "Georgia?" He squinted at them like a vampire unused to sunlight.

"Hey, David. Need a favor." Georgia just pushed past him, motioning Tessa to follow, and headed straight for his living room.

Which was mammoth, a large fireplace with a marble mantel. Overstuffed furniture with decorative pillows. Amid coffee mugs and unopened mail on the coffee table was a yellow flowerpot. The plant blooming from it had two stems, flowers that were such a deep purple they looked almost black drooping from the ends.

Familiar flowers. The orchids that bloomed on the foyer table at the Estate were that same velvety plum, with a vivid green in the middle. The orchids in the room she slept in with the Russian were a pinker purple, with yellow spreading in the centers.

"Who are you?" David asked Tessa.

"She's a friend of mine," Georgia said. "Her name's Tessa."

"How old are you?" he asked her.

"Fifteen," Tessa said, with no strength in her voice. David's scrutiny made her nervous.

Georgia tossed a magazine from the sofa and took a seat, patting the cushion for Tessa to join her. She perched on the edge and fought the urge to dash away. She wasn't even sure why she felt that way.

"You know Peyton was looking into human trafficking," Georgia said.

"I still can't believe it. How could she do something so dangerous without telling her husband?" His voice rose.

"I need to tell you about Tessa."

And she did. She talked about following Peyton's footsteps into the trafficking world. About Roman, Lito, and Jefe. About the massage parlor and The Orchid Estate.

"Jesus, George." David's glare seemed incredulous. "Why are you having anything to do with any of this?"

"Because someone had to! At least the police are involved now. Should be some arrests soon. Anyway. Tessa got hurt by one of the traffickers. She was in the hospital but left because the traffickers found her there. She's AMA. Can you check her out? Make sure she's medically okay?"

He ran a hand over his anemic hairline. "I don't keep a lab here. You should take her back to the hospital. At least reach out to the doctor who worked with her."

Tessa clutched the armrest. Georgia patted her thigh. "Can't do that, for obvious reasons. Just take a look at her. If you see something that concerns you, I'll get her somewhere for treatment."

"I'm fine," Tessa said, her voice tight.

David grumbled as he stood, motioning Tessa to do the same. He started with her face, examining the tiny stitches on her bottom lip and the bruised socket around her eye, which had faded to a dull green. The left wrist came next. "No swelling here. That's good. They may want to refit that cast."

"Ribs, too, David," I said.

Tessa lifted her shirt. His touch on her chest was surprisingly gentle. "Might want to wrap these for a few days," he said. "Mostly to prevent aggravation of the injury. But they're healing nicely."

When he rested a hand against her forehead, she startled like a scared filly.

"Sorry. Just checking for fever. You're doing remarkably well."

"Good," Georgia said.

"I'd get her some iron tablets. She's likely anemic." A blast of symphony music from the mantel surprised Tessa. David rushed to answer his cell phone. "Hey, Colby."

David's grip on the phone was white-knuckled as he carried it into the kitchen. Georgia stood and paced the room. Tessa followed her over to the fireplace. On the mantel, she spotted yet another orchid, this one a vivid white. "Weird."

"What's weird?" Georgia asked.

"In my whole life, I've seen maybe two orchids. But over the past ten days or so I've seen dozens."

"Where?"

She pointed at the mantel and the table. "And at the Estate. They're in most of the rooms. Behind the main building, there's a greenhouse full of them."

Georgia looked as perplexed as Tessa felt. "And on your arm," she whispered tightly.

Tessa's gaze fell on the loathed tattoo. "I guess Jefe likes them."

The sound of tiny footfalls drew their attention to the stairs. A preschooler with blond curls and bright blue eyes hurled herself at Georgia, a yellow bear tucked under her arm.

"How's my peanut?" Georgia scooped her up and embraced her, the child giggling in her arms as though it was where she belonged. Once she settled herself, Georgia said, "Lindsay, this is my friend Tessa. Can you say hi?"

"Hi," she said with a little wave.

Tessa leaned over and winked at her, which drew a dimpled, shy smile. This little girl had lost her mother when trying to help Tessa. The stark reality of this hit her right in the stomach.

David reappeared, pocketing the cell.

"I'm up, Daddy," Lindsay said.

"I see you are." His grin at her was a weak attempt.

"I'll bet you want a snack. Come on, Peanut." Georgia took Lindsay by the hand and motioned for Tessa to join them in the kitchen, where she served two glasses of milk and Fig Newtons. "Give me a few minutes with David," she said.

Tessa nodded and sat across from the little girl at a table surrounded by windows. Outside, the backyard look neglected, a lawn grown wild and bushes that needed trimming. So very different than the immaculate landscaping in front.

She could overhear a little of what the adults were saying. Something about how Georgia should have minded her own business and should turn Tessa over to Child Services. Georgia swatted down that idea like it was an annoying mosquito. "I'll mind my business when you mind yours."

The little girl, Lindsay, held up her empty cup. "Can I have more milk?"

"Sure." Tessa carried the cup to the stone counter beside a refrigerator that was as big as a Buick. The double stainless doors were covered with photographs, mostly of Lindsay, some of her mother, Peyton, and one shot of the two of them with David and a guy who had salt-and-pepper curls and a wide smile. *A smile like a shark's.*

Tessa snatched the picture from its magnet and carried it to the window for better light, not wanting to believe. Her finger traced the outline of the curly-haired man, a man she knew. She'd smelled his breath against her face. Felt his foot crushing her abdomen. She loathed him and feared him in equal measure.

This man was Jefe. Why was he on David's refrigerator? Did Peyton make this connection? Is this what got her killed?

Tessa drew a steadying breath and approached the child. "Hey, Lindsay, who is this man in the picture?"

Her tiny fingers gripped the photo. "That's Uncle Colby."

"Colby?" She'd only heard him called Jefe. *Colby* was the name David had just said into the phone.

"Can I have my milk?"

"Sorry." She hurried over to the fridge and filled the cup.

"Thank you." Lindsay slurped.

Tessa couldn't take her eyes off the photo. She had to warn Georgia. Suddenly everything about this house, with its cold granite counters and giant rooms made her itch. She was too close to him, even though he wasn't here.

"How about we go check on Aunt George." She pocketed the photo and reached for Lindsay's hand, noting how willingly it grabbed hers. She wanted to tell the child to be more careful with her trust, to watch out for people who might hurt her, even people she knew and loved.

Tessa approached Georgia. "We need to get going."

Georgia eyed her in confusion.

"You said we needed to pick up Elias. He's expecting us now." She released Lindsay's sweet little hand and marched to the door.

"Okay. Yeah, right. We need to go." Georgia stood and said to David, "You'll tell the peanut I'll see her soon?"

He nodded.

"Good."

Tessa hurried out the door, Georgia close behind. Once she got the AC going in the car, Georgia turned to her. "What was that about? Something wrong?"

She nodded, unsure how to tell Georgia. "Please. Get me out of here."

"Okay. Take it easy. You're about to hyperventilate."

Georgia eased out of the drive, Tessa working to calm herself as they got some distance from the house. Suddenly, Georgia pulled over. "Okay. Tell me what's going on."

Tessa handed her the photo. "I took this from David's refrigerator."

"Why?"

She tapped a finger on the smiling face. "You know him."

"Colby? Sure I do. He's David's brother."

Tessa closed her eyes. "He gave David the orchids. He grows them at the Estate. This man is the boss. He's Jefe."

CHAPTER FORTY-FOUR

I stared at the photograph Tessa had given me. This revelation shook me to my core. I didn't want to believe it. Colby was always nice to me. Kind. He'd even asked me out.

Wanting information, the counselor whispered.

Tessa looked as pale as I'd ever seen her, her gaze watching me with the vigilance of a trauma survivor. Needing to be believed.

"I've got to think this thing through."

"How long have you known him?"

"We met years ago, before Peyton got married. He moved away. Atlanta, I think. But came back a few years ago after his divorce." I remembered Peyton describing a welcome-home party at the Ribaults. How different Colby had seemed to her. "He gave his parents a new Jaguar. Like it was nothing. I guess Atlanta was good to him," Peyton had said.

"He apparently made a lot of money before the move."

"How?" Tessa demanded.

"I don't know. David was always vague about it. I know his parents had some financial concerns—investments went bad, I think—and Colby helped them out.

"Peyton must have figured it out. God. How awful that must have been for her. And it got her killed." Was this why she hadn't gone to the police? Because of what it would do to the family? It probably tore her up inside.

"You believe me?" Tessa sounded both fragile and furious.

"I absolutely believe you."

Go somewhere safe, the counselor said. I needed to think straight. I clawed through my purse and pulled out Lou Michaels' card. He answered on the third ring.

"I have news. Kinda big news."

"Hold on, I'll put you on speaker. Agent Warren is with me."

I did the same. Tessa deserved complete transparency.

"Something's happened." I told him how Tessa had seen a photograph and made the critical, heart-stopping connection. "The leader of the trafficking ring is right here. Colby Ribault is the reason my sister is dead."

The silence on the line made me think he hadn't heard me, but then Agent Warren said, "We know."

"You know?" I yelled. "You know and you didn't warn me?"

"It's complicated. The important thing is to get you and Tessa somewhere safe. Do not go home. Ribault probably knows where you live."

He was right about that.

"We're about forty minutes away," Lou continued. "Head to the police station and I'll meet you there."

At the words, "police station," Tessa stiffened.

Go see Elias, the advisor said.

"I have another idea. Call as soon as you get back to town."

"Okay," Lou relented. "But promise me you'll be careful. In the meantime, anything happens, and you can't get me or agent Warren, call 9-1-1."

I said I would, though I hoped I didn't have to.

I headed to Elias's house. Elias meant safety to me. Always had.

When we arrived at the brick bungalow, I was glad to see his black Jeep in the driveway. Just as I started to climb out of the car, the new garbly voice spoke.

Something wrong.

There were a helluva lot of somethings that were wrong. Elias's back door hung open just a crack. *Odd.* Elias was neurotic about locking himself in—a holdover from the wild druggie days.

Not. Safe. The new voice practically bellowed in my head. My heart was doing a hummingbird wing impression.

I glanced over at Tessa. "Listen." I tried to keep panic out of my voice. "I need you to wait here."

"What's wrong?"

I pulled my phone out and pointed to the redial number. "Here. If I'm not out in five minutes, call Lou. If you can't get through, call 9-1-1. Then you get the hell out of here."

Her eyes widened as she took the cell.

"Don't be scared. I'm just being cautious. Maybe even a little paranoid." I pointed to the phone. "But just in case."

Call them now. Sometimes the counselor is well intended, but she can be overly cautious. I hurried up the drive and down his front walkway. The rocking chairs on the front porch looked undisturbed. Orange marigolds overflowed his planters, the welcome sign hung neatly from the door. Which was open like the back.

I pushed it with my index finger to peek inside. Elias sat in his leather armchair, perfectly still. I started to say something, but when he spotted me, his eyes squeezed shut and his chin dropped to his chest. That's when I noticed the rope around his hands.

I backed out the door and into what felt like a brick wall. Someone gripped the back of my neck and shoved me. I nearly fell over Elias's coffee table.

"Sit!" an accented voice commanded, as though I was a dog in obedience class. I spun around to find a man standing over Elias, his gun pressed against Elias' head.

I sat.

"Are you okay?" I asked Elias.

He gave me an *"are you serious?"* expression that told me he was.

I prayed Tessa had done as I'd asked. If these pricks got their hands on her—

"What do you want?" I asked the Latino man.

He answered with a venomous scowl.

You sure screwed this up, the general scolded.

The man's cell phone buzzed, and he answered. After a few "Si, Senor's" he ended the call. The front door squeaked open.

Tessa. In the harsh grip of a man I recognized—the one who had followed me that night, the man whose face I saw on the photo stills from the hospital, the man she called Lito. The blank desolation etched on Tessa's face made something crumble in my chest.

You fucked up big time, little lady, the general snarled. His words cut deep.

"What are you going to do to us?"

Lito hurled Tessa toward the sofa. I grabbed her at the waist to soften the fall. She gripped her casted arm as though it hurt, and I prayed he hadn't injured it worse.

"Jefe says bring them to the Estate," the other man told him.

"Stan, get the van." Lito tossed keys to Stan, who hurried out the front door.

Our best shot at escape was when they took us outside. When Roman unbound Elias' hands from the chair, he flexed his fingers and gave me a long, hard stare.

I arched my brows, glancing at the door.

His head shake probably wasn't noticed by anyone but me. He thought attempting to escape was a bad idea. Maybe he was right—there were bigger and meaner than us—and they had weapons.

A few minutes later, a horn honked out front. Lito nudged Elias out of the chair with his gun. I helped Tessa stand before Lito could get his hands on her. Her arm vibrated in my grip. "I'm sorry," I whispered. "I'm so sorry. It'll be okay."

You'll get them both killed. You deserve what happens. Not them.

I tried to think around these growls. Now that I knew who

Jefe was, it might help us. Jefe might be a cold, greedy bastard, but Colby might be a different story. And Colby had to be inside the man somewhere. This might be our only hope.

They loaded us in the back of a utility van that smelled like sweat. I could imagine the other humans who'd been tossed inside—victims of this horrendous crime, ripped from their lives and from the people they'd loved. Taken to somewhere unfamiliar to suffer untold abuses. Why? So Colby could get rich?

Our ride was forty minutes of rocking, bouncing, noisy hell. Lito sat between me and Elias, the gun held securely on his knee. Tessa leaned against the back of the driver's seat, her eyes closed.

I wondered what they would do when we reached the Estate. If there was a way—any single thing—I could do to keep my friends safe.

CHAPTER FORTY-FIVE

More hours had passed, and Lillian had grown weary of the cool, damp room. She needed another bathroom trip, too--- the squatting in the corner idea had lost all appeal since the key had arrived. Perhaps she could sneak up the stairs and grab something from the kitchen. Jefe rarely came in there. His men would be busy with whatever he'd asked them to do.

She had to try.

The heavy door squealed when she opened it, but she heard no response from upstairs. She opted for speed and stealth, hurrying up the steps, slipping past the washer, the refrigerator, and the pantry.

She slipped into the tiny bathroom, grateful for the relief it brought. No flushing, she decided. As she pushed the lid closed, she heard muted voices in the front of the house—probably Jefe's office. She cracked open the door and listened.

"It's Vasily again. Want to talk to him?" Stan's voice.

"Shit. Don't know what I can tell him." Jefe sounded distraught.

"We don't have any new information for you," Stan said, presumably into the phone.

Whispering. Jefe talking to someone else. Javier?

"I'll tell him," Stan said. "It's bad, boss."

"What?"

"They said they were sending a picture. Check your phone."

Silence, then Javier said, "Who is the girl on the swing?"

"My niece. She's four years old. Fucking hell." A crash. The sound of breaking glass.

"This is just a threat, Jefe. If they had her, we'd know it."

"That's David's backyard. They were that close to her. We have to up security at his place." Footsteps coming toward the kitchen propelled her out of the room and down the steps. She secured herself back in the wine cellar.

So, Jefe had a niece, a young child. The Russians were threatening her. How did he keep this other life so private that even Javier didn't know?

What would Vasily do to the child? Lillian didn't want to think about it. Vasily could be more brutal than Jefe, and she would soon experience Jefe at his most murderous.

This world. There was no getting out of it alive.

Finally, mercifully, the van swayed to a stop. I wiped the sweat dribbling over my eyes. My wet hair slimed against my neck. We all could have used about a gallon of water.

Lito slid to the rear, his gun leveled at Tessa.

"We won't try anything," I said. "Please don't hurt her."

He opened the door. Roman and the one they called Stan stood behind the van, guns drawn. Beyond them, I saw a massive house with a slate roof, wide windows, and elaborate landscaping. I climbed out, my legs achy, and held Tessa's elbow as she stepped out of the van. Her continued silence worried me, but then so did everything else about our situation.

Another Hispanic man met us. This one shorter and wider than Lito. He indicated that we should follow him inside. We entered the mammoth house, and I scanned the plush furnishings, the shiny marble floors, and the immense windows, but what caught my attention was the orchids; a purple one on the foyer table. Pink in the dining room beyond. White on a shelf.

Somehow, these plants drove it home for me. *Colby Ribault is Jefe. The boss. Murderous. Evil.*

My sister's killer.

Elias positioned himself beside me. I put my hand on Tessa's arm, wanting her to know she wasn't alone.

A noise from somewhere above us drew our attention to the top of the stairs. I saw three women—girls, really—watching us. Lito said something in Spanish, and they hurried away, doors slamming shut.

There was considerable noise in my head; whispers, indistinct, like a crowded elevator, similar to the night after they found Peyton's body. I had a fleeting thought of Nora telling me it was *"best to avoid stress"* if I wanted to silence the voices. Yeah, right.

"Lock them in the cellar with La Señora," Lito said.

Stan pressed his gun against my back to nudge me toward what looked like a kitchen, my friends close behind. We went down some dark stairs to a basement. Lito unlocked a heavy door and shoved us into a small, dank room.

We weren't alone.

"Lillian?" I hadn't expected to see her. She sat on what looked like a wine case, her hair a mess, her eye makeup smeared, and the bleakest expression on her face.

"Georgia? Kitten? What the hell are you doing here?"

The door clanged shut.

"That's a long story." I offered an abbreviated version, explaining everything that happened when Tessa left the hospital.

Lillian turned to Tessa. "I'm glad Lito didn't find you, Kitten. Except . . . here you are."

"My name isn't Kitten. I'm Tessa." The kid spoke with a bold defiance that made me proud.

"Okay then, *Tessa.*" Lillian sounded profoundly weary. I wondered how long she'd been locked in here.

"Tell her what we learned about Jefe," Tessa said.

Just mentioning Colby's name made something sour in my stomach. This was all so hard. Too hard.

You're doing fine, the counselor said.

Lillian spoke. "My turn. I have news for you, too."

She talked about the Russian clients who had been at the Estate. The one who'd been with Tessa, a man named Vasily, had been very upset when Tessa disappeared. His anger was amplified when he found a video camera hidden in their room. "Did you know anything about that, Tessa?" Lillian asked.

"No. I had no idea."

"Neither did Jefe, but Vasily didn't believe him. He's furious. And he's got resources. He's made threats to Jefe's family."

"Jesus," I whispered, picturing David and their parents. Had they been warned?

"The Russians sent Jefe a photo of a little girl on a swing. He said it was his niece."

"Lindsay?" My peanut in danger? What the hell?

"They want the recording from the video camera. It's really small—probably just uses a micro-SD card. Jefe doesn't have it."

"You're sure he doesn't?" If I knew one thing about Jefe—*Colby*—it's that he was an outstanding liar.

The sudden opening of the door made us all jump. Stan stepped into the tiny room and pointed at me. "Jefe wants to talk to you."

I nodded. I had plenty to say to him, too. I whispered to Tessa, "I'll be right back," but leaving her worried me. I cast a glance at Elias who gave me a reassuring nod. He'd do whatever he could to protect her. But then, he was in danger, too.

I marched out the door, determined not to show fear. We climbed the dank steps up to the kitchen, then moved down the hall to a closed door. Stan knocked twice before opening it.

This space had an oppressive, opulent feel. A large antique desk with a banker's lamp rested at one end. In the center, a red Oriental rug and four leather chairs. Abstract art hung from paneled walls. From the recessed ceiling hung a crystal chandelier that likely cost four digits. Sitting under it was Colby Ribault, former friend. Current crime lord.

"Wait outside," Colby said to Stan, who closed the door behind him.

Emotions tangled in me as I glared at David's brother. Fury. Terror. Disgust. Profound betrayal.

He pointed to one of the chairs. "Please."

I sat, watching as Colby—*Jefe*—came around his mammoth desk to take the chair across from me. I wasn't sure how to play this, so I waited for him to take the lead.

"This isn't what I wanted." He spoke in a soft, Colby-like voice.

I looked around the plush office. "This?"

"You. Being here," he clarified.

"Then let us go, Colby." I used his name with intent. Colby had to still be in the man across from me.

"I like you. Always have." The gentleness in his eyes confused me. It was the man I knew, not Jefe.

"I used to like you. Then I found out you murdered my sister. Kinda changed things for me."

Careful, the counselor said.

"You are too much like her. Determined. Meddling where you shouldn't." He scratched at whiskers that were beginning to shadow his chin. "What do you know about my family? The family Peyton married into?"

"What do you mean?"

"The Ribaults. That name. What does it make you think of?"

"Old Southern family. Well moneyed." *Arrogant blue bloods,* but I didn't say that aloud.

"Well moneyed, right. Until Dad lost a fortune on bad investments and couldn't afford to keep his business or the house. Until David's practice was close to bankruptcy, and he nearly lost everything. Bet you didn't know about any of that."

I shrugged. I knew a little. I knew Peyton worried when David did. I knew most independent medical practices struggled to survive in the current economy.

"It was up to me to help them. So, I did. I took care of my family."

I studied him for a long moment, strategizing. I thought of Tessa locked in the cellar with Elias. Two people depending on me. I had to keep them safe.

"Let us go, Colby." I leaned forward, keeping steady eye contact. "Please. We won't tell the police about any of this. I promise."

"You promise." Another laugh. "I have no faith in people's promises. I cannot let you leave here."

He'll kill us. That cold reality tunneled through me. "I can't believe you are the man I liked. The man I trusted. The man Peyton loved as a brother."

He lifted a finger. "She could have let it go. Do you know how this started? It was such a little thing. A stupid thing. I had one of the workers from the farm come to my folks' house to do some gardening. Didn't know Peyton was coming over. Didn't know she'd cornered the girl and asked a bunch of questions."

"She figured out what you were doing?"

"Not right away. But she decided to do that project for school, and went to the farm where the girl usually worked, and that took her down the rabbit hole. Damn Peyton! We gave her every chance, but she couldn't quit nosing in my business. We warned her, but she didn't care. So damn stupid."

"Stupid?" I had to tamp down my anger at this. *Stay in control,* a voice said. "She was doing something good, Colby. She would never turn her back on those girls. You knew her. You knew she couldn't."

His face was drawn and shadowed. "And you picked up where she left off. I have no choice, George. This is about damage control."

A knock at the door interrupted us. He flashed a look of annoyance and yelled, "What?"

Stan entered. "Got some news, boss. Thought you'd want to hear it."

I wasn't asked to leave and guessed it didn't matter what I heard, since I wouldn't be around to use it.

"Russians reached out again. Sent this photo. Thought you ought to see it." He handed Colby a phone.

Colby stared at the image, his eyes wide, looking vulnerable in a way I never expected. "Jesus."

"What is it?" I asked.

He shoved the phone in my face. The picture sent ice water through my veins. Two men I didn't know. One staring at the camera. The other holding a little girl with giant blue eyes and a yellow bear tucked under her arm. *My Lindsay.* "Who are they? What do they want?"

"Leverage." Colby thrust the phone at Stan. "Their demands?"

"The SD card from the camera. You have thirty minutes."

"Thirty minutes? I can't even drive to town that fast."

"They're coming here." Stan pocketed the cell.

"Here? Jesus."

This information came at me like hurled stones. My breath stuttered. The voices swelled.

Calm down, the counselor said.

Your fault, replied the general.

"How . . . how did they know about her?" I demanded.

"They know everything." Colby turned an accusing gaze on Stan. "We had security on the house. How the hell did this happen?"

"They stormed the place. Outnumbered our guys. Knew exactly where she was and snatched her."

Snatched her. How terrified she must have been. What if they hurt her? Or worse?

Don't think about that, the counselor whispered. *Don't assume the worst.*

Worst is what she gets. The general's snarl filled my brain, overwhelming my synapses. I shook my head as though trying to shake it out.

"David? Is my brother okay?" Colby asked.

"Got a bloody nose from fighting them. He's lucky they didn't kill him."

"You have to give them the recording, Colby. You have to get Lindsay from them," I pleaded.

"Just one problem with that. I don't have it. I didn't put the camera in their room."

He had to be lying. Was he that desperate to hold onto the recording that he'd put his niece—our niece—in danger? "I don't believe you."

"What you believe doesn't matter."

"Wait." Desperation rang in my voice. "If you don't have the recording—then how do we get her back? Maybe you need to go to the police."

"The police?" His laugh held an edge as cold as steel. "God. You are clueless. They can't help. All they can do is destroy the little that I have left."

"But—"

"Stan. Get her out of here."

His grip on my arm bruised. The door slammed shut behind us.

CHAPTER FORTY-SIX

Lillian fingered the key in her pocket. She could unlock the door and free the three of them. Of course, they wouldn't make it up the stairs without getting caught; she could hear Jefe's men on the floor above them. No way he'd let them go.

"How long has she been gone?" Elias asked.

"Maybe fifteen minutes."

"Is that all?" Tessa asked.

He crossed over to the girl and squatted, giving her face a thorough study. "You doing okay?"

She heaved her good shoulder up in a shrug.

"Georgia is fine. And when she gets back, we'll find a way out of here."

She nodded but looked at Lillian. The two of them knew the truth. None would get out of here alive. Elias stood and circled the room again. Nothing had changed. No window had magically appeared. No phone that would work. Maybe he just needed to work off his fear.

When the door opened, Elias jumped, looking like he wanted to clobber whoever entered. The gun pointed at them stopped him cold. It was Lito.

He pointed at Tessa. "You. Come with me."

Lillian jumped to her feet. "Where are you taking her?"

His low voice resonated in the dank room. "Ain't none of your business."

"Lito . . . don't. Don't do this."

He grabbed Tessa's arm and snatched her up. As he approached the door, Elias jumped between them and Lillian winced, expecting gunfire. Instead, Lito smashed the revolver against Elias' skull. He collapsed in a heap on the floor.

"Lillian! Help him!" Tessa cried out, as Lito dragged her away.

She felt Elias' wrist, relieved to find a pulse. Blood trickled from a cut on his forehead and puddled beside him. She tore the bottom of his shirt to make an ill-fitting bandage and tried shaking him. Elias was out cold.

The thought of Tessa in Lito's hands horrified Lillian. He had a grudge against the girl and would be merciless. She slid her hidden key into the lock and turned it, careful to open the door so that it wouldn't make a sound. Just as she stepped through it, she hesitated, then carried the key back to Elias. She wrapped it in his hand and slipped out of the room.

Once she reached the top of the steps, she paused, listening for Lito or Roman or any of Jefe's men. Oddly silent.

The back door hung open. Where did Lito take her? Back to the toolshed? Before exiting, she grabbed a knife from the butcher block, praying to God that she wouldn't have to use it.

I was dragged to the dining room and dropped in a chair, Roman standing over me with a gun. "Can't I go back to my friends?"

"Shut up."

The voices became a stormy rumble in my brain. Colby was on his phone two rooms away. I could hear him yelling. Stan came blasting up the hall followed by Gunner, who was on his cell growling in Spanish. It felt like being in a beehive.

My head felt like that, too. I kept thinking about Lindsay. If anything happened to that sweet little life. She was all I had left of Peyton.

When Peyton figured out about Colby, did she confront him? And he killed her. He had not done it himself, of course. Colby didn't get his hands dirty like that. He'd simply issued the order and his men went after her. I pictured Peyton hiding Lindsay in the closet, desperate to keep her safe, but unable to do the same for herself.

And now Lindsay could suffer the same fate.

You screwed up big time, the general said.

She's doing her best, the counselor replied.

That's never been enough.

The voices spoke on top of each other. The synaptic volume knob at maximum. My head buzzed, the words swirling and echoing and making it very difficult for me to think. To move. To handle this.

And I had to handle it.

Handle what? Sacrifice yourself for your friends.

"Shut up," I whispered.

"What did you say?" Stan spun around to confront me.

"Nothing. Sorry."

Sorry. Yeah, you're sorry. Sorry. Sorry, The general chanted, the word riding my synapses, pushing out other thoughts. repeated this word in a chant. God, I wanted him to stop.

Tessa's arm was on fire. Lito's fingers dug into her flesh, just above the cast, as he tugged her through the backyard. Cruelty had always come too easily to him. He reached the garage. Tessa saw the Thunderbird parked there, the one Lillian drove, and wished she could hop inside and dash away. That she'd never driven before wouldn't stop her.

"We've had enough of you, Chica," Lito growled. "You have done much damage to Jefe's business."

"Good then." No need to try to placate him. She knew what was coming.

He shoved her down, her thigh scraping against concrete, pain slicing through her as her arm bounced against the ground. She closed her eyes and drew a deep breath, willing the influx of air to push away the pain.

She didn't want to die this way. Not by Lito's hand. Not on this property where her body had been sold. She'd tried so hard. She'd strengthened her body to prepare for escape. She'd chased away the dark moments when hope seemed lost to her. She'd clung to the belief that she'd find a life outside of Jefe's reach, she'd see her baby brother again. She'd put this nightmare behind her.

Lito loomed over her. The barrel of his gun glinted in the rays from the setting sun. No. She wouldn't focus on that. She wouldn't focus on his sweaty face or the devil's grin on the T-shirt he loved to wear. She lifted her gaze skyward. A few clouds spattered the sky. A flock of birds—geese maybe—soared above her. They looked peaceful, gliding along the sunset.

Maybe she'd know that peace soon.

The gun exploded.

The cry that bellowed out wasn't from her throat but from Lito's. She moved—but how? Scrambling back from him, away from him, and saw someone else there behind him.

Lillian.

Lito staggered back, looking oddly bewildered, and turned around. Blood gushed from the knife wound in his side. She'd stabbed him.

Lito staggered, aiming the gun at Lillian and Tessa. Lillian stumbled away from him, turning to run, but it was too late.

Lito pulled the trigger as he tumbled down.

Lillian fell a few feet across from him.

Tessa closed her eyes, thought of the soaring birds, and wished for that same peace for Lillian.

CHAPTER FORTY-SEVEN

Gunshots. Two of them. Staccato bursts from the backyard that made me jump. Stan and Gunner hurried up the hall and out the kitchen door. I tried to follow but Roman stopped me. "Don't you dare move."

Jefe came hurrying from his office. "What the hell?"

"I don't know, boss. The others are checking it out."

They're dead, the general said. *Your fault.*

No. Please God, no.

You failed them.

They were loud and filling my brain so there was little room for anything else. I wanted to cover my ears, to crawl into a hole, to drug myself so completely that no sound could reach me. The same black place I found myself when I learned Peyton had died.

"What's wrong with Chica?" Roman asked.

Elias. Tessa. Lillian. Who was dead?

Your fault. Your fault. Your fault.

Georgia, it will be okay. You can handle this. The new voice, the staticky edge gone. It was clear and female and a balm to my torment.

I need you to handle this. I'm counting on you. The voice was my sister.

Counting on you, Peyton repeated.

A scuffle from the kitchen. Stan and Gunner returned, Tessa gripped between them. She looked battered.

"Boss, Lito's down," Stan said.

Jefe's eyes flared. "Kitten killed him?"

"No. Lillian." Gunner spat out the words.

"Lillian?" He blinked, as though digesting this news. "Where is she?"

"She won't be a problem anymore," Stan said.

Something flashed across Jefe's face. Regret? Shock? But then the searing glare returned. "Take them back to the wine cellar," Colby said.

I didn't fight them. I kept my focus on Tessa, supporting her as we descended the stairs, careful to avoid her injured arm. I was eager to see Elias and prayed he was alright.

He is fine, Peyton said.

He met us when Stan unlocked the door. He wasn't fine. He had a nasty gash on the side of his head, but he was alive and conscious, and he wrapped his arms around me. "Are you okay?" he asked.

I nodded. The door clanged shut.

As soon as I helped her sit, Tessa filled us in on what had happened. "He shot Lillian in the stomach." Her words, like her eyes, held a disturbing bleakness. "She saved my life."

"Yes. I'm very glad she did, Tessa. Are you sure—"

She nodded.

"I'm so sorry." I told them about my niece, Lindsay, trying to keep my voice from trembling, trying to hold my shit together. Peyton was counting on me.

"What the hell?" Elias shook his head. "What are they going to do to her?"

"That I can't think about. Colby says he doesn't have the SD card. He said he didn't put the camera in the room."

"Then who did?" Elias asked.

"That's the million-dollar question. I thought Colby was lying but now I'm not so sure."

Tessa eyed the door. "There is someone—I don't know—someone who works for Jefe who tried to help your sister. And he's been nice to me a few times. Kind of implied things would be over soon. I wonder if maybe—" She shook her head. "No, that wouldn't make sense."

"What wouldn't?" I asked.

She hesitated, then went on. "I wondered if maybe he was working with the police or something. If he was, then he may have put the camera there. For evidence."

"And Colby—Jefe—wouldn't know about it." I thought back to the night Peyton disappeared. The Latino man who left a message for her, telling her the plan was off. Was he the same one? "Who is this man, Tessa?"

"Javier."

"Is he here now?"

"I saw him earlier, but not in the past few hours."

We could hear activity above us. Voices. Footsteps. What was Colby planning? I wanted to believe he'd fight to keep Lindsay safe, but I had very little faith in him. And the Russians sounded merciless.

"We don't have much time." I crossed to the door and tried to open it. Locked, as I suspected.

"This may help." Elias approached, holding a key.

"Where did you get that?"

He glanced sorrowfully at Tessa. "I think Lillian left it for me when I was out cold."

Tessa winced. She'd been through so much in her young life, and now this loss. But I couldn't afford to focus on that just then. We had to find a way to save my niece.

"Okay. We have to find Javier. He's our only chance. It sounds like they're very busy up there." I pointed above us.

"What does this guy look like?" Elias asked.

"He's not tall, but very muscular. He's got brown skin with black freckles across his face." Tessa ran a finger over her nose and cheeks to demonstrate.

"Thanks. That's helpful." I smiled at her. "Let's separate and see if we can find him. Deal?"

They nodded and we crept out of the room.

I prayed none of us got caught.

Tessa found it surprisingly easy to sneak through the foyer and up the stairs. Jefe's men had gathered in his office where there was a lot of yelling going on. The room Mei-Mei used was empty. She moved on to Venus's area, which was also empty. When she passed the begonia room, Dulce opened the door.

Tessa pressed a finger against her lips, silencing her.

"What are you doing?" Dulce whispered.

"Looking for Javier. Have you seen him?"

Dulce cocked her head toward Onyx's room. "He may be in there."

Roman's voice echoed downstairs, Stan mumbling something in reply. Dulce glanced toward them, then at Tessa.

"Don't tell them I'm up here," Tessa said.

Dulce looked her up and down, mulling.

"Please. This may all be over soon."

"Stupid Chica," Dulce said pushing past her, then stopping. "Be careful."

"I will." When Tessa reached Onyx's room, she heard noises inside. She rapped quietly on the door, expecting Onyx's voice saying, "Who is it?" but instead heard nothing. Drawing a breath for bravery, she stepped into the room.

"What do you want?" Javier stood by Onyx's bed, a cardboard box in his hand.

"I need to talk to you."

"I'm busy."

"Busy taking down the cameras?"

Something flashed in his eyes. Quick, almost unnoticeable. Then the calm control returned. "Why would you say that?"

Emboldened, she leaned against the bed. "I always thought you were going to help me. From that time you told me about Peyton, that you had been working with her. I kept thinking one day you'd get me out of the trailer and into a different life."

"You never did though."

His gaze softened. "You don't understand."

"I want to. What are you, police? Jefe said he wasn't the one to put cameras in the bedrooms, so I figured it was you."

He looked at the contents of the carton in his arms. "I gotta get going."

"Going? Where?"

He didn't answer but made a move to the door.

Tessa stepped in front of him. "Are the police coming here?"

He nodded.

"How soon?"

"I'm not sure."

"You know about the Russians? About Jefe's little niece? You know they have her?"

Another nod.

"Then how the hell can you go anywhere? You have what the Russians want! Give it to them."

He eyed the door. "I can't do that."

"You have to." She moved in closer, eye-to-eye with him, something she never did to men. "I met Lindsay. She's four, and smart, and innocent. And we both know what they'll do to her if you don't—" Tessa couldn't finish that sentence any more than she could bear to think about what might happen.

"There you are!" The urgent whisper came from Georgia as she slipped into the room. "I was getting worried."

"Sorry." Tessa kept herself positioned so that Javier couldn't leave without physically moving her.

"You must be Javier," Georgia said. "I'm figuring FBI? You were helping my sister, weren't you? Now her daughter needs your help."

Tessa liked how Georgia used a firm, expectant tone, as though nobody would dare defy her.

"We're all very sorry about your niece," Javier said.

"Sorry? I'm starting to hate that word." She looked at the box in his hand. "I need the SD card."

He let out an exaggerated sigh. "Like I explained to Kitten—"

"My name is Tessa."

"Tessa—I can't give it to you."

Georgia's smile held not the tiniest bit of warmth. "Oh, I think you can. Otherwise, I go downstairs and tell Colby and his men that you are the mole. That you've been surveilling them since—well— who knows how long. I'm thinking that would create quite a ruckus."

His dark eyes widened. "You'll get me killed."

"Not if you hand over the recording! You don't have to tell your boss you did. You can say I stole it from you. But you are going to help me get Lindsay away from those thugs."

He set the box on the bed and ran a hand over his face. Tessa almost felt sorry for him, for this predicament he was in, but a little girl's life was at stake. Nothing else mattered.

Tessa spoke softly. "You don't want her hurt. I know that. I know you are a decent person who wouldn't want anything to happen to that little girl."

He shook his head.

"Then help us save her."

He hesitated, then reached in his breast pocket and removed the small, square SD card. He dropped it in the box. "I have to leave the room for just a minute. It would be a shame if someone stole this while I was out." He moved to the door.

"One more thing." Georgia blocked his exit. "My guess is the FBI is going to storm this place soon. If the Russians are here with Lindsay when that happens she could get hurt. Delay them. Give us an extra thirty minutes. Y'all can go after the Russians once she's safe."

He didn't reply. They gave him room to slip by them.

"You think he'll do it?" Tessa asked.

"We'll know soon enough."

CHAPTER FORTY-EIGHT

My voices droned like a propeller blade in my head. I couldn't quiet them. The tense exchange with Javier hadn't helped. I so desperately needed to hold my shit together, but it was getting harder and harder.

Georgia. You can do this. Peyton's voice again. It held the warmth of the counselor but the strength of the general. It almost made me feel confident. I turned to Tessa. "Listen to me. I want you to take Elias to the wine cellar. Lock yourselves inside. I'll join you soon."

"What are you going to do?"

"I'm going to talk sense into Colby."

She hesitated, eyeing me with fear and concern. What an incredible kid.

"Go on. And you may have to tie down Elias. I'll come get you if I need you." I gave her a little shoulder squeeze and nudged her toward the stairs.

The SD card felt small and insignificant in my hand. How could this tiny thing cause so much damage? And how was I going to make sure Colby did the right thing?

He loves Lindsay. Peyton always, always had faith in me, especially when I had none in myself. I studied the SD card, formulating a plan.

I prayed it would work.

Five minutes later, I found myself at Colby's office door. I didn't knock but opened it and barged right in. Four guns drew on me like gunslingers in the Old West. Probably not the wisest way to enter.

"What the hell?" Javier looked genuinely surprised to see me. Good actor, that one.

"How did you get out of the wine cellar?" Stan demanded.

"That's not important. What is important is that I know where the SD card is."

Colby glared at me. "How?"

"Also not important. I'll make a deal with you. I'll give you the card if you agree to give it to the Russians and give me Lindsay. Once we're safely away from here, you can do whatever the hell you want to the Russians."

He rose from his desk and approached me, his movements oddly cat-like. "Give it to me."

I shook my head. The guns lifted—four of them, pointed directly at my face. "Yeah, y'all can kill me. But then what will you do?"

Colby gave me his dimpled grin, the same one I used to find endearing, because I am an idiot that way. "I think we want the same thing."

I met his glare. "Do we?"

He loves his niece, Peyton whispered.

"I want to believe that," I said. "I love Lindsay with every sorry inch of my heart. Do you feel the same way?"

There it was. Just a flash, a flinch, a second of soft vulnerability on his face. The Colby I knew was still in there somewhere. "I don't want her hurt."

"Then we do this my way. I'll get the card. I'm the one who gives it to the Russian dude when he puts Lindsay in my arms. Y'all stay back or do whatever they want you to do until the trade is made."

"These are serious criminals, George."

I almost laughed. I almost said, *so are you*. I knew Colby would kill me as soon as he could.

Javier cleared his throat. "It could work, boss. They may be less threatened by her."

"Only because they don't know her like I do." Colby looked out the window. Beyond the shrubs, the pool, and what looked like a greenhouse, was a large pad of concrete. The helicopter pad.

"When will they be here?" I asked.

"Any minute."

"I want to go see my friends before they get here. They need to know what I'm doing."

Colby nodded and gestured to Javier to take me away.

As Tessa descended the steps, she wondered where the other girls were. They had to be hiding, but where? Before heading to the cellar, she glanced out the back door to where she'd left Lillian's body.

"Kitten?" Onyx's voice halted her. She stood just outside the door, holding what looked like a bloody towel.

"What are you doing?"

"We are taking care of her."

"Of Lillian?"

She nodded. "She's . . . she's always been good to me."

"She saved my life."

"And we are trying to save hers," Onyx said.

"You mean she's—"

Onyx pressed a finger to her lips. "You must keep this to yourself."

Tessa nodded, a flutter of hope tingling inside. *Alive. Lillian's alive.*

"I must get back to her. Remember, tell nobody. We will do all we can."

Tessa nodded, shutting the door behind her. She hurried down the steps to the wine cellar where Elias waited.

"Well?"

"She said for us to wait here." Tessa locked the door behind her.

"Wait my ass." Elias grabbed the doorknob, thought better of it, and paced the tiny room again. "I'm not great at waiting. Especially when it comes to George."

"She seemed to know what she was doing."

"She did?" He shook his head. "She's got you fooled then. She gets herself into situations—I mean, she always means well, but—and this is a serious cluster. She might get herself killed."

Tessa gave him a long, hard look. "Maybe you should have more faith in her."

"Faith in her? I got all the faith in her in the world, except when it comes to her looking out for herself. She seriously sucks at that."

A few minutes later, the door opened, and Georgia entered with Javier. Elias shot him a look like he wished he was armed.

"It's okay. He's with us. I think," Georgia said.

"I'm with the FBI, but let's keep that quiet for now."

Georgia told them her plan that she would be the one to exchange the SD card for Lindsay.

"Oh hell no. No way, George," Elias practically growled.

"It's gotta be me. Lindsay knows me and trusts me."

"She's also less of a threat to the Russians. That might work to our advantage," Javier added.

Georgia eyed each of them, something pleading and apologetic in her gaze. "I'm sorry if y'all think this is the wrong call. The police and FBI will swarm this place as soon as I get Lindsay. It's the only way." She gestured to Tessa and Elias. "Javier, keep them safe. Promise me that. No matter what happens, they leave here unharmed."

"We'll do everything we can."

"And they'll stay right here till it's all over." Georgia shifted to Elias and hugged him. "Look out for Tessa, okay?"

He nodded. She moved to Tessa and placed a hand on her shoulder. "Let the adults handle all this. Promise me."

Tessa blinked, moisture building behind her eyes that she wasn't used to. She rarely let herself cry. She never let herself get attached.

Yet she threw her arms around Georgia and hugged her hard.

Georgia pulled away, wiping her own eyes, and said, "I'll see you both soon."

CHAPTER FORTY-NINE

Let the adults handle this. The general chuckled.

"Shut up," I whispered.

I needed to ignore him, and the whirring hive in my head, but it wasn't easy. I'd have to have words with Nora about how well her stress-management techniques were working. Of course, they weren't usually tested by kidnapping, human trafficking, organized crime situations. The SD card was where I'd left it, under a small planter just outside Colby's office. Orchids grew in the planter, of course. I was starting to really hate that flower. I slipped the recording into my pocket.

The sound of the helicopter landing rumbled through the house. I hurried to the back door and watched the giant craft perch on the concrete pad like a Terminator version of a dragonfly. I saw three men inside. I couldn't see Lindsay.

Colby and his men stood away from the landing, hands over their ears as the mammoth propeller blade slowed and stopped. Nobody moved, except me. I stepped up to where they were, gripping the card in my hand, willing the internal voices to be silent.

Sacrifice yourself, said the general. I thought maybe he was right.

You save my daughter. And don't get yourself hurt. The strength in Peyton's voice silenced the general. It calmed me. Steeled me.

"I will," I whispered.

A man exited the helicopter, wearing dark, expensive-looking shades. He was wide with fat, droopy cheeks, an air of being both in charge and merciless. He saw us, removed his sunglasses, and approached.

"Where is it?" he demanded.

"Where is my niece?" Colby screamed over the helicopter noise.

The Russian turned back to the craft and motioned with his hand. Another man climbed out, taller, broad-chested, with thick brown hair. He held Lindsay in his arms.

"Thank God," I whispered. She looked at the man, at the propeller blades stilled above her. She looked well. She looked whole.

"Bring it to me." This had to be Vasily. The one who'd been recorded with Tessa.

"I have it," I yelled.

He eyed me curiously. "Who are you? Police?"

At the same time, Lindsay saw me. "That's my Aunt George!" she reached out to me.

I wanted nothing more than to run to her, to scoop her up, to get her away from these evil brutes, but I had to be careful.

Good girl, Peyton said.

"Bring it to me."

I tamped down my fear. One step, two. I glanced at Colby who's eyes were fixed on the Russians. Three steps. Four.

Lindsay squirmed in the man's arms. "Give me Aunt George!"

"Easy, sweetie. I'm coming to you." I could scarcely be heard over all the noise.

Another Russian climbed out of the helicopter, this one holding a gun. It looked to be about five feet long and probably held a thousand bullets, but then terror makes me exaggerate.

Finally, I reached them.

Vasily held out his hand.

I showed him the card but didn't turn it over. "Her first. Hand her to me."

The man with the gun inched closer, the barrel pointed at my head.

It occurred to me then, that I had everything to lose. They could shoot me, grab the recording, and fly away with my niece. There was nothing I could do to stop it.

"Same time," I said in a rush. "You get the SD card, I get Lindsay."

Vasily mulled. He took in the men behind me, assessing.

I drew a breath. Inched closer. "Now!"

I shoved the SD card at him and grabbed for Lindsay. Her tiny arms and legs clung to me like a limpet as I swung around and ran from the Russians.

"That's it, Vasily. We're done," Colby yelled.

Vasily laughed. "Are we?" The helicopter blades turned again. The deafening whir vibrated in my chest. Vasily climbed into the craft. I covered Lindsay's ears as they took off.

She's safe, Peyton whispered.

And then.

Sirens blared. Men and women in tactical clothes thronged us like ants, assault weapons poised. Colby's men drew their guns and opened fire.

I fell to the ground, Lindsay beneath me. My hands shielded her ears to muffle the gunshots. My body guarded her against being trampled by the dozen police and FBI that infiltrated the grounds. I didn't let her see blood pooling under Roman's crumpled body. The shouts and sporadic bursts of gunfire continued for what felt like weeks, but finally, blessedly, all quieted.

I braved a glance at Colby. Handcuffed, bleeding from his forehead. I didn't want Lindsay to see that. Stan had taken a bullet in the leg and moaned in pain. Another man looked dead—I didn't want to see who it was.

"You okay, Peanut?" I whispered.

She nodded, her nose pressed into my chest.

I felt a presence beside me and dared to open my eyes. Detective Lou Michaels was on his knees, a blanket in hand. "Hey, George. You okay?"

I nodded. "We're okay."

"Then let's get you away from all this." He used the blanket to shield us from seeing the carnage and for that I was grateful. He led us inside, to the living room, to where Tessa and Elias waited. They hurried to embrace the two of us.

And then a voice whispered inside my head. The one I hoped never left me.

Thank you, Peyton said. *Thank you.*

CHAPTER FIFTY

"Ready, Tessa?" I stood in the doorway to her room. A suitcase lay open across her bed with jeans, tops, and underwear not-so-neatly folded on one side. A huge black cat filled the other.

"Fenway wants to go with me," she said.

I scooped him up and plopped him on the floor, ignoring his annoyed cry.

"Can I bring the hairdryer you got me?"

I smiled. "It's yours, isn't it?" She'd gotten into feminine things over the past few weeks. Hair clips. Clothes. Nail polish. Nora said this was a good sign. Tessa might slowly return to the adolescence she'd had stolen from her. Recovering from the years of trauma might take a long time—decades even—but she was off to a great start.

Her arm had a bright red spot from her third laser treatment to remove the tattoo. Only a faint outline of the orchid remained, and it would be gone soon. Tessa monitored the progress with obsessive vigilance.

The doorbell interrupted us. I caught her startled flash of panic. That vigilance wouldn't leave her for a while. "Elias," I reassured her. She nodded as I went to answer the door.

It wasn't Elias. My ex, Ben Reeder, stood in my doorway, looking a hell of a lot better than the last time I'd seen him. A small scar across his cheek and the cane he leaned on were the lone remnants of his assault. "Damn. This is a surprise," I said.

"Thought I'd check on you. Hear you've had an adventure."

"You could say that." I didn't invite him in. Ben was, above all else, a reporter; once he learned I had Tessa staying with me, he'd drive us crazy trying to get her story. And she didn't need that. She'd have to relive her nightmare in therapy—then at trial—but not before. Not if I had anything to say about it.

"You okay, George?" He studied my face. I didn't look away.

"I'm good."

Javier had recorded over a hundred encounters at the Estate— prominent businessmen. Foreign royalty. Two US senators and a governor from the Midwest. He had evidence of bribery, purchased votes, and government contracts bought for sex with juveniles. The tremors from this explosive bust would be felt for years.

Colby was in a federal facility awaiting trial and scared for his life. Too many powerful people wanted him dead. His men—those who survived the FBI assault—had been imprisoned in various jails across the country. Tessa asked often about Drew, the man who recruited her into Jefe's operation. So far, he'd not been caught, much to Tessa's disappointment.

The stunning surprise had been Lillian. When nobody could find her body, they saw that the Thunderbird she always drove was missing. The girls—Onyx, Dulce, Mei-Mei, and the others—denied any knowledge of what had happened to her. I hoped, and prayed, she'd gotten away and recovered. She wasn't innocent, I knew that— but she'd been trapped in a life she couldn't escape.

"How is Lindsay?" Ben asked.

"She's safe," I said, because that was the most important thing. "David has her in therapy, but she seems pretty well recovered from her ordeal." David—and the other Ribaults—were also being investigated. If they didn't know what Colby was up to, they turned a blind eye to it and reaped its rewards.

A familiar black Jeep pulled up in front of the house. Ben spotted it and frowned. "Elias."

"Yep."

"Guess I'll get going then." He pivoted against the cane then looked at me again. "I'm proud of you, George. You are one gutsy lady."

The compliment took me by surprise. I found myself at a loss for words.

He hobbled down my steps and out to his car. Elias came in, carrying a paper bag which he opened on our dining room table. "Sandwiches."

"Excellent." I cleared seats for the three of us while he fetched beverages from the kitchen.

He handed me a glass but held on to it. "So. Chorus still quiet?"

I smiled. "Mostly. It's odd," an understatement. The voices had been a regular companion since my teenage years but ever since that afternoon, when the Russian held a gun at me, most of them had faded away. I had heard nothing from the general. The counselor commented now and then, but the new voice, the one I loved the most, had become a regular. Every word Peyton spoke made me smile inside.

Nora had been ecstatic about this development. "The others may not be gone for good, but you asserted your power over them. You showed them how strong you can be," she had said, grinning like a proud parent at a piano recital.

"What's the plan?" Elias asked. "You're taking Tessa to see her brother, then what?"

"She's too important a witness for the solicitor to let her permanently leave South Carolina. I'm her temporary foster parent through the trial. After that, it's her choice." I still couldn't believe they'd let me have her. Clancy had pulled some strings, and Lou had weighed in, too. Turns out, trafficking victims are hard to place in regular foster care, so they gave me a shot. We had a caseworker who would stop in every few weeks and get reports from Nora.

I liked having Tessa here. I liked watching her heal, though it would be a slow, difficult journey. Maybe it helped to have me around, someone flawed, struggling, and getting better. I hoped the others would recover, too. "Her brother has been adopted by his latest foster family. It's good he's got a stable home. Maybe they'll offer the same thing to Tessa."

"Or maybe she stays with you permanently."

I nodded, surprised at how much I liked that idea.

Tessa joined us from the bedroom. She opened a bag and helped herself to one of the sandwiches.

"I should bring you food every day. God knows what George is feeding you."

She laughed. "Takeout mostly. I think I'm going to learn how to cook."

"Elias needs to install a drive-through at his restaurant," I teased.

"Quit your bitching. You get personal delivery. That's a Georgia Thayer deal nobody else gets."

I smiled. "And I'm lucky as hell."

Eleanor Wallace shifted into fifth gear as she passed the truck on Highway 601, headed north. She wouldn't speed, not this time, not in this under-the-radar life she lived. She didn't know where she was heading but getting out of South Carolina had filled her with such relief she'd nearly wept.

She had so much to get used to. The brown tint to her now-short hair. This new name, complete with ID, was purchased from a guy who knew a guy in Charleston. The limited movement was caused by the not-quite-healed gunshot wound in her side, the one that almost killed her.

No matter. She had lived. With the help of her girls, she had escaped, leaving Jefe and his troubles behind. Onyx had taken a burner cell when she stole the money from Jefe's desk to give Lillian (now Eleanor). Onyx told her they'd been moved to a halfway house. Immigration would help some of them return to their home countries after they testified. Onyx chose to stay in the States. She hoped to go to school, and Eleanor had no doubt it would happen. Onyx was a force of nature.

Eleanor knew she'd committed many crimes, but she couldn't turn herself in. It would mean doing time. But the bigger threat was what she knew. Jefe's more powerful customers wouldn't let her live long enough to testify against them, not that she would. If any of them ever found her. No, escape was the only way to stay alive.

Passing a BP station Eleanor saw a girl standing by the pump— petite, coal-black hair, in a short dress and heels. For a second, she thought it was Violet, but then she remembered. Violet was gone, like the others who'd displeased Jefe. The girls she didn't try hard enough to save.

She had to put that life behind her. She was out of South Carolina, away from Jefe's reach, and she could go wherever she chose, be whoever she wanted to be.

Funny thing, you get so used to not having freedom, you forget how much it means.

To Eleanor Wallace, it meant everything.

ACKNOWLEDGMENTS

I wish to thank a million people, but that would fill all the pages, so I'll narrow it down to Ed Damron, Beth Johnson, Ashley Warlick, Tim Conroy, Marly Rusoff, Dartinia Hull, Steve Eaonnou, Mary Jane Reynolds, Rachel Silver, Pam Knight, Marly Rusoff, the WFWA Write-Inmates, Paula Benson, Scott Burditt, George Mavroftas, Stephanie Thompson, Jane Schwantes, Gabi Coatsworth, my remarkably patient husband, Jim Hussey, and the amazing folks at Koehler Books.

This book is in honor of all survivors of human trafficking: wishing them strength and hope in their recovery. A portion of the author's royalties will be donated to Doors to Freedom, which helps survivors recover and reclaim their lives. They offer housing, treatment, education, and support—you should check them out here: www.doorstofreedom.com.

CPSIA information can be obtained
at www.ICGtesting.com
Printed in the USA
BVHW050503130922
646692BV00003B/14

9 781646 637638